D0046100

PRAISE FOR BARRY EISLER

The Killer Collective

"Impossibly cool."

—*Entertainment Weekly*

"As usual with an Eisler novel, the plot is full of twists, the prose is muscular, and the action unfolds at a torrid pace. The result is another page-turner from one of the better thriller writers since James Grady published *Six Days of the Condor* in 1974."

—Associated Press

"In this crackling-good thriller from bestseller Eisler, Seattle PD sex crimes detective Livia Lone, assassin John Rain, and former Marine sniper Dox form a testy alliance to combat a vile conspiracy involving corrupt and toxic government agencies . . . The feisty interplay among these killer elites is as irresistible as if one combined the Justice League with the Avengers, swapping out the superhero uniforms for cutting-edge weaponry and scintillating spycraft. By the satisfying conclusion, the world has been scrubbed a bit cleaner of perfidy. This is delightfully brutal fun."

—*Publishers Weekly* (starred review)

"Vicarious pleasure for anyone wanting to see the scum of the world get its due."

—*Kirkus Reviews*

"Eisler does a great job of creating individual personalities and tics with this group of uniquely trained professionals. A solid recommendation for fans of Robert Ludlum's Jason Bourne and Daniel Silva's Gabriel Allon."

—*Library Journal*

"Riveting . . . Barry Eisler pulls off an *Avengers*-like feat . . ."
—*The Mercury News*

"Eisler turns the heat up like never before to deliver a fun, fast-paced thriller that's tailor-made for fans of nonstop action."
—The Real Book Spy

"The fun of Eisler's super thriller is in the excitement, the chase, and the survival. *The Killer Collective* binds it together into a blazing adventure of espionage escape fiction, perfect to start the new year."
—*New York Journal of Books*

"Eisler's *The Killer Collective* packs a punch like a sniper's rifle. A solid grounding in up-to-the-minute technology and current affairs makes this a hot read for thriller lovers."
—Authorlink

"A heart-pounding home run . . . Eisler has created a more literary version of *The Expendables*—the movie series that brought together Stallone, Schwarzenegger, Jet Li, Chuck Norris, Jason Statham, Dolph Lundgren, Bruce Willis, and other action heroes . . ."
—*It's Either Sadness or Euphoria*

"Demonstrating the extraordinary expertise in the art of espionage and special operations—including surveillance detection, cover, elicitation, operational site selection, and more—that his fans and fellow practitioners have come to venerate, Eisler delivers another brilliant, fast-paced thriller, full of well-developed characters who remind me of the special operations and intelligence officers with whom I served and in some cases against whom I worked. For a retired senior CIA Clandestine Services officer still nostalgic for his espionage operations of bygone years, Eisler's thrillers full of intrigue, adventure, and suspense are a most welcome opportunity to get as close as is now possible to the real thing."

—Daniel N. Hoffman, retired Clandestine Services officer and former CIA Chief of Station

The Livia Lone Series

"An absolutely first-rate thriller . . . Emotionally true at each beat."
—*New York Times Book Review*

"An explosive thriller that plunges into the sewer of human smuggling . . . Filled with raw power, [*Livia Lone*] may be the darkest thriller of the year."

—*Kirkus Reviews* (starred review)

"Readers may be reminded of Stieg Larsson's beloved Lisbeth Salander when they meet Livia Lone, and will be totally riveted by the story of this woman on a mission to right the wrongs in her past."

—Bookish

"You won't be able to tear yourself away as the story accelerates into a Tarantino-worthy climax and when you're left gasping in the wake of its gut-wrenching vigilante justice, you'll belatedly realize you learned a lot about a social travesty that gets far too little attention . . . *Livia Lone* is a harrowing tale with a conscience."

—*Chicago Review of Books*

THE
CHAOS
KIND

ALSO BY BARRY EISLER

A Clean Kill in Tokyo (previously published as *Rain Fall)*
A Lonely Resurrection (previously published as *Hard Rain)*
Winner Take All (previously published as *Rain Storm)*
Redemption Games (previously published as *Killing Rain)*
Extremis (previously published as *The Last Assassin)*
The Killer Ascendant (previously published as *Requiem for an Assassin)*
Fault Line
Inside Out
The Detachment
Graveyard of Memories
The God's Eye View
Livia Lone
Zero Sum
The Night Trade
The Killer Collective
All the Devils

Short Works

"The Lost Coast"
"Paris Is a Bitch"
"The Khmer Kill"
"London Twist"

Essays

"The Ass Is a Poor Receptacle for the Head: Why Democrats Suck at
Communication, and How They Could Improve"

BARRY EISLER

THE CHAOS KIND

THOMAS & MERCER

Text copyright © 2021 by Barry Eisler
All rights reserved.

Published by Thomas & Mercer, Seattle

www.apub.com

Amazon, the Amazon logo, and Thomas & Mercer are trademarks of Amazon.com, Inc., or its affiliates.

ISBN-13: 9781542005616 (hardcover)
ISBN-10: 1542005612 (hardcover)
ISBN-13: 9781542005593 (paperback)
ISBN-10: 1542005590 (paperback)

Cover design by Rex Bonomelli

Printed in the United States of America

First edition

For Dan, Kim, Jerron, and Nathan

The object of power is power.

—*George Orwell*

prologue

MANUS

Marvin Manus walked up a steep flight of stairs in Seattle's Freeway Park, his breath fogging in the damp morning air. He didn't know why they called it a "park." There were trees and grass, yes, and a series of artificial waterfalls, too, but the heart of it was sheer blocks of concrete, arranged like a scale model of windowless, doorless buildings, all of it as dull and gray as the autumn sky. It reminded him of the juvenile facility they'd put him in after what he did to his father. Like someone had taken the prison walls and tried to refashion them into art.

He'd read there had been problems with street crime here, and he could understand why. For one thing, he knew that places like this echoed. So you could hear a potential victim coming from a long way off. There were multiple vantage points from which to assess the victim's suitability. And with all the mazelike concrete walls, the victim would have nowhere to go other than forward or back.

He paused and looked around. He could see a good deal of the labyrinth, but still there were numerous blind turns. It really was well designed for criminals, and he was surprised the woman would use it for her runs even in the morning. Maybe she liked all the stairs.

He pushed the thought away and started climbing again. Beyond what the woman looked like, he didn't want to know anything about her.

In his previous life, details about an assignment hadn't bothered him. He'd believed in Director Anders. He did what the director asked, to whomever the director needed it done. But then the director had wanted him to surveil an NSA specialist named Evelyn Gallagher. Evie. Who had a deaf son, Dash. Manus had met them, as he was supposed to. The director had then told him to do more. And Manus . . . couldn't.

At the top of the stairs was a wall where the steps turned left. Amid the smell of damp concrete and mold and moss, Manus caught a whiff of body odor. By reflex, he dropped his hand to the Cold Steel Espada clipped to his front pocket, and moved to the right to create more space between himself and whatever might be beyond the ambit of his vision.

He reached the landing and glanced left. An old homeless man in a tattered down vest was sitting on a folded blanket, his back to the concrete wall. Had Manus not been at the far right of the stairs, he might have run into the man. It was a bad place to sit—too easy to startle someone coming up the stairs. And there were people in the world who, when startled, reacted badly.

As Manus moved past, the man said something, but he had a scraggly beard that covered too much of his mouth for Manus to see what he said. Probably asking for loose change. Manus would have given him some, but most people ignored such pleas, and Manus didn't want to do anything that was likelier to be remembered than to be forgotten or overlooked.

He kept moving. The sky had gotten darker and he smelled a coming rain.

At the next landing was another homeless man, this one younger and standing with a shoulder to the wall. The bladed stance could have been tactical, and Manus gave the man more attention than he had the one who'd been sitting. He read the man's lips—*Spare a few bucks?*—and shook his head once in response. The man frowned and spoke again: *Fuck you anyway.* Manus met his eyes. The man looked away and said nothing more.

Manus was used to the reaction. It wasn't just his size. When he looked at someone who might be trouble, he didn't feel anything. If the person didn't want to be a problem, Manus would keep going. If the person wanted to be a problem, Manus would go to work. Most people, when he looked at them, understood. Usually they preferred the first option.

He hadn't felt this way in a long time. Hadn't looked at people this way in a long time. He didn't like it. And he didn't like how easily he had slipped back into it. But what choice did he have? They'd told him if he didn't do what they wanted, they would tell Dash everything. About what Manus was. About the things he'd done. And even if all that had been before, how would a fourteen-year-old boy understand the difference?

Evie knew, of course. She'd known a lot even before he told her all of it, on that night he'd come undone by Dash's trust and Evie's gentleness. He'd signed *good night* to Dash, returning the boy's hug, something that had become natural for Manus after months of it being more one-way, and waited while the boy climbed into the loft the two of them had built together. Evie watched, smiling, then walked to the loft, stood on her tiptoes, and kissed her son good night. She'd followed Manus out, turning off the light and closing the door behind them.

There was a chair in her small bedroom, and Manus sank into it, staring at the floor, gripped by a sadness he couldn't name, as though he was grieving about something that hadn't even happened.

Evie knelt in front of him and touched his knee. He looked up.

I love the way you are with him, she'd signed. *And the way he is with you.*

At those words, Manus began to cry. He tried to stop himself, but it only got worse. Evie, her expression alarmed, signed *What is it?*

You don't know the things I've done.

Yes, I do.

No, you don't.

And then he'd told her. Told her everything. As though some part of him was trying to warn her, save her, drive her away.

She'd listened. When he was done, when it had all come out of him, she said, *You're not that person anymore.*

Then who am I?

You're the man Dash and I love.

Which dissolved him into another spasm of sobbing.

Evie hadn't said anything more. She stood, turned off the light, and pulled Manus to the bed. Manus hadn't understood why—they never turned the lights all the way off. They liked to see each other, and besides, without any light they couldn't sign and he couldn't read her lips. But then he realized that was the point, they were done with words. Words didn't matter.

They made love in the dark, Evie on her back underneath him, and when it was done, he cried again and she held him. They fell asleep in each other's arms and afterward never spoke of what he'd told her.

After that, there was nothing more important to Manus than being worthy of the way Evie trusted him. Wanted him.

Loved him.

And Dash even more. Both of them had been deaf from childhood— Dash, from meningitis; Manus, from a beating at the hands of his father. But the feeling between them was more than that. The boy's father had never learned sign. Even before the divorce, Evie had told Manus, the relationship had been strained. Dash needed a father. And Manus . . .

He didn't know what he needed. Not a son, exactly. But someone . . . someone he could teach the good things he knew. The three of them were living together now, in a modern saltbox Manus had built on land they'd bought near Emmitsburg, in Maryland just south of the Pennsylvania border. Evie was done with NSA. The new director had offered her an early pension, the implicit quid pro quo being that she would forget what she knew about his predecessor's rogue spying and assassination programs, the former of which had built on Evie's video surveillance and facial recognition work, and the latter of which had involved Manus. And Evie had taken it, both to signal her agreement to their terms and to discourage them from seeking some other means of obtaining her silence.

Dash had helped build the house—on weekends, holidays, and all during the summer vacation before eighth grade. Manus was proud of how fast Dash had caught on, and how well they'd worked together. And grateful that Evie had entrusted him with making sure Dash knew how to use Manus's tools safely. Once, when Dash was running a length of plywood through the table saw, Manus had caught Evie looking on, her arms folded across her chest, her expression worried. He had signed, *He's okay.* And she had nodded and signed, *I know.*

In the end, maybe it didn't matter what the bond was built on. What mattered was . . . Dash believed in him, in what he wanted to believe about himself. All he knew was that the way Dash looked at him . . . he needed to be what Dash saw.

So he didn't have a choice. He would do what they wanted. The problem was, once they learned they could get him to do this, they would make him do other things, too.

Which meant that taking care of this woman would only buy him time. For what, he wasn't sure. An opportunity. An opening. Something.

He reached the apex of the structure and looked down at the maze of concrete. They'd told him it had to look natural, or at least reasonably natural. Well, it wouldn't be hard for someone running through here to fall. The pavement was wet, the stairs slick in places. The fall itself might be enough. If he had to do more, he would.

But he hoped he wouldn't.

ONE WEEK EARLIER

chapter one

HOBBS

"A ll right," the president said, coming to his feet. "See you all next week."

As though a switch had been flipped, the attendees all rose, and the hushed room was suddenly filled with the simultaneous creak of dozens of leather chairs and a collective murmur of "Thank you, Mr. President." To Hobbs, who had visited numerous black congregations when he'd been considering a run for Congress in South Carolina's first district, the refrain always sounded like some weird cousin of call and response. Well, certainly there was enough ambient reverence in the White House Cabinet Room to make you feel you might be in church.

There was a moment of silence—another unconscious echo of religious devotion—as the president headed briskly toward his private exit at the south end of the room, his footfalls noiseless on the plush carpet. On those infrequent occasions when the president lingered, everyone else did, too, vying for a scrap of his attention. But the instant he was gone, all the august personalities who served at his pleasure would devolve into gossiping, backbiting courtiers, and as he closed the mahogany door behind him and the heavy brass latch clacked into place, the room erupted into a dozen scheming conversations. Power was like a magnet, keeping everything rigid and straight and proper. But without the magnet, it all collapsed into disorganized scrap.

The secretary of the interior saw his opportunity and zeroed in on the vice president, whose traditional position was directly opposite the president's and on whose left it was Hobbs's place as attorney general to sit. Hobbs caught the vice president's wince at the Interior guy's approach, probably in preparation for turning down a golf outing or some other invitation. Most of the time, the vice president would stick around after a meeting to enjoy the attention he received in the president's absence, but if he left now it would be bad. It would elevate Hobbs himself as a beacon for the cabinet's various lesser barons, and while ordinarily Hobbs was indifferent to their attention, today it would be a hindrance.

But no, the danger of the vice president exiting too soon was moot, because there was Devereaux, the director of National Intelligence, coming around the north end of the table, half a head taller than the people he was passing, a factotum on his heels. Perfect. Hobbs slipped past the small queue lining up behind the Interior guy and pulled abreast of Devereaux as he passed through one of the exits. Devereaux wasn't walking particularly quickly, but the man had a long stride, and Hobbs struggled to match his pace.

"Pierce," Hobbs said, keeping his voice low. "Have you got a few minutes? There's something I think might interest you." It wasn't so much that Hobbs was worried about someone overhearing; more that he wanted to signal the delicacy of the topic he needed to broach. And of course, a conspiratorial tone was engaging in its own right—engaging to anyone, and especially to America's top spy.

Devereaux stopped and glanced at his watch. Hobbs knew the reflex was theater. Information came with a price tag, and the shrewd players were careful to conceal their eagerness to buy.

Devereaux tilted his head lower and looked at Hobbs through a pair of wire-rimmed spectacles. "What's on your mind, Uriah?"

Hobbs, the shortest male cabinet member, was used to people towering over him. He'd hated it when he was young. But now he was the country's top lawyer, and that was the view that mattered.

He paused while the chief of staff, another favored target of the sycophants because his office was in the White House and he was the president's gatekeeper, passed by, the secretaries of Commerce and Labor attached to him like suckerfish. The pause was another small signal that Hobbs's information was valuable. Besides which, Devereaux's glance at his watch deserved to be answered with a gesture equally nonchalant.

"Not here," Hobbs said, when the chief of staff and the hangers-on were out of earshot. "I think you'll want to be sitting down for this."

chapter two

LIVIA

N ow underhook the ankle," Livia said, circling around and leaning forward. "No, not your hand, catch it in the crook of your elbow! Tighter! It's not his ankle anymore, it's yours!"

Jorge, a muscular former gangbanger and one of Livia's brown belts, had nearly fifty pounds on Diaz, but the ankle hook instantly stopped him from lifting her more than a few inches off the mat. He strained for a moment, Diaz's legs crossed behind his waist, then settled back into her.

"Again!" Livia said. Jorge crowded in, spread his feet, took hold of Diaz's gi collar, and started to arch toward the ceiling. But before he could get anywhere, Diaz hooked the ankle and stopped him cold.

Livia patted Jorge on the shoulder. "Okay."

Jorge disengaged and scooted back. Diaz sat up.

"You see?" Livia said.

Diaz nodded, but she looked more worried than pleased. Livia, who had worked with dozens of victims as a Seattle PD sex-crimes detective and who lived with her own childhood wounds, recognized what Diaz was trying to work through. Especially for trauma victims, it could take years of familiarity before the mind began to accept that a weapon would actually work. Even Livia, who had begun training in jiu-jitsu as a teenager and who in college had been an alternate on the US Olympic judo team, sometimes had dreams where an attacker would laugh off her arm bars and strangles and spine locks, or where bullets would plop uselessly from the muzzle of her duty weapon and the knife she carried would turn to rubber. When she had those dreams, she would hit the mat extra hard the next day, or spend hours at the range, or hang a cut of meat from a tree branch and slash and stab it to pieces.

"And remember," Livia said, "you can also just open your guard. Because what does Jorge need to slam you?"

"He needs to lift me."

"Right. And what does he need to lift you?"

"My closed guard."

"Yes. *You* decide whether someone can slam you."

Diaz looked at Jorge as though she wasn't buying it. "Were you really trying?"

Jorge laughed. "*Órale jefita*, I almost gave myself a hernia." He stood and started heading toward the door, shrugging off his gi top along the way. "Okay, ladies, gotta run. Promised the little one a bedtime story."

"Thanks for being a good attacker," Livia called after him. "And for sticking around after class."

Jorge stuffed the gi top into a gym bag and smiled. "Anything for you, Livia." He pulled on a tee-shirt, stepped into a pair of flip-flops, and slipped through the door, pulling it closed with a loud thud behind him.

The room was suddenly silent. A half hour earlier, the mats had been crowded, the small space reverberating with the shouts of twenty women students and of the three men who'd stuck around after their MMA class to serve as attackers. But now it was just Livia and Diaz.

Livia sat. "You're getting the hang of it. But if you want it to mean anything, you have to train with men."

"I just trained with Jorge."

13

"You spent the whole class avoiding him. I had to inflict him on you as he was trying to leave."

Diaz chuckled. "Someone should write a story about the power of jiu-jitsu to bridge human divides. Look at you and Jorge. Woman and man. Thai and Mexican. Detective Livia Lone and Jorge, former criminal gang enforcer."

Before being trafficked to America at thirteen with her little sister, Nason, and then being serially abused by Fred Lone, the wealthy Llewellyn town father who had "rescued" her, Livia had grown up in the forests of Thailand's Chiang Rai province. She was ethnic Lahu, not Thai, but the difference wasn't relevant to Diaz's point. Beyond which, Livia didn't talk about her childhood.

"Don't change the subject."

"No, really. And you'd be a good-looking couple, too, if he weren't married. Pretty and petite . . . I heard that's Jorge's speed."

"I'm serious."

Diaz dropped her head. "I'm working on it, okay?"

Livia looked at her. At a glance, Diaz would have been easy to underestimate. She was on the shorter side, with jet-black hair and a beautiful face, and though she was thirty-two, in casual clothes or a gi she could have passed for a college student. But when she put on a suit and heels for court, she radiated competence, focus, and smarts. She was known for her dedication to her work. But Livia knew it went deeper than that. Alcoholics needed to attend meetings. People like Diaz needed to put predators behind bars. Just as Livia sometimes needed to put them in the ground.

Livia had taken all the psych classes in college and understood that being a cop, and punishing rapists, whether through the law or on her own, was all just sublimation, a primitive part of her mind trying to propitiate her guilt over having failed to protect Nason. Over having inadvertently doomed her. Trauma never went away. You could try to block it, or bury it, or bludgeon it into submission. But something with that much power couldn't really be contained. The best you could hope for was a way to channel it.

So Livia could guess at what was behind Diaz's choice of career, and her bravery in bringing cases against rapists no matter what, and her attraction to jiu-jitsu and simultaneous discomfort rolling with men. But Livia respected Diaz's secrets, as she insisted on keeping her own.

Livia smacked her on the leg and Diaz looked up. "Hey. I wouldn't push if I didn't think you could handle it."

"I know. I'm just not very . . . confident on the mat."

"Were you confident the first time you argued in front of a judge?"

Diaz laughed. "I almost puked."

"But now?"

"Well, I still almost puke. But only before. Never during."

Livia laughed, then glanced around, even though she knew it was just the two of them. She leaned closer. "Any more fallout about Schrader?"

"No, it seems under control. I told you, my boss was pissed. But you were right about making sure the arrest got a lot of press. After Epstein, no one wants to be seen doing favors for another rich child rapist. Especially one as connected as Schrader."

chapter three

HOBBS

"Andrew Schrader," Hobbs said, leaning closer. "You know the name?" Devereaux sipped his coffee. "Sure, the investor. He was arrested recently."

They were seated in a discreet corner table of the White House Mess, a wood-paneled basement restaurant next to the Situation Room and run by the Navy. The space had a low acoustic ceiling, thick wall-to-wall carpet, and tables covered in patterned linen, all of which served to dampen noise even when the restaurant was full. But it was late now for breakfast, and lunch was still an hour away, so the usual crowd of commissioned officers and Cabinet secretaries and their guests and hangers-on was currently sparse.

"Do you know anything else about him?"

Devereaux shrugged. "Got his start with a software company he sold for a ton of money. Politically connected. Owns a bunch of trophy properties and likes to throw parties. A weakness for beautiful women."

Was Devereaux being just a touch *too* nonchalant? Hobbs couldn't be sure, but he thought so. Good.

"Well," Hobbs said, "he does like to appear at parties with models half his age or younger. But that's a smokescreen. His real interest is in girls. As in, underage girls."

Other than a judicious sip of coffee, Devereaux didn't react. Hobbs admired his discipline. You had to be careful with these intel types. Devereaux had been career CIA before his ascension to the top job, and he understood the power of silence to loosen tongues.

Or to conceal his own fear.

"In fact," Hobbs went on, "six years ago, he was indicted in South Carolina. A joint FBI-local law-enforcement investigation. He was having teenaged girls brought to his Kiawah Island mansion at an almost industrial scale. The indictment wasn't just for sex with underage girls. It was for trafficking."

Devereaux peered at him over his glasses. "Wasn't that when you were the US Attorney in that district?"

Hobbs was glad for the riposte. It felt fearful, like a veiled *Maybe I'm implicated, but then so are you.*

"Level with me," Hobbs said. "Have you ever heard of Schrader's indictment?"

"No."

"Well, that's good. Because we buried it. We let him plead out— one charge of solicitation of a minor. A non-prosecution agreement. No prison time. No publicity."

Devereaux set down his coffee and cocked his head, as though unsure why Hobbs would offer up something so incriminating. "Like what they did with Epstein in Florida."

Hobbs nodded. Everyone knew about Jeffrey Epstein. Which was of course part of Hobbs's concern about Schrader. "Something like that."

"That would have been a big case for you, if you could have made it stick. A celebrity prosecution like that."

"You want to know why I buried it?"

Devereaux offered a tight smile at the directness of the question. "Sure."

"Schrader is one of the world's great networkers. A lot of powerful friends he's been collecting for decades. Politicians. Corporate titans. Media barons. Friends of ours."

Devereaux nodded in appreciation of the gravity of what he had just heard. The thing was, what he thought he understood wasn't the half of it.

"What, then?" Devereaux said. "You were protecting the innocent from embarrassment? Guilt by association?"

"I was protecting them from videos."

Devereaux's expression was neutral, but Hobbs detected the effort behind it. *I've got you, you son of a bitch,* he thought.

But Devereaux said nothing, so Hobbs continued. "Schrader had hidden cameras installed in every bedroom of his six homes, to which he was always happy to fly his rich and powerful friends on his private jet."

"That's appalling."

Hobbs wasn't sure whether Devereaux was referring to the cameras, to the behavior they recorded, or to the stupidity of anyone who would allow himself to be captured in such compromising circumstances. Probably there was self-reproach in the mix, as well.

"But how did you know . . . ," Devereaux started to say, then caught himself.

Hobbs offered a sympathetic smile. "It's okay, Pierce. This is explosive stuff. If you want to pretend it doesn't matter to you, it's fine, but I'll know you're full of shit."

Devereaux gave him a *touché* laugh. "Fair enough. You saw these videos?"

"Highlights. Yes."

A beat. Hobbs thought he might ask directly, but Devereaux was too canny, and said only "How bad?"

Hobbs couldn't help admiring the performance. It was a close imitation of someone who was concerned about the tapes only in general. Not specifically that he himself was in them.

"Professional quality. Every kind of depravity. With girls as young as thirteen."

Devereaux looked at him and for a moment said nothing. Not in a *power of silence* way—the man was simply speechless. Then he shook his head as though to clear it. "These videos . . . they're extant?"

"Very much so. Including one of a man who, when the video was made, had been only a lowly senator. But who at the time of the indictment happened to be president of the United States."

chapter four

LIVIA

As was often the case, things seemingly going smoothly made Livia uneasy. "What about Meekler?" she said.

"Oh, he was definitely trying to scare me off. But no way he was going to openly order me to not indict."

"Wait, let me guess: 'Alondra, you've got such a bright future with the department . . . I just want to make sure you're not getting out over your ski tips on this . . .'"

Diaz laughed. "You know our US Attorney, right down to the clichés. It was all, 'Schrader is rich, he'll have an army of thousand-dollar-an-hour lawyers . . . One tiny mistake and they'll shred you.' But then we reviewed my witness list, the trafficking and racketeering elements . . . And when he saw how extensive the case is, he backed off. Those girls you interviewed—their testimony is going to be devastating."

"Did he say he wants to meet with them?"

"Of course."

"Can you prevent him?"

"No. But I've prepped them. They know what he's going to say: 'We're all so grateful to you . . . Schrader is going to sic private investigators on you and your family, he's going to drag your name through the mud . . . Most girls in your position are afraid to testify, but you're so brave!' Like he's their friend and just trying to warn them."

Livia knew the Meeklers of the system well. And hated them. "When in fact he's trying to warn them off."

"Yeah. Most of the girls I contacted were already too scared to come forward. The ones who are cooperating are terrified, too. Meekler knows he might be able to scare them into withdrawing their testimony. Cut the legs out from under my case."

"Any chance it'll work?"

There was a beat while Diaz considered—or struggled with something. Then she said, "I told them what they're going to hear from Meekler . . . It's all true. It really will happen. And that men like Schrader—and Meekler—count on the threat of the secondary assault, the publicity assault, to intimidate us into silence."

Of course, *us* might have referred simply to women. But Livia sensed Diaz was using the plural pronoun to signal something more particular than just gender.

"They'll testify," she said. "For you."

"And for you," Diaz said. "I know you could have gone with King County, but I'm glad you brought it to me. The interstate aspects are going to be the most damning, and we needed the Bureau's resources."

"I didn't bring it to you just for the Bureau's resources," Livia said. "I brought it to you because I knew you wouldn't wilt."

Diaz started to say something and then stopped, perhaps realizing that Livia had expressed more than just a compliment. Livia understood. It was unnerving when someone saw past the façade everyone else bought into.

"Anyway," Livia said. "When are you going to indict?"

"Statutorily, I've got thirty days. But I'm shooting for seven."

"Another fait accompli for your boss?"

Diaz nodded. "And Meekler, too."

"They're not going to forgive you."

"I don't want them to forgive me. I want them to fear me."

21

Livia had no doubt they would, and suspected they already did. What worried her was how far the powers that be might go. They'd killed an FBI agent, and tried to kill Livia herself, to cover up a Secret Service child abuse ring and the high-ranking politicians it implicated. What would stop them from trying to eliminate an assistant US Attorney?

She'd tried to get Diaz to be more careful. But real personal security was a hard lesson for people to internalize if they hadn't lived through the actual need for it. And Diaz, a public school kid from Washington Heights in New York, whose parents had died when she was a toddler and who had done more to raise her little brother than the aunt and step-uncle who had taken them in, was more street smart than most. Still, dealing with predators was one thing. Professionals were a whole different level.

They stood and headed toward the door. "What about Schrader?" Livia said. "Are you sure—"

"We've been over this. Extra guards. Multiple cameras. Everyone's afraid of another Epstein being suicided in prison. So for anyone thinking to try . . . it's not an option."

That was good to hear. On the other hand, anyone who couldn't silence Schrader directly might decide that removing the only person serious about prosecuting him would be a sensible Plan B.

"I have an extra helmet," Livia said. "You want a ride?"

Diaz shook her head. "It's barely a mile."

"It's cold."

Diaz laughed. "You know what it's like in New York this time of year? It's never cold in Seattle. Just wet."

Livia took a good look through the window at the front of the academy before opening the door. Not so long before, this is where the conspirators had ambushed her. That was her first encounter with the really deep water, the currents Carl and Rain swam in. She'd fought her way out. But the best way to beat an ambush was to see it coming. Or to avoid it entirely.

They stepped outside and Livia locked the door. Her bike, a Ducati Streetfighter, was parked behind the building, and if she'd been alone she would have gone out the back. But she wanted to try one more time.

"Alondra," she said. "Are you sure—"

"You said you wanted me because I don't wilt."

Livia glanced around. "You can stand up straight and still look behind you."

"Fuck that. *They* need to be looking out for me."

chapter five

HOBBS

Devereaux shook his head, plainly stunned. "Schrader had videos of the president? When you were the South Carolina US Attorney?"

"Correct."

"But he . . . That was the other party. Why would you—"

"This isn't about parties, Pierce. And even if it were, I assure you, the issue is thoroughly bipartisan."

Devereaux looked at him. Hobbs knew what he was thinking: *At last. The matter at hand.*

"Now you're starting to get it," Hobbs said. "You see, back then, Schrader had video of only one president cavorting with a teenager." He paused for dramatic effect, then continued. "Now he has video of a second."

Devereaux glanced upward as though he might see the Cabinet Room, or even the Oval Office, from where they were sitting. "You mean—"

"That's right. Before he got into politics, when he was just an ordinary billionaire business baron. By the time these guys rise to national prominence, they seem to realize their association with Schrader isn't good for their brands. But by then it's too late."

"Schrader's blackmailing the president?"

"No, that's the thing. The basis for the non-prosecution agreement, in fact. Schrader isn't interested in leverage. There's nothing he wants and can't buy. Except one thing."

"To stay out of jail."

"Bingo."

"That's the deal you made with him?"

Hobbs nodded. "Schrader's got a high-powered lawyer, Sharon Hamilton, and she made it clear that Schrader had created the material purely as a get-out-of-jail-free card, to be played only under the narrowest of circumstances. If those circumstances were to disappear, the material would never surface."

"You believed that?"

"What choice did I have, really? But yes, I believed it. Schrader had been compiling the material for years. He could have used it sooner if he'd wanted to, in a variety of ways, but he never did. And the material inculpates Schrader as much as it does the subjects captured. Those videos aren't a gun. They're a doomsday weapon."

The waiter came by and refreshed their coffees. When he was gone, Devereaux said, "What's changed, then?"

Hobbs appreciated that Devereaux was being polite. The more direct version of the question would have been *Why are you telling me this?* Or even *What do you want from me?*

Hobbs took a quick glance around, but it was reflex—there was no one within earshot. And of course, the entirety of the White House was swept constantly for bugs. This was as safe a place as any to talk.

"After the non-prosecution agreement, Schrader made himself scarce in South Carolina. He bought new property—on Bainbridge Island, in Washington State. Built a twenty-eight-million-dollar compound, with mooring for his yacht and a helipad. And went back to doing what he does. He owns an Airbus ACH130 helicopter that delivers six girls at a time, a ten-minute flight from Seattle."

Devereaux said nothing, and after a moment, Hobbs continued. "Three days ago, the FBI arrested Schrader in the Western District of Washington State. Turns out an assistant US Attorney there has been spearheading an investigation for the past year. And lord almighty, does she have the goods. Schrader's got no way out."

"Except one."

"Ah, but here's the problem. This AUSA, Alondra Diaz. She's a zealot. I explained to the US Attorney in the district—good guy named Meekler—that Schrader can't be prosecuted. I didn't give details, but Meekler got the gist, and recognized there would be rewards for cooperation. He told me he'd make sure Diaz understood she had caught the wrong fish and that she'd throw him back in the water."

"And?"

"Meekler talked to her. Standard *Are you sure we have our ducks in a row* talk. Nudge-nudge, wink-wink. Diaz was adamant. And she'd made sure to have lots of reporters present when the FBI made the arrest. Meekler's afraid if he pushes too hard, someone's going to start writing stories about it."

"What about your non-prosecution agreement?"

"Only binding in the district in South Carolina."

"Schrader agreed to that? That he could still be prosecuted anywhere else in the United States?"

"He didn't like it. But if we had tried to run it through main Justice, the whole thing could have been shot down. The perfect as the enemy of the good. Schrader settled for staying out of jail in South Carolina."

"And you settled for letting him go hunting anywhere else in the country. Like the Vatican and those priests."

"What would you have done, Pierce? Prosecute him, and let those videos loose? Do you know how damaging that would have been?"

"Are you in those videos?"

Hobbs laughed. He'd been expecting the question, and he'd rehearsed his response. "No."

He waited, but Devereaux didn't ask the question Hobbs sensed he was dying to: *Am I?*

"I told you," Hobbs went on, "this isn't about parties. It isn't about the players, it's about . . ." He paused and looked around the prosperous, wood-paneled enclave, then back to Devereaux. "It's about the whole game."

"Still. If Diaz prosecutes, your role in South Carolina is going to be headline news."

Translation: *Even if you're not in those videos, it's your ass, too.*

"Yes. If Diaz prosecutes, I expect I'll be one of the casualties. Though I also expect my decision not to prosecute Schrader will be slightly less fascinating to the public than videos of the implicated men fucking teenaged girls in various of Schrader's mansions."

Devereaux blanched, then got ahold of himself. He said, "I would think . . . after what happened to Epstein, Schrader must be worried someone could try to get to him."

"Oh, he certainly is. Or at least was. His lawyer says he has the videos protected with some sort of dead-man switch. If something happens to Schrader, the material gets uploaded. News outlets, YouTube, social media . . . everywhere."

"You believe that?"

"Enough so that if I were—hypothetically—thinking about how much better off the world would be without Schrader, I'd be afraid to try to make it happen."

"Which is why you're focused on Diaz."

Hobbs nodded, but said nothing more. It wasn't just intel types who understood the power of silence.

Finally, Devereaux said, "What are you asking of me, Uriah?"

"Diaz won't respond to reason. Maybe she'll respond to pressure. Justice hasn't been able to dig up anything. But no one has the kind of resources you do. Maybe you can find something. Some videos Diaz is in. Who knows?"

"General Motors tried something like that with Ralph Nader, back in the day. They found nothing and the whole thing backfired."

"General Motors was using private investigators. And that was the sixties. You're the director of National Intelligence. In the twenty-first century. I'm betting you can do better."

Devereaux rubbed his chin. "Threats are never useless. They're either effective or they make things worse. What if we find something and push, and Diaz pushes back?"

Hobbs was relieved to hear Devereaux talking about *we*. The man was in. Of course he was. Now it was just a question of how far.

Hobbs waited a beat, then said, "I'm open to suggestions."

There was another beat. Devereaux said, "I want to see these videos."

"I don't have a copy. Hamilton showed me something on some sort of encrypted website. So what are we going to do?"

Devereaux's expression was impassive, but Hobbs could tell the man didn't like having to go on Hobbs's word. Or not knowing exactly what Hobbs had seen.

Devereaux sighed. "I'll talk to Lisa Rispel."

Hobbs nodded, pleased. "I've heard she's very . . . effective."

"That's right," Devereaux said. "She was my most dependable case officer when I was head of the Counterterrorism Center, and my deputy when I was director of CIA. I told the Senate committee she would make a great successor, and she has. But you knew all that."

"I meant the black-site interrogations. People say she was willing to do whatever it took. Even eager."

Devereaux frowned. "No one was eager, Uriah. We did what needed to be done."

"The word is, she went to lengths that made even some of her colleagues queasy."

"As I said: Lisa did what needed to be done. And if some of her colleagues weren't willing to do the same, that's on them, not her."

"I don't have a problem with it," Hobbs said. "We want someone ruthless for this, don't we?"

He might have added, *And with her history, if push comes to shove she'll be an ideal cutout, too.* But Devereaux would intuit that. No need to make him uncomfortable by saying it out loud.

"All the resources of Justice are at your disposal," Hobbs said. "I don't know if we'll ever be in a position to tell anyone what we've done here. What I do know is that whoever figures out a way to fix this will have the president in his debt."

He wondered if Devereaux would appreciate how discreet he was being. How many face-saving asides he had offered. Because even if he couldn't prove it in court, he sensed in his gut the truth of what Devereaux had been working so hard to conceal.

Devereaux knew Schrader. Well enough to be worried about appearing in those videos.

He only hoped Devereaux hadn't figured out the same about him.

chapter six

KANEZAKI

Tom Kanezaki sat in a plush chair across from DCI Lisa Rispel in the corner of Rispel's spacious seventh-floor office, a pot of tea and two cups and saucers arrayed before them. On the wall opposite were dozens of photographs of Rispel with presidents and potentates and plutocrats, all hung so as to dominate the view, regardless of where Rispel might seat a visitor. Today, Kanezaki would have preferred the seat across from her desk. That she had invited him into the corner suggested a faux intimacy. Her warmup—a few banal thoughts with regard to his upbringing in the States by nisei parents; fulsome congratulations on ops well executed; and respectful murmurs about an impressive twenty-year rise in the ranks overall—only deepened his suspicions. Well, nothing to be done but to sip the tea, politely deflect the praise, and wait for her to arrive at whatever was the real matter at hand.

"By the way," she said, leaning back as though the real business was done and they were now just chitchatting, "I understand that from time to time you've employed a contractor, a former Marine sniper—nom de guerre Dox."

He offered a friendly smile to conceal his unease. "When it comes to contractors, aren't we trained to neither confirm nor deny?"

She smiled back. It was a warm smile, one he imagined she had practiced many times in front of a mirror, along with the vaguely regal bearing he assumed she'd cultivated as part of an *act as if* philosophy. In fairness, the image had carried her to CIA's top job before her fiftieth birthday, even in the face of widespread political concerns about her treatment of detainees.

"We are," she said. "But I believe that's more for testimony before the Senate."

Kanezaki chuckled at the intel-insiders joke. He had learned early on that the key to power within CIA and the broader intelligence community was to develop your own network—for information, of course, but also for action—and Dox was one of the proverbial jewels in the crown. They'd been working together for years, initially at arm's length, and then increasingly on the rare and surprising basis of trust. He didn't know how Rispel had learned about the connection. Her own network, he supposed. Spies among the spies.

"I've worked with him a few times, yes. Discreet and reliable. Why?"

The smile faded and she eyed him coolly—a duchess losing patience with a favored retainer.

"Is he effective?" she said.

"I thought that would go without saying."

He didn't know why he was sparring with her. The rope-a-dope would have been smarter. Maybe because he felt protective of Dox. Not that the big sniper needed anyone else to protect him.

"Can you contact him?"

"I can try," he said, remembering his training: *It's not enough to know your way in. You have to know your way out.* "He doesn't always respond."

"I thought you said he was reliable."

"About carrying out a job. Not necessarily about accepting one."

"Compunctions, then?"

"I don't know him that well. Sometimes he says yes. Other times no. I don't recall him ever offering reasons."

There was a pause, and when Kanezaki didn't respond to the silence, she said, "There's a man who needs to cease and desist. A formidable man best persuaded permanently, and from a safe distance. I'd like you to engage your contact Dox to do the persuading."

Kanezaki thought he had heard all the euphemisms in the world, but *persuasion* was a new one. "Who's the man?"

"His name is Marvin Manus. He's military- and Agency-trained, although you'll find no records of any of it. You see, before his untimely death, NSA director Theodore Anders employed him as something of a Praetorian guard. Anders did an admirably thorough job of deleting Manus's personal history from government files. But we can give your contractor Dox the necessary intel on where he can be found, and when."

Kanezaki might have pointed out that knowing the exact where and when was an impressive feat with regard to a target who sounded like a well-practiced ghost. But there was no upside to revealing his thoughts, or to the plans that might flow from them.

"All right," he said. "What does Manus need to be persuaded to cease and desist about?"

"The thinking is that Director Anders's untimely death was at Manus's hands."

"The Praetorian guard turning on the emperor?"

"I suppose you could put it that way."

"But that's not a cease-and-desist. It already happened."

Rispel offered a chilly smile—something that, like the warm one, Kanezaki sensed had some practice behind it. "What did you say about this Dox discussing his reasons?" she said.

"Just that I couldn't recall him offering any."

"Exactly. You see, Tom, sometimes it's safer to have nothing even to recall."

chapter seven

KANEZAKI

K anezaki glanced around and immediately saw Maya sitting in the right back corner of the theater. He walked up the aisle stairs past her, munching on the popcorn he had bought, and took a seat immediately behind her. The movie wouldn't start for another fifteen minutes, but the place was already half-full. An installment in one of the superhero franchises that had opened just a few days before.

He leaned forward. "Anything?"

She turned her head toward the aisle, away from the people to her left and in front of her, and rested her left cheek against her folded hands. "Taped to the bottom of my seat. Lean forward whenever you like and it's yours."

"Summarize it for me."

"The man, Manus, is a ghost, like you said. All his records purged. Not many people could have done that, so yeah, the idea that he reported to then-NSA director Anders makes sense. Whether Manus killed Anders, I couldn't say."

"But they're tracking him now. They say he's in Seattle."

"Again, not something I could confirm. But if it's true, I'm pretty sure I know why he's there. Remember what we talked about with Guardian Angel?"

Guardian Angel was a massive system of government surveillance. It monitored emails, phone calls, cellphone movements, credit card payments, Internet searches . . . everything. It was one of the few programs Snowden hadn't known about, in part because it was so compartmentalized. The architects knew individual pieces. Only a very few had the complete picture.

"Of course," he said.

"Well, someone was using the system to monitor someone named Alondra Diaz. She's an assistant US Attorney, who just—"

"Announced a case in connection with the arrest of Andrew Schrader, yes."

Maya glanced back at him. "You know?"

If he hadn't been so troubled by what Maya had found, he might have been amused. She was the most capable Science & Technology whiz kid he'd ever come across, and cultivating her had been a coup. Most of the seventh-floor people tried to develop lateral assets—other chiefs, deputy chiefs, assistant deputies. But those were political sources, when what Kanezaki wanted was information. So he wasted little time in Headquarters's more rarefied realms, preferring to troll the facility's basements and subbasements instead. In his experience, the maid often knew more than the lord of the manor. Certainly Maya did. But that didn't mean she didn't have blind spots.

He gave her a gentle smile. "Don't let yourself get so distracted by what's stamped *secret* that you forget to read the news."

She chuckled. "Good point."

Not for the first time, he was bewildered to find himself someone's mentor. It seemed like not that long before, the helplessly green recruit had been him. He wished Tatsu could have seen the transition. He wished the wily Keisatsuchō cop, who as part of Japan's national police force should have been an adversary but who instead had treated Kanezaki as a son, could have known before he succumbed to cancer that the naive kid he had taken under his wing now navigated his own fraught moral waters, with Tatsu's example as his compass.

"Anyway," she went on, "I think that's the connection. There's more in the file. But . . . I mean, an assistant US Attorney, do you really think . . ."

"I don't know yet. I'll read the file. But that was a great idea you had, a backdoored hidden log file to monitor which Guardian Angel searches were being deleted."

"What goes into the shredder is what's most revealing."

"Exactly."

She rolled her eyes. "Yes, exactly. You're the one who told me that."

Had he? Maybe, though not in those words. "Well, it's true."

"What I'm saying is, the back door was your idea."

He wasn't sure where she was going. "I was just thinking out loud. You're the one who told me it could be done. And who found a way to do it. Credit where it's due, that's all."

"Yeah, well, if you give me too much credit, I might think you're trying to snow me. And you don't need to, Tom. I believe in you."

He nodded, thinking *touché*. Here he'd been teasing her about the importance of paying attention to the news and not just to matters stamped *secret*. While himself forgetting something more important— not to underestimate people.

"You're right," he said. "I'm sorry. I believe in you, too."

She smiled. "Obviously. Now, are you taking off? One of us should, and I was hoping to watch the movie."

chapter
eight

DOX

Dox stood under a gray drizzle at the apex of Freeway Park, observing the weird concrete labyrinth below. It was hard to know what to make of it. He'd been to most of the great city parks of the world—Lumpini in Bangkok, Güell in Barcelona, Beihai in Beijing. Not to mention your more local candidates like Central in New York and Golden Gate in San Francisco. But this one . . . Well, it was sui generis, as the lawyers liked to say, you'd have to give it that. He wondered what was behind the design—a crazy architect, thinking what the world needed most was a Brutalist version of Angkor Wat or the step-wells of India? Maybe. The problem was, two great tastes didn't always taste great together. He liked sriracha plenty and he loved durian, too, but he wouldn't pour the one on the other.

But he'd told Kanezaki that, based on the intel, he had a feeling the park would be the place to look for this hombre Manus, and so here he was.

It was a strange job for a sniper. Hell, it was a strange job for any respectable killer for hire. More a humanitarian mission than the kind of reach-out-and-touch-someone engagement Kanezaki ordinarily had in mind.

Of course, that didn't mean the job was free of Kanezaki's signature manipulations. The man just couldn't help himself. Though somehow, the fact that Dox knew what he was up to, and that Kanezaki knew Dox knew, tended to make the habit tolerable.

The way Kanezaki had initially pitched it, for example, when he'd reached Dox on the satellite phone in Bali two days earlier. He'd said, "I have something that needs looking into in Seattle. Livia would be right for it, but I thought you'd want to know first."

Thought you'd want to know. True enough, of course, but it obscured the larger story, which was that there was no way Dox would allow Labee to face danger if he could face it himself. Labee, Livia's real name, which she'd told him when he told her his was Carl. He loved the sound of it. Loved saying it, even to himself. And he loved that only he got to call her that.

"That's very courteous of you," Dox had told him, half-annoyed, half-grateful.

"In fairness," Kanezaki said, "I was instructed to retain you for the job."

"Instructed? By who?"

"DCI Rispel."

That threw him. When the hell had he become a plaything for people as high up as Rispel? And why would Kanezaki even consider Labee for something like this?

"Should I be honored?"

Kanezaki chuckled. "I doubt it. It's clear to me Rispel's primary concern, with effectiveness as a given, is disposability."

"At least my effectiveness is a given. For a minute there, you had me worried."

"She pitched the job as retaliation. But that's bullshit. Someone brought in a contractor to make a run at a government official. They want to use you to cut the thread."

"Assassinate the assassin?"

"That's how it looks to me."

"Classic. But I wouldn't even consider it."

"I've always admired your ethics."

"It's not ethics, son. It's professional courtesy. With maybe a little concern for karma thrown in. Who's this official, anyway?"

"An assistant US Attorney named Alondra Diaz."

"Pretty name."

"Livia knows her."

The thought of Kanezaki monitoring Labee put him on edge. "What? How? And how do you know?"

"Just incidental collection. Diaz's cellphone history shows a periodic nexus with Livia. I didn't look into it more deeply, but I think Livia trains her. Martial arts or women's self-defense or whatever."

He sensed the *didn't look into it more deeply* was an attempt to mollify him, but he was still irritated. "Son, if you want to call it 'incidental' for public consumption, I can't stop you. But please, don't piss down my back and tell me it's raining."

"I don't track Livia, Dox. Out of respect for her, and for you. And for myself. I've seen too many people in this gig get addicted to the voyeurism."

"Sure, loveint and all that."

"Loveint is the least of it. People lose sight of the purpose. I'm not going to let that happen to me."

The truth was, Dox didn't find the declaration reassuring. It felt to him like protesting too much. But he had bigger concerns for the moment than Kanezaki's self-awareness about the allure of power. "Is Livia in danger?" he said.

"I don't have any reason to think so, no."

"You're sure?"

"Based on everything I can tell, I think Rispel believes Diaz is the problem, and that eliminating her will solve it. She's probably right, too. Assuming they can make it look natural."

"Natural? Wonder why they didn't reach out to John? Or maybe they did. But he's retired, and besides, he won't take a job if it involves a woman."

John Rain, half-American and half-Japanese, was once so adept at "natural causes" that he had been the go-to man for elements of the Japanese government and for the CIA. But age, conscience, and maybe the love of an ex-Mossad agent named Delilah had conspired to impel him to find a way out of all that. Still, pound for pound, even now Rain was the most formidable urban operator and tactician Dox had ever known.

"I don't know if they tried Rain," Kanezaki said. "My guess is they didn't. The guy they're bringing in is more deniable. A ghost named Marvin Manus. Whose only known connection is to former NSA director Theodore Anders."

"Didn't Anders drown a few years ago?"

"That's the official story. The truth is, he was crushed to death. Back broken. Rispel says Manus did it, but who knows?"

"And Rispel says she wants me to, what, drop this guy for killing Anders?"

"Correct. But I think what she really wants is for you to drop Manus after he kills Diaz."

"And what do you want?"

"I want you to stop him."

"You mean preempt him?"

"No, not like that. Not kill him. Just . . . stop him."

"By what, sweet-talking him?"

"Look, I'm not going to micromanage you. I don't want Diaz dead, and I don't want Manus dead, either. He's more valuable to me alive."

Dox didn't even have to ask why. With Kanezaki, it was always about the information.

It wasn't his kind of job. And he didn't need the money. He realized that's why Kanezaki had mentioned Labee. *Go ahead and turn me down,*

I'll just call in that marker your girlfriend owes me. Yeah, of course that was it. It had worked, hadn't it?

Not that Labee was his girlfriend exactly. He didn't know what label to put on it, and wasn't inclined to try. Whatever it was, it was about as unlikely a thing as he could have imagined, which is probably why the gods or fate or the universe or whatever had decided to have a laugh by making it happen. Dox had been in Cambodia, hunting for a guy named Sorm as part of a contract. And Labee had been in Thailand, where she had tracked down the men who had trafficked her and her sister, Nason, when they'd been girls. They'd run into each other, some-how gotten past their initial suspicions, and realized they had the same objectives, albeit for different reasons. Then they'd killed a bunch of people who had it coming and then some. She'd told him things about her past, things she'd never told anyone but that he needed to know to understand the forces they were up against. Maybe it was the way she'd trusted him. Or how brave she was. Or beautiful. But the truth was, when it came to love, you could come up with all the articulable reasons in the world and in the end it wouldn't mean a thing. But he did love her, he knew that. He'd never said it for fear of scaring her off, but he did.

When it came to Kanezaki, though, none of that mattered. What mattered was what might be negotiated on Labee's behalf.

"If I take this thing," Dox said, "it squares Livia's debt with you?"

"I wouldn't say squares, but—"

"Squares, son. That's the deal. I save Ms. Diaz via less-than-lethal means, and Livia owes you nothing, not even a cup of coffee if you happen to be in town. You want it or not?"

There was a pause. Kanezaki, with his theatrical pauses. If things didn't work out at CIA, he could always teach a course on negotiation.

"All right," Kanezaki said. "Do this, and Livia and I are square."

Dox spotted the loophole. "Not just square to date. Square forever. Even if she asks for your help again, with Guardian Angel or whatever."

He was aware he was revealing too much, that Kanezaki would use it as leverage next time. But the damn rascal was already using how much he cared about Labee. And besides, the point wasn't to protect himself. It was to protect her.

"Come on, Dox. I don't know what she might ask of me in the future."

"Neither do I, and I don't care. Those are my terms."

"Okay. But then next time she asks me to go out on a limb for her, what's my incentive?"

Damn, he hadn't thought of that. "All right. But whatever she might ask of you going forward, when it's time to collect you come to me first, you son of a bitch." Which of course Kanezaki was going to do anyway. After all, he'd just done it now.

"Deal," Kanezaki said, probably with a suppressed smile. "Are you going to bring in Rain?"

Dox was glad they were done haggling. The truth was, he had certainly considered asking for John's help. And it was funny, when they'd first met in Afghanistan, a lifetime earlier, they hadn't gotten along well, at least not personally. Dox talked too much for John's taste, though from Dox's perspective, the problem was that John talked too damn little. But then they'd met again in Rio, where some government dumbasses thought they could get Dox to betray an old comrade in arms for money. They turned out to be wrong, in the dead-wrong sense of the word, and afterward, realizing he could trust someone had just about melted old John's brain. But they'd had each other's backs ever since, stumbled into a few adventures—sometimes with Kanezaki's help, other times at his instigation—did a good deed or two, and somehow even managed to make a little money along the way by outsmarting a few bad guys.

"Nah," Dox said after a moment. "He and Delilah deserve some peace. He's always going on about how he's retired. It's high time someone acted like he means it."

"Does he?"

"He thinks he does."

"Then who?"

"My God, the calumny. Maybe I'll just handle it all by my capable self, you ever consider that?"

"Come on, we both know less-than-lethal is likely to be more complicated. Who?"

"Sources and methods, son."

Kanezaki laughed. "That's my line. Let me guess. Daniel Larison."

Larison had fallen in with them a few years back in connection with a series of false-flag terror attacks initiated by some of America's most esteemed political personages. It hadn't been a great fit initially, and in fact they'd all nearly killed each other before finding a way to work together. And now Larison was on the very short list of people Dox trusted to have his back. More amazing still, he knew, was that Larison felt the same way.

Dox smiled. "Not much I can hide from you, is there?"

"Not if I'm looking. You don't think Larison might be . . . too much?"

"I'd rather use a soldier as a diplomat than a diplomat as a soldier. But I'll tell the old angel of death to dial it down this time."

"Remember, we don't want death here. We want Manus motivated to tell us what he knows."

"Oh, it's *we* and *us* now, is it?"

"For all the things that matter? Yes. It is."

Dox couldn't deny that. Kanezaki was an ace bullshitter, but that didn't mean he never told the truth.

And now here he was, just two days later. Not an ideal amount of time to prepare, but he and Larison knew each other's moves and they were managing.

His cellphone buzzed in his back pocket. He pulled out the unit and glanced at the screen. Caller blocked. Well, of course. The phone was an encrypted burner, and only Kanezaki had the number. He pressed *Answer* and raised the phone to his ear.

"Hello."

"She just left her apartment," Kanezaki said. "As soon as it was clear she was heading toward the park, they called me with instructions to have you in position near Pike Place Market."

"Why there?"

"They say Manus spent the night at a hostel in the neighborhood and they expect him to be there again later this morning. I'm betting that means he's at the park now. They don't want you to have those coordinates because they want you to remain ignorant of what he does to Diaz. A federal prosecutor falls and cracks her head or gets mugged or whatever in the park, you drop a guy near Pike Place Market, no one ever makes the connection. Congratulations, I think you called all of it."

He had called it, hadn't he? Well, a killer just knows a killer. Kanezaki's people had assembled Diaz's cellphone history. She didn't have a lot of reliable patterns beyond home and office, neither of which would present an attractive option for something intended to look natural because of too many witnesses and too much known connection with the target. But it turned out she had a habit of using Freeway Park on some of her morning jogs. Dox and Larison had agreed that if they were looking to take her out, and especially if it had to look at least seminatural, this was the spot they would use to make it happen. And if they were thinking that way, it was reasonable to expect Manus would be, too.

"What's your intel on the man based on?" Dox said.

"What do you mean?"

"I mean, are we talking national technical means? Or are there other operators in the vicinity?"

"He's carrying a burner they dialed into. I gather foot surveillance against this guy would be difficult. Especially this early in the morning, without many people around."

That was a relief. Too many cooks and all that.

"We're here already," Dox said. "My partner's out having a look-see as we speak. But are you sure you're not going to take any shit for this not turning out per your boss's request?"

"Who can say what went wrong? Manus didn't do the job. He never showed up where they told me to instruct you to wait, or at least you didn't see him. Etc."

"Fair enough. Just wish you could have told me more about this guy. But okay, with the rain and the early hour, the park's pretty empty right now. Shouldn't be too hard to spot him."

"Keep me posted."

There was a nervous edge to Kanezaki's voice. Dox smiled. Nothing new there. "Don't I always?" he said, and clicked off.

It was weird being back in Labee's city. Even under normal circumstances, she wouldn't have appreciated it. She liked her space and didn't like surprises. Other than the time he'd come here to help her with those Child's Play conspirators, all their get-togethers had been on neutral ground. He badly wanted her to visit him in Bali, but she'd been noncommittal when he'd asked and he was afraid to push it.

He saw Larison approaching along one of the wet concrete walkways, wearing a rain parka that nicely concealed the Glock 17 he was carrying in a small-of-the-back holster, but that did considerably less to hide his weight lifter's bulk. Deployed above him was an umbrella Kanezaki had provided—functional, but with a forty-inch lead-lined hickory stem.

Beyond its potential utility as a long and nasty nightstick, Dox had hoped the umbrella might help make Larison look like an innocent tourist determined to visit the iconic park no matter the weather. But he could see now the ruse was weak. It wasn't exactly that mothers would pull their babies to their breasts and slam the shutters closed at his approach, but Larison was definitely one of those operators with an unmistakable air of *fuck with me and die*. If Dox ever had to tangle

44

with him—and back in the day he almost had—he'd do all he could to ensure it was from a quarter mile out and an elevated position.

But what couldn't be concealed could sometimes be used to distract. In fact, once upon a time, the KGB had deliberately shadowed CIA officers in Moscow with obvious surveillance. The officers would focus on what they could see, get clear of it, and then overlook the real surveillance that clung to them all the way to a dead drop or something else operational. So let Manus focus on Larison's rattlesnake vibe. That would soak up all his attention, while Dox ghosted in from his flank.

He wished again that Kanezaki could have provided a little more intel on what Manus looked like. On the other hand, Dox had yet to meet the operator he couldn't make. John might be an exception, true, but he was smaller than Dox and Larison, which was an advantage in these things. And unless this Manus had John's level of grappling expertise, he must have been a sizeable specimen himself. Even if the story about how he had crushed Anders to death was bullshit, the man must have been large for a rumor like that to take hold.

Other than the patter of rain on wet concrete and the rush of the waterfalls below him, the park was quiet. He couldn't even hear the traffic from I-5, over which the park was built.

He watched as Larison got closer. Nothing in the man's demeanor had changed from twenty minutes before, when he'd set off to have a look around. Or nothing Dox could have easily articulated, anyway. But there was something—some extra level of alertness. A narrowing of focus. A purposefulness. Like a jungle cat's stillness in the instant it catches the scent of prey.

Larison reached Dox's position and paused to scan the area. In his low rasp of a voice he said, "He's here."

chapter nine

LARISON

In response, Dox offered only a simple nod. Larison was glad. Rain, for all his impressiveness as a leader and a tactician, had a tendency to micromanage. Not that Larison, who had his own trust issues, could fairly object to the habit. But Dox was different. Once you'd earned the big sniper's confidence, there was no second-guessing.

"What's your take?" Dox said.

"A reloader, no doubt."

Reloader was a term he'd picked up from Dox. It meant someone so formidable you'd empty the whole magazine into him, eject, reload, and empty the second magazine, too, just to be sure.

"Oh, hell," Dox said. "Not another sumo? My insides are still healing from the time one of those boys rammed me damn near into low-Earth orbit. I'm telling you, these less-than-lethal parameters are the worst."

Larison chuckled, still scanning the area. Dox had told him the sumo story many times. "Not sumo-sized. But big. And . . . solid. Rooted. You'll see. He's circling the park now. I'm guessing when he's done with the perimeter check, he'll head here for the view from the high ground. What about Diaz?"

"According to Kanezaki, she's on her way. We were right about our Mr. Manus wanting to do it here. Too good a spot to pass up."

"Listen," Larison said, closing the umbrella. "I'm not about to get rammed, into low-Earth-orbit or anywhere else. If he doesn't like the look of us, or the sound of whatever you're planning to say to him, I'm using the Glock, not a damn umbrella."

Dox frowned. "If we have to drop him, we'll drop him. But my deal with Kanezaki was less-than-lethal methods in exchange for he won't go pestering Livia. I mean to hold up my end, if at all possible."

Not for the first time, Larison was impressed by the man's loyalty. And, if he was being honest with himself, moved by it. In part because of the wonder of knowing it now extended to him. Before he could overthink it and change his mind, he said, "She's lucky to have you."

Dox smiled. "Maybe." And then, as though reading Larison's thoughts, added, "But then so are you."

Larison didn't disagree, but he wasn't going to give Dox the satisfaction of saying so. "Well?" he said, extending his left hand toward Dox's right. "You ready to get into character?"

Dox took hold of his hand and smiled. "My whole life."

They walked off, hand in hand. It had actually been Dox's idea. There were a lot of patterns an operator might run to spot opposition—sniper hides, elevated positions generally, flanking maneuvers . . . the list was long and varied. But whatever this guy Manus might be alert to, two men walking openly hand-in-hand probably wasn't part of it.

And this was another thing Larison was still struggling with. Decades in the closet. His sexuality a lifelong torment he had worked so hard to conceal—from the military, even from his estranged wife. But Dox, and Rain . . . they knew. And just didn't care. It mattered to them about as much as whether he was left-handed or right. If it meant so little to them, why was he still so . . . private about it? Nobody could hurt him with it anymore. And nobody who mattered wanted to. So why couldn't he let it go? Something that was once a vulnerability no longer was. Why was that anything but a wonder, a relief?

They strolled along, seeing no one but an occasional jogger or vag-abond. Dox kept up a medley of cover-for-action small talk—blather about Brutalist architecture and urban renewal and whatever else he'd learned about the park while researching it online. Larison had never known a sniper who liked to talk even half as much as Dox did. Most of them were as quiet as Larison himself. It had taken a while to get used to. The weird thing was, he'd actually come to enjoy it.

Now and then Dox would pause to extend a cellphone in front of them from a selfie stick as though snapping a picture. Another of Kanezaki's toys—the phone was a dummy, while the stick was a twenty-six-inch extensible steel baton. Then they would link hands again and continue walking. Dox was carrying his own small-of-the-back pistol—the Wilson Combat Tactical Supergrade he favored—but there had been no need to discuss whose right hand would be free. From behind a scope in low light at a half mile out, there was no one better than Dox. But for pistol work, everyone recognized Larison was in his own league.

Though as Dox had said, hopefully it wouldn't come to that.

They walked. Dox talked and Larison periodically grunted responses, heart pounding steadily the way it always did in the moments before action, eyes sweeping the terrain.

They went around a corner. And there, fifty feet away, was Manus, coming straight toward them.

chapter ten

DOX

The instant Dox saw Manus, he knew. Larison had been right: a reloader for sure.

Even under the rain parka the man was wearing, Dox could see he was thick-boned and heavily muscled. And while Larison had the build of someone who pumped a lot of iron and took supplements on top of it, and while Dox himself had once played tackle on his high school football team, Manus . . . It was like one of his parents had been an oak tree and the other a bank vault. For a second, Dox pictured the sumos and wondered what would have happened if they'd charged this guy. Whatever the outcome, it would have been the proverbial irresistible force and immovable object.

But none of those thoughts made it to the surface. If there was one thing he'd learned from John, and he'd learned more than a few, it was not just to act as if, but to feel it. And his feeling was, he was just a tourist taking a walk in the park, not a care in the world, enjoying the outdoors despite the steady drizzle. And if his heart was beginning to beat hard, well, that was only because he was excited to be here side by side with Larison, his special friend.

Forty feet. Manus didn't seem to be watching them particularly closely. But Dox could feel his attention. Could feel the way Larison's danger vibe was pinging his radar.

They kept moving. Dox disgorged all the facts he had learned about the park. Larison responded with *uh-huhs* and *reallys* and *you don't says*.

At thirty feet out, there was a ripple in Manus's energy. It was nearly invisible, and maybe it even was invisible, but Dox knew what it meant. It was like a Doppler shift, the change in frequency you could sense when a man went from asking himself a question, to being an instant away from answering it.

And not answering in a good way.

The original plan had been for Dox and Larison to get close—but not too close—and then to politely introduce themselves. *Hello there, Mr. Manus, you don't know us, but we're here to tell you the thing with Alondra Diaz is a setup and the people who hired you want you dead. What can we tell you, you just can't trust management these days, it's unfortunate but that's the state of our modern world. Would you care to join us for a cup of delicious Seattle coffee so we can put our heads together and maybe find a way to watch each other's backs?*

But he could tell now that ship had sailed. He should have known the effect Larison's presence would have on a potentially delicate situation. Should have realized that in telling himself Larison could provide a useful distraction, he'd been rationalizing. He hadn't wanted to bother John. But for all his lethality, there was a stillness to John that had a way of reassuring people. And as he watched Manus looming closer and closer, he would have happily paid good money for a way to keep the man calm, and mentally kicked himself for not having one.

Well, he could do the after-action report later. Hopefully.

Fifteen feet. Manus was no longer pretending not to notice them. He was watching intently, his eyes leaving their faces, where he could read whatever was available in their expressions, and settling on their torsos, which would give him a peripheral-vision view of hands and therefore an early warning of a reach for weapons. Probably the only thing that had kept him from taking action already was the incongruity of Dox and Larison holding hands, and maybe of Dox's banter.

But that would last only for another second, if that.

Manus's hands were empty, which was good. And while he was wearing a backpack, that wouldn't offer ready access to a weapon. But Dox could see the clip of a folding knife in the man's front pocket. And who knew what he might have behind his back, or under his rain parka.

Ten feet. Dox could feel Larison beginning to tense up, seeing where this was going, determined to stay ahead of the action-reaction curve. *Shit.*

"Pardon me," Dox called out, improvising. "I wonder if you could advise on the location of the world-famous Seattle Space Needle?"

Ordinarily, giving a person's brain one additional thing to process could buy you a precious extra second. But it was like Manus didn't even hear him. The man's eyes never left their torsos. And even as the words were leaving Dox's mouth, Manus's left hand was coming forward, his body blading off, his right hand dropping to the clip of that folding knife in his front pocket—

Everything slowed down. The sound of the rain faded out. Dox felt Larison letting go of his hand and breaking right, saw the umbrella dropping to the ground. He didn't have to look to know Larison was clearing leather. The miracle was that he hadn't done so already.

Manus had taken hold of the folder. It was coming out of his pocket now. And coming. And coming. God almighty, what the hell kind of knife was this?

In his peripheral vision, Dox could see Larison bringing around the Glock.

Without thinking, Dox dropped the selfie stick—judging from the size of this guy, getting hit with it would probably have done no more than make him mad—and rushed in. "Don't shoot him!" he yelled.

Manus had cleared the knife but hadn't yet opened it. Still, the damn handle itself looked almost a foot long.

A crazy thought raced through his brain: *Please God not another sword fight—*

And then he slammed into Manus, coming in low under the free arm, hitting him in the gut with his right shoulder like a linebacker trying to blast through to the quarterback. The force of the impact knocked Manus back—not by much, but enough to buy Dox just enough space to wrap his hands around Manus's hand and wrist and pin the knife to the man's hip. They struggled for a second, and Dox realized with a tinge of panic that even with a two-on-one grip and bearing down hard, he was having trouble controlling the knife hand. Worse, if he had two hands occupied, it meant that Manus—

He sensed the elbow blurring in a second before it landed and managed to get a shoulder partly in the way. Still, the shot glanced off his head and he saw stars.

"We're here to help you, goddamnit!" he shouted. "Listen to me!"

But Manus didn't listen. He brought in his free hand, grabbed Dox's right wrist, and began to pry it back. Good lord, the man's grip was like the damn jaws of life. Dox couldn't see Larison and was afraid he was angling off for a shot. "Don't shoot him!" he yelled again. "Get in here and help me!"

Dox struggled desperately to hang on. Manus's hand was slippery from the rain, and if he broke Dox's grip, an instant later that knife or sword or whatever the hell it was would be in play.

"Listen to me!" Dox shouted again. "We're not trying to hurt you!"

His arms started to shake with the effort of trying to control Manus's knife hand. And just as he was sure he was going to lose it—

Larison crashed into Manus from the opposite side. He took hold of Manus's free hand and dragged it back. Now each of them had a two-on-one grip. They circled clockwise for a moment, like dancers locked in a weird waltz, everyone taking little mincing steps so as not to slip on the wet pavement. Somehow they managed to shove Manus back against one of the concrete walls. They tried to pull his arms wide, but the man was so strong the most they could manage was a stalemate, everyone hanging on to whatever they had.

Well shit this is certainly going well—

And then Manus seemed to tap into some hidden reserve of strength. Gritting his teeth but not making a sound, he started to retract his left arm. Larison braced and pulled the other way, grimacing with the effort, eyes bulging in disbelief, but inch by inch Manus hauled him closer until he'd gotten him in front of Dox. And then he began to drag the knife hand back, using Larison's body as a kind of brace.

"Goddamnit, can't you tell we're not trying to hurt you?" Dox shouted. "What are you, deaf?"

From just behind him, he heard Larison say, "Oh, hell."

Dox thought, *What?*

And then Larison was gone, disengaged. Instantly Manus seized Dox by the throat with his freed left hand. He started to squeeze. Dox turtled in his chin to save his trachea from being crushed but still he couldn't breathe—

"Dumbass . . . we're . . . trying . . . to . . . help . . . you," he rasped.

But Manus ignored him. Dox could feel his grip on the knife hand slipping—

And suddenly Manus stopped, as still as if he'd been turned to stone. Dox jerked his head back, coughed violently, and sucked in a huge, heaving *thank-you-sweet-lord* breath. He glanced right. There was Larison, five feet back, angled out, the Glock up in a two-handed grip and pointed directly at Manus's face. The danger vibe was gone, replaced by pure ice. The angel of death himself, and Dox had never been gladder for his company.

"Can you read lips?" Larison said.

Manus looked at Larison. There was a long, frozen moment. Then he gave a single nod.

"Drop the knife," Larison said. "You can have it back after we've talked. If we wanted to kill you, you'd be dead already."

Manus eyed Larison. He wasn't struggling with Dox anymore, but he wasn't complying, either.

Dox stole a quick glance in Larison's direction. "Tell him I said please."

"What?" Larison said.

"Tell him."

"No."

"Damn it, tell him. I'm not letting go of his wrist until he drops the knife. And my hands are getting tired."

There was a pause. Larison said, "My partner says he doesn't want me to kill you."

"That's not what I said!"

Another pause. "He says please."

But they were still stalemated.

"Tell him I'm not letting go of his wrist until he drops the knife. And of the two ways he might drop it, I'd prefer he chooses the one where he can pick it up again when we're done talking."

"Either you drop the knife on your own," Larison said, "or you drop it because I've shot out your brain stem."

"That's not what I said!"

"It's what he needs to understand."

A long moment went by. Dox didn't know what to do. If the man didn't believe Larison would kill him, it would be a hell of a last mistake.

But whatever Manus saw in Larison's stance and in his eyes, he must have known what it meant. Dox felt the man's wrist flex. An instant later, the knife hit the wet pavement with a clang. Dox kicked it away, released the wrist, and took a long step back and to the side, making sure he didn't get in the way of Larison's line of sight.

"Thank you," Dox said, looking at Manus. "Can you understand what I'm saying?"

Manus gave a single nod. It was unnerving, how silent and still and expressionless the man was. It was hard to tell what he might be thinking. Was he willing to listen? Or was he just waiting until he saw an opportunity to gut them both?

"Please, think about it," Dox said. "My partner's pointing a gun at you. I've never seen him miss, not even from a lot farther than he's standing right now. If we were here to kill you, or hurt you, why wouldn't we have done it already?"

Manus watched him for a moment. Then he said, "What do you want?"

The voice was a bit monotone, but overall not so unusual. He must not have been born deaf.

"We know what you're here for," Dox said. "Alondra Diaz. We were sent to kill you after you did the deed. But we're not going to do that. You're being set up. Do you understand?"

Manus looked at him, expressionless. "No."

"I know, it's confusing. Look, I'd like for us to put our heads together. Can we do that?"

"Can I pick up my knife?"

"Do you mind if I hold it for a while instead? I'm recently phobic about swords. It's a long story."

Manus didn't respond. Dox knelt and retrieved the knife. Now that the craziness of the moment was past, he recognized the model. He would have liked to open it, but under the circumstances that would have been unduly provocative.

He held it up and faced Manus so the man could read his lips. "The Cold Steel Espada," he said. "Very nice. The extra large?"

He'd been hoping to establish a little rapport with that, but Manus only looked at him.

"I've always thought of it as a novelty," Dox went on. "Due to its size. Never heard of someone actually carrying one. But I can see it suits you."

Still Manus only looked at him.

"Anyway, I'll look forward to handing it back as soon as we've gotten to know each other better and I'm less paranoid about you trying to fillet me with it. Does that seem reasonable?"

Manus said, "All right."

It might not have been much, but they were talking at least. A little.

"Thank you," Dox said. "And if I were to politely ask whether you might be carrying any other hardware, would you be truthful with me on short acquaintance?"

"Would you be with me?"

That was fair. "Probably not. Trust doesn't come easily in our trade. You should have seen my partner and me back in the day. But look at us now. Holding hands and everything."

He was hoping for some kind of reaction to that—maybe not an outright belly laugh, but something. But Manus just looked at him.

A woman in a jogging outfit turned the corner behind Manus and started running toward them. She saw the tableau and stopped short. For a second, Dox was afraid it was Diaz. But no, this woman was white, with short, sandy-colored hair.

"Police matter," Dox called out to her. "I'm sorry, ma'am, but I'll have to ask you to take an alternate route this morning."

Manus glanced back. Without a word, the woman did a 180 and was on her way. Manus looked at Dox again.

"Obviously that was for her benefit," Dox said. "We're not really police."

"I'm deaf. Not stupid."

Oops. "Of course. I apologize. I have it on reliable authority that when I'm nervous, I can talk too much. Anyway, I think we should go. And at the risk of being rude, could I first trouble you to lift that parka high and spin slowly around? You can see my friend is still tense, and I think you might put him at ease that way."

Manus complied. Nothing under the parka.

"And those pants. Maybe just lift them up a few inches so I can see your ankles?"

Manus complied. Nothing but a pair of socks around ankles as thick as a normal man's knee.

"Thank you," Dox said. "And forgive me, but I'm about eighty percent sure that's a push-dagger buckle on your belt. As it happens, I'm wearing one myself. I'm hoping your pants will stay up without it, and I can give it back to you along with the Espada when we're done talking?"

Manus removed the belt and tossed it underhand to Dox. Dox caught it and took a look at the buckle.

"Don't recognize this one," Dox said. "You make it yourself?"

Manus nodded.

Dox shoved the belt in one of his parka pockets. "Looks like fine work. Maybe sometime you could show me how."

No response to that. Well, rapport didn't always come easy.

Dox knew there might be more hardware. In fact, if the man were anything like Dox, he'd have at least three other sharp and pointy things hidden on his person. But they'd been here too long already, and even with the foul weather it was lucky they'd had to deal with only a single civilian. There wasn't time for a more careful search. The good news was, there was no reason to think Manus would favor another skirmish without first hearing what they had to say. And besides, Larison wasn't likely to let the man close enough to offer the opportunity.

Dox glanced over at Larison. Larison nodded and holstered the Glock.

"Okay," Dox said. "Time for us to scram. As it happens, I know a delightful coffee emporium, about five miles south of here—All City, it's called. Maybe we can regroup there and talk?"

Manus nodded.

Dox wished the man would say more. His calm silence was spooky. But maybe he'd loosen up once they were past the current unpleasantries.

"Oh," Dox went on. "Just one thing. You should toss that burner you're carrying. It's how they're tracking you."

Manus looked at him. "I'm not carrying a phone."

Dox glanced at Larison. Larison looked past Dox and said, "Oh, fuck."

chapter
eleven

MANUS

When the wingman said, "Oh, fuck," Manus followed his gaze. The woman jogger was back, flanked by two burly men. None of them was running. They were intent on Manus, the wingman, and the talker, methodically closing the distance from fifty yards away. As they walked, each kept a fist resting on a hip—quick access to a weapon.

He looked in the other direction. The wingman was looking the same way now. Three more large men, approaching from that side. Same distance, same fist-on-the-hip methodical walk.

The talker pulled a gun from behind his back and said something to the wingman. His back was turned so Manus couldn't read his lips. Probably they were discussing options.

It occurred to Manus that the whole thing could be an elaborate setup. It didn't feel likely, but—

The talker turned to him. "Sorry I don't have an extra pistol," he said. "But here you go, and let's hope you can put it to good use." He tossed the Espada underhand and Manus caught it.

The feel of the Espada back in his hand settled it for Manus. The wingman and the talker were no longer a problem. The other six were.

The talker laughed. "On the plus side, with all these blocks of concrete, at least we've got cover. Never really cared for Brutalist architecture before, but call me a convert."

The talker didn't seem afraid, or even nervous. Manus had the sense that unlike the wingman, the talker would be easy to underestimate. That in fact, the talker might prefer it that way. Probably the holding hands thing had been his idea. It had worked, too—for one second too long, the incongruity had confused Manus and delayed a proper response.

Without any need for consultation, the three of them started backing away at ninety degrees from the approaching teams. Obviously, the wingman and the talker understood a pincer maneuver and how to avoid it. That was good.

The two teams crept closer. Manus could imagine several reasons for the care they seemed to be taking in their approach. They might have been familiar with his reputation, or with the wingman's and the talker's. And although they had superior numbers, they were moving across open grass. There were some trees, but they hadn't reached them yet. So they might have been concerned about their relative lack of cover. They might also have been concerned about a drawn-out gunfight rather than a quick massacre, and the attention the noise would bring.

The three of them stopped just short of one of the sheer walls of concrete blocks. The talker and the wingman were almost shoulder-to-shoulder, the talker positioned on the right and monitoring the approach of the team on that side, the wingman performing mirror-image duty on the other side. Manus drifted to the left and put his back to the wall. He wished he could see their faces better to read their lips, but it was more important to have something solid behind him.

There was an opening for a stairway a few feet to their right. The wingman glanced toward it, then went back to watching the team on the left. He said, "Don't like the stairs. Don't know what's down there. They could be funneling us."

The talker turned and glanced at the team coming from the wingman's side. "Agreed. And I don't fancy giving up the high ground, anyway." He went back to watching the team on his side.

Manus thought the wingman was right about the stairs. And the talker was right, too, about not ceding the high ground. And either or both theories could also explain the slow, deliberate approach.

The problem was, if another group flanked them from below, they'd be penned in on three sides without any escape route. If Manus had been carrying, he would have preferred a frontal assault against one of the pincer groups. Attack the ambush, fight your way through it. But he had left the Force Pro, his customary carry, back in Maryland. He'd gotten lazy. Lazy and stupid. Acting like a civilian, even after they'd made him go operational again.

The good news was, he had visited the park several times already, and had studied it closely. He'd gotten stupid, yes, but he still reflexively examined terrain for routes of ingress and egress, still ran constant when/then scenarios.

It was too bad about the Force Pro. But there was a lot he could do with the Espada.

chapter twelve

DOX

Dox was castigating himself over his earlier hubris—had he really assured himself he'd yet to meet the operator he couldn't make, right before that damn jogger turned out to be anything but?—when Manus pulled himself up onto the concrete wall behind them, flattened out on top of it, and rolled over the other side.

"He's gone," Larison said. "Can't blame him. Sucks to have nothing but a knife at a gunfight."

Despite himself, Dox was surprised by the quiet suddenness of Manus's exit. But there were more important matters to consider. For example, the two teams still approaching, now about thirty yards away.

"Which way do you want to play it?" Dox said. "I don't like how slowly they're moving. I think they're waiting for something, and I don't want to be here when it happens."

"I think they're not sure of their orders," Larison said. "Look. They stopped."

Dox watched the woman jogger pull out a cellphone and speak into it.

"Could be that," Dox said. "Could be she's calling for reinforcements. I say it's time to blast our way through one end of the pincer or the other."

"Agreed. Which side?"

"It's all the same to me. You have a preference?"

"No."

"Well shit, what are we going to do? Eeny, meeny, miny, moe?"

The woman put away the phone. All six pulled out pistols and started moving again.

"Looks like their orders have been clarified," Dox said.

"Okay, let's take the three approaching from your side."

"Why aren't they shooting yet?"

"Could be from that far out they're afraid they'd miss and we'd go down the stairs."

"Or like you said, they could want us to go down the stairs."

"What difference does it make?"

Dox couldn't argue with that. His heart started beating harder.

"You ready?" he said. "One. Two—"

chapter
thirteen

MANUS

Manus hopped from one giant vertical concrete block to another, scanning the area for another team or for anything else suspicious. Other than two elderly Asian women doing tai chi despite the rain, the area was clear.

When he knew he was well past the righthand team's position, he jumped down and made his way to the stairwell at the park's south end. He raced up the steps three at a time, crouched at the top, and darted his head around the corner.

He saw the three-man team, their backs to him fifty feet away, still moving methodically forward to close the pincer. Their hands were in front of their bodies now. From the way they were moving, he could tell they were all righthanded, and all holding pistols at high compressed ready. Obviously, they were trained.

If he approached from behind and to the right, the biomechanics would be awkward for them. The distance was farther than ideal, but manageable. The problem was, the other team would see him coming. If they got off a warning, it could be bad.

But he saw no other options. He didn't even consider leaving. He didn't want the talker and the wingman to be killed. He wanted to know what they knew. Who was behind this whole thing. Why they had set him up.

Most of all, whether Evie and Dash were in danger.

The thought terrified him. He judged his current odds of success at about sixty-forty. And while he could accept those odds for himself, if he died, who would protect Evie and Dash?

His heart pounding uncharacteristically hard, he opened the Espada, manually depressing the folding mechanism to mute the click he knew the blade would otherwise make. He couldn't be sure how loud the sound would be, or how far it would carry.

He felt the blade lock into place. He took a deep breath, stood, and charged from behind the corner.

Fifty feet. He raced over the wet grass, knowing there was a chance they might hear or even feel his footfalls. But he couldn't afford stealth. Speed was everything. Speed and violence of action.

Thirty feet. Someone on the opposite team saw him and began frantically waving his arms.

Twenty feet. The three team members stopped. Checked their flanks.

Ten feet. The man farthest to the right started turning clockwise. He must have sensed Manus's footfalls because his right shoulder began to come up, his head turtling in—

Five feet. Manus brought back the Espada like a tennis player about to hit a blistering forehand. The man kept turning, turning, his face rotating toward Manus now, his gun swinging into view—

Manus whipped in the Espada. The man's throat and the lower part of his face were protected by his shoulder, but it didn't matter, the blade blasted into the bridge of his nose, cut through his eyes, and sheared halfway through his skull. The man's body convulsed and Manus yanked the blade free.

The man was falling but there was no time to wait; Manus shoved him to the right as the next man kept turning, turning, his gun coming around—

Manus brought down the Espada like a hatchet, aiming for the man's wrist but connecting halfway up the forearm. The blade sliced through tendon, muscle, and bone. The man shrieked loudly enough for Manus to hear, and the gun, the man's hand and wrist still attached to it, dropped to the wet grass.

The woman, the jogger, had turned her head all the way toward him. Her eyes were desperate, shocked, afraid. It meant nothing to Manus. All he cared about was the gun, and the woman had now brought it nearly all the way around—

Manus shoved the second man aside and leaped forward, to the left of the gun, smashing into the woman's right shoulder, jamming her arm into her body, catching the nape of her neck to keep her from being thrown back by the impact. She struggled to bring the gun around and Manus launched the Espada from hip level as though he was throwing an uppercut, arcing it up under her arm and spearing it up behind her chin and into her brain. The force of the blow lifted her off the ground and for an instant her body twitched as Manus held it aloft. Then he jerked the knife the other way, and she collapsed backward, limbs twitching, insensate.

The second man was on his knees, blood spurting from the stump of his right arm, pawing for the gun with his remaining hand. Manus strode over, raised the Espada overhead like an ice pick, and plunged the point down through the back of the man's head. The man's face slammed into the sodden grass like a cannonball, muddy water spraying up around it. Manus jerked the blade free. The man listed left and folded to his side.

Something buzzed past Manus. He realized it was a round. An instant later there was the crack of a gunshot, loud enough for him to faintly hear. Another. A third.

The other team was shooting at him. And where he stood, there was no cover.

chapter fourteen

DOX

Over the years, Dox had seen his share of blood and guts. Still, what Manus did with that Espada in five short seconds was a wonder to behold. Dox was so stunned by the man's sudden reappearance, and by the havoc he wreaked, that for a moment he froze, thinking he wasn't seeing things right. Fortunately, the sounds of gunshots from the team on the left brought him out of it.

He spun and brought up the Wilson. Larison was already engaging. Dox was so adrenalized he barely heard the report of the Glock—just a muted *pop, pop, pop*. Something snapped back the head of one of the three men and the man went down. Larison, dialing in a head shot.

The other two raced forward, firing as they ran, trying to get to the trees. Dox knew the chances of someone hitting what he was aiming for while running flat-out were decidedly poor, but still, having rounds flying even at random did tend to pose a challenge to your own ability to aim. He took a deep breath, put his front sight on the torso of the man on the right, let the breath ease out, and pressed the trigger. The round caught the man in the shoulder. It threw off his stride, but the man managed to keep his footing. Dox adjusted. The next shot caught the man in the midsection. The man flinched like he'd been punched hard in the gut. He tried to get his gun up and back into play, but Dox had zeroed him now and put three more rounds into the man's chest. The man twitched, staggered, did a half pirouette, and went down.

The last man, number six, had managed to make it to a tree—with the current angles, better cover than Dox and Larison had. Without anything needing to be said, they raced for their own tree, both laying down suppressing fire as they ran. They got behind the trunk just in time to avoid a fusillade of shots. The tree, which had looked plenty thick from far away, suddenly seemed like a sapling.

Larison swapped in a fresh magazine. "You want to show this guy what a pincer is all about?"

Dox swapped in a fresh mag, too. "Hell yes. Who goes first?"

"You."

"Had a feeling I shouldn't let you choose."

"Just about who's the better shot. No offense."

"None taken. Though if something happens to me, I'd be grateful if you'd kill him dead after. Of course, before would be my preference."

"Shut up and go."

Dox sucked in a long breath and dashed out from behind the tree—

Larison popped partway out from the other side and began firing—

The remaining man fired back—

Dox felt a round whiz past him, another, and then—

He was behind the next tree. It was no thicker than the previous one, but still he'd never been so grateful for the proximity of nature. The last line of a poem zipped through his head—*But only God can make a tree*—and he almost laughed.

He glanced back at Larison. Larison nodded. Dox took a deep breath, stepped right, and started firing. In his peripheral vision, he could see Larison sprinting forward. This time, the sixth man didn't even try to return fire. Maybe he was swapping in a fresh mag. Maybe he was shitting his pants. Maybe all of the above.

Larison made it to the next tree. Their three positions now formed a scalene triangle, with Dox and Larison at the base and Dox closer to number six's position.

There were more trees ahead. If Dox had been the man, he would have found the options depressingly bleak. Dox and Larison could just keep leapfrogging closer and closer until they flanked him, one keeping him pinned down while the other moved. Absent a hell of a lucky shot, at this point it was only a matter of time.

Number six must have been doing the same math. Because just as Dox was about to dart to the next tree, the man went tearing off in the opposite direction, zigzagging as he moved. But his zigs and zags weren't as random as they might have been, and Larison, stepping out from behind his tree, brought up the Glock, took a moment to track the man's movements, and fired. The round caught the man in the back and staggered him. Dox fired twice, nailing him both times. Larison shot once more and the man went down.

The two of them did a quick 360-degree sweep of the area. No more threats. No more anyone, other than Manus. But there would be plenty of visitors soon enough, most of them wearing blue uniforms. People could rationalize or otherwise ignore a single gunshot, maybe as many as three or four. But even if the city hadn't set up one of those fancy acoustic gunshot detection systems, and probably it had, a running firefight between this many combatants in a public park was going to get called in.

Larison walked over, his head still swiveling, scanning the park. "You all right?"

Dox took a moment to inspect himself. He didn't see any holes. "Yeah. You?"

"You want to make small talk, or you want to get the hell out of here?"

Dox laughed. Once you got to know him, Larison actually had a fine sense of humor. "Don't see why we can't do both," he said.

They looked over at Manus. The man was heading their way from fifty feet off, the dripping Espada still gripped in his right hand. It looked like someone had tossed an entire bucket of blood onto him. Which, as Dox considered, was more or less what had happened.

Neither of them said anything as Manus approached. Dox, who had planned to holster the Wilson, found himself keeping it in a retracted low ready position. As it happened, Larison was doing the same.

Manus reached their position. He glanced at their pistols. Then he closed the Espada, and for the first time, Dox saw him smile.

"Don't worry," he said. "If I wanted to kill you, you'd be dead already."

chapter
fifteen

LARISON

Larison couldn't decide whether Manus was serious or joking. Even Dox, who had an answer for everything, was momentarily stymied and just stood there silently, the Wilson frozen in purgatory.

Whatever. Probably Manus meant it both ways. Larison holstered the Glock and looked at Dox. "Stick together, or split up?"

Dox glanced around, then back to Manus, either so Manus could read his lips or because Dox was afraid to look elsewhere.

"Three big guys," Dox said, finally holstering the Wilson. "One scary, one covered in blood, and one devilishly handsome. See if you can guess who's who. Anyway, overall the description is apt to be a lot like whatever witnesses might report."

"Yeah," Larison said. "But on the other hand—"

"I know, on the other hand, if anyone runs into another team, I'd rather it be the three of us together. It's hard to imagine whoever's behind this sent more than six, but still, let's take our chances with witness descriptions until we're clear of the area. Then we'll split up, and regroup later and debrief. Sound good?"

It sounded good to Larison. And apparently to Manus, too, who said, "Let's go."

They all popped up their parka hoods. Larison said, "Wait, let's not leave the toys. I told you it was going to be talking or shooting and nothing in between." They grabbed the umbrella and the selfie stick and started moving.

There were a lot of ways in and out of the park, so unless there were quite a few more than the six they'd already dropped, Larison didn't expect to run into any more opposition. They'd already thoroughly reconnoitered and knew the surroundings well, and without any discussion headed out the east side, the less trafficked part of the park.

Larison scanned the area as they moved, eyeblink-ready to pull the Glock if he saw anything the least bit suspicious. But the park was quiet.

He was half-horrified, half-relieved that he hadn't shot Manus when he had the chance. A sequence kept replaying in his mind: when he had hesitated, the trigger half depressed, then holstered the Glock, tore in empty-handed, and engaged an obviously formidable operator struggling to deploy a giant knife. Why? To help Dox, of course, but a head shot would have been the right way to do that. He realized it was Dox's determination to stay within the less-than-lethal parameters for the sake of his lady. But that was Dox's deal. When had Larison become so devoted to Dox, and to Rain, that he would compromise his own instincts just to demonstrate his loyalty?

It was disturbing, and he'd have to think about it. For now, he was glad he'd made the right call. Or at least the lucky one.

They had made it down the stairs and had just cut onto Ninth Avenue when they saw a woman in a jogging outfit come running up the street straight toward them. Of course. Alondra Diaz.

chapter sixteen

DOX

Larison and Manus kept their heads down and their feet moving, but Dox couldn't help looking back as Diaz passed them. Ah, shit, she was turning onto the stairs and heading straight up into the park.

He shook it off and continued along the street. She was probably safe for now. There couldn't be another team in the park at this point, could there? A cleanup crew, something like that?

Of course not. He was being ridiculous. But—

"Don't," he heard Larison growl. The man had gotten to know him too well.

Dox tried to listen. Tried not to think about how he would feel if something happened to the woman. And couldn't help imagining her walking right into the kind of ambush he and Larison had just prevented.

"Don't," Larison said again, louder, but it was already too late. Dox turned back. She was halfway up the stairs and about to go around a corner. He called out, "Ms. Diaz!"

She stopped and looked at him. He heard Manus's and Larison's footfalls moving steadily away. He couldn't blame them. He just hoped they wouldn't blame him.

"Please, ma'am, don't go running in the park this morning. There are people there who were planning to hurt you. They can't now, but there might be others. You need to watch your back. I think it's about that big case of yours. Some powerful people who aren't happy about it."

"What?" Diaz said. "How do you . . . How do you know who I am? How do you know about my case?"

"You need to stay clear of that park," Dox said. "And anywhere else people might expect you. Now, if you have any sense at all, you'll listen to what I just said."

He turned and walked away, fast but not too fast. He made a quick right, then another right onto a series of quiet stairs that led to more stairs and a walking path behind some apartment buildings. One of the bugout routes they had agreed on earlier. In under a minute, he'd caught up to Larison and Manus. He looked back and was relieved Diaz wasn't trying to follow them.

Manus was walking point and didn't say anything. Not that his silence meant much. Dox got the feeling the man was even quieter than Larison, and besides, he probably hadn't heard Dox coming. But Larison glanced back and said, "What the hell was that?"

"You know what it was."

"I agreed to save her. Not die for her. Or get arrested. She can describe you now."

"My hood's up. I don't think she got much of a look."

"No, just enough to tell the cops, 'He was a big guy who sounded straight out of Abilene. And he was with two other big men.'"

"How come you're the men and I'm just the guy?"

"I'm not fucking around."

"I know, I'm sorry. A lot just happened and I'm trying to improvise."

"You want to be a knight in shining armor, do it when it's not my ass, okay?"

"I said I'm sorry, all right? Let's just keep moving."

They passed some early-morning commuters, but with the rain, everyone was walking hoods up and heads down. A few were sheltering under umbrellas. No one paid them any heed.

At the top of the path, they emerged back onto the street. They headed into an alley between a pair of apartment buildings and ducked behind a Dumpster.

"Partial as I am to All City Coffee," Dox said, his eyes going from Manus's face to the tip of the Espada protruding from his front pants pocket and back again, "I think we'd be better off reconnecting outside the city limits. How'd you get here and how were you planning to leave?"

"No," Manus said. "I don't want to split up."

"Well, it's not my first choice either, but—"

"I want to know who's behind this. Who hired me. Who hired you. Who sent those people."

"Fine, we can talk about that when—"

"I'm not taking a chance on you two ghosting. We stick together until you tell me what you know."

"Hey," Larison said. "I don't want to hear your demands. We just saved your ass back there."

Manus shook his head. "I saved yours."

"Why the fuck would we ghost? The only reason you're not dead right now is because someone wants to know why you were sent to kill Diaz."

"You want what I know?" Manus said. "You go first."

Larison took a step back and to the side. "No. You."

Well, that wasn't good. A typical posturer would have stepped in to make a point. When Larison stepped offline, it was the opposite. He wasn't making a point. He was going to shoot you.

"Hold on," Dox said. "Hold on. We're all a little upset and we need to take a deep breath. Mr. Manus, my name's Dox. And this here is Larison."

"Jesus," Larison said. "Why don't you just give him our driver's licenses?"

"You're right that we need to put our heads together," Dox went on. "And we want the same thing you do. So I'll tell you what. We have a car—a minivan, as it happens. One of us can drive, the other two can lie down. When we get somewhere quiet, we can park and all sit in back and debrief to our hearts' content. Maybe even bring in a little takeout. I don't know about you, but I always get hungry after surviving a gunfight."

"What are you doing?" Larison said. "We had a bugout point, why are you changing the plan?"

Good God, anytime something seemed to be cooling off, Larison had to turn a damn flamethrower on it. "Because, in case you haven't been keeping up on current events, so far this morning not one thing has gone according to plan."

"Bullshit. You want to stick around because you want to see Livia."

That riled him, mostly because it was true. He stared at Larison. "Why are you saying her name in front of him?"

Larison took a step closer. "You can say mine and I can't say hers?"

In spite of everything, Dox couldn't help but smile at that. In contrast to what he'd done with Manus, Larison had stepped closer to Dox to emphasize his anger.

"Remember when we used to fight?" Dox said. "We'd be an eyeblink from shooting each other. And now? All you're thinking to do is punch me in the face. That's some kind of in-group we've formed, and I for one am proud of it."

For a second, Larison stared at him, incredulous. Then he started laughing. "I give up," he said. "You crazy bastard, I'll get the van."

chapter
seventeen

DIAZ

For a long moment, Diaz stood rooted to the steps, watching the now-empty street, unsure of what to do. Had that man really told her not to go into the park? That people were trying to hurt her in connection with . . . what, with Schrader? There had been three of them, hadn't there? But suddenly she was unsure. It felt so surreal, she wondered if it had even really happened.

Just a few minutes earlier, as she was approaching the park, she'd heard what sounded like gunfire. It hadn't been very loud, though, and there had been so much of it that she'd dismissed it as something else. Kids with firecrackers or something. But the park was designed to suppress the sound of the highway it was built over. Could the design suppress the sound of gunshots, too?

She realized she was afraid to go in. And that decided it for her. She turned, marched up the stairs, and walked into the park.

She saw it all immediately. Bodies. Several of them.

She froze, her heart suddenly hammering so hard it seemed she could hear it. "Shit," she said. "Shit, shit, shit." Her voice sounded unnaturally high, and she realized her throat had constricted. Still, it was a comfort to hear herself saying something, anything.

She jerked her head right, afraid whoever had done this was still here. Nothing. She jerked left—and saw another cluster of bodies, the ground around them soaked with blood. She stood staring for a moment, shocked, sure she wasn't seeing correctly.

They're statues. It's a joke. It's, it's . . .

She tried to pull out her cellphone but her arms were frozen. She tried to say *shit* again, but nothing came out. Confused, she tried to move her feet. They were stuck. She heard a roaring in her ears, as though water were rushing past. It was like one of those nightmares where you're glued to the ground or sinking into it—

The freeze, she heard Livia saying. *A normal survival reflex. But to break it, you have to take external action. Say a word. Flex your hand open and closed. Take a step.* Something. *And make that one external action lead to another.*

She tried to say *shit* again, but it was as though her throat was locked tight, her jaw wired shut.

"Sh . . . sh . . . ," she managed. She felt her stomach clenching and she pushed harder, managing to draw out the sound: "Shhhhhhhh . . ."

And then the word broke through. She said it again and again, afraid if she stopped, her throat would close again. "Shit, shit, shit, shit, shit . . ."

She was talking. She could talk. "Move, Alondra," she said, panting. "Fucking *move* . . ."

But she couldn't. Her legs wouldn't listen. She imagined her toes. Tried to wiggle them. She made her foot turn back and forth, as though stubbing out a fallen cigarette. She forced the foot forward, an inch, another, two more, like someone confirming the ground would support her weight. She managed a shaking step. Then a second. And suddenly the freeze was gone. It was as though she'd burst free of a straitjacket, an invisible cocoon.

Her hands were shaking so badly she couldn't reach into her jacket pocket, and when she finally did, she nearly dropped her cellphone. She managed to punch in 411 and was about to press *Call* when she realized that was information, it was 911 she needed. She deleted the entry, got the correct digits in, hit *Call*, and raised the phone to her ear.

One ring, then: "911, what is your emergency?"

"This is Alondra Diaz," she said. Her voice was still high and shaky and she fought to control it. "I'm an assistant US Attorney. I'm in Freeway Park. There are . . . bodies here. Five. No, wait, six."

"Ma'am, are you sure—"

"I'm sure. I'm looking at them. I don't know what happened. There's blood on the ground. Lots of it."

"Are you in danger?"

She remembered what the man had said: *You need to watch your back. I think it's about that big case of yours.*

"I don't . . . I don't think so. I don't think anyone else is here."

"Okay. We're sending a patrol car now. Wait for them, but only if you're sure you're safe."

"I'm fine. Just . . . please, hurry."

She clicked off and stared again at the bodies and the blood, still trying to convince herself she was seeing something other than what it obviously was. Were those guns on the ground? Yes. She'd been right. A gunfight. A big one. Gangs? Seattle had its share. But as soon as she considered it, she knew it was her mind, looking for another way to deny what she didn't want to accept.

You need to stay clear of that park. And anywhere else people might expect you.

On impulse, she speed-dialed Livia. Her hands were still shaking. But her mind was suddenly clear.

I'm coming for you, Schrader, she thought. *You just fucked with the wrong prosecutor.*

chapter eighteen

RISPEL

Devereaux was shouting so loudly that Rispel had to hold the secure-line receiver away from her ear.

"This was not a complicated op!" he barked. "You couldn't have had more complete intel. How could you have fucked this up?"

Rispel deliberately glanced around her office: one wall, a second, a third. It was a technique she used when she needed to slow things down. Absent that discipline, she might have felt too keenly her shock at the indignity of Devereaux addressing her as though she were some green recruit. She might have given in to the temptation to shout back.

But if there was one thing she had learned in this man's world, it was the danger of doing anything that could be disparaged as "emotional." Men could shout, they could rant, they could even cry, and they were just being assertive, or passionate, or caring. But for women, the same behaviors were bitchy. Or unhinged. Or worst of all, weak.

"The intel wasn't complete," she said. "It was—"

"I didn't say it was complete! Intel is never complete. I said it couldn't have been more complete."

Along with the shock, she felt irritation now, struggling to get a foothold. The interruption. The pedanticism. And the condescension.

"Which is why I used two teams," she said. "We couldn't be sure—"

"Does Diaz suspect? How could she not? She was on her way to the park for her morning jog and two teams of operators get wiped out there?"

Her irritation secured the foothold it had been trying for. She knew she should try to dislodge it. But she was beginning to not want to.

"She wasn't there when it happened," she said, managing not to raise her voice. "And the team was sterile, of course. Even their finger-prints were wiped from military databases. There's no way anyone can connect them to anyone."

"Jesus Christ, Lisa, do you really not understand? They might as well have been carrying business cards saying 'Private Military Contractor'! Fine, no one can prove who they were, but what do you think Diaz is going to guess? And if she winds up with additional security as a result, or she moves up the indictment against Schrader, or who the hell knows what, what excuses are you going to come up with then?"

She'd heard Devereaux talk this way to subordinates before. He was known, after all, for kissing up and kicking down. But during all the years he had mentored her, he'd always treated her like a favored child. And to have him turn on her like this . . . She was surprised at how much it hurt.

Surprised, and angry.

"I'm not offering excuses," she said. "I'm trying to engage in a con-structive conversation intended to redress the matter at hand. But if that's less important to you than berating me, by all means, go right ahead."

That shut him the hell up. Which felt so good she realized it had been what she was after.

Don't let him make you stupid.

"I'm not interested in a conversation," he said after a moment. "I'm interested in hearing you tell me exactly how you're going to rectify the most grievous personal fuckup I've witnessed in thirty years in intelli-gence. And I hope you have something compelling to tell me, Lisa. I really do. Because if this thing doesn't get unfucked, and fast, you are going to be facing a long line of people, all with pay grades even higher than mine, looking to take your scalp."

Did he not understand she would recognize the framing? They were taught as recruits never to threaten openly. Instead, they were taught to pose as the target's protector and ally. *Even if the target understands the subterfuge,* the training went, *he'll still feel respected that you offered a fig leaf rather than a naked display of your power over him.*

And then she realized: *Of course he understands.*

The shock, and hurt, and anger, were all suddenly underscored with fear. Had Devereaux really . . . turned on her like this? So quickly? So decisively?

"Help me," he went on. "Help me help you. Because I don't know who else is going to."

Got it the first time, you prick.

In fact, she did have a backup plan. Already assembled and ready to go. She almost blurted it out, and then was ashamed of the reflex, recognizing it as a vestige of the past, when she'd been new and Devereaux had taken her under his wing. Well, it was natural for adult children to revert to old patterns in the presence of their parents. But natural wasn't the same as desirable. Or useful.

And besides. Something was suddenly telling her there would be no advantage to cluing him in about the backup plan. That in fact there could be opportunities lost. And other potential downsides.

"I'm putting together the facts of what happened," she said. "It's complicated by the exceptional compartmentalization. I need to understand how Kanezaki's sniper contractor wound up in the park—he should have had no knowledge of the location, or of what was planned there. And I need to understand who his partner was. And how and why they were talking to Manus when the plan was for the contractor to kill him."

"How much does Kanezaki know?"

"That's another thing I'm trying to determine. Why don't I get back to it, all right? And then I'll get back to you."

"For Christ's sake, Lisa, you better have a hell of a Plan B."

He hung up. After a moment, she did the same.

She didn't want to believe it. She could feel herself trying not to. But how could she not have seen it coming? It was almost funny: the plan had been to dispose of Manus after he'd completed his job. And now they were going to throw her under the bus for failing to complete hers.

All those times Devereaux had told her how the intelligence community needed more women. More diversity. *A three-hundred-sixty-degree optic,* he liked to say. *How are a bunch of incestuous old white guys going to achieve that?*

And she'd actually believed him. Because she agreed, of course, and because it was so flattering to find herself the vessel by which all women would advance in the ranks of the IC.

God. The things she had done. At the black site in Thailand. To prove she was as tough as any of them. No, tougher. She'd needed sleeping pills ever since.

She replayed the conversation in her mind. Devereaux had been angry, yes. But now . . . What she'd initially thought was only anger felt more like . . . fear. She realized she'd been so hurt and afraid herself that she'd initially misinterpreted it.

Fear of what, though?

Well, the videos, certainly. When she'd asked who was on them, he had said only *People we know. Schrader's been at this for years.* The threat, it seemed, wasn't to any particular individual. It had to be wider than that. How else could it justify the deletion of an assistant US Attorney?

But the fact that the threat was widespread didn't ipso facto mean—

He's on those tapes.

The instant the thought blossomed in her mind, it felt right. Even obvious. The insight had the kind of clarity she experienced only when a faulty assumption, suddenly swept away, had been occluding it.

Of course. That's why he's so afraid. And trying so hard to conceal it with anger.

How many assets had she known who, hands-over-heart, had protested that they were spying for America only out of political conviction, when in fact it was the money, or the excitement, or the promises of resettlement for them and their families? Or any one of a dozen other personal reasons, including fear of what CIA could do to them if they refused to cooperate?

Devereaux could protest all he wanted about how this was really about protecting the club. And maybe on some level, it even was. But what he was really trying to protect was himself.

She could see now the precariousness of her position. She had understood she was to function as a cutout, yes. In the course of a long career, she'd become accustomed to that. But there was a thin line between cutout . . . and fall guy.

Devious little bastards, she thought.

And then she smiled at the irony. They were trying to exploit a woman to clean up a mess that was caused by, and that by definition was only a threat to, other men.

She remembered something her father, before his untimely heart attack himself a career CIA man, had told her when she was a girl: *If you want to get something you never had before, you have to do something you've never done before.*

She thought about everything Devereaux had told her. About how Schrader had used the videos only once before this, and both times only as a get-out-of-jail-free card.

But if the videos included footage of men like Devereaux . . . if they included footage *of* Devereaux . . . then for all these years, Schrader was in possession of assets that he was vastly underutilizing.

What a waste, to make so little use of something with so much potential power. It was like keeping a race car forever in the garage.

But race cars weren't built for garages. They were built for drivers.

She'd been right to refrain from mentioning the backup. Devereaux wanted a Plan B? He had no idea.

chapter
nineteen

LIVIA

Livia was on her way into the morning briefing at headquarters when her cellphone buzzed. She saw it was Diaz and immediately felt uneasy that Alondra would be calling at such an early hour. She peeled off toward the elevators and raised the phone to her ear.

"Hey. Everything okay?"

"I'm okay," Diaz said. "I'm okay."

That sounded not okay at all. Beyond which, Alondra's voice was breathless and shaky.

The elevator doors opened, and Livia's lieutenant, Donna Strangeland, emerged with her trademark giant coffee thermos. "Hey," she said in her outsized Brooklyn transplant accent. "You're going the wrong way. Big shooting this morning in Freeway Park. Come on."

"Be right there," Livia said. And then, when Strangeland was safely out of earshot, "What's going on?"

"I was on my way to Freeway Park for my morning run. I thought I heard gunshots, and . . . there are bodies. I think six."

The corridor seemed suddenly ten degrees colder. "You're in the park now?"

"Yes."

"Did you call 911?"

"Yes. They're sending a car. Or cars."

"Are there people around?"

"A couple now, yeah. I think they called 911, too. Now they're just . . . staring. Taking pictures with their phones."

"That's good. With that many dead, I doubt any who got away would be coming back. Plus there are witnesses now. You should be okay."

"I don't think this was gangs."

"What, then?"

"There was this guy. I was going up the stairs, after I'd heard the shooting. He told me not to go in the park. Because there were people there who were planning to hurt me. And he called me by name. 'Ms. Diaz.' I mean, he also called me ma'am, but he knew my name. I'm sure of it."

No. It's not possible.

"He called you ma'am?"

"Yes. So what?"

"Did he say anything else?"

"He said it was about 'that big case of yours.' What else could that be but Schrader?"

"I don't know. What else did he say?"

"He told me . . . I need to watch my back. And not go anywhere where people might expect me. He was with two other men, or at least two . . . I didn't get a good look at any of them. They were big, though, I could see that. And the one who warned me had an accent."

Livia closed her eyes. "What kind of accent?"

"I think Southern. Maybe Texas. I'm not sure."

Without thinking, Livia said, "When the detectives take your statement, leave that detail out."

"What? Why?"

"Just don't mention it. You can always remember it later."

There was a pause. Diaz said, "Do you know something about this?"

"No. But I know some people I can ask. Just trust me for now, okay?"

"Okay. Can you come?"

"I'm on my way into the morning briefing and my lieutenant just saw me. I don't want to advertise that we're in touch about this and I don't want to make up an excuse. Just forget that you called me for now. I should be there in an hour at most. Okay?"

"Okay. Just come as soon as you can. I swear, if Schrader was behind this . . ."

"We'll find out. Stay cool. I'll be there as soon as I can."

She clicked off and headed back toward the conference room. She badly wanted to call Carl, but she couldn't do that from her regular phone. And besides, whatever his involvement in what had happened at the park, the conversation was bound to be fraught. She knew he'd been waiting for her to call him again. But she hadn't. One month had become two, and then three, and then six, and she was just too . . . afraid.

It couldn't be him. It couldn't.

It felt like him, though. The accent. The *ma'am*. The chivalry.

But if it was him, he'd protected Alondra. Warned her. And he would have useful information. He could help Livia get to the bottom of this, and make sure Schrader and any coconspirators got what they deserved. If Carl was involved, it was good news, not bad.

So why was she so enraged?

chapter twenty

DIAZ

A guard unlocked the door and Diaz walked into the SeaTac Federal Detention Center interrogation room. She'd called ahead and Schrader was already there, sitting in one of the room's two chairs, his wrists manacled to the rectangular table.

The guard walked out and pulled the door closed, and for a moment the painted cinder-block walls echoed with a metallic clang. Everything echoed in these places. The doors, the gates, the locks . . . the constant, background exclamation points. She secretly hated all of it.

At least the FDCs didn't smell like the local jails. Though as bad as decades of accreted sweat and urine could be, the federal devotion to unlimited ammonia and bleach was only a marginal improvement.

She pulled the second chair away from the table and sat. Schrader's chair was bolted to the floor and his ankles were manacled to it. *You own the room,* they'd taught her. *Make sure the subject feels it.*

She made him wait for a moment—you never know what a prisoner might say. But Schrader offered nothing. He just sat there, watching her, his expression perplexed. The orange jumpsuit, which could make the hard cases look even harder, on Schrader was more like a clown costume. And the missing hairpiece—a constant in the society magazine photos, but confiscated upon his arrest—was worse. Without it, he looked older. Exhausted. Exposed.

"Surprised to see me?" Diaz said.

He did look surprised, but not in the way she'd expected. He shook his head. "My lawyer told you. I'm not going to plead. And where is she, anyway? Isn't she supposed to be here if you're talking to me?"

She had hoped he wouldn't ask. A request for a lawyer turned a gray-area conversation into something black-letter inadmissible. Well, there was no one else in the room. Not even any cameras. And besides, she hadn't come for a confession. She just needed to confront him. Stare him down.

"We already have you on child trafficking," she said. "Racketeering. Sex with underage girls, at least some of whom were drugged when they were assaulted. So why not add conspiracy to commit murder? I guess you figured you had nothing to lose."

"What?"

He really did look surprised. And worried. But not in that *Shit, they're on to me* way she'd learned to spot. This was something else.

"Come on, Andrew. Six people are dead in Freeway Park. Six people who were waiting for me. You going to tell me you didn't know anything about that?"

He shook his head, his mouth hanging open. *Shit,* she thought. *He really doesn't know.*

He didn't just look surprised, though. He looked . . . scared.

"I don't know what you're talking about," he said.

"You really think murdering me is going to get you out of here? I just gave an interview at Freeway Park in front of a battalion of television reporters. It's going to be nonstop speculation about what happened in the park and your potential involvement. You had some support before, I'll admit it. Your money. Your connections. But I'm untouchable now, do you understand that? Got any ideas for what that means for you?"

Did he lose some color at that? Yes, he did. *Good.*

"I didn't do anything," he whined. "I didn't do anything. I don't know anything about this."

It sounded like some sort of self-comfort mantra. She sensed an opening and decided to press it.

"You know what happened at New York's Metropolitan Correctional Center on the night Epstein died? Two out of three cameras malfunctioned. The third was pointed in the wrong direction. What video they did have was subsequently accidentally deleted. Oh, and two guards forgot to check on the prisoner the entire night. What do you make of all that?"

He shook his head. "I don't know."

"You want to know what all the beefed-up video outside your cell and the rotating guard checks cost the state? You want to know how many of the higher-ups have pressured me to get rid of it all because they say it's too expensive and you're not worth it?"

Framed as a question, it wasn't a lie. But the truth was, no one had pressured her. The precautions were coming from FDC management as much as they were from Diaz.

The room was cool, but beads of sweat had sprung out on Schrader's scalp. "I didn't do anything," he said again. "I don't want to hurt anyone. They know that. They know that."

Damn it, what was he talking about?

"No, Andrew," she said. "They obviously don't know that. And unless you want the Bureau of Prisons to remove all the extra safeguards I've fought to have installed for your protection, you better help me out here."

"They wouldn't hurt me," he said. "They wouldn't."

He was wobbling. She could feel it. One more solid punch.

She stood. "It looks like we're going to find out." She turned and smacked her palm against the door. "Guard! We're done here."

The guard's face appeared behind the glass square.

"Wait!" Schrader said.

She kept her back to him. "Like hell. You've wasted enough of my time."

"Tell them . . . if anything happens to me . . ."

There was a loud metallic clack as the guard turned the lock. The door opened.

"Just wait!" Schrader said again.

Diaz glanced back at him, then at the guard. "Give us a minute."

The guard seemed to be resisting the urge to roll his eyes. But he left, locking the door behind him.

Diaz turned back to Schrader but stayed on her feet. "If anything happens to you, what?"

Schrader stared at her, his expression both frightened and petulant. "They know. They know what will happen."

"You said you want me to tell them something."

"They already know."

"They do? That's great. Then you don't need all the protection. We'll remove the cameras. The extra guards. You'll be fine."

"If something happens to me, it all comes out. They know. They know."

"What comes out?"

"All of it."

"All of what?"

"They know."

"Who knows?"

"All of them."

"I don't have time for games." She turned back toward the door.

He pounded the table. His manacles clanked. "Wait!" he said again.

She turned to him. "Last chance, Andrew."

"The things they're saying about me," he said, his eyes pleading. "It's not . . . it isn't fair. They all know it isn't fair."

"Who are you talking about?"

"Everyone. Everyone in the videos."

chapter
twenty-one

MANUS

M anus, Dox, and Larison had parked the van in the lot of a
Puyallup Costco, forty-five minutes south of Seattle. Dox and
Larison were in the back seats facing forward; Manus sat on his backpack facing them on top of the folded-down middle seats. Manus was
fine with the arrangement. He needed to see their faces to understand
them. And tactically, it was better to have them both in sight.

While they'd waited for Larison to get the van, Dox had made a
call. He stayed facing Manus while he spoke. Manus wasn't sure, but he
sensed it was out of courtesy, so Manus could read his lips. Most hearing
people forgot to do that. Manus wondered if this guy had spent time
with deaf people. If not, he had good instincts.

"I'll make it quick," Dox had said. "On the one hand, things went
well. We made contact and established rapport." At this, he smiled at
Manus. "On the other hand, while we were there, six operators showed
up and tried to gun us down. They're all dead now. You'll be seeing it
on the news soon enough."

A pause, then, "No, we're all fine. Together. Getting the hell out
of Dodge, and when we're safe we'll debrief. I'm going to destroy this
burner now. I'll call you on one of the backups later on. I sure hope
you'll have some insights about what the hell just happened."

At that, he'd stomped the phone to bits and tossed the fragments into the Dumpster. He looked at Manus and said, "We're good? Not going to try to kill each other, at least for now?"

It was a strange question. Why would the man trust any such assurance from Manus? Manus wouldn't trust it from him. But the straightforwardness didn't feel devious. It felt . . . straightforward. He couldn't think of any other way to answer, so he simply said, "We're good."

"Great. Then pardon me while I get the shakes. 'Cause that was a very near thing back there."

At which point, as promised, he started trembling. After a minute of breathing deeply in and out, he held up his hands. When he seemed satisfied they were steady enough, he said, "That doesn't happen to you?"

"It depends."

Dox smiled. "Okay, good. We've only just met, and I wouldn't want you thinking less of me."

Manus couldn't tell if he was joking. Why would Manus think less of him? The man was obviously competent. Shaking was just what your body did after you'd been scared. There had been times Manus was so scared he'd pissed himself. That was just something your body did, too.

Dox nodded toward Manus's pack and said, "You got any extra clothes in there? There's enough blood on you for me to smell it."

It was true—Manus could smell it, too. He changed into his spare shirt and pants, returning Dox's courtesies by moving slowly and emptying out the pack rather than letting his hands disappear inside it. He hadn't liked getting undressed in front of Dox. It wasn't that he was modest. It was the temporary helplessness of having his boots off, the Espada momentarily out of reach.

The feeling was more reflex than anything else, though. He didn't sense that Dox was a threat anymore. In fact, Manus thought the man might be . . . okay. Like a dog that could be dangerous but that was more inclined to be friendly. As long as you didn't give it a reason not to be.

When he was dressed again, he stuffed the bloody clothes into a contractor's bag he had brought in case of a contingency like this one. He'd get rid of them somewhere far away.

While they'd waited, Dox had asked about his hearing. "If you don't mind my saying," he said, "you don't sound like you were born deaf. What happened?"

Somehow, the frankness of the question didn't seem rude or presumptuous. In fact, it reminded Manus of Dash, and how unaffected he was about not being able to hear.

"An accident," Manus had responded, to which Dox once again showed courtesy by simply nodding and asking no further questions.

The other one, though. Larison. He reminded Manus of some of the boys at the juvenile prison. The mean ones. The ones who the only way to get them to leave you alone was to hurt them so badly they would never forget it.

And sometimes, even that wasn't enough. Sometimes Manus had needed to do more than just hurt them. He hoped it wouldn't come to that with this Larison. But if it did, it did.

They wolfed down sandwiches Larison had brought in from the Costco. Manus was glad for the food. Dox had been right. A fight always made you hungry.

Dox briefed him on what he and Larison knew, leaving out the name of their CIA contact. The omission was fine. Manus would have been surprised if Dox had shared the name, and in fact would have distrusted that level of openness.

The problem was, they didn't know much. Or at least claimed not to. CIA Director Lisa Rispel had coordinated the attempted hit on Manus. The reasonable inference was that Rispel was also behind the planned hit on Diaz.

"But on whose orders?" Manus asked. "What's Rispel's interest?"

"We're not sure," Dox said. "We're speculating that it's related to the arrest of this guy Andrew Schrader. Diaz is the prosecutor behind it."

"Who's Schrader?"

"Some big-time hedge-fund manager and political donor. Lots of low friends in high places. Diaz is making a case against him for trafficking underage girls. So either the interference with Diaz is a favor to a friend, or it's more they're afraid of being associated with a guy whose hobby is raping children."

Something must have shown in Manus's face, because Dox looked at him and said, "Any of that mean anything to you?"

During his first week in the juvenile prison, three older boys had raped Manus. He killed two of them and crippled the third. That helped. But still.

Manus looked at him. "I don't like rapists."

Dox waited a beat, then nodded. Manus had said so little. Had Dox . . . understood?

"Anyhow," Dox went on, "maybe they're afraid Schrader would offer information about other powerful people in exchange for a reduced sentence. Whatever the explanation, Schrader is likely why they want Diaz gone. She's the one carrying the football, and without her playing, the game's over."

Manus considered, then said, "Why not kill Schrader?"

Dox frowned. "You mean, why don't we kill him? As a way of protecting Diaz?"

"No. I mean, why wouldn't they kill Schrader? If your speculation is right, Schrader dead would solve their problems permanently. Diaz might be carrying the football. But Schrader *is* the football."

Dox glanced at Larison, then back to Manus. "Well, that's a good question. I should have thought to ask it myself. I mean, he's in custody . . ."

Larison turned to Dox and said something. Manus couldn't see his face.

"Hey," Manus said. "You need to look at me. Even when you're talking to him."

Larison turned back to him. "I don't need to do anything."

Manus wasn't worried. He'd seen Larison adjust his carry for quicker access when they sat. But he knew he could have the Espada open and its seven-and-a-half-inch blade through the man's xiphoid process and into his diaphragm before the gun would be in play. Action beats reaction.

"I can't understand you if I can't see your face. So when you turn away it means either you're hiding something, or you're a rude asshole. Which one?"

Manus watched. Any tiny tell—a narrowing of the eyes, a thinning of the lips, a subtle shift of the hips—and Manus would kill him.

A beat went by. Larison stared into Manus's eyes. Manus couldn't tell what the man was thinking. He couldn't even tell if he was afraid.

And then Larison surprised him by laughing. He leaned back—which was fine with Manus, as it made access to the pistol more difficult—and said, "Maybe both. But okay. Point taken."

Manus relaxed a little. Consciously or unconsciously, had the man been testing him? If so, it seemed Manus had passed.

"What I was saying," Larison went on, facing Manus now, "is that custody could cut either way. Depending on where they're holding him, what the security arrangements are, who the guards are, etc. Maybe it would be easy to get to him. Maybe it would be hard. If it's hard, they look at Diaz as an acceptable Plan B."

Manus nodded. He didn't like Larison, but the man wasn't stupid.

"And there's another possibility," Larison added. "Schrader might have something on his 'friends.' With a dead-man switch set to release the compromising material if anything happens to him."

That also made sense to Manus. And the confidence with which Larison had suggested the possibility made Manus wonder whether the man had ever employed a dead-man setup himself.

"It might not matter," Dox said. "Maybe they can't get to Schrader, maybe they just won't take the risk. Either way, it's Diaz they're focused on. But look, Mr. Manus—"

"Manus is fine."

Dox nodded. "Manus then. The thing is, my partner can be a little more direct than I am, but he was right when he said the reason we were sent to talk to you instead of killing you, or trying to kill you—in fairness, who can really say how it might have turned out, though I'm sure we all would have acquitted ourselves heroically no matter the results—is because our handler didn't like what Rispel was up to here and was hoping you could shed some light on it. But now it seems we're all in deeper water than we'd anticipated, and in it together, too. So whatever you can tell us about who approached you, when, what they said, all that . . . Well, in my experience we could kill a lot more bad guys if we share information instead of siloing it."

Manus waited. Dox was obviously a talker, but it seemed he also knew when to shut up. And Larison, too, had enough sense, or discipline, not to be drawn in by silence.

After a few more seconds, Manus said, "There were two of them. I don't know who they were. They felt like former military to me. Contractors. They knew a lot about me. About my life. They told me if I didn't take the Diaz job, they would . . . do something to hurt people I care about."

It was strange. He hadn't once felt anything from Larison other than menace. But for an instant, something shifted in the man's expression. His jaw tightened, or his eyes narrowed. It was too subtle for Manus to be sure. But . . . something.

He'd planned to stop there but found himself adding, "I haven't done these things in a long time. And I knew once they saw they could pressure me into one job, they would try to pressure me into others. I was trying to buy myself time."

Dox said, "Time for what?"

Manus looked at Larison.

Larison said, "Time to kill whoever's behind this."

Manus nodded.

"Your people," Larison said. "Are they in danger now?"

Manus had already been over and over that. He couldn't see any advantage for anyone in moving against Evie or Dash. It would get them nothing, other than Manus's implacable rage. Still, it was hard not to worry.

"I don't think so," Manus said. "And I can't . . . If I tried to warn them, I don't think it would help. It would only be . . . upsetting."

Larison nodded. "That's good. Back to Plan A, then. Kill whoever's behind this."

Manus wasn't sure why Larison would care. And maybe he didn't. But at least he understood.

"So Diaz was too high-profile," Larison went on. "You were supposed to be a one-off. Disposable."

Manus nodded again. "I was worried about that, too. They were guarding their information tightly. They never gave me a name. Only a description. They told me the woman liked to run in the park, and I should wait there early every morning. They gave me a burner and said they would text me photos when she was on her way to me. Several different ones, distance and telephoto, all taken just before being sent."

"To make confirmation easier and more reliable," Dox said. "You see the clothes she's wearing, whether her hair was up or down, everything. They were supposed to do the same thing for us with you, though I suppose that's been overtaken by events."

"What about the cellphone?" Larison said. "You weren't nervous they were tracking you?"

"They'd tracked me already. Besides, they knew I would be in the park every morning. So I wasn't worried about them doing anything before I killed Diaz. That's what confused me when I saw the two of you. I knew something was off, but it was too early. Plus you were holding hands. That was smart."

"My idea," Dox said. "Just saying."

"I knew it was high-profile," Manus added. "They told me they wanted it to look like she'd fallen. Or was mugged. Not like an assassination."

Dox looked at Larison and nodded, then turned back to Manus. "Yeah, we figured it would be that way. Our guy tracked her cellphone, too, and we decided that for natural, the park was the best option."

Manus tried to imagine a different explanation, but there was nothing that made sense. It felt like Dox was telling the truth. "That was smart, too," he said.

"If we're so smart," Larison said, "why do we keep pissing off the wrong people?"

Dox laughed. "You know why. You just enjoy it."

Larison looked as though he was going to protest, then just shrugged.

"The person who sent you to stop me," Manus said. "Can he tell us more?"

"I hope so," Dox said. "I'll get details when we're done here and safely away."

Larison looked at Dox, then seemed to remember himself and looked back at Manus. "What about 'She who must not be named'?"

Dox scowled. "Stop that."

"You know you were going to see her anyway. And Diaz is a prosecutor. Your lady might know something about this. And she's sure as hell going to hear about what happened in the park this morning. What's she going to make of it when Diaz describes the chivalrous Texan who warned her of danger in the park?"

Dox shook his head and looked genuinely pained. "I do want to see her. But the whole point of this was to keep her out of it."

"Well, you're batting five hundred."

Dox nodded. "All right. Shit, I hope I'm not rationalizing."

"And there's someone else we should call. In case whatever we're up against is even bigger than we think it is. Which is probably the case."

"Yeah? Who's that?"

"Rain."

chapter twenty-two

LIVIA

The morning briefing was excruciatingly long. All Livia could think about was how badly she wanted to call Carl and debrief Diaz. Her anxiety was made worse when one of the detectives, Suzanne Moore, showed everyone a live television interview she had pulled up on her cellphone—Diaz, talking to a gaggle of reporters. Diaz hadn't mentioned the Texas accent, thank God. But she did recount the rest—three big men, one of whom had warned her by name that this was about her case.

Livia couldn't deny that the impromptu press conference was a clever move. Anyone hoping to bury the Schrader prosecution by killing the prosecutor would know that any subsequent attempt would have the opposite effect. With luck, Alondra was now untouchable. Which probably meant Schrader himself was at increased risk. Among the many things Livia urgently wanted to discuss with Alondra was how to increase Schrader's protection.

The moment the briefing was done, Livia headed into the corridor and toward the elevators. She checked her phone—three calls from Diaz. *Shit.* She was about to call back when the screen lit up with an incoming *Blocked Caller*.

She answered, simultaneously hoping and afraid it might be him. "Hello?"

"Hey, darlin'. It's me and I'm so sorry to bother you. Can you talk?"

At the sound of his voice, her heart started pounding. His voice, and his way of talking to her—the solicitousness, the gentleness. It was good when they were together. Why couldn't she just accept that and not overthink it? Why did it always also make her so afraid?

"Where are you?" she said.

"Well, that's why I'm calling. You see—"

Fifty feet ahead, the elevator doors opened. Chief of Police Charmaine Best emerged and turned left. She saw Livia and nodded. The nod felt like more than a greeting. It felt like an *I want to talk to you.*

Livia barely had time to think *Shit.* She returned the nod and said softly into the phone, "Call me back in fifteen. And fifteen after that, if I don't answer. Keep trying." Then, louder, "Okay, good talking to you. Bye."

She clicked off and pocketed the phone. "Chief Best. Hi."

Best gave her a quick once-over, as though she might spot some incriminating evidence. "How was the briefing?"

Ordinarily, the chief summoned people she wanted to see. If she had come to talk to Livia—and Livia sensed she had—it would be in the nature of an ambush, an attempt to deny Livia time to prepare.

But prepare for what?

Livia shrugged. "The usual. Other than a big shooting in Freeway Park."

"Yes, the preliminary findings are certainly unusual. Six victims, five men and a woman. All carrying untraceable firearms and none carrying ID. Phones all burners, used only to call other burners."

"We were briefed on the same. Not gangs. Likely some sort of professional operation."

"That had the misfortune of running into someone even more professional. What do you think, Detective Lone? Was this really aimed at AUSA Diaz?"

"I was just briefed myself," Livia said. "I don't know."

"Of course. Still, I was hoping you might have some insight."

"Insight?"

"Well," Best said, with a smile she might have intended to be disarming, but that for Livia had the opposite effect. "That attempt on you at the martial arts academy. Those snipers across the river from your apartment. And those operators who came at you in Utah, and the ones shot to death at the Salton Sea, before your heroic rescue of Sherrie Dobbs. You just seem to have a nose for this kind of trouble."

Livia realized she should have seen this coming. She had been mixed up in too many messes, had too many convenient excuses, and had emerged with too many medals. Best was a good cop and respected her results, Livia knew that. But a chief was at least fifty percent politician, and the politician in Best was perennially troubled by Livia's mysteries and determined to solve them. The problem was, what the woman thought she knew was bad enough. What she didn't know was significantly worse. And if she ever grabbed on to a thread and started pulling, the entire tapestry could come apart, leaving Livia exposed beneath it.

"Do you want me assigned to this?" Livia said. "I know Alondra. She takes my women's self-defense class. If she's at risk, I'd like to—"

"No, I don't want you assigned to this. That would be Lieutenant Strangeland's call, in any event. And besides, I don't imagine you need to be formally assigned to be involved."

Livia didn't mind the passive-aggressive jibes. She recognized them as a pressure release, an outlet for Best's frustrations. The real worry would be if they stopped.

An elevator opened and several detectives got off. They nodded nonchalantly to the chief while doubtless gleaning whatever they could from the fact of her corridor conversation with another cop. Instinctively, Livia waited to say anything until they were out of earshot.

"Well, do you want me to—"

"What I want," Best said, "is that nothing should happen to AUSA Diaz, do you understand me? What I want is for that predator Schrader to not be able to bribe or bully or God knows what his way out of justice. That is what I want. And I'm not particularly concerned about how. So if you know more than you're letting on here, and of course you do, that's fine. By now I'm used to it. I just want to know we're on the same page."

For a moment, Livia was taken aback. Had she misread Best's intentions? Was this . . . détente?

"I . . . want those things, too."

Best nodded. "Then do what you do, Livia. I don't need to know the details." She paused, then added, "And maybe I don't want to."

chapter
twenty-three

DELILAH

Delilah was with John in Little Red Door, a bar they liked in the Marais. Like so many things in their life these days, it was a compromise, though not a bad one. They spent part of the year in Kamakura, and part in Paris. They frequented places that were lively, for her, and more serene, for him. She preferred dinner late, so evenings out often began with a cocktail on the earlier side. Which was fine because early meant uncrowded, and uncrowded meant a seat facing the entrance—one of the areas about which she knew John would never compromise, not even for her.

But facing the door was fine. It was no more than common sense, really. The other habits—the ones that had been gradually waning—were much more extreme. The insistence on varying routes and times. Never making a reservation. Always reconnoitering the exterior of a place before going in—and then doing a thorough scan inside, as well. There were still vestiges that would occasionally reappear, moments when the old John would seem to startle awake before realizing that all was well and it was safe to return to sleep. And while she knew that some of his newfound demeanor was an organic consequence of increasing distance from the life—obsolete reflexes growing dull from lack of stimulation, old neural pathways being rerouted, replaced, rewired by new ones—she also understood that some of it was deliberate. A thing he did for her.

Of course, she could make an argument that he owed her. He had wanted out of the life before she had been ready, when she was still in the grip of a one-way allegiance to her birth country, Israel, and her employer, Mossad. He had given her an ultimatum that backfired. And out of stupid male pride had disappeared from her life for years afterward, before finally coming to his senses and crawling back.

He took a sip of his drink, something called a madre de dios. Watching him in profile, she felt a wave of affection. She knew she could be difficult with him. Partly because he put up with it. Once, she'd told him she recognized the dynamic, that she was grateful for how he had learned to stay cool even when she was running hot. He had laughed and told her it was all about survival. She'd mock-punched him for that. And, then, more seriously, he had told her it was something called *amaeru*.

"Which is what?" she had asked.

"A kind of . . . relationship glue. All humans have it, but it's more central in Japan. Which is why they gave it a name."

She was intrigued. John rarely talked about the Japanese half of his heritage, and when he did, it was always as *they*, never *we*. Though in fairness, he never talked about America as *we*, either.

"All right," she had said. "Tell me about this glue."

"It's . . . when you want to test whether someone really cares about you. And foster that caring, too. You behave a little selfishly. Even childishly. And the other person puts up with it. Because he loves you."

"Is this your way of telling me that I'm selfish and childish?"

He had smiled at that. "Or that I love you."

She glanced around the bar. She cherished this place—the exposed stone-and-brick walls, the eclectic upholstered seating, the subdued lighting. The feeling of being here with this man she loved. This thing they had, which he had once called a nation of two.

He looked at her. "What are you thinking?"

She took a sip of her drink—an Art Deco, another of the bar's specialties—and smiled. "I was thinking I like that it's whisky in Kamakura, and cocktails in Paris."

"Is that really what you were thinking?"

There were several ways she might have answered. But the most eloquent was also the one she most wanted. She kissed him. She knew he liked when she did that, liked how physical she was with him, even in public. It had taken a while for him to become comfortable with it, to trust how much she enjoyed touching him. Once upon a time, her specialty for Mossad was honeytrap operations, and some aspect of John's survival instincts, or maybe just his cynicism, had clung to the suspicion that she might be playing him long after she no longer was.

She felt her phone buzz. It was another compromise between his distrust of cellphones and her insistence on real-time accessibility. She took it from her purse and glanced at the caller ID. "Blocked," she said. She didn't get many calls, and she could feel his instant unease.

It buzzed again. "Go ahead," he said. "Otherwise, we'll just be in suspense."

She answered. *"Allo?"*

"Delilah. Am I catching you at a good time?"

She recognized the voice instantly—gravelly, like the shake of a rattlesnake's tail.

"Daniel. It's good to hear your voice. Is everything all right?"

She could feel John's unease increase at her mention of Larison's name. He was probably worried it was something about Dox. For that matter, so was she.

"Everyone's fine," he said. "I'm not calling too late?"

"No, it's evening where we are. You're sure everything is all right?"

She saw John do a quick sweep of the room—the entrance, the hotspots, the other patrons with backs to the wall. Stimulus, response.

"All right enough. Dox and I took on a little job that turned out to be not as little as expected."

"I see."

"He didn't want to bug you guys. But I think we could use backup."

Alongside her worry, she felt a surge of irritation. "Daniel. What is wrong with you two? You don't need the money. You have a good life, a person who loves you."

"Stop. I already feel guilty."

"Not guilty enough."

"Can we talk about my feelings another time?"

"I wish we had talked about them sooner."

"I wrote up the details on the secure site. I don't know when you'll be able to check it, but in the meantime, read the news out of Seattle. That was Dox and me. And the gist of it is, we think there's more where that came from."

The irritation escalated to an adrenaline rush surreal in its familiarity. "What's the plan?"

"I'm not sure yet. Other than my sense that we're not going to resolve this playing whack-a-mole. We need to figure out where the problem is coming from and take it out."

John was looking at her. She knew he wanted the phone. But he was the one who refused to carry one. And besides, she wasn't done. "What about Tom?" she said. "Can he help?"

"He's the guy who hired us. He's finding out what he can."

"Is Livia involved with this?"

"No. Well, not yet. Dox is going to see her."

She tried to suppress her resentment. "Of course."

"Is John around?"

Her resentment worsened. "Yes, he's right here."

"Listen, I really am sorry to bug you. But if the two of you were thinking about visiting the States, now might not be a bad time."

chapter
twenty-four

DUNLOP

Dunlop didn't recognize the two FBI agents who were there to escort Schrader to the local Bureau field office. That didn't concern him. The marshals who routinely shuttled prisoners to and from the courthouse, everyone got to know. But no one could keep track of Bureau business. Probably not even the Bureau itself.

He squinted at the court order again. There was nothing wrong with it. It was properly filled out and stamped, and signed by District Judge Ricardo. And the agents' IDs were legit, too.

But still, a day pass for an off-site interrogation was unusual. Plus Schrader was the FDC's premier celebrity guest. That nice prosecutor, Alondra Diaz, had been by to meet with him not thirty minutes earlier. It all made Dunlop feel a little . . . twitchy. He wondered if he should maybe contact her. But no, a court order was the last word, and if Diaz objected, there would be nothing he could do and all he would accomplish would be to get her pissed at him. Dunlop had been with the Bureau of Prisons for eighteen years and had never made a major mistake, and all he cared about at this point was keeping it that way so he could enjoy his pension while doing nothing but drinking beer and catching fish and watching football. So no, no sense calling Diaz. But if there was an *i* here that hadn't been dotted, he was damn well going to make sure it wasn't his ass that got bitten for it.

"How come you guys didn't call ahead?" he said, looking up from the court order. "Usually people call ahead when they're going to pick up a prisoner. Sometimes it takes us a while to locate them, believe it or not. Unless they're in the SHU, which this guy Schrader is not."

The two agents glanced at each other. Both white guys, both early thirties and fit-looking, both with that cocksure Bureau attitude that rubbed everyone the wrong way. "You gotta be kidding," the taller one said. "They were supposed to call ahead. Like an hour ago. Jesus. How long is it going to take to locate this guy . . . What's his name? Schrader?"

"Well, I don't know. He's probably back in his cell now. We had him out just a half hour ago to meet with the prosecutor. But say, Agent . . ."

"Robinson," the tall one said.

"Right. Agent Robinson. The thing is, this is an unusual request. I'm just going to call the ExA—the executive administrator—and make sure it all checks out."

"Do what you gotta do," Robinson said. "Sounds like we're already going to be late and it's none of our faults. It's the idiots who didn't call ahead."

Five minutes later, the ExA, a pencil neck named Nulty, was out front, personally reviewing the court order and the agents' credentials. Nulty would understand that Dunlop had called him to cover his own ass, of course. But that was fine. He'd also understand that the ass at risk now was his own.

"Everything seems to be proper," Nulty said, still staring at the paperwork. "Have you checked to make sure it's in PACER?"

Shit. Dunlop hadn't thought of that. "Uh, no. Give me just a minute."

He logged on, but couldn't find the order. "Nothing by case number. Nothing by Federal Register Number. And . . . nothing by name. It's not entered."

"Huh," Robinson said. "Maybe they haven't gotten to it yet or whatever. Can you call the court?"

Nulty nodded. "Sure, we can do that." He glanced at Dunlop to indicate that by *we* he meant *you*.

"Just do me a favor," Robinson said. "On the assumption everything checks out, which it should, can you bring out the prisoner so we can get a move on? We're on bullshit detail all day, and this isn't our only stop."

Dunlop looked at Nulty. Nulty nodded. Dunlop called the SCO. "Bill. We got a court order here and a couple of feds waiting to transport prisoner number 45047-177. One Andrew Schrader. Yeah, I know, he's popular today. Can you bring him up front ASAP? The chief's waiting, too."

He hung up, got an outside line, looked up the court number, and dialed. A woman's voice answered: "United States District Court, Western District of Washington. How may I direct your call?"

"This is Fred Dunlop calling from the SeaTac FDC. I'm trying to confirm the presence of a court order that hasn't been entered in PACER yet."

"That would be the clerk of court. Hold, please."

Dunlop heard a click, and the line went over to Muzak. Why people felt the need to torture you while you were on hold, Dunlop would never understand.

The Muzak stopped and a different woman's voice came on. "Clerk of court, Western District of Washington. How may I help you?"

Dunlop repeated the request. A moment went by, and the woman said, "Yes, temporary release order for prisoner number 45047-177, Andrew Schrader. Signed by Judge Ricardo this morning."

Dunlop looked at Nulty and nodded. "They've got it."

Nulty returned the nod. Dunlop thanked the woman and hung up.

"Looks like you were right," Nulty said, turning to Robinson. "Just hadn't been entered yet."

Robinson rolled his eyes. "I'm surprised they even had a copy of it. Half the time the left hand doesn't have a clue what the right is up to."

Nulty laughed. "Tell me about it."

Something still felt . . . off to Dunlop. But if the chief was okay with it all, it wasn't Dunlop's problem. He printed out the release paperwork and slid it over to Robinson with a pen.

Robinson glanced at the other agent. "Look over the paperwork, will you? Make sure it's in order." He looked at Dunlop. "No offense. Just don't want any more glitches."

Dunlop shook his head. "None taken." Which wasn't exactly true. But whatever.

A few minutes later, a klaxon sounded, an electronic lock clacked, and the barred door to the prisoners' area slid open with a mechanical whine. Two guards brought out Schrader, hands and ankles regulation-manacled.

Schrader looked at the two agents, then at Dunlop. "What's going on?"

"Court order," Robinson said, bending to sign the release paperwork. "Your presence is requested at the Seattle field office."

"Why?"

Robinson didn't even look up. "You're asking the wrong people. We just drive the car."

"Does my lawyer know?"

"You'll have to ask her. Come on, guy, we're already behind schedule. Let's go."

After they left, Dunlop still felt a little bothered—more than he had at the outset. He didn't know why. He'd checked every box. Called the chief and everything.

A half hour had passed before he realized what was bugging him. Those agents—they were a couple of paper pushers, like him. Just there to pick up a prisoner, nothing more than that. Robinson had barely even remembered Schrader's name.

So how had he known Schrader's lawyer was a woman?

chapter twenty-five

LIVIA

Livia was in the parking garage, about to jump into her Jeep, when the phone buzzed. Alondra. She picked up and said, "I was about to call you. The morning briefing—"

"He's out!" Diaz said. "I just got a call from the desk officer at the FDC. He said there was a court order, but I called the court—"

Livia tried to control her shock. "What do you mean, *out*? Schrader? How?"

"That's what I'm saying. They released him. The desk officer, Dunlop, he says there was a court order and they confirmed it with the court, but I just called the court myself and it's bullshit, there's no court order, the clerk spoke personally with Judge Ricardo and there's no fucking court order! What is going on?"

"I don't understand. He just walked out of the jail? Who did they release him to?"

"Two FBI special agents—Robinson and McBride."

"Did you—"

"Of course. I called the local field office. There are two agents with those names, but I spoke to one of them, and he told me he didn't know what I was talking about, he had no orders, he'd been nowhere near the FDC, he had nothing to do with Schrader. What the fuck is this?"

Livia tried to focus. "Does anybody know where Schrader is?"

"No one I've spoken to. I don't know how someone could pull this off. Dunlop said the court order was totally legit—stamped and everything. Even Ricardo's signature is a match!"

Think, Livia. Think. "Where are you now?"

"On my way to the courthouse to find out what the hell is going on. And listen. Not a half hour before this went down, I was at the FDC, interviewing Schrader."

"What? Why?"

"That thing at the park. I just . . . I was spooked. I needed to confront him. But that doesn't matter. What matters is, he told me he has video. Of all these powerful men having sex with kids. Raping them, though of course he didn't put it that way. He said everyone knows if anything happens to him, the videos will be released."

As Livia tried to process that, she heard an incoming call beep. She checked the screen—*Caller Blocked*.

"I have to take this," she said.

"Wait, we need to figure out—"

"Listen to me, Alondra. Don't go home, do you understand? Don't go back to work. Don't go anywhere you might be expected."

"Livia, what the hell—"

"Just do as I say! And don't go to the courthouse. Hold on, I have to take this call."

"Wait, what—"

"I'll be right back." She switched over to the incoming call. "Yes."

"Hey," Carl said. "Can you talk?"

"It's better if we meet. Are you around here? But don't say where."

"Yeah, way ahead of you. You know that beverage place I once told you I like? And you told me it was one of your favorites?"

He was talking about All City Coffee in Georgetown. But she got her coffee there routinely and they all knew her. "Yes."

"Would that work?"

She thought for a second. "Make it the park northwest of there. When can you be there?"

"Inside a half hour."

"Okay. If I'm late, wait for me. I have to go."

She switched back to Diaz. "Alondra?"

"What's going on?"

"Not on the phone. Now pay attention. I've tried to get you to be more careful and you haven't listened. That's my fault, not yours, I should have pushed harder. But I am pushing now. You got lucky at the park this morning and we can't rely on that kind of luck again. Ditch your phone right now. I don't care what you do with it, but you can't keep it on your person. Go straight to a public place, stay there, borrow someone's phone, and call me in an hour. You can't have a phone right now, it's too easy to track."

"What about you?"

"Don't worry about me. Just call me in an hour. From a random person's phone, do you understand?"

"Okay."

"Don't go confronting your fears again. Brave is great. Brave and dead is stupid. We are up against heavy opposition and we need to be smart."

"Who? Up against who?"

"That's what I'm trying to find out. Now do as I say—get rid of your phone right now, and call me in an hour."

chapter twenty-six

LIVIA

Livia parked the Jeep at the north end of Georgetown Playfield park. She saw Carl immediately—he was straddling the bench at a picnic table under an awning, casually scanning the area. Her heart started beating hard and she felt a surge of irritation—at him, and even more at herself for the effect he had on her.

Just before she cut the wipers, she saw him spot the Jeep. She flipped up her hood, got out, and started toward him. The park was empty, and everything was muted by the soft patter of the rain. He stood and watched her, grinning like an idiot.

She came in under the awning and pushed back her hood. She had no idea what she was going to say. "What are you doing here?" is what came out.

"Labee," he said, shaking his head. "God, I missed you. I'm sorry, I promised myself I wasn't going to say anything mushy, and now I've gone and blown it."

I missed you, too, she thought. But it didn't come out.

"Damn it," he said. "This is unbearable. I'm just going to hug you for a minute, all right? You know you don't have to hug me back."

"Carl," she said, but he already had his arms around her and had pulled her in close. She felt that surge of irritation again, and something hot like anger, and she was aware of his warmth, and the feel of his body, and his smell. One of the jets from nearby Boeing Field went screeching overhead, obliterating the sound of the rain. And then he was kissing her, and she was kissing him back. Hard. And her anger boiled over.

She shoved him away. "Stop. We have to stop. What is going on?"

He shook his head, whether to indicate he didn't have an answer or to clear it, she wasn't sure. The roar of the jet receded, and the soft drumbeat of rain faded back in. He did another quick scan of the area. "I'm sorry," he said again. "I . . . damn. You want to sit?"

She glanced back at the empty parking lot. "How did you get here?"

"Took a cab."

"From Freeway Park?"

"No, from farther out. I'm with Larison, and now this new guy Manus, too, and after the park we decided to get clear of the city. They dropped me off at SeaTac. I didn't want to ask them to come all the way back. Just in case."

"A taxi driver could remember you."

"Ah, you know me. Not that it's easy, but I can be unmemorable when I set my mind to it."

"Did you not know you don't sound like you're from around here? Diaz certainly noticed."

"Good news," he said, replacing the Texan with something as ridiculous as it was unspecified. "I made sure to address the driver in the humiliating accent I'm using with you right now. If you find it sexy, though, I'll keep doing it."

He stood there, grinning at her. She almost said, *What am I going to do with you?* but realized he would probably offer at least several answers, none of which she was ready to deal with.

They straddled the benches on opposite sides of the picnic table. The table was good—they could each see behind the other. With one leg in and one leg out, they could move quickly if necessary. And she needed some distance, the presence of something solid between them.

He briefed her on what had happened in the park, and everything that led up to it. While he spoke, she alternated between rage and relief, and struggled not to interrupt. But by the time he was done, she felt clearheaded and relatively in control again.

"Why did Kanezaki go to you?" she said. "I owe him. He knows that. You even told me once he would come to collect. Why not me?"

He blew out a long breath. "Well, maybe he just, uh . . ."

She knew he was a good liar, at least operationally. That he could offer nothing in response to her question suggested either that he didn't want to lie, or that she was throwing him off his game as much as he threw her off hers.

"Don't bullshit me, Carl. I could at least have warned Alondra."

"Would she have listened?"

Livia thought of the way Diaz had blown off her attempts to get her to be more tactical. But she wasn't going to concede the point. "We'll never know now, will we?"

"Well, I warned her."

"Yeah, after the fact."

He smiled. "Better late than never?"

When she didn't respond, he said, "I'm sorry, I don't mean to make light. Look, Kanezaki said he was going to involve you. And I told him not to, that I would take care of it myself."

"Why?"

He threw up his arms. "What am I supposed to do, let you get mixed up in this shit?"

"It's not your call. And besides, I am mixed up in it."

"Well, I tried. To spare you. You want me to apologize for that?"

"I don't need you to protect me."

"I never said you did."

"Then stop acting like it."

"Fine. I called you, didn't I? So now you're involved. I hope you're happy."

"Stop sulking. We need to figure this out."

"I'm not sulking."

"I've never seen you look sulkier than when you said that."

For a second, he stared at her, looking exasperated enough to pop. Then he broke out laughing. "I guess you've gotten to know me pretty well."

"Don't change the subject."

"See what I mean?"

"Listen to me. It's worse than you think." She told him about Diaz's call, about Schrader being released.

"I'll be damned," he said when she was done. "They're going to kill that boy for sure. He's probably dead already."

"I don't know. What about the videos?"

"Right, I expect he's going to endure some unpleasant questioning en route to coughing up whatever he knows. The good news, maybe, is this gets Diaz off the hook. Plus being tortured to death over blackmail materials couldn't happen to a nicer guy."

"We need to talk to Alondra. Schrader was saying if anything happens to him, those videos will be released."

"You mean like a dead-man switch? Larison was speculating about that."

"I don't know. And the people who took him—maybe they don't know, either. Or they don't know about the videos at all. Maybe you're right. Maybe they've already killed him. We need to find out more."

"Well, if there is a dead-man switch, and they killed him, I expect we'll find out soon enough."

"Who could have taken him? They had to forge a court order, fake FBI credentials, spoof a phone line out of the prison . . . This was a sophisticated operation."

"My first guess would be Rispel. She's the one trying to kill Diaz, or at least she's the cat's-paw. So when things went sideways for her in Freeway Park, she busted Schrader out of jail as a Plan B. But . . . could be another player entirely. Different agenda, different plan. Hard to say."

"Can Kanezaki help?"

"I already talked to him. He's trying to find out what he can. While dancing around Rispel's suspicions."

"What about Rain?"

"Larison's calling him. John's not going to have any intel, though."

"I don't want him for his intel. We don't know what we're up against."

"Yeah, I know. I just feel bad. John's trying to retire, or at least he thinks he is. I didn't want to bug him. That's why I called Larison. Larison loves this kind of shit. If trouble didn't come looking for him, he'd go find it on his own. And I didn't want . . . I'm sorry, Labee, I know you don't need protecting, I really do. It's just, if I can save you from something, I just . . ."

His voice trailed off and he looked away, his expression so forlorn it almost made her feel guilty.

"Carl. You have to stop making this about me. About us. It's bigger than that. Okay?"

He looked at her and nodded slowly. "There's not a lot for me that's bigger than us. But . . . point taken."

"You know what I mean."

"I do. That's the problem."

She wished she could tell him how much she . . . cared about him. She wished he knew how much she wanted to say it. But all she did was look at him, hoping he would somehow understand.

"You know," he said after a moment. "It occurs to me, maybe psychologically I've just been trying to get your attention. And if we could see each other more regularly, like normal people, then I wouldn't be so motivated to get up in all kinds of political skullduggery as my only hope of ever being with you."

She folded her arms and stared at him.

"I'm joking, of course," he said. "And by joking, I mean eighty percent serious."

Her phone buzzed. Someone named Jill Ehrman. *Diaz.* "Hello."

"It's me. I borrowed a phone."

"Are you someplace safe?"

"Storyville Coffee."

"The one at First and Madison?"

"Yes."

"I'll be by in ten minutes. Look for the Jeep. Make sure you confirm it's me driving. I'll have a passenger, too, but don't worry about that. When I pull up, come out and get right in."

"Livia—"

"I don't care if it sounds paranoid. Just do as I say."

"It . . . doesn't sound paranoid. Not anymore."

chapter
twenty-seven

RISPEL

There was a knock, followed by Rispel's admin opening the door. "Director Rispel, Director—"

Devereaux barged past her. "Thank you," he said. "And now please leave us."

The admin looked at Rispel. Rispel nodded, and the admin left, closing the door behind her.

"Pierce," Rispel said. "I was just going—"

He slammed his palms onto her desk and leaned all the way over it, putting his face just inches from hers. "What the fuck is going on, Lisa?"

Flecks of spittle hit her and she might have flinched—might have reverted to their past dynamic. But she'd imagined this eventuality and had mentally rehearsed it. So without even attempting to conceal her disgust, she wiped her cheeks, looked into his eyes, and said firmly, "Sit down, Pierce."

"Are you fucking kidding me? I said—"

"Put your ass in one of those two guest chairs right now, or I will call security and have you escorted from my building."

He looked at her, his mouth agape but for once nothing coming out of it.

"Sit," she said again. She realized she had deliberately addressed him in the same way she did her cocker spaniel, and that she had enjoyed doing so. She reminded herself to keep her ego in check.

After a moment, he straightened and took a step back. To save face, he said, "You better have a damn good explanation." He sat.

She knew perfectly well what had brought him, but there was no upside, only risk, to going first. "Explanation for what?"

He reddened, and for a second, she thought he might go into another tirade. But he didn't. He must have known she was serious about having him escorted out. And he must have been afraid of his current position. She had him. He might try to bluff, but she had him. She felt herself wanting to relish the knowledge, and suppressed the feeling.

"It's a shitshow in Seattle," he said. "The press is crawling all over the US Attorney, Meekler. The district judge is receiving death threats. There are QAnon protesters in front of the damn courthouse, claiming some sort of deep state conspiracy to release a rich pedophile! So please. Just tell me. Where the hell is Schrader?"

It was what she had been expecting. "That's why I was going to call you. I thought this was you. Some kind of Plan B."

He looked half-desperate, half-incredulous. "You're saying you had nothing to do with it?"

"That's exactly what I'm saying. Are you saying the same?"

He went pale, and his lips moved as if to form words, but nothing came out. She wondered if he was going to be sick.

"Lisa," he said. "Look, I'm not upset. Maybe it's good. I just need to know what's going on, okay?"

"You seem upset." *Don't toy with him. That's not the point.*

"No. No. Just . . . agitated. But . . . come on. Who else could have done this?"

"Are you joking? Are you seriously asking me who could have been motivated to acquire a set of doomsday blackmail videos involving prominent Americans? And who could have had the means to do it?"

He shook his head as though to clear it. "You're saying . . . FSB?"

"Of course. And if not Russia, China would be my next guess."

He put his hands to his temples. "This can't be happening. It can't."

"Pierce. Listen to me. We need to prepare for the very real possibility that whoever is on those tapes is now subject to blackmail by the FSB or MSS. Those people need to be warned. We need contingency plans."

He laughed slightly hysterically. "Contingency plans? There are no contingency plans for something like this. Do you know who we're talking about?"

"That's what I'm asking you."

"For starters? Try the president of the United States."

Rispel stared at him. She didn't have to pretend to be shocked. The feeling was real.

Be bold, and mighty forces will come to your aid. That was another thing her father had liked to say.

Well, she'd been bold, all right. But it wasn't triumph she felt. Because her mother had a preferred expression, too. *Don't bite off more than you can chew.*

She was suddenly afraid it was her mother's wisdom she should have heeded.

chapter twenty-eight

SCHRADER

Schrader knew something was wrong as soon as the agents began driving south on I-5. "I thought you said we were going to the FBI field office," he said. "Isn't that in Seattle?"

The wipers made a soft *thump thump*. The one called Robinson glanced at him in the rearview mirror, then back to the road. "We have different field offices. We're taking you to Tacoma."

But a few minutes later, they exited the interstate and started heading southeast on surface roads. Schrader looked around, not understanding. The windows of the car were dirty, and with the rain it was hard to see. "Where are we going?" Schrader said.

"You'll know when we get there," the one called McBride said, not even glancing back. "Now do us all a favor and shut the fuck up. Our job is to drive you, not to make small talk."

They hit a pothole and the handcuffs bit into Schrader's wrists. "I want to talk to my lawyer," he said, trying to control his growing unease. "Sharon Hamilton. You can call her for me. I'll give you her number, she's right here in Seattle. Could you do that? Please."

McBride turned back and looked at him. "Tell you what, buddy. If one more word comes out of your mouth, we're going to pull over and I'm going to gag you."

"But it's not fair! I don't know where you're taking me and I want to talk to my lawyer!"

Without a word, Robinson pulled over onto the shoulder and stopped. McBride got out. He was holding some kind of long white cloth—a bathrobe belt? Schrader was suddenly terrified.

"Okay, okay, I'm sorry! I won't say anything else! I'll stop!"

McBride said nothing. He opened the rear passenger-side door, leaned in, and pulled the cloth across Schrader's mouth. Schrader wanted to twist away, but he was afraid of what they might do if he tried to resist. "Wait, wait, *wuhwuhwuh* . . . ," he said as McBride secured the belt behind his head. He tried to ask them why they were doing this, why they wouldn't just call Sharon, but all that came out was the *wuhwuhwuh* sound. The cloth was rough against his tongue and the only way he could avoid gagging was to bite down to keep it from invading deeper into his mouth.

McBride took him by the chin and looked in his eyes. "No more noise from you," he said, his tone weirdly gentle. "Do you understand? Unless you want to get hooded, too. Do you want that?"

Something in the kindness of the tone undid Schrader. He shook his head and started to cry.

McBride patted his leg. "That's good. We'll be there soon. You're going to be fine."

They started up again. Other than the *thump thump*, *thump thump*, the car was silent now. The handcuffs hurt and the cloth belt was worse. Schrader had to concentrate to keep from gagging. He felt something running down his chin and realized it was drool.

Robinson turned on the radio, some country-and-western station. McBride said, "I hate this shit. I choose on the way back." Robinson laughed.

The farther they drove, the more Schrader knew something was badly wrong. The areas they passed through were increasingly remote. There were barely any houses, let alone FBI field offices. He realized he had to pee, and he couldn't even ask. Not that they would have listened. He breathed through his nose and tried not to gag.

The pine trees grew taller and thicker. They passed a big body of water. Schrader thought it might be Lake Tapps, but he'd lost track of where they were heading.

They turned onto a twisting gravel road and stopped at a gate. McBride got out and unlocked and opened it. Robinson drove through, then waited while McBride relocked the gate and got back in the car.

Robinson turned off the music. Schrader hadn't liked it, but the silence that replaced it was much worse. *Thump thump, thump thump.*

They came to a two-story green house. It had a pair of white garage doors in front. One of the doors opened. But no one in the car had pressed a button. Someone inside must have been waiting. Watching.

They pulled inside. The wipers stopped. The garage door closed behind them with a loud mechanical rumble and a thud. For a moment, they sat there in the dark and the quiet. Schrader didn't know where they were. Or what was happening. All he knew was that it was very bad. He tried to hold in his pee, and all at once he couldn't.

A man came out. He flipped on a light. He was wearing jeans and a fleece jacket. He didn't look like an FBI agent.

The man opened the rear passenger-side door and pulled Schrader out. "Jesus," he said, looking at Schrader's wet prison jumpsuit. "You guys couldn't pull over and let him take a leak?"

McBride came out and looked. "Oh, come on." He looked at Robinson. "I am not cleaning that up."

Robinson came around and looked, too. "Oh, hell. Whatever. We'll throw some towels over it. Keep the smell down."

Schrader stood there, ashamed and humiliated. He realized he was still peeing. There was nothing he could do. He started crying again.

"Why'd you gag him?" the new man said. "He could have choked." It didn't sound like he cared about Schrader. It sounded like he cared about . . . something else.

"Hey," McBride said. "You want to take the gag off, go for it. Good luck finding another way to shut him up."

The new man chuckled and patted Schrader on the back. "Well, we don't want to shut him up, do we?" He looked Schrader up and down, as though measuring him for something. "We want to hear everything he has to say."

chapter twenty-nine

KANEZAKI

When Kanezaki's admin told him the DCI wanted to see him immediately, he wondered if it was connected to DNI Pierce Devereaux's presence in the building. The word was, Devereaux had come to see Rispel, and her admin had heard shouting from behind Rispel's closed office door. When it came to gossip, at least, in an intelligence agency there were no secrets.

He was actually glad Rispel had summoned him. From what he'd seen on the news, Seattle was boiling over, and Dox, Larison, and Manus were flying blind without him. A meeting with Rispel would be a chance at more intel, or at least more insight. Beyond which, the anxiety of wondering how she was going to play it with him had been an unpleasant distraction. Best to get past it.

No cozy seat in the corner this time. Rispel didn't even get up from behind her desk when the admin let him in. Or say anything after the admin had left and closed the door. Kanezaki sat, suppressing the urge to speak. *You go first,* he thought. *You're the one who wanted the meeting.*

"I've just received some quite disturbing news from DNI Devereaux," Rispel said after a moment. "About Seattle."

Well, he'd been right. It was about both Devereaux and Seattle. "Yes?"

"I'm afraid that, through no fault of my own, I've put you in a bad position."

That, he hadn't been expecting. "Yes?"

"This . . . Manus matter. I was given to understand it was a payback operation, as I told you. It seems in fact it was related to Andrew Schrader, who as I'm sure you've seen on the news has been waltzed out of his prison cell by mysterious forces."

Kanezaki had already planned on playing dumb, and despite Rispel's unforeseen gambit he saw no reason to change the plan now. "I was wondering why I never heard from you this morning."

"I had operators in the area tracking Manus. Six of them. They were massacred in a park."

"I saw it on the news. Those were your people?"

She nodded. "Are you certain your man Dox had nothing to do with this?"

Your man. He recognized the trap she was laying out—an easy opportunity to claim that Dox had never been anywhere near the park. But Dox had told him there had been a scout, a woman posing as a jogger, and he couldn't be sure of how much Rispel might know. So all he said was "I can't imagine why he would have been involved."

"Have you been in touch with him?"

Another potential trap. "Of course. He wanted to know what happened to the target. Why he was 'all dressed up but didn't have a prom date,' is I think how he put it." At any rate it sounded like something Dox would say.

Rispel nodded. He could tell she wasn't convinced.

"Well," she said after a moment. "It seems I've been used. Not for the first time. But that's another story. For now, suffice to say that it seems this Manus thing wasn't about payback for Anders, as I was given to understand, but rather about securing, or silencing, Schrader."

He remembered something one of his instructors had told him: *The best way to conceal a lie is to wrap it in truth.* "I don't understand."

"I'm not sure I do, either. Did Dox say anything else?"

He saw risks in the truth and risks in the lie. He chose the lie. "Just that he had the same concerns you do about current events. Told me the job wasn't worth the per diem."

"He's in the wind, then?"

"Are you asking if I can contact him?"

"Or track him down, yes."

"I can try. But when he doesn't feel like answering, he doesn't. And if I try to contact him another way, I doubt he'll feel it's friendly."

She sighed. "It's strange. The team I had monitoring Manus. Before they were all annihilated, the leader checked in with me. She said she saw two men in the park bracing Manus. Could that have been Dox? If it was, then he and Manus must have been cooperating. There's no other possible explanation for how Manus could have prevailed against a team of six trained operators."

Another thing he hadn't seen coming. "Manus was in the park? You had me position Dox near Pike Place. The fish market."

"Yes, Manus had spent the night in a hostel nearby. Dox didn't mention any of this to you?"

"No. He told me he waited all morning near the market, heard the news about the shooting and then the prison break, and pulled the plug." He realized he was being too reactive, giving her too much leeway to shape the conversation. "But if you had six operators . . . why did you even need Dox?"

She frowned. "Compartmentalization, for one thing. Deniability, for another."

"Who were the operators?"

"Honestly, Tom, what difference does it make?"

"You have a lot of questions about Dox, but none about the operators?"

129

She pursed her lips. "Your man Dox is alive. The operators are dead. I'd say they've proven their bona fides. Dox, on the other hand, is an open question."

She looked away for a moment, drumming her fingers on her desk. "The DNI has informed me that Schrader is likely in possession of some extremely compromising material regarding some extremely highly placed people. I don't know the details. But the DNI is afraid this . . . prison break was engineered by Russian forces. Or possibly Chinese."

He'd tried hard to game out all the possibilities, but that one he hadn't seen coming. "Wait a minute . . . You mean the DNI told you to take out Manus as a payback operation, and now he says he thinks, what, the FSB or MSS broke Schrader out of prison because of black-mail videos? Did he explain any connection between the two? Or try to resolve the discrepancy?"

"I asked him about exactly those subjects. He's keeping me in the dark. Telling me just enough to make me frustrated, but not enough to make me useful."

"I can imagine," Kanezaki said. He couldn't resist, but he immediately regretted it.

Rispel chuckled. "Fair enough. As I learn more, so will you. In the meantime, see if you can get in touch with Dox. Try to find out what he knows. If there's a storm coming, we want to batten down the hatches."

RISPEL

After Kanezaki had left, Rispel considered.

He'd been lying, of course. The team leader had described the men in the park, and one of them fit the photographs Rispel had of Dox from when he'd been a Marine. The leader also described him as having a Texas accent.

Of course, in theory it was possible Dox was lying to Kanezaki rather than Kanezaki lying to her. But there was no way a contractor like Dox could have independently developed the intel to track Manus. It had to have come from Kanezaki.

But how could Kanezaki have acquired it?

By tracking Manus's phone? But the man wasn't carrying his own phone. Only a CIA-provided burner. And Manus's exceptional surveillance consciousness was the very reason Rispel had wanted such a large team on the ground to monitor him.

Through Diaz, then?

Diaz was easy to track. If Kanezaki had keyed on her, he would have considered the park a likely nexus, just as Rispel had.

Why, though? What was Kanezaki's interest?

She couldn't answer that. Couldn't imagine what advantage he would see in thwarting her.

All right. Forget why. How?

She couldn't answer that, either. Diaz wasn't difficult to track, but how would Kanezaki even have known to do it? Unless . . .

Guardian Angel.

No. She'd deleted all the searches related to Diaz. Deletion was unlawful, of course, but Rispel had people, trusted people, she could rely on to circumvent the safeguards.

But given that there were ways to get around the no-deletion protocols . . . could there also be a way to log the deletions themselves?

My God.

She reminded herself that she was only speculating. There was no reason to panic. She didn't really know.

But nothing else made sense.

Who, though? Kanezaki couldn't have done it himself. He didn't have the technical chops, any more than Rispel herself did.

She had her people. Who would be Kanezaki's equivalent?

She didn't know. What she did know was that no one could get in and out of Guardian Angel without leaving footprints. And her people were excellent trackers.

chapter
thirty-one

DOX

The rain had stopped, and while they waited for Diaz to come out, Dox wiped off the sideview so he could better watch for tails. The other hand he kept on the butt of the Wilson. He didn't expect any problems and didn't see any, but he wasn't taking chances, either.

Diaz came out, and Dox held the door for her as she jumped in back. He got in, and Labee was pulling away from the curb even before he had the door closed. She made an immediate right, checking the rearview as she drove.

"You," Diaz said. "You're the one I saw outside the park."

"Yes, ma'am," Dox said. "I'm sorry I didn't have a chance to properly introduce myself. It's been a hectic morning. You can call me Dox."

"Did you kill those people?"

Dox glanced at Labee. She made a left, again checking the rearview, and said nothing.

"I'm just glad you're safe," Dox said. "And I hope you'll believe me when I say, I'd like to keep it that way."

Labee made another left, then a right into something that was more alley than street, squeezing past a delivery truck on the way. As soon as they were past the truck, she gunned it, throwing Dox back against the seat and making him wonder whether he'd exercised good judgment in leaving his seatbelt unbuckled in case they ran into opposition. She turned the wrong way onto a one-way street, gunned it again, and cut back onto a main thoroughfare. Dox checked the sideview. As far as he could tell, they were clean.

Twenty minutes later, they were sitting on the mats in one of the martial arts academies where Labee taught her women's self-defense classes. Classes were at night, and for the moment, the place was empty.

"What did Schrader tell you?" Labee said to Diaz. "About the videos."

Diaz looked at Dox as though uncertain of what to say. That was fine. He felt uncertain about her, too. He wasn't in the habit of chatting with federal prosecutors right after gunning down a bunch of bad guys in a public park.

"You can trust him," Labee said. "And not just because you have to."

There was a long pause. Diaz said, "I tried to scare him. I mean, I *did* scare him, obviously. I told him that people had tried to kill me, and failed, and that now I was going to be untouchable. Which meant the next move by whoever sent the people in the park would be to silence him. I told him one word from me, and the BOP—" She glanced at Dox. "The Bureau of Prisons would remove all the protection he was getting. No more cameras, no extra guards. He said no one would hurt him, because he has videos of various powerful men having sex with underage girls."

"Children," Labee said. "Alondra, I don't care how they get referred to in statutes, underage girls are children."

Diaz grimaced. "Bad habit. I don't say *child prostitutes* anymore, either. Prostituted children."

Labee nodded. "What men?"

"He wouldn't give me that. I got him to say a lot—more than he meant to, I'm sure, because he was scared and trying to please me—but he wouldn't name names. But I could tell he was worried. I kept pressing him, saying how would they know, and why should they believe him. And he said his lawyer told Hobbs."

"Uriah Hobbs?" Dox said.

Diaz nodded. "That Hobbs."

"Well," Dox said, "that's not great. I mean, it was bad enough when it was just Rispel and the CIA. But the attorney general runs Justice, and Justice runs the FBI. This is turning into a lot of opposition for our little band of brothers."

"There's more," Diaz said. "Schrader says the videos will be released unless he resets an automated system."

"Dead-man switch," Dox said. "Like Larison suspected. Not just the angel of death—smart, too. Did Schrader offer any details? How the system gets reset, or where, or by whom?"

Diaz shook her head. "I tried. All he would say is if I didn't get him out of jail right away, there would be what he called 'a shot across the bow.'"

Dox had heard that kind of thing before. "Well, he would say that, wouldn't he?"

Labee looked at him. "That doesn't mean it isn't true."

"Fair enough," Dox said. "I guess we'll find out soon enough. Unless the people who took him can get him to reset the system beforehand."

Diaz looked at Dox. "Who are you? How are you involved in this?"

Dox gave her a quick rundown, doing his best to leave out anything that could be used against him in the proverbial court of law.

When he was done, Diaz said, "I can't believe this shit goes on."

"Me neither," Dox said. "And I'm part of it."

They were quiet for a moment. Labee said, "But why would Hobbs have believed Schrader's lawyer? I mean, would they really have conspired to murder an assistant US Attorney, and to break Schrader out of prison, based just on the lawyer's say-so?"

"No," Diaz said. "Schrader said the lawyer showed Hobbs excerpts. Proof."

Dox realized something. "Wait a minute. If the damn lawyer has some kind of highlight reel, anybody who's trying to roll this thing up by disappearing Schrader is likely to make a run at the lawyer, too. Do we know who or where this person is?"

"Yes," Diaz said. "Her name is Sharon Hamilton. She's been in Seattle since Schrader's arrest. Staying at the Four Seasons."

"And where's that?"

"Downtown," Labee said. "Fifteen-, maybe twenty-minute drive."

Dox pulled out his burner. "Larison and Manus might be able to get there faster than that. And if we all get there together, it'll be good to have backup. Alondra, do you know Hamilton's cellphone number?"

"Yes," Diaz said. "But . . . shit, it's on my phone. I left it in the library near the courthouse."

"Good," Labee said. "That was the right move."

Dox's mind was racing. He was getting a bad feeling about Hamilton. He looked at Diaz. "Can you get it from someone in your office? Or by calling Hamilton's office?"

"Maybe."

"Not Meekler," Labee said. "I don't want you talking to him right now, or having to answer his questions. We don't know who's in on this."

Dox thought of Kanezaki. "Well, try who you can," he said. "And even if you can't manage it, maybe my contact can get the number just from Hamilton's name, and he can track it for us, too. But let's get someone over to the hotel first." He called Larison's burner.

Larison picked up instantly. "Everything okay?"

"Copacetic. I mean, *copacetic*'s a relative term this morning, but you know what I mean. You getting along okay with our new friend?"

"We're fine. Nice to spend time with someone quiet for a change."

Dox would have laughed, but he was too concerned about Hamilton. "Okay, here's the deal. I need the two of you to get over to the Seattle Four Seasons pronto."

"You want us back in Seattle? After the park, I thought the idea was for us to stay out."

"Hey, we've been improvising on everything today, why should we stop now? Anyway, Schrader's lawyer, Sharon Hamilton, is staying at the hotel. And for reasons I don't have time to get into right now, I think she's in danger."

"Well, what do you want us to do?"

"I'd say for starters kill anything that looks dangerous." He covered the microphone and said to Diaz, "*Kill* being a euphemism, of course."

He put the phone back to his ear. Larison said, "At least this time you're not asking me to just hit someone with an umbrella."

"I don't care how you do it. The main thing is, if we want to figure out where this opposition is ultimately coming from, we need to know what Hamilton knows. That'll work best if she's alive and not disappeared by whoever took Schrader. Now head over there double time. I'm doing the same, and I'll see if K. can confirm a cellphone location, too. If Hamilton's not at the hotel, I'll call you back."

He clicked off and looked at Labee. "You got a nav system in that Jeep of yours? I don't know how to get to the hotel."

"I'll drive you."

"No, I don't think that's—"

"I'll drive you."

If there's one thing he'd learned about Labee, it was the futility of arguing. "Can Alondra stay here?"

Diaz said, "I'm coming, too."

Labee shook her head. "Bad idea."

"I'm the only one Hamilton knows," Diaz said. "She won't listen to you. Or go anywhere with you."

Dox said, "How about if you just call her at the hotel? See if you can reach her in her room and tell her to stay put and not answer the door."

"Even if I reach her, if you go without me, she won't know who you are."

Dox stood and called Kanezaki. "Well, whoever's going, let's make it quick. I got a bad feeling about Hamilton, and we might be too late already."

chapter thirty-two

DOX

Labee drove and Dox rode shotgun. Diaz, in the back, used Dox's burner to call the Four Seasons. She asked for Hamilton's room, waited, then shook her head and clicked off. "Not in the room," she said.

Dox had already tried Kanezaki but hadn't been able to reach him. And no one in Hamilton's office had been willing to share the cellphone number. "Damn," he said. "If she's not at the hotel, and someone else is geolocating her cellphone, we're wasting our time. Alondra, you said you have the number in your cellphone. You left it in a library? Where?"

"Near the courthouse," Diaz said. "Just a few blocks from the hotel. Livia, swing by. I'll use it just to call Hamilton. I can ditch it again afterward."

Labee glanced at Dox, obviously not liking it.

"It's a small risk," he said. "Remember, it's not just that we need Hamilton's intel. If whatever she knows falls into the wrong hands, that's doubly bad."

Five minutes later, they pulled up in front of the public library. There were people marching past with signs—SAVE THE CHILDREN and THE STORM IS COMING and DEEP STATE PROTECTS PEDOPHILES. Schrader's bizarre prison release was in the news, and it was stirring up the QAnoners.

Diaz moved as though to get out. "No, ma'am," Dox said, scoping the area. "Tell me where the phone is and you stay put. Just in case there are any unfriendlies in the area."

"Behind a book called *Recursion*, by Blake Crouch. Level three. Fiction."

Dox went in while Labee circled the block. He found the phone no problem and made it back to the Jeep without incident. "Haven't turned it on yet," he said. "Let's wait until we're moving."

They pulled away and Diaz called Hamilton. Dox eyed the sideview. He didn't see anyone tailing them, but there was too much traffic to be sure.

"Sharon," Diaz said. "This is Alondra Diaz. I—no, I didn't have my cellphone with me, I just picked it up. Listen—no, I don't know where Schrader is. I had nothing to do with—listen to me, this is important. It's critical that I meet you right away. Where are you?"

A pause, then, "Where in the hotel? I tried you in the room."

She glanced at Dox. "The restaurant? That's—" A pause. "I don't know why you can't reach Meekler, I haven't been to the office. Are there other people in the restaurant?"

Another pause. "Can you just answer me? I think you're in danger. Did you not hear about what happened in Freeway Park this morning? It's not just about me. They might be coming for you, too."

Another pause. "I don't care if you think I'm being paranoid. Will you just stay put? In the restaurant. Near other people. I'll be there in a few minutes and I'll tell you more. Okay? Good. Just a few minutes."

She clicked off and powered down.

Dox called Larison from a burner. "Where are you?"

"About a minute from the hotel. You?"

"Not far behind. We reached Hamilton. She says she's in the hotel restaurant. I couldn't reach K., so I don't have independent confirmation, but there's no reason to think Hamilton's lying. Why don't you pull up and send Manus in to have a look. You stay with the van. It's not personal, just—"

"I know. I get noticed."

"It's one of your charm points. I'll be right behind him. If it all looks good, we'll send in Diaz, who'll be functioning as our bona fides, and we'll escort Hamilton out."

"Understood. By the way, we're passing protestors. I think they're heading to the courthouse."

"Yeah, we saw a bunch, too. Schrader's release and all the denials, I guess. The good news is, it'll probably draw police resources. Give us a little more room if we need it."

"Agreed. Call me if anything changes."

He realized he wouldn't know Hamilton even if he saw her. "What does Hamilton look like?" he asked Diaz. He handed her his phone. "Here, see if you can find a photo."

Diaz worked the phone, then handed it back to him. It was the cover page of Hamilton's law firm website—Hamilton, Barrett & Brown. An exceptionally thin, fiftyish white woman standing between a couple of men who, other than their jowls, looked cut from the same corporate cloth. Long brown hair, arms crossed confidently as she smiled for the camera.

Two minutes later, Labee stopped at a traffic light. "The entrance is on Union," she said, pointing. "One block up. But see that shop across the street, Fran's Chocolates? You can access the lobby through there."

"Roger that. And since Larison is already by the lobby, can you swing around and wait in front of Fran's? Better to have options."

"Yes. Be careful."

He smiled. "I love when you show you care."

She punched him in the arm. "Get out."

He cut across the street and went into the chocolate shop. It was an upscale place, the chocolates laid out under glass like jewelry. A pretty brunette was standing behind one of the displays. "Hello," she said, with a nice smile. "May I help you with anything?"

Dox looked around as though perplexed. "I'm sorry, I thought this was the hotel."

"Oh, you can access the lobby right there." She pointed to a double set of wooden doors.

"Well, thank you," Dox said. "I'm pressed right now, but I hope to be back to sample some of your delicious-looking confectionaries."

He hadn't intended any double entendre, but the way she smiled again made him think maybe it had come across that way. "I hope so, too."

She really was pretty. He was never going to stop loving women. Unfortunately, the one he was in love with seemed unable to conquer her ambivalence. Well, thoughts for another day. He put his hand on the butt of the Wilson and went through the doors and into the hotel lobby—

A large man was standing there, facing the chocolate shop entrance, his back to a pillar and his hand inside his jacket. Dox made him instantly. Unfortunately, he made Dox just as fast. Also unfortunately, action beat reaction, and on the assumption that the hand inside the jacket was already holding a gun, there was no way Dox could beat him to the draw.

Dox glanced around the lobby. It was bustling with tourists and an early lunch crowd. He looked at the guy and smiled. "Well, what do we do now?"

The guy didn't smile back. "We wait."

"Couldn't we just talk through our differences? Why does there have to be so much hostility?"

If there was one thing Dox was good at in this world, it was rattling someone with insouciance and non sequiturs. Well, in fairness, he was a hell of a marksman, too. And he liked to think he knew how to make a woman happy. But this was a moment for the insouciance and non sequiturs.

The guy was pretty cool in response. "I'm not hostile. Just doing a job."

"Happy in your work?"

"Never really thought about it."

"They say the unexamined life isn't worth living."

"Yeah? I think my chances of living are good. Yours, not so much."

Dox saw movement along a flight of stairs above where the guy was standing. He glanced up and saw Manus on the way down. Manus paused, watching them.

The guy saw where Dox was looking but didn't follow his gaze. "You think you're going to make me look? What's next, my shoelaces are untied?"

"Of course not," Dox said. "I can tell you're way too smart for that." And then he kept moving his lips, but without making any sound. *Use the Espada. No noise.*

"What's that?" the guy said.

"Sorry, I'm just praying to the good lord. I mean, what else can I do"—he started enunciating very carefully—"with you holding a gun on me under your jacket and all." And then silently, *Drop him right now, please.*

For a big man, Manus moved remarkably smoothly and quietly. He continued down the stairs. As he came to the landing just behind the pillar, Dox caught a flash of the Espada's steel blade. Manus was holding it like an ice pick, close to his body.

Manus turned the corner. He did a quick witness check, left and right. He pulled abreast of the pillar and into the guy's ambit of vision. The guy saw him and started to turn. Too late. Without any hesitation at all, Manus drove the Espada backhanded up into the guy's midsection. The blade must have pierced the diaphragm, because the guy folded up instantly, making not a sound beyond a single loud wheeze. Dox rushed in and grabbed the guy's right arm. But there was no need—the guy wasn't trying to get his gun out, he wasn't trying to do anything except maybe make the wheezing sound and twitch and shudder.

"I like my chances fine, asshole," Dox said. He reached inside the guy's jacket and took his pistol. He got some blood on his sleeve in the process but it wasn't too bad, he was just glad old Manus hadn't cut the guy's throat. They lowered the body to the floor, Manus leaving the knife in until the last moment to keep the blood flow down.

Dox heard a woman's voice from the lobby behind them. "Oh my God!"

He looked up and saw a woman in a floor-length leather jacket watching them, her expression horrified. He realized he'd gotten more blood on himself than he'd thought. "Get a doctor!" he called out. "This man's bleeding. I think it's hemorrhagic fever, probably Ebola!"

The woman backed up so fast she might have been jerked with a rope. Dox passed the pistol to Manus. "I think they were waiting for Hamilton to leave so they could snatch her nearer the exit," he said, so softly he was practically just mouthing the words. "Meaning there's likely to be more opposition nearby, here or right outside. You ready?"

Manus nodded once. Larison was right, the man was quiet. And even more, reliable.

They stood. A cluster of people had gathered, chattering in confused tones and watching. The staircase concealed some of what was happening, but it was clear there was a body on the floor. And a lot of blood.

"I wouldn't get too close," Dox said. "Thankfully I'm immune to Ebola from my time combatting the disease in Africa, and am no longer infectious myself. I'm pretty sure."

"Ebola?" he heard someone say, and the cluster was suddenly gone. But the lobby was abuzz now with agitated voices.

He and Manus came from around the stairs and headed toward the restaurant. The people who had seen them with the body gave them a wide berth. Everyone else was looking around, confused and uncertain. A guy in a blue blazer, probably hotel security, rounded the front desk and rushed past them. Dox kept his head moving, looking for more opposition, but so far he didn't see any.

No way to get Diaz in here now. Well, so much for their bona fides. They were going to have to improvise again.

chapter
thirty-three

LARISON

L arison was directly across from the hotel, standing inside the glass doors of a place that arranged brewery and roastery visits for tourists. He'd asked if they wouldn't mind his waiting for a friend there, just to get in from the rain. It wasn't raining anymore, but they told him no problem. He might not have had Dox's ability to go unnoticed, but people didn't like to argue with him, either.

He'd parked illegally just around the corner. He wasn't worried about a ticket—they had rented the van using fake credentials. And he wasn't expecting to be there long enough for anyone to get a tow truck.

He saw two people rush out of the hotel. They started talking urgently with the bellman while pointing back into the lobby. Several more people rushed out behind them. Something was going on. Maybe Hamilton had decided not to come quietly.

To the right of the hotel was a viewing deck looking out over the waterfront, and a long flight of stairs alongside it. Two big men came racing up the steps and toward the hotel entrance. Larison glanced left, to the street corner, and didn't see any other problems.

He walked out of the tour shop and crossed the street, head swiveling. Still no one else who looked like trouble. He broke into a jog as the two men reached the hotel entrance. They got stuck there for a moment because more people were running out. One of the men eased a pistol from a waistband holster. Larison was already holding his, covered by the rain parka draped over his arm.

The men squeezed through the doors, Larison just behind them. Inside, he saw Dox and Manus, about to head into the restaurant. Amid the weirdly incongruous lobby music, the atmosphere was agitated. People looking around anxiously, a lot of confused chatter about Ebola. He smiled. *Fucking Dox.*

He scanned and saw a body to the left, a sizeable pool of blood around it. His smile broadened. *Manus.*

One of the men nudged the other and pointed to Dox and Manus. The second man eased out a pistol.

A woman with two kids crossed in front of Larison. He sidestepped and closed on the two men. They were less than twenty feet from Dox and Manus now.

Ahead, Larison saw a guy in a wheelchair take note of the two men. The guy's gaze zeroed in on one of their pistols. He pointed and yelled, "He has a gun!"

There was more shouting. Dox started to turn. The two men brought up their pistols—

Larison capped each of them in the back of the head, the two shots so rapid it sounded like a double tap. The lobby erupted in screaming and Dox and Manus spun and brought up pistols—Dox, the Wilson; Manus, presumably something he took from the guy he'd killed. They saw it was Larison and checked their flanks.

Dox turned to Manus. "I'll get the woman. You two git!"

Larison scanned the lobby. Pandemonium. People stampeding toward the exit. "What if there are—"

"I'll handle it. Just go!"

Dox strode into the restaurant. Larison thought, *Fuck that.* He caught up to Manus and looked inside. For a second, he thought the place was empty. Then he realized—everyone had taken cover under the tables.

Dox looked back at him. "Get the van!" he said. "I told you, I got this!"

Larison scanned the room. He didn't see any problems but didn't want to leave. But Dox was right. More important to have the van running and ready to go.

"Watch his back," he said to Manus, and he was surprised to realize he trusted Manus to do it. "I'll be in the van, right outside the entrance."

chapter
thirty-four

DOX

Dox glanced around the restaurant. There wasn't a person to be seen. Everyone was sheltering under the tables, even the waitstaff.

He thought about calling Hamilton's name, but with all the shooting and panic she must have been terrified. What was she going to do? Stand up and say, *Oh, here I am!*

One of the tables by the windows had a laptop open on it alongside a sheaf of papers. Someone had been working there, obviously. Next to it was a half-eaten salad. Dox thought of the thin woman in the law firm website photo. He hustled over to the table and squatted next to it. There she was, shrunk back against the wall, looking at him fearfully.

"Sharon Hamilton?" he said, extending his hand. "Come with me if you want to live. Hah, I always wanted to say that. I loved it in those *Terminator* movies."

She shook her head and pressed herself harder against the wall. Well, so much for breaking the ice with humor.

"My name's Dox," he said. "I'm with Alondra Diaz. She's waiting outside. She was going to come in herself, but there were people here to ambush you and things got a little crazy. Anyway, they can't harm anyone anymore, but there are others where they came from. You need to trust me, all right?"

She shook her head again.

"Ma'am, I'm not here to hurt you. I'm a friend. And with the people you've pissed off with those videos, believe me, you need one."

She looked at him. He extended his hand further.

This time, she took it.

chapter thirty-five

HOBBS

I don't care what the media claims," Hobbs said, his breath fogging in the cold night air. "And the crazies are going to believe whatever they like, facts be damned. I'm just telling you, I spoke with Judge Ricardo personally. No one presented him with an application for Schrader's release. He didn't issue a court order. The courts, and the DOJ, had nothing to do with it. The question is, who did?"

He and Devereaux were strolling on the Mall near the steps of the Lincoln Memorial, their security details paralleling them front and back in the dark. The meeting had been Devereaux's idea—he said he didn't trust the secure phones, but Hobbs suspected it was because the man had grown so paranoid he was afraid anything said on the phone might be recorded by the other party. Certainly the same thought had crossed Hobbs's mind, and more than once.

"Rispel believes it was the Russians," Devereaux said. "Or possibly the Chinese."

"Do we have actual evidence of that?"

"No evidence to the contrary."

They passed a knot of protesters. Their signs were backlit by the lamps lining the Reflecting Pool, and Hobbs couldn't read them. But the *Deep state protects pedophiles* chants were clear enough. He felt vaguely sorry for them. Of course there was a "deep state," or whatever else people might want to call it—not just in America but in every country. How could a society function without a semipermanent core of experts committed to stable governance? As for "protecting pedophiles," the fact that these people genuinely believed such a thing was real was proof of the need for a club of pragmatic insiders. No one was trying to protect pedophiles. People were simply trying to protect themselves—and by extension, of course, the country.

When they were out of earshot, Devereaux said, "What about Hamilton?"

"No one can reach her. Not even her law firm. Have you tried—"

"Of course. She was using her cellphone heavily at the Seattle Four Seasons until early afternoon, West Coast time."

"My lord. You mean—"

"Yes," Devereaux said. "Where there were more killings today. Her cellphone history shows calls to the Federal Detention Center, the Seattle District Court, and her law firm. Presumably she was as stunned as everyone else by her client's mysterious release and was trying to figure out what the hell was going on."

For the thousandth time that day, Hobbs thought, *How could this have happened?*

"Any other calls?"

Devereaux shook his head. "Some incomings from Diaz, and from another number we can't pin down. But Hamilton is nowhere to be found. And Diaz is also missing."

"Can you track the phone?"

"No. It's either destroyed or in a Faraday case. I don't know what the hell to make of this, I really don't."

They walked in silence for a moment. There had to be a way to manage this. There had to be.

"All right, look," Hobbs said. "I'm just a lawyer. You're the director of National Intelligence. You tell me it's Russia, okay, I'll go with Russia.

151

But we need something. Even if it's only to feed the media. Justice is facing a ton of questions, and I can't keep dodging reporters."

Hobbs heard a cellphone buzz. His, or Devereaux's? He reached into his coat pocket to check and saw Devereaux doing the same.

There was a text message. Hobbs didn't recognize the number, but there was a photo attached. For some reason, he felt suddenly queasy. Devereaux was looking intently at his own phone. He must have received a message, too.

He punched in his passcode and the message opened. It was a photo of an empty room. It looked familiar. He wasn't sure why.

Then he realized. It was the guest room in Schrader's Kiawah Island mansion. The one where Hobbs had . . . where he had . . .

His heart started pounding and a wave of dizziness washed over him. He fought to conceal the reaction. And then realized that Devereaux was paying him no attention at all. Because the man was so focused on a text message of his own.

He looked back to his phone. There was something printed below the photo. It said, The next transmission won't be an empty photo. It will be video! With people in it. And it won't be released just to you. Live and let live. With a little smiley face at the end.

No, he thought. *Lord, no.* It was perfectly horrible. And somehow, the smiley face made it worse.

Devereaux turned away. Hobbs thought he was trying to shield his expression. But then the man doubled over and vomited.

For whatever reason, it was comforting to know it wasn't just him. That his suspicions about Devereaux had been right. And that, for whatever it was worth, Devereaux at least wouldn't be able to judge him.

Devereaux stood and wiped his chin. His security detail had closed in, and Devereaux waved them away.

"I didn't know," he said. "I thought . . . they told me she was eighteen."

Hobbs knew it was the truth. Because they'd told him the same thing. Or had they? Had he just assumed? It didn't matter. He was afraid to answer.

"Don't be an asshole," Devereaux said. "I saw your face. You got one, too."

Hobbs was too rattled to deny it.

"Is the president really part of this?" Devereaux said. "And his predecessor?"

Hobbs felt a renewed wave of panic. "Of course he is."

"Stop lying to me, you grubby little prick."

Hobbs realized it didn't matter anymore. "I had to," he said. "You wouldn't have helped me."

"I'm helping you now."

"I didn't know before . . . that you had a personal stake in this, too."

"You made it all up. The president. Both parties. 'It isn't about the players, it's about the whole game.'"

"The president isn't involved. Or his predecessor. As far as I know. But the rest is true. You think you and I are the only ones implicated?"

They were quiet for a moment. Hobbs said, "What are we going to do?"

Devereaux spat. "I don't know."

They walked in silence again, past the protesters, past the skeletal trees. Hobbs heard a police siren in the distance, then a helicopter overhead. The chants of the protesters faded behind them. Somehow, the shadows were comforting. He wished he could just keep walking. In the dark. Where no one could see him.

"I'm thinking," Devereaux said. "Rispel might have a point. All of this . . . It does have the classic signs of a Russian active-measures campaign. Fake news, disseminated by our adversaries."

Hobbs felt a stirring of hope. He didn't give a damn that it was horseshit. It was the kind of thing the media would eat up and disseminate, and for the moment that was all that mattered. "And if something comes out about the . . . blackmail?"

"You mean *kompromat*. Another hallmark of Kremlin active measures."

The buzzwords would do the job, all right. Everyone knew the best disinformation campaigns in the world were American ones masquerading as Russian, and the con would never get old. But still.

"*Kompromat,*" Hobbs said. "Fine. Maybe we can mitigate. But how do we get back on offense?"

Devereaux nodded. "I . . . suggested a contractor to Rispel. Someone named Manus. I thought he would be deniable. And disposable. But I think . . . Rispel may have turned him."

Hobbs was horrified. How off course had this thing gotten? And how were they going to straighten it back out?

"What are you telling me?" he said. "Rispel is playing a separate game?"

"Maybe."

Hobbs said nothing. He thought it might be his turn to puke. He breathed deeply for a moment, the cold air calming him somewhat. After a moment, he said, "Then what the hell do we do?"

Devereaux paused, then nodded as though confirming an internal judgment call. He looked at Hobbs. "Manus has people he cares about. Maybe . . . maybe there's a way we can get him back onside."

chapter thirty-six

EVIE

E vie was grading tests in her office while she waited for Dash.
Cross-country practice wasn't over yet, but the light outside was
already fading. Autumn was always a sad time of year for her—the days
so short, and still getting shorter.

But whenever she was feeling blue, she reminded herself of all
there was to be thankful for. And there really was a lot. First was Dash,
of course. Her beautiful boy had become a handsome teenager, with
athletic gifts he had inherited from his father more than from her,
thank God. He was only in eighth grade but had made the high school
cross-country team. The coach wanted him for the 101 weight class on
the high school team when wrestling season started, too. And while
baseball was his favorite, and Evie knew there was a good chance he'd
make that team a year early, too, Dash was nervous. She didn't think
that was a bad thing. Of course, after the meningitis, the deafness, and
the divorce, she wanted everything to come easily for him. But she knew
it was better that he had to work for it, that he didn't take anything for
granted.

And while teaching high school math at Dash's school and computer science at Mount St. Mary's wasn't as cutting-edge as what she had
been doing at NSA, she was relieved to be clear of her former employer.

What had happened there, what Anders and his goon, Delgado, had tried to do to her, still gave her occasional nightmares.

The saving grace, of course, was Marvin.

She had never thought of herself as particularly bold in bed, but there was something he brought out in her that she loved to indulge. She didn't know what caused it. She was attracted to him, no doubt— had been since the first time she'd seen him—but the alchemy had more to do with the effect she had on him. There were times he would look at her, and there was something so primally . . . hungry in his eyes, so beyond his control, that it thrilled her, and filled her with a confidence she'd never known with anyone else.

And he was so good with Dash. So good *for* him. Watching him teach Dash how to use tools, how to help build their house, had sometimes moved her so much that she'd had to look away and wipe her eyes. And of course Marvin had taught her, too, and she'd helped out, as well. Which was fun and gratifying. But it was nothing compared to watching the two of them together, experiencing the bond they had. And not just for how much it did for Dash. For what it meant to Marvin, too. She knew the horrible things he had done in the past. She was glad he was different now, glad he was done with that part of himself. With everything about that life. These days, he sometimes felt to her like a giant bear who harbored no ill will toward anyone, and wanted no more than to be left alone.

But God help anyone who might try to hurt his cub. And she had no problem with that. No problem at all.

Her phone beeped. She glanced at it, expecting a text from Dash. Instead, it was an alert from the camera network she had installed around the house.

She was surprised. She'd tested the system, of course, but its AI had been trained to ignore her face, Dash's, and Marvin's, and it had never picked up anything else.

She tapped in her passcode. In the dying light, she saw a man in a UPS uniform standing at the gate to the driveway, holding a package, looking at the house. He checked a tablet as though confirming an address. Behind him was the familiar brown truck. It all looked completely normal. Except that the house was owned by a corporate front a lawyer had helped them set up, and she used the school to receive all their mail and packages. You didn't have to be former NSA to understand that the first rule of privacy was to ruthlessly separate your residence from your mailing address.

The man looked around. Anyone who might have been watching would think he was just trying to figure out how to get to the house to drop off the package. But it was doubtful anyone was watching. The property was on five acres at the end of a cul-de-sac. There were only two other driveways, each of which led to houses set back as far as theirs. The rest of the area was surrounded by woods.

Alongside their driveway was a sign declaring **LIBERTY TOWNSHIP CRIME WATCH IN EFFECT**. The UPS guy put out a hand and leaned against it, as though trying to see through the trees to the house. Then he shrugged, went back to his truck, and drove away.

Evie realized her heart was beating hard. Something was wrong. She could feel it.

She panned the camera and zoomed in on the back of the sign. There was something attached to it. She zoomed more and saw it was a small camera, probably with a magnetic mount.

It all came flooding back. Delgado, the syringe, the back of the van. His hands on her. His smell. The things he said as he—

He's dead, she thought, the words mantra-familiar. *You shot him. Marvin split his head with that hatchet. He's dead.*

She closed her eyes and for a moment just breathed. *Okay.*

She reversed the footage. There—the truck license plate. If she'd still been at NSA, she could have run it down in thirty seconds. And tracked the truck's movements, as well. She suddenly felt helpless.

She thought of Marvin. He'd been gone for days, working on a construction site near Pittsburgh. He didn't travel often, but there were crews who would bring him in for jobs involving built-in shelving, which was one of his specialties. Some had in return lent a hand when Marvin had built the house. She knew he wasn't mixed up with the government anymore. She'd never even worried about it.

Although this time . . . he'd seemed not himself when he left. Stressed, somehow. Distracted. Still, they'd FaceTimed every night since then, and he'd seemed fine. Was he, though? Maybe she'd been trying to convince herself.

She tried to tell herself it was nothing. Just a coincidence. Marvin was fine, the camera on the sign was just a way for UPS to know when someone was home, so they could come back later and deliver a package that had been sent to the wrong address . . .

Her heart started pounding again, and she closed her eyes and breathed deeply for a minute, trying to calm down. It had been years. She'd really believed it was done.

A text message popped up. Dash. **Practice is over. Should I come up? Or meet at the car?**

The parking lot was well lit and there would be lots of people there. Parents waiting for their kids. Kids finishing soccer practice, cross-country practice, other after-school activities. But she was suddenly frightened.

Meet me up here? she texted back.

Sure. Be there in five.

She texted back a thumbs-up emoji. Though she felt anything but.

What were they going to do? She was afraid to go home. She hated to admit it. But she was afraid.

She FaceTimed Marvin. He didn't pick up.

Shit.

She suddenly wished they had Find My Friends or some other cellphone tracking app enabled. But she knew too much about how exploitable those features were.

She texted him. Hey. I'm worried about something and I'm afraid to go home. Can you text or FT me right away?

She tried to tell herself again that everything was fine, that she was being paranoid.

But she couldn't convince herself. Couldn't even come close.

chapter thirty-seven

MAYA

Traffic on the GW Parkway was moving at a crawl, and Maya realized she should have taken Chain Bridge to Canal Road. Her fault for not checking Waze first—an embarrassing lapse for a CIA Science & Technology specialist. Usually she left a lot later, when the Parkway was the fastest route. But at rush hour, apparently it was the slowest.

Maybe Key Bridge. You can still make it. And if you're late, it's okay. He'll wait. Maybe it's even better. You'll seem . . . nonchalant.

She didn't feel nonchalant, though. This guy was really hot. They'd been flirting for weeks on Tinder, and tonight he was flying in from touring in Chicago, and they were going to meet at Lapis, an Afghan restaurant not far from her apartment. At 6:00. Less than thirty minutes.

She checked Waze. Okay, Key Bridge was better. But only by two minutes.

She wanted to shower and even put on a little makeup. Twenty minutes, minimum. Seven-minute walk to the restaurant. And she was still fifteen minutes from home.

Twelve minutes late. That's not bad.

But she had to walk Frodo. The service took him to the park at lunch, but there was no way he would make it until she was back from dinner. Even if dinner was over early—which she was definitely hoping would not be the case.

Maybe Ali. They had been in the same class at CIA, they both lived in Adams Morgan, and they were both *Lord of the Rings* fans. Ali even had a terrier mix like Maya's that she'd named Pippin, and they covered for each other on dog care. Pippin had been visiting with Ali's parents for the last few weeks, so lately Ali had been there more for Frodo than Maya was for Pippin. But Ali missed Pippin, and never seemed to mind walking Frodo anyway. Plus she would understand the reason . . . if she was home . . .

She called. A ring, and . . . success. "Hello?"

"Ali? Hey, I have to ask a favor . . . are you home?"

"Not quite. I'm on Mass Avenue."

"Yeah, I should have gone that way myself. Listen, I'm running late, and I have a date . . . that guy I told you about."

"The jazz dude? Dave something?"

"The trumpeter. Yes. He's back in town and I'm meeting him for dinner at Lapis—"

"Score!"

"Hah, well, we'll see. But—"

"You want me to walk Frodo?"

"If you could. You have your key, right?"

"Of course. Want me to feed him?"

"No, he can wait until I'm home."

Ali giggled. "What if you're home late?"

"You're bad."

"Trumpeters. I hear they can do magic things with their mouths."

Maya laughed. "You're extremely bad. Okay, if you could feed him, too. I'll totally pay you back."

"You can pay me back by having a great night."

"Deal."

"And then telling me all about it."

161

Maya laughed again. "Hey, first there has to be something to tell."

"I have a good feeling."

"Anyway, I should be home in . . . thirteen minutes. And out the door twenty after that."

"I'll come by after you're gone. Don't want to interfere with the preparations."

"There are no preparations! Okay, maybe just a few. But thank you so much. You're a lifesaver."

"Can't wait to hear about it . . ."

"We'll see. Bye!"

Exactly thirty-three minutes later, Maya rushed out the back of her apartment building. Ali was coming the same way.

"Don't hold the door!" Ali said. "Just go, we're good."

"Thank you again! Don't forget, he—"

"Likes a little chicken with the regular food. I know, you spoil him. Go!"

Maya cut through the parking area behind the building and zig-zagged west. She wondered if she should call Dave. What time was it? She reached for her phone and realized she had left it in her other jacket—the navy peacoat. At the last minute, she had decided the leather looked cooler.

Shit. She almost went back. But she was so late already. But what if he was trying to reach her, and couldn't? Or what if Ali needed to reach her?

Well, worst case, she could always borrow his cellphone. And she was so close already.

But when she got there, she didn't see him. The hostess confirmed that yes, they did have a reservation for two under David Teller, and offered to seat her.

She waited a half hour. Had he come and gone already? But no, the hostess would have told her that. Besides, she was late, but not that late. She would have waited for him at least that long. In fact, she just had, and then some.

Maybe he'd been trying to call her, or to text. She could have borrowed a phone and tried him, but she didn't remember the number. And anyway, wouldn't that look desperate?

Well, it was less than a ten-minute walk. She could just go back, check her phone, and decide at that point. She wished she hadn't called Ali. She could have walked Frodo herself. They could have taken a long one.

She came in through the back of the building and let herself into her apartment. Ordinarily, Frodo, hearing the key in the lock, would be waiting at the door. But not this time. The lights were on, but the apartment was silent.

"Frodo? Where are you, boy?"

No response. She felt a little uneasy. Could Ali still have been walking him? Not impossible, but . . .

The peacoat was hanging by the front door. She reached into the pocket and pulled out her phone. A text from Dave—sent just a minute after she'd run out, naturally. His plane had been delayed, but they had landed and he was on the way. He could still meet her if she wanted, or another time. She smiled, and realized she'd really been worried that he'd blown her off. But . . .

"Frodo?" she said again. He always greeted her. Ali was still out with him. That must have been it.

She saw lights flashing against the venetian blinds. She went to the window and peeked through.

There were police cars all over the street. An ambulance. People standing around at the periphery. And at the center . . . Oh, God, was that someone lying on the sidewalk?

She bolted out the door, down the stairs, and through the front entrance. Yes, someone was on the sidewalk. But there was yellow tape strung up and people in the way and she couldn't get close enough to see.

She heard whimpering. Frodo. She turned and saw a uniformed cop, a woman, holding him.

"Frodo," she said, running over. "Frodo, I'm here, boy."

"Yours?" the cop said.

"Yes. Yes. Come here, boy. Oh, my God."

The cop handed him over. Frodo whimpered and licked her cheek. She turned and looked at the person on the ground again. But there were still too many people, and shadows from the lights flashing from the patrol cars. She tried to tell herself she was wrong, it was someone else, but the clothes, and who else could have been with Frodo . . .

"Do you know her?" the cop asked.

Maya was suddenly aware she was crying. "Yes. I mean, I'm not sure. Oh, my God, what happened?"

"Detective," the cop called out, holding up a hand. "Over here." One of the people kneeling near the person on the sidewalk stood. He clicked off a flashlight and started over. As he ducked under the yellow tape, Maya saw a tough-looking guy with a dark goatee and a badge hanging from a lanyard. "Someone who knows the deceased," the cop added.

"Deceased?" Maya said. "What, no, that isn't possible . . ." She looked again. She had to fight the urge to shout at Ali to get up, this joke wasn't funny . . .

"I'm Detective Pacquiao," the goateed guy said. "Do you know Ms. Watkins?"

"Oh no," Maya said, shaking her head. Frodo was licking her tears, but she barely felt it. "No, no."

"I'm sorry. Believe me, I know how shocking this can be. Do you know her?"

"Yes. But . . . I don't understand."

"She was shot. She was with the dog . . . Yours?"

"Yes. She was walking him for me. I had a date. Who didn't even show up. But . . . why? Why would anyone shoot Ali?"

"At the moment, we think a mugging. I'm so sorry. Take a minute, and we'll have a few questions for you, okay?"

Maya tried to answer, but she was crying too hard. She thought, *I shouldn't have asked you. You'd be fine now, none of this would have happened, it's my fault.*

She realized with relief tinged by shame that if she hadn't asked, probably she herself would be the one on the sidewalk.

I don't care if it would have been me. It should *have been me.*

And then a crystal-clear shard of a thought cut through her confusion and grief:

It was supposed *to be me.*

She didn't know where the thought came from. She couldn't have articulated the basis.

All she knew was that she had to call Tom.

chapter thirty-eight

RAIN

It was past midnight and they were back in Delilah's apartment. Rain was at the laptop. He'd read the secure-site update from Larison. And he'd seen more fallout on the news: Schrader, mysteriously released from prison; three men killed in the Seattle Four Seasons; QAnon protests sprouting in major cities all over the States. He needed to go. But there were no flights until morning.

It was strange to imagine them all doing something without him. He'd wound up as the group's de facto leader twice before. It wasn't a role he had asked for, or one for which he considered himself well suited. But at the same time, the thought of them operating alone was . . . worrisome. Was he just flattering himself? Or looking for an excuse to get back in the game?

"Just so you know," Larison had said, "Dox thought about bringing you in at the outset. But it sounds like you've persuaded him you're serious about being retired. So you can blame this on me. I'm not as solicitous. Plus I don't really believe you. Look at me, I live in paradise with someone I love. This is the kind of thing I do for a vacation. I don't think you're so different."

Rain had thought about protesting, but then didn't. What would it have accomplished? Beyond which, he was afraid Larison could be right. And that protesting would prove it.

He looked over at Delilah. She was sitting on the couch on the other side of the room, pretending to read. It was strange to have to coordinate on something like this. There had been a time in his life when there was no need to compromise, when he had lived alone, aloof, apart. But when he looked back on that time now, he realized all of it was itself a giant compromise, one that, while protecting his body, had been steadily suffocating his soul.

He started to say something, then stopped. She'd stymied all his earlier efforts to discuss it with an impenetrable wall of *It's fine*. He didn't blame her. She was done with Mossad. Done with the life. So as fond as she was of Dox, she resented the big sniper for refusing to get out as she had. And even more, she resented Livia, who in her mind had once before pulled Dox, and therefore all of them, into her war against child abusers.

But as he sat silently in front of the laptop considering his options, apparently she couldn't abide the silence any longer. She closed her book and walked over. "All right, tell me. Is this coming from Livia?"

Well, at least they were talking. Though the silence suddenly felt safer.

"No."

"She's leading Dox by the nose again, isn't she? So all of us will be dragged in as a result."

He closed the laptop. "It's not that simple. Livia didn't ask for Dox's help. She didn't even know about whatever this is until after the fact. It's coming from Kanezaki." Earlier, he'd tried to brief her on what Larison had told him. This time, she let him.

"It's a distinction without a difference," she said when he was done. "That Dox, always having to protect the damsel in distress."

"I wouldn't call Livia a damsel."

"Tell that to your friend. He's the one who needs to hear it."

"He's your friend, too."

"He doesn't come to me. He comes to you."

Rain tried to control his exasperation. "He didn't come to me. He tried to keep me out of it."

"Another distinction without a difference. He brought in Larison. Larison called you."

"He called you. You're the one who insists on carrying a phone."

The moment it came out, he regretted it. When Delilah was pissed, there was no winning move. Your only option was to try to find a way not to play.

"Don't you see how impossible this is?" she said. "It doesn't matter who it starts with. In the end it's the Three Musketeers, or four, or however many. One for all and all for one. How many rounds of this game are we going to play before someone gets killed or winds up in prison? I don't want to save the world anymore. I want to be normal. I want some peace. Don't you?"

"Yes."

"No, I mean it. Do you really?"

"Yes."

But it was obviously a rhetorical question, because she continued. "There's a part of you that doesn't want to let it go. The danger, the edge, whatever it is you're afraid to lose. Everyone recognizes it but you."

"Who's everyone?" he said, the realization that she'd succeeded in drawing him in coming an instant too late to stop the words.

"Dox, for one. He once told me a stupid joke he says is a parable about you. A hunter in the woods—"

"Yes, and the bear. He's shared it with me. Along with a bunch of others."

"And you don't think there's anything to it? You don't see that the hunter is you?"

"I try not to think of myself that way. Look, you know if you were in trouble, Dox would help you."

"I don't get myself in trouble the way he does."

"He wouldn't care."

"I wouldn't ask."

"You wouldn't have to. And you wouldn't be able to stop him."

On cue, her phone buzzed from where she'd left it on the couch. She stalked over, snatched it up, and brought it to her ear.

"Allo." She turned and looked murderously at Rain. "Hello, Tom, what a nice surprise." A pause. "No, I wouldn't want you to have to go through the secure site, it's more efficient to use his secretary." She walked over and handed Rain the phone.

"Everything okay?" Rain said, watching Delilah.

"They're all fine," Kanezaki said. "And, uh, sorry if I've caused a problem over there."

"It's okay."

"I know Larison already called. Already asked you to come to the States. That was smart. I should have thought to do it myself."

"Tom," he said, watching Delilah, "I'm retired. At some point you have to believe me when I say that."

Delilah watched him, shaking her head. If he thought she'd appreciate his response more than whatever had precipitated it, it was a clear case of the triumph of hope over experience.

"I need your help," Kanezaki said. "Anything you want in return, you can have. I won't haggle. I put someone in danger. I need you to protect her."

"I already told Larison—"

"This is about the same thing." He briefed Rain on a young CIA Science & Technology officer named Maya, and how she had helped uncover the plot Dox and the rest of them were now embroiled in, and how earlier that evening someone had tried to kill her, and mistakenly killed another young officer instead.

Even beyond the fact of the dead girl, it sounded bad. They weren't containing this thing. It was metastasizing.

"You're sure it was an attempt on Maya?" Rain said.

"The murdered girl was her friend. Walking Maya's dog as a favor in front of Maya's apartment while Maya was out for a date. They look enough alike. And Maya forgot her phone. Think about it. A hurry-up operation. You're going on nothing more than a photo and a description. It's dark. You key on the girl, on the dog, on the place, the cellphone tracker confirms location—"

"But why?"

"Maya's a hacker," Kanezaki said. "She figured out a way to see what requests were being illegally deleted from Guardian Angel. She figured out Rispel was trying to protect Schrader by having Diaz killed. But she must have left footprints, footprints one of Rispel's people traced back to her."

"So this is about Maya knowing too much?"

"Exactly."

"What about you?"

"Don't worry about me."

"I do, actually, though I try not to. If Rispel made a run at Maya, why wouldn't she make one at you?"

"I'm a little more security-conscious than Maya. Or than I was when you first met me."

They'd originally crossed paths in Tokyo, when Kanezaki had been a green CIA case officer and almost fatally naive. But he'd learned fast. From Rain, from Dox, and most of all, Rain knew, from Tatsu, who before his death from cancer had looked on Kanezaki as a son. They'd been through a lot together, and occasionally Rain was surprised to find himself feeling proud of who Kanezaki had become. Proud of whatever he himself had contributed to it. And he knew Tatsu would have been even prouder.

"What about your family?"

"I'm not worried about them. This isn't about revenge. It's about a cover-up. But yeah, Rispel is moving fast and she's making mistakes.

Anyone who's near me is at risk. I'm not going home until this is resolved."

"Is Maya with you?"

"No. She's with Yuki."

Yuki was Kanezaki's sister. Rain had met her years before, when Kanezaki needed an outsider to get Rain and Dox out of a jam. A soccer mom with something of a mysterious past, she was impressively cool and capable.

"She can't stay with Yuki," Rain said. A statement, not a question.

"No. For the reasons I just said."

Rain didn't resent the implicit calculus. There were pieces on the board Kanezaki would risk, and ones he wouldn't.

But then Kanezaki surprised him, adding, "I'm sorry. It's not just Yuki. It's my nieces, too. I can't."

Rain remembered two adorable girls. "How old are they now? Ten? Twelve?"

"Hah. Fourteen and sixteen."

Rain shook his head. It was hard to believe it was that long ago.

He sighed. "What do you want me to do?"

"Whatever it takes to keep Maya safe."

"Look, I don't know what that would entail, but I can't even get there until—"

"I have a Gulfstream waiting for you right now. Check the secure site."

"Wait a second."

He muted the phone and looked at Delilah. "Remember you once told me that my attachment to the finer things—good jazz, good coffee, good whisky—was a substitute? A salve for my lack of attachment to people?"

She didn't respond, which made him think this might be the right approach.

"You said, 'If you live only for yourself, dying is an especially scary proposition.' You know, at the time, I resisted the notion. I did. Dismissed it as sentiment. But now I see you were right."

Still she didn't respond. Okay, maybe he was using the wrong approach.

"If I were in trouble," he said, "and I needed you, you'd be there, wouldn't you?"

She glared at him. "You ask as though this is some kind of hypothetical."

Okay, the other approach was better.

"No, you're right. It's not. You have been. I know. And you know it's the same in the other direction. But . . . I can't say no to this. I don't have many people. I never thought I was going to have any, didn't think I needed any, but somehow I wound up with these few. And I want my time with you, and my peace with you, and everything we have together. Our life together. But if something happens to one of these people, and I could have prevented it and didn't, I'm not going to have any peace."

"And if you try to help, and something happens to you, what peace will I have?"

He looked at her. He loved her. He really did. It was so improbable. So precious.

And so fragile.

"I don't know what to do," he said.

She shook her head. Started to say something. Shook her head again.

Finally, she sighed. "Tell him you're coming."

He looked at her, not knowing how to respond.

"And that I'm coming with you, you idiot."

He felt a surge of love, and gratitude, and relief. "Delilah—"

"And tell him that if he gets you killed? I'm going to kill him."

chapter
thirty-nine

LIVIA

Livia hoped no one was trying to reach her. After what had happened at the Four Seasons, her unavailability wouldn't look good. But if she checked in, there might be questions she wasn't ready to answer. She decided to hold off.

Carl had used fake credentials to get a room at the Motel 6 in Issaquah, about twenty minutes east of Seattle. Livia had recommended the place because it was outside the city and the rooms had exterior doors, which would allow the six of them to file in without having to go past a front desk. They'd driven separately—Manus and Larison in the van; the rest in Livia's Jeep. Hamilton was badly freaked out, and being with Diaz, an adversary but at least a familiar face, seemed to be reassuring her somewhat. The two of them were sitting next to each other now on one of the double beds, across from Livia and Carl. Manus had pulled over a chair and sat perpendicular so he could read lips. And Larison was keeping watch through the curtains.

"I don't understand," Hamilton said, even though Livia had already explained. "I didn't do anything. I don't know anything."

"Yes, you do," Diaz said. "You know about the videos. We know you met with the AG."

Hamilton looked at her, plainly surprised. "How—" she said, then stopped herself.

"Your client told me," Diaz said. "Now you need to stop thinking about confidentiality and attorney-client privilege and all that bullshit. Right now. And start thinking like someone who wants to stay alive. Do you understand?"

"Are you threatening me?" Hamilton said.

Diaz threw up her hands. "Are you really this stupid? I'm not your adversary. We're past that. We need to help each other."

After a moment, Hamilton said, "All right. I met with Hobbs. Andrew . . . He told me Hobbs would be receptive."

"Why?" Livia said. She hadn't minded Diaz softening Hamilton up, but she wanted to manage the Q&A herself.

"Presumably . . . ," Hamilton started to say, then stopped. She glanced around at each of them. "I'm sorry, I don't know who you people are. I mean, this is completely insane. What are we, in some kind of Motel 6 safe house? Look, even if we're not adversaries, okay, but why should I tell you anything?"

"It's up to you," Larison said from his spot by the window. "In fact, you can leave right now. But the next time you're enjoying a dandelion salad or whatever in your favorite restaurant, and a pair of gunmen ghost up from behind to punch your ticket, we won't be there to bail you out. You like your odds without us? Take them. Personally, I don't give a shit."

Livia glanced at Larison. It wasn't the first time the men in this group hadn't followed her lead in eliciting information.

Larison shrugged. "Just my two cents."

Manus glanced back at Larison, then at Livia. She realized he hadn't been able to follow the exchange, and summarized for him. Then she looked at Hamilton. "Why would Schrader believe Hobbs would be receptive to a message about those videos?"

There was a pause. Hamilton said, "Presumably because Hobbs brokered the South Carolina non-prosecution agreement six years ago."

Livia glanced at Diaz. "Did you know about this?"

"No," Diaz said, staring at Hamilton. "There's an NPA from the district in South Carolina? From when Hobbs was US Attorney there?"

Hamilton nodded. "They didn't clear it with main Justice."

"Why not?" Livia said.

"Because," Diaz said, still staring at Hamilton, "main Justice might not have cleared it."

Hamilton nodded again. "That was our thinking at the time."

Livia felt a vortex of rage spiraling up inside her. She tried to tamp it down, and couldn't. "They had him six years ago, and you got him released? With videos? Of other men raping teenaged girls?"

"I'm not the judge," Hamilton said. "There's a system, okay? How I feel personally can't enter into it. Every person accused of a crime is entitled by the Sixth Amendment to the assistance of—"

"To the assistance of a lawyer," Livia said. "Not to blackmail videos that are themselves evidence of other crimes being committed by other powerful men. How many girls have been raped, all over the country, because of you?"

"That's a fair question," Carl said. "Very fair. But could I respectfully suggest that for the moment we might do better to focus on solving the immediate problem at hand, which is stopping the people who seem intent on killing all of us?"

Livia knew he was right. But she wasn't done with Hamilton. Or Schrader. No matter how this thing turned out.

"I don't know if I should say anything more," Hamilton said. "If you're accusing me of a crime, or . . . Look, Detective Lone, you're a cop. And Alondra, you're part of the Justice Department. I don't know how you're mixed up with these people. I don't think I want to know."

"Don't worry about that," Larison said from by the window. "I trust you. I know you would never compromise anyone in this room. Ever." He smiled at her. "Isn't that right?"

Hamilton nodded quickly. "Yes."

"Great," Larison said. "Now how about if you go on telling Livia everything you know, just so no one starts to think maybe you're playing for the wrong team."

Everyone was silent for a minute. Larison looked at Livia. "Sorry."

She didn't like it. On the other hand, that bone-chilling smile had its uses. She summarized again for Manus.

"If I may," Carl said to Livia.

She looked at him and nodded, not minding the interjection. She trusted his instincts. And unlike the case with some of the others, also trusted his ability to mesh his own efforts with hers rather than just going his own way.

He leaned forward, toward Hamilton. "You said Schrader told you Hobbs would be receptive now because he was receptive when he was the US Attorney in South Carolina."

Hamilton nodded.

"All right," Carl went on. "But why was Hobbs receptive back then?"

No one said anything.

Carl leaned back. "I mean, I suppose it could be anything. But it wouldn't surprise me if Mr. Guardian of American Justice and Values makes a personal appearance in those videos. You sure your client didn't say anything about that?"

"No," Hamilton said. "He didn't."

"Did he give you any specifics at all?"

"No."

"Well, what did he tell you?"

Hamilton looked at Livia. "He told me he had designed the system so that if anything happened to him, the videos would be uploaded."

Diaz nodded. "He told me the same."

"There's more," Hamilton said. "The system . . . He has to operate it himself. It's not like a normal account, where you can log in from anywhere if you know the URL, the username, and a password."

"What do you mean?" Livia said. "Operate it himself how?"

"He has keypads in his houses. Look, I'm not technical, I don't know the details."

"Okay," Livia said, suppressing her excitement. "But what did you tell Hobbs about the system?"

"Why does that even matter?"

"Because," Carl said, "there's a substantial likelihood that right now, your client is being tortured for information about this system you say he set up. And it would be handy for us to have some idea of what he might be telling his torturers, and what they might then do about it."

"The initial plan was to kill me," Diaz said. "In Freeway Park this morning. Without me to spearhead the indictment, the whole thing would have fallen apart. Schrader would have walked."

"But when that didn't work," Livia said, "they shifted to some kind of alternative plan involving Schrader himself. Given that Schrader was the secondary plan and not the primary, we've been operating on the assumption that Schrader told someone about the dead-man switch. It sounds like that person was Hobbs, through you."

Hamilton nodded. "Yes."

"Okay," Livia said. "But now it sounds like they can't stop the system without going to one of Schrader's houses. Is that right?"

"Yes," Hamilton said. "But it's more than that. Andrew said he has to personally reset it."

"Biometrics," Carl said. "That would be my guess. Although I hope for Schrader's sake he didn't rely on just a fingerprint reader. Otherwise, they're not going to escort him to one of his nice houses. Just his hands in a bucket of ice."

Hamilton lost some color. "No, it's more than just fingerprints. Andrew said there's something about a voice-stress analyzer, too. To make sure he's not being coerced."

"Whoever has your client," Larison said, "you better hope they're invested in keeping those videos suppressed. Because if what they want is for the videos to be released, all they have to do now is snuff him and let his system do its automated thing."

Livia had been thinking along the same lines. "It's possible," she said. "But they didn't need to break him out of jail for that."

She summarized for Manus. He said, "I think Larison is onto something."

Everyone looked at Manus. He'd been quiet for so long.

"Rispel wanted me to kill you," he said to Diaz. "And wanted Dox and Larison to kill me after. So that Schrader could go free, the way he did six years ago. When that didn't work, they broke him out of jail. But being let out, and being broken out, aren't the same thing. The second one doesn't take the pressure off him. He can't enjoy his houses, his lifestyle, his rape parties. It's not what he wants. It's not what Hamilton was playing for when as his lawyer she tried to make a deal with the attorney general."

Everyone was quiet for a moment, digesting that.

"In other words," Manus went on, "the first plan was to give him what he wanted. The second is to get someone else . . . what they wanted."

Livia nodded, thinking Manus might have made a good cop. "We know it was Rispel who hired you," she said. "You think someone else broke Schrader out of prison?"

"It's a different plan," Manus said. "With a different objective. That could mean a different party. Or it could mean Rispel changed her mind. She was playing for one thing, and then decided to play for something else."

It was a sound framework. What they needed were more inputs.

"Okay," Livia said. "If the current plan is to cause an automatic upload, Schrader is probably dead already. If the plan is different . . . getting control of the videos for blackmail, something like that . . . they're going to have to take Schrader to one of his houses. Ms. Hamilton, do you know where those houses are?"

"You can call me Sharon."

"I'll call you Ms. Hamilton."

Hamilton looked taken aback. It would never stop amazing Livia. The collaborators. The enablers. The familiars. They never felt culpable.

After a moment, Hamilton said, "Yes. My firm sets up the entities through which the real estate is purchased and held."

"How many houses are we talking about?"

"Six. The Bainbridge Island compound here in Washington State, which is the primary residence. The others are in Los Angeles, New Mexico, Aspen, Wyoming, and New York."

Livia looked at Carl. "We don't have the resources. Not even with . . ." She had almost said Rain, but even after Larison's admonition to Hamilton, thought first names would be safer. "Not even with John. The houses are a good lead, but we need more information."

Carl took out a cellphone and popped in a battery. "Can you fire up that satellite hotspot?" he said to Larison. "Virgin burner, no SIM card, Wi-Fi connection. Unless there's an AWACS plane overhead, no one can geolocate, so nothing to worry about, we're good to go."

A few configurations later, Dox had the phone to his ear. "Tom," he said. "Glad I'm able to reach you. We got some more intel, and we're hoping you can make it a little more actionable."

He briefed Kanezaki. When he was done, he said, "You all right? You sound a little . . . not yourself."

Livia watched as he listened for a moment. His lips were pursed, and Livia tried not to worry. "Damn, I'm sorry to hear that. But I'm glad John's going to be able to help out." A pause. "No, I think following the recent unpleasantness, and given the obvious resources of who we seem to be up against, no one's going to be leaving a phone on. But I'll check the secure site every chance I get. All right. Let me know what you find. And give my best to John and Delilah. Oh, and tell her I tried to keep John out of this. I love her, but I think she's apt to be peeved."

He clicked off and powered down the phone. "There's a young officer who works for Tom," he said. "Someone tried to kill her this evening
in DC. But they made a mistake and killed the wrong girl. Now Tom's
afraid to go home to see his own family. Thinks Rispel is behind the hit,
and is going to make a run at him, too. John and Delilah are coming,
and Tom's going to hand off his officer to them to make sure she's safe."

Manus looked grim. Carl said, "You thinking about your people?"

Manus nodded.

"For what it's worth," Carl said, "Tom's not worried about anyone
deliberately trying to hurt his family. Mostly he's worried about another
mistake. He wants to be far away from the people he cares about in case
someone takes a shot at him and misses. Plus right now he's not hugely
inclined to show up at places where he might be expected."

Livia didn't know Manus, but she didn't think he was going to
buy that. She turned to Carl. "Can Manus use your satellite hotspot to
check in with them?"

"Any of us can," Carl said. He looked at Manus. "Would that help?"

Manus nodded.

"Okay," Carl said. "Just make sure your phone's cell reception is off.
Connect it through the satellite hotspot like I just did."

Livia knew these guys all understood cellphone security—even
better than she did. Even so, the use of phones made her nervous. She
said, "Let's clear out right after, all right? I think we've been here long
enough."

"Agreed," Carl said. "I'll tell you, I don't like the order of battle right
now. We need to shake up the board, and good. Because when order is
your enemy, chaos is your friend."

chapter forty

SLOAT

Sloat sensed that the latest round had gone on long enough. "Okay," he said. "Unwrap him."

Tyson set down the watering can. Two gallons, lime-green plastic, $4.97 at Walmart. He began undoing the towel. Taupe, also purchased from Walmart, $3.97 with "upgraded softness," a feature doubtless lost on Schrader. Not that Sloat blamed him.

The instant the towel was off, Schrader puked up a bolus of water. He managed to turn his head, but because he was tilted backward over the bathtub, a lot of it had nowhere to go but over his face. He drew in a huge, convulsing breath, then puked again. Tyson glanced at Sloat, his expression concerned.

"He's fine," Sloat said. Tyson was new to waterboarding, but for Sloat it had gotten routine. He'd long ago lost count of how many detainees he'd done. Twenty? At least that many. Maybe thirty. The reactions tended to be similar. Crying, vomiting, pants-pissing. As long as you knew when to unwrap the towel, there wasn't a lot to it.

The materials were pretty simple, too. The watering can and towel, of course. Restraints, for which Sloat favored hook-and-loop cable ties. An adult diaper was a good idea, because no one could be subjected to more than a few sessions without losing bladder control, and sometimes more. The only big-ticket item, if you could call it that, was a plywood board. Which Sloat liked to deploy with the low end over a bathtub and the high end propped on a dresser or chair. He'd used all the purpose-built stuff at the black sites, but it was no better. The do-it-yourself worked just as well.

"Please," Schrader sobbed, his chest heaving. "Please. No more."

Sloat stepped in closer, so Schrader could see his face. "We don't want to do more, guy. This is no fun for us. Just tell us how to shut down those videos and we're done. You get a nice warm bed—dry bed—and no more of this shit. Okay?"

"I told you," Schrader said, crying. "I can't shut it down! I can only reset it. Oh, God, I wish I could shut it down, I wish I could, I wish I could, please, no more, please don't do it anymore, please . . ."

"Shhh," Sloat said, patting him on the shoulder. "Shhh. Tell you what, we'll take a little break." He looked at Tyson. "Stay with him. I'll be back in a few."

He went out to the garage and called Rispel from an encrypted burner. She answered instantly. "Did you get it?"

"No," he said. "Not only did we not get it, I don't think he has it."

"What do you mean?"

"What I told you before. He says he set up the system with this kind of scenario in mind. If he doesn't reset it within a specified time frame, the system uploads whatever it's programmed to upload."

"Then get his passcode and reset it yourself. It'll buy us time, at least."

"He already gave us the passcode. Twelve-digit number, nothing complicated. But he claims he can only reset it from encrypted keypads installed in his various houses. And—"

"He has a house that can't be more than a thirty-minute chopper ride from where you're standing."

"Look, first, I don't want to go someplace where US marshals are likely to be looking for him, okay?"

A pause. She said, "What about the other houses?"

"And second, he says the keypad requires biometric credentials. Fingerprint, retina scan—"

"Then take him personally and press his finger and his eyeball wherever they need to go."

"And a voice-stress analyzer. You get it? We could take him to one of his houses and press his finger and stick his eyeball and whatever else, and put a gun to his head and make him say the magic words, and the voice-stress analyzer is going to say, *Fuck off*. This guy anticipated duress. And prepared for it."

There was a pause while she absorbed that. "I'm not buying it," she said. "Why didn't his lawyer warn anyone of this?"

Sloat considered that. "You said they let him go six years ago, right?"

"Yes."

"My guess? They were expecting the same thing would happen this time. Or at least hoping."

She didn't respond, which he knew from experience meant she didn't disagree.

"But then at some point," he went on, "maybe he sees what happened to that guy Epstein. And decides he needs to be more careful. Some kind of dead-man setup, just in case. Maybe he goes even further, and architects it not just to protect against someone suiciding him, but to ensure everyone's motivated to get him out of jail ASAP. And to ensure he can't be under duress. Give the guy credit, it's clever."

"Maybe too clever. You don't think he's making it up?"

Sloat considered. "While we were boarding him? No."

"You and I both know people will say anything to make it stop."

"That's my point. What he's telling us isn't making it stop. It's making it continue. We've done him six times now. He's crying, he shit himself . . . If he could give a dark web URL where we could log in and use the passcode without him, something like that—I think he would have told us by now."

Again, she didn't respond. He waited, then said, "So what do you want to do?"

"I need to think about it. Ultimately, we're probably looking at taking him to one of his houses and verifying his story that way. But first, I want you to up the treatment."

He'd sensed that might be coming. "I don't really think that's—"

"Don't go wobbly on me, okay? We need to be sure. Do his fingers. No wait, make it his toes. In case the biometric story is true."

Shit. He wondered if she'd specified the toes to prevent Sloat from later lying about having done it. Waterboarding left no physical evidence. Fingers and toes . . . not so much.

But orders were orders, and as his sergeant used to say back in the day, *You don't have to like it. You just have to do it.*

"I'll let you know what we get out of him," he said. He clicked off and headed back in.

chapter forty-one

MANUS

M anus was trying not to show it, but he was frightened and angry. Frightened for Evie and Dash. Angry at himself for downplaying the possibility that they could be in danger.

And he was confused, too. He'd lied to Evie about where he was. But now maybe the lie had put them in danger. Maybe *he* had put them in danger. If anything happened to them, it would be his fault.

You've been over this. They're fine. There's no reason anyone would want to hurt them.

He connected the phone's Wi-Fi to the satellite hotspot. Immediately, a text from Evie popped up:

Hey. I'm worried about something and I'm afraid to go home.
Can you text or FT me right away?

His heart started slamming. What happened? Why would she be afraid to go home?

He checked the text. It had been sent a half hour earlier. Enough time for anything to have happened. *No,* he thought. *No, no, no . . .*

He blew out a long breath. *They're all right,* he told himself. *The school is safe. And* afraid *to go home means she hasn't. She's being careful.*

He glanced around and realized he had no good place to prop up the phone. He looked at Dox. "Can you hold it for me? I need my hands free."

Dox nodded. "You bet."

Manus FaceTimed Evie and handed the phone to Dox. She answered instantly. He waited while she adjusted the angle of her phone.

Hi, she signed. *Did you get my text?*

Just now. Are you and Dash okay?

Yes. We're in my office at the school.

Dash stuck his head in the frame and waved. *Hi, Marvin. When are you coming home?*

Manus felt a wave of relief. Followed an instant later by an undertow of fear and regret. He should have been with them. He shouldn't have left. He shouldn't have lied.

Soon, he signed.

We have a meet on Saturday. Can you come?

I hope so. I like watching you run.

Me, too. I run faster when you're there.

I know. Your parents named you Dash because you're fast.

It was what Dash had told Manus when they'd first met, at an Orioles game, where Manus, who had been surveilling Evie at Director Anders's request, caught the Manny Machado walk-off home run ball and then without thinking handed it to Dash.

Dash laughed. *I don't really say that anymore.*

I still like it. Can I talk to your mom for a second?

Sure.

And then he was gone again, and it was just Evie. She looked away for a moment, and he realized she was watching Dash. Probably waiting for him to get back to his homework or an electronic game so that he wouldn't see what she was signing.

After a moment, she started up again. She told him about a UPS truck. A camera by their driveway. She wanted to believe she was just being paranoid, but she didn't. Still, what could it mean? She'd taken the pension, they'd kept quiet. Everything had been fine. They hadn't done anything, had they?

He felt panicked and fought to control it. *Don't go home,* he signed. *I think something bad is happening. I'm trying to fix it.*

She looked at him. Was it worry in her eyes? Or . . . betrayal?

Where are you? she signed.

I can't explain now. But I will when I'm with you. I'm sorry.

When will you be here?

I'm not sure. Sometime tomorrow. As soon as I can. But don't go home. Not until I'm there.

What is happening?

I'll tell you everything when I'm back. I . . . He felt self-conscious, even though Dox wasn't watching him, even though in all likelihood the man couldn't read sign. *I miss you. And Dash. So much.*

I'm scared.

It's okay to be scared. Just be careful. I'm so sorry.

Don't be. You didn't do anything wrong.

That hurt. *How do you know?*

I know. But where should we go?

For all he knew, that UPS truck might have been in the parking lot that very moment. *Can you just stay there?* he signed. *At the school?*

Yes. Dash could stay in the dorm with one of his friends—

No. Stay with him.

She looked frightened at that. He added, *I'm just being careful. Stay with him until I'm back. I might not be able to text you, but I'm coming.*

Okay.

But don't stay in your office. Someplace else.

He could tell he had frightened her again. He hated it. But the alternatives could be worse.

I don't know, she signed. *There are couches in the faculty lounge—*

No. Not a common place. Not a place someone else would expect. And don't take your phones with you.

She nodded. She would know not to take the phones, of course. She knew more about that kind of thing than he did. More than almost anyone. He was scared for them, that's why he had said it. He realized his hand had dropped to the hilt of the Espada. He was going to find the people who were behind this.

He glanced at Dox again. He was still holding up the phone, and still looking away. Not for the first time, Manus was impressed by the man's instincts.

He looked at Evie. *I love you. Be careful. I'll be home soon.*

He took the phone, clicked off, and powered it down. "I have to go," he said to Dox. "Right now. Drive me to the airport."

"The airport?" Dox said. "Are your people all right?"

"No." He told them about the UPS truck and the camera.

"Look, they're all right for now," Dox said. "Let's take just a minute to think this through. Where are you flying to?"

"Washington."

"Okay, fine. But even if you can get a red-eye tonight, you won't land until tomorrow morning. By the time you get to them, it'll be, what, midmorning at best?"

Manus was getting irritated at how much the man talked. "The sooner I leave, the better my chances. Do you want to drive me, or should I call a cab?"

"What I mean," Dox said, "is that according to K., John and Delilah are landing in DC late tonight. They're going to pick up K.'s young officer, the one someone made the attempt on earlier. They could keep watch on your people, too, at least until you're back."

Manus hated that Evie and Dash were so exposed, but he didn't like Dox's suggestion. "I don't even know who they are."

"What you need to know is this," Dox said. "I've been running and gunning with John for a long time. He knows all there is about how to make someone dead. Which makes him the person you want most when it comes to keeping someone alive."

chapter
forty-two

DELILAH

Delilah was still trying to doze off when she felt a jolt and realized the plane had touched down. Her ears had been popping, but she hadn't expected to arrive so soon. She checked her watch—not quite four o'clock in the morning local time.

She pressed the button to raise the seat. John stirred across from her, still reclined. Ordinarily he was a light sleeper—a survival reflex, she knew. But when he felt safe, as apparently he did inside an airborne private jet, it was a different story.

The plane began to decelerate. John opened his eyes, stretched, and raised his seat.

"Well," she said. "At least you got some sleep."

He pinched his nostrils, closed his eyes, and blew out to pop his ears. "I'm guessing that makes one of us?"

She nodded.

"I'm sorry."

"It's all right. If I'd stayed behind, I wouldn't have slept any better. And I would have been pissed on top of it."

"Does that mean you're not?"

She sighed. "I was thinking . . . I wasn't being fair. It used to be you who tried to pressure me to get out of the life. And I wouldn't, because I wasn't ready."

"You had your reasons. I shouldn't have pressured you."

She laughed. "Yes, that's true. But I could be a little more understanding myself. I care about Dox, too. You know that. Livia . . . I'm mixed on."

"Only because you're protective of Dox. That's no vice."

He was right about that. "He's a good friend."

"The best. But don't tell him I said that. When the opportunity presents itself, I still need to be able to give him shit."

"What you said before . . . about how, if I needed help, I wouldn't be able to stop him."

John looked at her. "It's true."

She nodded. "I know it's true. No one could. I don't want to lose sight of that. Or anything else that really matters."

While the plane continued to taxi, John used the bathroom. Delilah followed suit. When she came back, he was closing the laptop. He would have connected, she knew, through the plane's satellite hotspot.

"All good?" she said.

"Yeah. Turns out we have two more people to pick up, not just this girl Maya."

For a second, she thought she'd heard wrong. "You're kidding," she said. But it was a reflex. John never kidded about that kind of thing.

He told her about the other two—Marvin Manus's woman and her boy. The woman had seen something worrisome and was afraid to go home. Manus was flying in to be with them, but he wouldn't land for a few more hours.

"Is this really necessary?" she said. "This Manus . . . we don't even know him."

"Dox told him we'd do it."

"Shouldn't he have checked with us first?"

"I'm sure he had a good reason. And it's only for a few hours." He paused, then added, "I'm sorry."

She suddenly had a bad feeling about all of this. It had been a nice moment on the plane after they landed. But now she could see in his eyes that the relaxed demeanor of Paris and Kamakura was gone. In its place was another facet of his personality, the facet she had first encountered a long time ago in Macau. She wanted that part of him to be confined to the past, and it was upsetting to see it abruptly recrudesce. It reminded her too much of how cold he had become, how much he had reverted, when that megalomaniac Hilger had rendered Dox. But she realized she was being stupid. They were operational now, whether she liked it or not. Did she want him to be sloppy?

She told herself there was nothing to worry about. This wasn't like the thing with Hilger. Dox wasn't being held. There was no gun to his head, at least not literally. John wasn't going to spiral. They would pick up these three passengers, babysit them for a little while, and go back to Paris as though none of it had ever happened.

She hoped.

They got off the plane directly onto the tarmac less than fifty meters from the terminal. They were at Leesburg Executive Airport, about forty miles northwest of DC. Dulles would have been the more obvious choice, which was of course part of the reason Kanezaki had used this smaller regional outpost instead.

Just ten minutes after landing, they were driving out of the airport in the car Kanezaki had left for them—a Honda SUV she assumed he had selected because of its popularity in the region, and therefore its unobtrusiveness. Delilah was behind the wheel. She preferred to drive, and was glad John didn't have the typical male need to be in control of the car. Besides, he was a better shot than she was, so it made sense that he would be their first line of defense with one of the two Glocks Kanezaki had left for them under the two front seats, each with a bellyband holster.

It was only a few miles to the meeting point—a Hampton Inn motel in Leesburg. But they took a circuitous route involving surface roads and several quiet neighborhoods. On this, she deferred to John's instructions. She had never known someone with better countersurveillance instincts. Traffic was light, and it was easy to confirm they weren't being followed.

They pulled into the motel parking lot and drove to the periphery, where there were fewer cars. She saw the vehicle they were looking for—a silver minivan. It was in one of the center spaces, no car left or right, room to drive forward or back as circumstances required. A good tactical spot. But that wasn't unexpected.

"Pull up next to it," John said. He was holding the Glock. "Slowly. So I'm next to the driver-side window. And be ready to gun it."

She rolled forward as he'd asked, giving it almost no gas, her foot poised to mash the pedal if there were any problems.

As they got closer, she could see the driver. An attractive Asian woman. Kanezaki's sister, John had said. Yuki. And a pretty brunette in the passenger seat. Maya, presumably. Was she holding a stuffed animal? No, it was an actual dog, some kind of terrier. Good God, they weren't here just to babysit. They were going to be dogsitting, too.

They stopped. Yuki nodded and rolled down her window. John did the same.

"Hey," John said. "It's good to see you." There was a surprising note of warmth in his voice.

Yuki smiled. "Isn't one of us supposed to say *The moon is blue* or something like that?"

John laughed. "I think that's only for people who don't know each other."

Delilah was surprised—John hadn't mentioned that he knew Kanezaki's sister. And the laugh was a little unlike him, too. Under any circumstances, and especially now, when he'd been so focused.

"You look good," Yuki said. "The greeting card business must agree with you."

Delilah recognized the reference to the old *Get Smart* series. Was this woman flirting with John?

"I'm retired, actually."

This time, it was Yuki who laughed. "That explains it. I was wondering what you were doing here in the Hampton Inn parking lot at ass-dark thirty picking up one of Tom's, uh, State Department colleagues."

"Same thing a soccer mom is doing dropping her off."

Delilah didn't know what that meant. Some kind of inside joke. God, they really were flirting. And just a half hour earlier, she'd been worrying about how he was reverting to his old, killing self.

Delilah leaned toward the passenger-side window. "Hello," she said. "I'm Delilah."

"Good to meet you," Yuki said. "Tom said you'd be coming."

John glanced toward the back of the van. "The kids aren't here this time? Rina and Rika, right?"

One quick exchange—which Delilah herself had initiated—and she was just the driver again, an afterthought.

Yuki nodded. "You have a good memory. They stay up later these days than when you met them, but not this late. Actually, they're going to be waking up soon. Luckily I have an understanding husband who's going to take them to school while I sleep in."

Delilah wondered whether the husband reference was for her benefit. It irritated her to think she might have unintentionally shown something the woman was responding to.

"Maya?" John said, leaning forward to look past Yuki.

The girl nodded. "Yeah."

"Tom told me what happened tonight. I'm sorry."

The girl nodded again. The dog whined and licked her face.

John got out, holding the Glock low alongside his leg, and scanned the area. Then he walked around to the passenger side of the van and opened the door.

"Come on," he said. "Let's keep moving."

The girl came out, holding her dog. John escorted her to the back of the SUV, his head swiveling as they moved. She looked exhausted, her face puffy, no doubt from crying. He closed the door behind her, then went to Yuki's window.

"You should go," he said. "Your brother is careful, and I seriously doubt anyone would have followed you—they would have been here already. Still, you might want to take an indirect route home. Go through some residential neighborhoods where there's no traffic. If it seems like anyone is following you—"

"I can handle myself."

"Sorry."

"It's okay. Tom says you micromanage."

John did another scan of the lot. Now that they had Maya, he seemed focused again. "He's probably right," he said.

Yuki looked past him toward the back seat of the SUV, then back at John. "Take care of her. She's really . . . She's having a rough time."

John nodded. "It was good seeing you."

"Same." She glanced at Delilah and added, "It was good meeting you, Delilah. Thanks for helping Tom."

"Of course," Delilah said, trying to inject a note of warmth into it. "It was good meeting you, too."

Yuki rolled up the window and drove off. Delilah watched as the taillights hit the street. "Nice woman," she said.

John nodded. "Yeah."

The taillights disappeared. Delilah pulled forward. "Attractive, too."

He was looking at the sideview. "Yeah," he said again.

Okay. Either he was being deliberately obtuse, or he was focused, as he needed to be. Or both.

Probably she should drop it. Or at least, bring it up later. After they'd picked up the other two and were done caring for all these strays that had been thrust upon them.

chapter
forty-three

LARISON

After dropping off Manus at the airport, Larison had driven to the Silver Cloud Inn—a hotel overlooking Commencement Bay in Tacoma. Dox had suggested it as a random place to regroup and spend the night. Larison knew the randomness had something to do with it, but figured if it overlooked a body of water, Dox was hoping for a little ambiance, too. The man was so head-over-heels about Livia it almost pained Larison to give him a hard time about it. Not that a little pain was a sufficient impediment, of course.

They'd cut Hamilton loose at the Motel 6. Nobody wanted to babysit her, and being around the five of them was obviously causing the woman freak-out levels of cognitive dissonance. They'd told her she needed to take a vacation—*Don't go home, don't go to the office, don't use your cellphone or credit cards*—until they'd figured out how to put the proverbial toothpaste back in the tube. She seemed to get it. But Larison thought there was at least a fifty percent chance that once she was away from them, it would all start to seem unreal, and she would rationalize what had happened at the hotel, rewrite the rest of it, and go back to her life and the normality most people clung to. He didn't particularly care one way or the other. The one thing he knew she wouldn't forget was what he'd told her before he and Manus headed out.

"I want you to know something," he'd said, looking at her so she could see it in his eyes. "From my standpoint, you have no more benefit to offer us. Meaning you're pure liability. So if it were up to me, I'd leave you here with a bullet in your head. The only reason I'm not doing it is because some of these people have qualms I don't, and I respect them enough to go along with their wishes. Sometimes. But if you ever say a word about any of us, next time it'll be purely up to me. And I promise, I've killed people a lot harder to find than you, Sharon Hamilton."

He'd held her gaze for a moment after saying it—just long enough to see the color drain from her face.

On the way back from the airport, he'd picked up takeout from a place called Indo Asian Street Eatery—dumplings, rolls, satay, rice bowls. He'd dropped off half for Dox and Livia. Now he and Diaz were sitting on the floor in their room, eating their half. Well, Larison was eating. Diaz was devouring.

"I'm glad you like it," he said. "I didn't know what you'd want, but it's better to stay off the phone."

She swallowed what she'd been chewing. "Sorry. Yeah, I was starving. This is great."

He liked that she was hungry. Some civilians, when they found themselves suddenly in the shit, broke down. Stopped eating, stopped sleeping, got withdrawn. Set themselves up for a vicious cycle. Others were more adaptable. Larison had no patience for the former variety. He wasn't like Dox, who had weird scripts running through his head about the importance of protecting the weak. For Larison, if you couldn't carry your own weight, it wasn't up to him to carry it for you.

"So you know Livia?" she said, around a mouthful of Thai basil chicken.

Larison nodded. "Mostly through Dox. You?"

"Through work. And I take her classes. Women's self-defense."

Larison nodded again. He didn't think much of most self-defense classes he'd ever come across. But if Livia was teaching, it would be all right.

"What's up with her and Dox?" Diaz said.

"What do you mean?"

"You know. She never mentioned him to me. I mean, her private life is pretty mysterious, and I'm beginning to understand why."

"I don't know. They've got some kind of on-again, off-again thing."

"There's some kind of connection there. I can see it when she's looking at him."

Probably the topic was harmless, but Larison wasn't comfortable discussing Dox's love life. Maybe because of the danger it would lead to questions about his own. And while he'd gotten used to what Rain and Dox and company knew about him, that didn't extend to the rest of the world. At least not yet.

"She's complicated," he said. "What about you? How'd you get into this line of work?"

She shrugged. "I hate bullies," she said. "People who take advantage of other people just because they can."

It felt like a PR statement, probably one she'd trotted out in every job interview she'd ever had. People claimed all sorts of high-minded motives for the shit they did. The truth was usually something else.

Still, there was a coldness in her eyes that made him wonder if there was something more to it. Just because she might deploy it as some kind of résumé mission statement didn't mean it was only that. And maybe it was such an obvious bromide, so appealing an explanation for someone in her line of work, that she used the glittering public-relations aspect to distract from some darker foundation of truth.

"That ever happen to you?" he said.

She looked at him, and he could see she was put off by the question. He smiled. "I don't mean to pry. But hey, you brought it up."

She looked away. A beat passed. Then she said quietly, "My stepfather. When my brother and I were small."

It was obviously something she wouldn't ordinarily share. He wondered why she was trusting him with it now. Probably the feeling of the everyday world in abeyance, the four of them, and now just the two, at sea together, adrift, detached. When Larison had been a soldier, he had hitchhiked a lot. And was frequently astonished at the personal stories people would share after picking him up. One guy, who had been having an affair with his own sister-in-law, had said to Larison, "I don't know why I'm telling you this. Well, I guess, who are you going to tell, right?" The truth was, most people had a deep-seated need to unburden themselves. It was just a question of the right timing, and circumstances, and confessor.

"Where is he now?" Larison said.

"Dead."

"That why you became a prosecutor? Because you couldn't punish him?"

"What are you, my therapist? Anyway, what makes you think I didn't punish him?"

Larison doubted it, but he said, "I hope you did."

There was a pause. She said, "Well, I didn't."

"I'm sorry."

"What about you? How did you get into . . . whatever it is you do?"

He swallowed a mouthful of chicken and rice. "Long story."

"Are we going someplace?"

He smiled. He liked Diaz. She wasn't as tough as she thought she was, but with a little luck, she would be.

"It started with the rah-rah stuff," he said. "Flag and country and all that. But really, I just didn't want anyone to ever be able to fuck with me. You know. 'Yea, though I walk through the valley of the shadow of death, I will fear no evil, 'cause I'm the baddest motherfucker in the valley.' But it didn't take long to figure out the rah-rah was just bullshit and marketing. A racket."

"Well, at least you got the baddest motherfucker part, right?"

He laughed. "I don't know about that. But yeah, people tend to leave me alone if I want them to. And if they don't, I can make them."

For a moment, her eyes were far away. "I wish I could have done that," she said, and he knew she was remembering the stepfather.

He nodded. "There's a cost, though."

"What?"

He shrugged. "Parts of you wind up . . . cauterized."

He stopped, amazed he had said so much. Well, the hitchhiker principle worked both ways.

"I'm sorry," she said.

"Don't be. These people have been good for me. That fucking Dox . . . He can wear you down. Anyway, what about you? What are you going to do when this is over?"

"What do you mean?"

"Are you going to be able to go back to the law, and the rules, and all the sanctimonious bullshit and pretend it's not all just, you know, a racket?"

"It's not all a racket," she said.

He liked her enough not to want to disabuse her.

"Anyway," she said after a moment. "I knew Schrader had allies. Livia warned me about what I'd be facing with an indictment. But even she didn't see . . . how far they'd go. Although maybe she did. She kept trying to get me to be more careful. I thought she was being alarmist. God."

"There's a saying I like. 'Denial has no survival value.' If you're going to play, you have to at least recognize what the game is."

She nodded. "Well, now I know."

"And on the bright side, there's a good chance Schrader spent the last hours of his life screaming for it to stop. And who knows? Maybe they're not done with him. Maybe he's screaming right now."

"Somehow that doesn't feel like justice."

"It beats someone killing you, and Schrader walking free."

She smiled. "Well, when you put it like that."

He smiled back. Yeah, she was all right.

"This whole thing," he said. "It's about the videos, right?"

"It seems that way."

"That's what all the bigshots are playing for. But maybe the videos will wind up with you. Who'll be the baddest motherfucker then?"

"That's not what I would do with them. Those videos are evidence of crimes. I'd use them for new prosecutions."

"Well, that's one way. But you want to hear another expression I like?"

She didn't answer, and he went on.

"'Don't bring a lawbook to a gunfight.'"

chapter forty-four

EVIE

Evie was at the checkout desk in the library. Other than the flicker of the computer screen and the ambient glow from the parking lot lights outside the windows, the cavernous space was dark. It was so quiet she could hear the hum of the computer, and the air had a trace of must—that unmistakable book smell, which she had always found comforting but that now felt surreal and discordant.

Dash had passed out on a couch, under the multicolored afghan Ms. Symons typically kept folded across her lap and that, along with her overlarge glasses, had become her trademark as the school librarian. Evie was relieved he was sleeping. He'd reacted better than she had feared: if Marvin said they shouldn't go home until he could make sure the house was safe, they shouldn't go home. Evie couldn't answer his questions beyond that, so he would save them for Marvin, who he trusted so completely.

But the first questions would be only the beginning, and when the answers proved unsatisfactory, the questions, and the doubts, would grow. Dash wasn't a little boy anymore, to be bought off with stories about scavenger hunts and games as the reasons they had been on the run, or vague explanations that Delgado was a bad man who had been trying to hurt them because he thought Evie had information Delgado wanted, and that Marvin had made Delgado go away. Dash had always believed Marvin's vague assurance that he had been one kind of contractor, for the government, and now had become another, the kind that builds houses. And while she knew Dash wouldn't indulge those fictions forever, she had always hoped he would hold on to them for longer.

She glanced at the clock on the screen. Not yet five. She was tired, but she didn't want to go to one of the couches, or even to nod off. After the custodians had finished cleaning and left for the night, she had put her and Dash's cellphones in her office as Marvin had instructed. But with a twist—she had turned on FaceTime on each phone, and was now monitoring the feeds from the checkout desk computer. If anyone entered her office, she would know.

Not that she was really expecting anything like that. But . . . it couldn't hurt to be careful. Just in case.

Dash moaned in his sleep and she glanced over at him. Curled on the couch in the faint light from the parking lot, he looked smaller than he was. Like the little boy he'd been and not the teenager he'd become. She felt a wave of desperate love for him. And an underlying ripple of terror that somehow, she had put him in danger.

She rubbed her eyes. She wished it would get light. Everything would feel better then. More sane.

Through the computer speaker, she heard a soft electric buzz. It stopped, then started again.

She looked at the feed. She didn't see anything. But whatever sleepiness she'd been feeling was instantly gone, replaced by an adrenalized alertness.

The buzz continued, then abruptly stopped. She heard the unmistakable sound of a lock clicking open.

Her heart started hammering and her mouth was instantly dry. She stared intently at FaceTime through the camera aimed at her office door.

The door opened. A man came through. Her heart was beating so hard she was afraid someone would hear it.

She had left a desk light on in the office. It wasn't enough to make out the man's features. But she could see the brown uniform. The UPS guy she had seen at the house.

He was holding something in his hand. It might have been an electric toothbrush, but she knew better. It was an electric lock-pick gun. That's what she'd heard buzzing. The man slipped the pick gun into a pocket and began moving stealthily through her office.

She was convulsed by a wave of terror. *911,* she thought. *Call 911.*

But the cellphones were in her office—

She realized that in her panic, she'd forgotten all about the landline. She grabbed the receiver, shocked at how badly her hands were shaking, and brought it to her ear.

No dial tone.

Wait, wait, you need an outside line. Hurry—

She managed to punch the *9* button. Dial tone. *Thank God.*

She punched in the three digits. A single ring. Then a man's voice: "911. What is your emergency?"

"My name is Evelyn Gallagher," she whispered. "I'm a teacher at the School for the Deaf. There's a man in my office. I think he's going to hurt us."

"Where are you now, ma'am?"

"At the school."

"In your office?"

"No. In the library. But I think—he's looking for us."

"All right. Stay where you are. We're sending units right away. Do you want me to remain on the phone?"

"No. I have to wake my son. Just please, hurry."

She placed the receiver back in the cradle, her hand still shaking badly. She got up to go to Dash, but heard a faint buzz through the FaceTime feed, different from the sound of the pick gun. She glanced, and saw the UPS man reach into his uniform and pull out a cellphone.

He held it to his ear and listened. "I don't know," he said quietly. "Maybe she heard me. Doesn't matter. I'll meet you there."

She shook her head, confused. Meet who, where?

The library.

She felt a fresh wave of terror. They'd spoofed the phone line. Probably had a dirt box simulator set up outside to intercept cellphone transmissions, too.

She'd meant to call 911 . . . and had told them exactly where she and Dash were hiding.

That feeling of waking up in the van, nauseous, confused, Delgado telling her the horrible things he would do if she didn't cooperate . . . It all came back in a dizzying rush.

Get it together, Evie, get it together—

A weapon. She needed a weapon. But what could she use? It was a library—was she going to throw books at them?

She pulled open one of the desk drawers. The computer screen's glow was too dim to see inside the drawer, and she couldn't very well turn on the lights. And of course she didn't have her cellphone to use as a flashlight—

Come on, come on . . .

She squinted and reached into the drawer, groping for something, anything. A letter opener. Something heavy like a paperweight. Or—

Scissors. The kids in here were always making posters about books. They had to have scissors.

She yanked open another drawer and groped inside. Pencils. A ruler. Nothing useful.

A third drawer. A stapler. A hole punch. A container of glue.

God what kind of library doesn't have a fucking pair of scissors—

It was taking too long. She ran from behind the desk and over to Dash. The main library entrance was on this floor. The second-floor entrance was always locked and wasn't even marked. So they'd come in here, right? If she and Dash took the internal staircase to the second floor, maybe they could slip out before anyone saw them. They could find a different place to hide. She didn't know where—all the doors were locked at night. She only had keys to the library, the faculty lounge, and her office. They might think of the lounge. Marvin had been concerned about that. There were stenciled metal signs alongside each door. Could she remove the one for the faculty lounge? But then that would be the only one missing . . .

She was thinking too much. They'd find something. A bathroom, maybe. A closet. Or they could get to an exit and run out of the building. Get to the street and pound on someone's door. But first they had to *move*.

She leaned over Dash and shook him briskly by the shoulder. He flinched and opened his eyes.

We have to go, she signed. *Right now.*

He looked around, obviously confused and still half-asleep. *Is Marvin here?*

No. Not yet. Come on. And quiet, all right? Like a ninja.

Where are we going?

Up the stairs.

I have to go to the bathroom.

Later. Come on.

She pulled him to his feet and they walked quickly to the stairs. They were almost at the top when she heard the vibration again, in the library door.

The lock-pick gun. They were out of time.

chapter forty-five

RAIN

Rain scanned as Delilah drove, the weight of the Glock reassuring in his hand. The neighborhood around the school was residential, and unlike the highway, where they had passed a few cars, these streets were still empty, the streetlights revealing nothing but early-morning mist. They circled twice and saw nothing, not even a jogger or suburbanite walking a dog.

According to Google Maps, there were two parking lots, one at the north end of the campus, the other at the south. Manus had told him to use the north lot, alongside the main building where the woman, Evelyn Gallagher, had her office. But it always made sense to see the balance of the terrain before arriving at the destination.

"Turn here," he said to Delilah. "Swing through the south lot first."

They did. Not a single car. There was a baseball diamond nearby, and farther off, a football field. Probably the south lot was used more for athletic events.

"Go back out," he said. "Left on the street, then left again. Let's enter the north lot at the northeast end."

"All right," she said. She didn't ask why. He was glad. He couldn't always explain why he preferred one approach over another. And when he was focused, he didn't want to have to try.

He took a quick glance back at Maya. She had been extremely quiet, but he saw she wasn't sleeping. She was holding her dog in her lap. Her knees were pressed together to create a kind of seat, and she was leaning forward, her arms around the animal as though to protect it.

"What's her name?" Rain said. "Or his."

"His. Frodo."

"He seems like a good dog."

She didn't respond.

"You okay?" he said.

She nodded. "Yeah."

He knew she wasn't okay. But his job was to make sure she was safe. Someone else would have to help her with the trauma of what she'd been through earlier. In the meantime, he was glad she had Frodo.

As they got closer to the parking lot, he forgot about Maya. He focused on how he would do it if Gallagher were his target, rather than someone he was here to help. Where he would park. Where he'd position sentries. Where he would set up for a counter-ambush. But he saw nothing that set off any alarm bells.

They pulled in. At the far end, there were two vehicles. One, a Prius. The other, a UPS truck.

"A little late for a delivery," Delilah said, mirroring his thoughts. "Or a little early."

"Just keep going," he said. "Past the vehicles. Make a right when we get back to the street. Don't even slow down."

If someone was looking, they'd already been spotted. But that didn't mean you decloak. Better to act *as if* until you had no choice but to break cover. Sometimes riding out the subterfuge could buy you a little more time.

Delilah kept going. The Prius was parked nose-in, and in the yellowish pall of the streetlights shone in early-morning dew. The UPS truck was nose-out, for a more efficient departure. And covered with no dew at all.

Rain's heart rate kicked up a notch. This wasn't going to be a simple pickup like the girl. Someone was already here.

"They haven't been here long," Delilah said, again mirroring his thoughts. She must have been extremely unhappy about this development, but she said nothing else, and for a second, he understood her irritation at Dox. He loved the big sniper, and would do anything for him if he was in a jam. *Had* done anything for him, things he preferred not to remember. As Dox had done in return. But a favor for a friend was one thing. A friend of the friend was another thing entirely. And this favor was looking to be a lot bigger than originally advertised.

Fifty feet up the street, he said, "Stop here." He would have preferred something farther away. But he didn't think they had time.

Delilah waited until they were past a streetlight, then pulled to the curb along a line of brick rowhouses in the shadow of a cluster of trees. "We go in?"

"Just me."

"John. Don't be stupid."

"I'm just going to take a look. If anyone's looking back and I have to come running, I don't want to have to wait to start the engine."

"You don't know what's in there."

"They're here for a schoolteacher and a teenaged boy. They didn't send a whole battalion and they're not expecting one in return."

"Just because the woman saw only one man outside her house doesn't mean—"

"No time to argue. If you have to move, circle the block. But look for me here."

He jumped out before she could say more, easing the door closed with a hip check to keep the sound low.

He slipped the Glock into the bellyband and started fast-walking toward the school, keeping to the shadows, his breath fogging in the morning air. His tactical analysis wasn't crazy, of course, but neither was hers. The truth was, there was no way to be sure. All he knew was that he couldn't put her in more danger than he already had. They'd fight about it later. And he would remind himself of what a privilege that was—to be alive, to be with her, no matter what.

He stopped at the end of the line of rowhouses, crouched, and eased his head past. This was the edge of the campus. At ninety degrees to his left and continuing straight ahead was an iron fence. But it was obviously for demarcation, not to keep out determined intruders.

He waited for a moment, listening. Nothing. Just the faint roar of traffic on Interstate 70 a mile south. *Okay.*

He vaulted the fence easily, eased out the Glock, and ran forward. He paused again alongside a tree to look and listen. Still nothing.

Ahead was the main building and the parking lot with the Prius and the UPS truck. The building was a rectangle with its length running north and south, meaning the main entrances were on the long east and west sides, and the side entrances were on the short north and south ends. Other things being equal, they would have used the north side—the entrance closest to where they'd parked.

Most of the building was dark, though he could see some light spilling out from the west entrance doors. Presumably, room lights were turned off at night; corridor lights got left on.

There were no more trees or other cover between his position and the building. But no trees meant no autumn leaves on the ground, only soundless grass. Just fifty feet in the dark. Unless they had a sentry and night-vision equipment, he ought to be okay. He tried not to think about how many people had died with *unless* as their last thought, or about how his analysis of their numbers and defensive posture was a hunch based on not much data.

He ran forward at a low crouch and reached the corner of the building in seconds. He paused, reassured by the feeling of the stone façade against his back. He looked and listened. Nothing.

Ten feet along was a lightless ground-floor window. If someone was inside looking out, there was no way to pass unobserved. The chances were low. But the penalty for missing could be high.

He took a quick breath and darted past the window, stopping at the edge of the north entrance. No reaction he could detect from within.

Light was showing through the door's windows. He flash-checked inside. Nothing.

He scanned again—all quiet—and turned his attention to the door. It was open a crack, and he immediately saw why: a magnet attached to the top of the metal jamb. A simple alarm reed-switch bypass. They'd located the alarm magnet with a laminated sensor shim and left everything taped in place for a quicker exit. Maybe not an operation sophisticated enough to knock over a bank, but not the Keystone Kops, either.

But they weren't expecting opposition. And/or they didn't have numbers. He guessed two inside, maybe three. More than that, and they would have left a sentry at the entrance.

He eased open the door and scanned the corridor left and right. Nothing. He slipped inside and soundlessly returned the door to its position.

No cover here, and with the lights on, no concealment, either. He turned right and fast-walked to the end of the short corridor, staying on the edges of his feet to muffle the sound of his footfalls on the waxed floor. He paused and darted his head around the corner. The long corridor was empty.

It would have been convenient to have some information about where to find Gallagher and her son. But Manus himself didn't know. He had told her not to stay in her office, which was smart. Beyond that, though, they could be anywhere. Of course, human behavior was far from random, and *could be* rarely lined up neatly with *would be*. Here, the primary question was, Where would be most comfortable for a mother to spend the night with her teenaged son? Places with a couch. And common places, rather than someone else's office, which psychologically would have felt like an intrusion. It would have been easy enough to just call the woman and provide the bona fides Dox had communicated over the secure site. But Manus had told her to leave her and her son's cellphones in her office. Again, smart, but also again, the security came with complications.

He moved forward, the Glock up, checking signs. **BARBARA CLOONEY—ENGLISH. JERRY SACHSEL—MATH. MARIA TRZEPACZ—SOCIAL STUDIES**. He tried doors as he moved. They were all locked.

He was a third of the way up the corridor when a door opened on the left twenty feet ahead. A man stepped through. He was wearing a UPS uniform.

chapter forty-six

EVIE

Evie and Dash got to the top of the stairs just as the door opened below. She grabbed Dash's shoulder and pulled him behind one of the shelves. It was shadowy, but there was enough light from outside to see. She pressed her fingers to his lips.

Why? he signed.

There's a man downstairs. We can't let him hear us.

Maybe they could have made it to the second-floor doors. But it was hard for Dash to move quietly—he had no way of gauging whether he was making noise. And in that silent space, there was no way they would be able to make it through the doors without being heard.

A man stepped in, silhouetted by the corridor light. Peeking through the books, she could make out only his shape, not his features.

"Anyone in here?" he called out, holding the door. "We got a 911 call."

Yeah, Evie thought. *I'll bet you did.*

"Evelyn Gallagher?" the man called out. "Are you in here?"

She looked around wildly. There was a metal cart just behind them, its three shelves loaded with books. The floors were carpeted. But if the wheels squeaked . . .

"Evelyn?" the man said. He let go of the door and it closed behind him with a firm clang, cutting off the light from the corridor. He walked to the checkout desk and glanced behind it.

She wondered why he wasn't turning on the lights.

Because then you'll see he's dressed as a UPS man, not as a cop.

But that wouldn't last. When he didn't see them, he'd abandon the act.

She looked at Dash and signed, *Don't move!* Then she got on her hands and knees and crawled toward the cart.

"Evelyn?" the man called out again. "The dispatcher said we could find you here. Come on out, ma'am, you're safe now."

She reached under the cart and felt for the wheels. They were aligned in the wrong direction. Of course. She rotated them a hundred and eighty degrees. The cart was heavy, and she grimaced with the effort of moving the wheels without making noise.

"It's really all right, ma'am. You can come out."

For a second, she felt herself wanting to believe him. The alternative was too terrifying.

No. That is never going to happen to you again. Never.

She put her hands low on the end of the cart, just above the wheels. She pushed. It didn't move.

She gritted her teeth and pushed again, harder. Again she couldn't budge it. What was wrong? With all those books, it was heavy, but not that heavy.

She saw Dash crawling toward her. She waved for him to go back, but he ignored her. He reached under the cart and started doing something to the wheels. She wanted to tell him she had already aligned them, that he should stay where no one could see him—

The wheels, she realized. Did they have some kind of locks?

She reached under, felt around, and found the mechanism instantly. A simple lever. She pulled one, then the second. She looked up. Dash was looking at her. He signed, *Safety locks. Like on Marvin's tools.*

She nodded frantically. *Okay. Go back.*

He crawled away, but toward the tables, not behind the shelf. She waved frantically, but he couldn't see her—

The lights came on. She froze, feeling suddenly, horribly exposed. From behind the cart, she couldn't see the man. But did that mean he couldn't see her?

She was ten feet from the stairs. She'd wanted to move the cart closer, but with the lights on, she didn't dare.

She looked to her right. Dash was under one of the wooden study tables. He was doing something to one of the legs. She couldn't tell what. *Please, God, please don't make a noise . . .*

She strained to listen. She could just make out footfalls, soft on the carpet below. He was moving toward the back of the first-floor space. Of course. Past every shelf, then a return on the opposite side. And when the first-floor search proved fruitless, he'd move to the second floor.

And find them.

The sound of footsteps faded. She wished he would call out again so she could have an idea of his position. But he must have recognized the 911 gambit had failed.

She glanced at Dash again. But he was ignoring her, intent on the underside of the table.

Seconds passed. Crouched behind the book cart, she could see the landing at the top of the stairs, but nothing below it.

Over the pounding of her heart, she heard footsteps again. Closer. Louder.

The cadence changed. She realized she could now hear not just the footsteps, but the soft rustle of the material of his clothes.

He was coming up the stairs. And he was close. Any second, and he would see them.

chapter
forty-seven

LIVIA

C arl and Livia sat on the floor, eating the takeout Larison had brought them. "The angel of death," Carl said. "Moonlighting as DoorDash delivery. Who'da thunk it?"

Livia didn't answer. She wasn't sure about the sleeping arrangements. Would Alondra be comfortable with Larison? Maybe Larison and Carl should have taken the other room. Or was she just telling herself that as an excuse, because she was afraid of what staying with Carl might mean? As usual with him, she was overthinking everything.

But also as usual, her silence didn't dissuade Carl. If anything, it encouraged him. "I hope the room's okay," he said, looking around. "I got the last one with two queen beds for Larison and Diaz. All they had left was these honeymoon-suite types, with the king beds and water views and hot tubs. I guess we'll just have to try to make the best of it."

Again, she didn't answer.

He said, "I'm kidding, they did have some with two queens, but none of those faced the water. But you know the floor's okay by me, if you'd prefer."

She looked down. She didn't know what she preferred. They'd shared a bed before—literally as well as otherwise—and she'd gotten used to having him next to her throughout the night. She even . . . liked it. Or wanted to. She wished she could explain to him that whenever she caught herself feeling happy, it terrified her. The lesson seared into her psyche being that she could never trust anything good. That it would all be ripped away from her. And with Carl . . . there were moments when she'd never been happier. But the terror was correspondingly bad.

"What's our next move?" she said, wanting to change the subject.

He took a bite of satay and chewed, his expression contemplative, then swallowed. "Hard to say without more intel. You heard anything more from SPD?"

She shook her head. "The chief is giving me a lot of room for once, meaning she's not pressuring my lieutenant, either. I don't want to risk any of that by getting in touch. If anything changes, I'll hear from them."

Carl nodded. "Sleeping dogs, I get it. Well, no matter what, it seems to me we need to either get ahold of those videos, or confirm they're destroyed. Or at least confirm they're inaccessible by anyone, which amounts to the same thing. I don't think any of this is emotional for the people we're up against. They're just trying to acquire something that's important to them, whether because it's valuable or because it's a threat. If they get it, we don't matter anymore. If they realize they can't get it, same thing. Of course, if we get the videos, and they know we have them, or they think we do, anyway, they're not going to leave us alone. We'll have to make them."

That all made sense to her. Of course, the question was how.

"What about Schrader?" she said.

"What about him?"

"You think he's alive?"

He looked away for a moment. "I have a hunch he is, yeah."

"Why?"

"Because he knows the only thing keeping him alive is those videos. If he gives up his credentials, they'll kill him for sure."

"But if they're torturing him, at some point he'll break."

"True. But even then, they wouldn't kill him right away. Because if it turned out the information he gave them was false—and by the way, information you torture out of someone is typically unreliable—they'd be shit out of luck. It's like if you tortured the combination to a safe out of someone. You'd be wise to open the safe before killing the person. Sorry to be so gruesome, but it's true."

"Plus there's the dead-man switch."

"Right. If you want those videos to use as blackmail, they're not much good once they've been released into the wild. Are you thinking what I think you're thinking?"

"What am I thinking?"

"Well, if Schrader dies, one way or the other, and there is a dead-man switch like he told Diaz, the switch gets triggered, the videos get released, and we're all off the hook. I mean, if I knew for sure there were a dead-man switch, I'd happily shoot the sumbitch myself. And I figure, all the men in those videos would have their reputations destroyed, which seems only fair. On top of which, every one of those videos is a crime and evidence of a crime, right? So with the videos out, Diaz could prosecute a whole lot of people."

Livia didn't answer. He was right—some of it was what she had been thinking. But he wasn't seeing the whole picture.

"But here's the thing," he went on. "We don't know about the dead-man switch. If it's a bluff and we kill Schrader, then we have no way to take control of those videos. Someone else could get ahold of them. Or they could be lost forever. Either way, the men who appear in them would go unpunished. And we'd need a way of persuading the people who are after the videos now, like Rispel, that we don't have them. It could be tricky."

All true. But he still wasn't seeing it. She didn't blame him. This was her world, not his.

"There's something you're missing," she said.

"Tell me."

"The girls. If those videos are made public on the Internet, it's forever. That kind of thing is a nightmare for the victims. For the rest of their lives, every time they see a strange man looking at them—in a supermarket, in a restaurant, at work—they wonder if it's someone who has watched them being raped and degraded online. So yeah, I'd like to kill Schrader. And I'd do it, too. But not if there's a dead-man switch. Not even to take the pressure off us. And I don't want you or Larison doing it, either."

He nodded. After a moment, he said, "I hadn't thought of that."

"It's not your fault. But now you know."

"You know I'm with you. Larison might take some persuading, though. His focus tends to be narrower than mine."

"I know. And I don't like it."

"Don't judge him too harshly. He hasn't had the easiest life himself. And he has a lot of respect for you and your work."

"Then he won't do anything that would risk those videos being uploaded."

He nodded. "I'll make sure he doesn't."

She looked at him, conflicting emotions roiling inside her.

"What?" he said.

"Sometimes you're so good to me it makes me want to hit you."

He smiled. "Well, you could if you like. It's not necessarily my thing, but I'm notoriously open-minded."

She laughed, then said, "I'm serious."

"Larison'll be fine. And I'm happy to talk to him."

"I'm sorry I'm so . . . difficult."

"I don't find you difficult. I love being with you, no matter what. Maybe that's what you find difficult."

She was too tired to spar with him. And what he'd said was too true. "Maybe."

He smiled. "Tell you what. You want to make it up to me? I mean your difficultness and all that."

"Maybe," she said again.

"Lie down on the bed with me. And touch my face the way you do."

"Yeah, we both know where that leads."

"Past performance is no guarantee of future results."

"But also hope springs eternal."

He laughed. "Fair enough."

She tried to think of what to say. What came out was "It's okay. I want to, too."

He looked at her, his expression so open it almost hurt. "You mean, touch my face?"

She shook her head. "Everything."

"Well, *everything* could cover a lot of ground. I didn't bring a Wonder Woman outfit or a golden lasso, but there might be a place open around here even at this hour."

She laughed again. She'd never known anyone who made her laugh the way he did. She loved it, even though it also always made her sad.

"I just don't know what it means," she said.

"What *what* means?"

"Us . . . being together."

"I don't know, either."

"Yeah, but what do you want it to mean?"

"Why don't you let me worry about that?"

"I feel like I'm . . . I don't know. Leading you on."

"Please refer to my previous sentence."

She laughed again, but she felt like he was deflecting. "You don't feel that way?"

"No."

"I know I . . . vacillate."

"That's fair."

"It feels unfair."

"You've never been unfair with me."

She looked at him. "Why don't you ever get frustrated with me?"

219

"I do. All the time. I just don't show it."

"What? Why not?"

"Because that wouldn't be fair to you."

"But see? Then I'm the one who's being unfair."

He shook his head. "No, you're not. You're just trying to figure things out. And who could blame you for that?"

"You really don't?"

"No."

"But what if I never do? Figure things out."

"If you're asking if I'm ready to quit you, the answer is no. Especially not immediately following your offer to do everything with me right here and now in the Silver Cloud Inn honeymoon suite."

She laughed. Then she leaned in and kissed him. And for that moment, it really was lovely. Like a wave gently hitting the beach. Without any undertow at all.

After a moment, he broke the kiss. He looked at her and said, "I've been thinking."

"Yeah?"

"You know, I don't always have to be so gentle. I mean, you tend to bring that out in me, but we could try it the way it was that first time, at Saeng Chan Beach."

She felt embarrassed talking about it. "I think . . . it might feel artificial."

"What if I provoked you?"

She was surprised to find the thought excited her. "What if you did?"

"See, I'm doing it already. Putty in my hands."

That excited her more. "Bullshit."

She didn't remember what he said next. It was eclipsed by what came after.

chapter
forty-eight

RAIN

Rain trained the Glock's sights on center mass. "Keep your hands where I can see them," he said. The tone was neither loud nor belligerent. Just an if/then equation: the *if* being failure to comply, the *then* being death an instant later.

The guy was so plainly surprised that for a moment he just stared at Rain, his mouth agape.

"Hands up," Rain said, moving slowly in, his tone still deadly calm. "Palms forward. Fingers splayed. Anything else and you're dead right there."

The guy raised his hands. "What the hell is this?" he said. Loudly. Loudly enough to alert a partner.

Rain didn't answer. The only reason he hadn't dropped the guy yet was the hope that he could get close enough to crush his skull silently with the gun butt, rather than alerting whoever else might be around with gunfire.

Rain hugged the wall to his left and kept moving forward. If the guy was righthanded, which was statistically likely, this way he'd have a harder time deploying a weapon for an accurate shot. He flash-checked his right flank and kept the Glock sights on center mass.

The guy was ten feet away now. Point-blank.

Rain raised the gunsights to the guy's face. "Make another sound," he said softly, "and you're done."

But the guy must have reasoned that if Rain was concerned about sound in general, he'd be concerned about gunfire specifically. Maybe so concerned that he was bluffing. In an even louder voice, the guy called out, "Who are you? Why—"

He didn't get to finish the question. Or even to learn that the bluff he'd meant to call was—*oops*—not a bluff at all. Rain pressed the trigger. The corridor echoed with a giant *BAM!* and a small hole appeared in the guy's forehead. An expression of perfect, vacuous astonishment rippled across his face. He shuddered as though from an electric shock, fell back into the door behind him, and slid bonelessly to the floor.

Well, so much for the element of surprise. But one less of the enemy to deal with. And though whoever was left would now understand there was opposition, they wouldn't yet know who had shot whom. They'd come in here with a plan. Now they'd be improvising. Though in fairness, of course, so was Rain.

And then, somewhere down the corridor, a woman screamed.

chapter
forty-nine

EVIE

Evie crouched behind the cart, staring through the space between the books, her heart hammering. The sound of footsteps came closer. Closer . . .

She felt paralyzed with fear. What if she tried to ram him too early and he got out of the way? Or too late, and it didn't knock him down the stairs? She had only one chance, just this one chance . . .

She saw brown hair. A forehead. A narrow set of eyes, a stubble of beard—

He looked right at her. Smiled. "Caught you," he said.

She bunched her shoulders and tensed to shove the cart forward—

Bam!

A gunshot. It had to be. From out in the corridor below. The man turned to look, his hand going inside his jacket—

Evie screamed and blasted out of her crouch, shoving the cart toward the stairs with all her strength. The man turned his head back toward her, seeming to move in slow motion now, his hand coming from inside his jacket, holding a gun—

Evie kept screaming, driving the cart forward like a battering ram. The man's eyes bulged, he brought up his free hand, and flinched away—

The cart went past the landing and bounced down the stairs, Evie losing her balance now but still keeping all her weight behind it. It crashed into his side with a satisfying crunch and he fell backward, the cart barreling over him. Evie lost her grip and tripped as she hit him, and then she was tumbling down, tangled up with him, everything spinning past her, the ceiling, the lights, the stairs. The back of her head hit something and she saw an explosion of fireworks. And then she felt a giant *thud* through her body and all the movement stopped.

The man was on his back on the floor right next to her. He rolled to his side. Got his knees under him. "You fucking bitch," he groaned.

Evie sucked in a huge breath. She saw his gun, on the carpet just a few feet away. And saw him see it.

He started crawling toward it. Without any thought at all, she shrieked and scrabbled onto his back, trying to hook her fingers into his eyes, to tear them out of their sockets—

The man screamed. He shook his head frantically left and right and grabbed her fingers, ripping them away from his face. He reached back, got a hand in her hair, and pulled her forward. She tried to hang on, but he was too strong, and he dumped her over his shoulder onto the floor. She barely felt the shock of impact, she was too focused on his eyes again, on getting her fingers in them. The man shook his head again to keep clear, then reared up, raised a fist—

She saw a shape loom above her. Something arcing through the air. There was a loud *crack*, like the sound of a home run hit. The man went flying off her. She rolled to her knees and saw Dash, moving in on the man, cocking back a club, no, the leg of the wooden table, like he'd just stepped up to the plate and was about to swing for the fences. The man scuttled back, trying for the gun, and Dash screamed and swung again. The man got his hands up, but the table leg whipped around and blasted the man's hands into his face and knocked him onto his back. Dash stepped in, still screaming, bringing the table leg back again, but the man managed to grab him around the knees and rolled into him, knocking him down—

Evie tensed to launch at him. But the gun, it was right there—

Dash tried to hang on to the table leg but the man was too big. He yanked it out of Dash's hands, reared up, raised it over his head like a stake—

Evie grabbed the gun, spun on her knees, and pointed it with both hands the way Marvin had taught her. She squeezed the trigger. There was a *BAM!* and the gun jumped in her hands. The man twitched— she'd hit him! But he didn't go down.

She heard Marvin's voice in her head: *You don't shoot once and then check. Or hit once, either. You keep going until the threat isn't a threat anymore.*

She fired again. And again. Each impact caused the man to twitch, but he was still holding the table leg, still on top of Dash—

She fired a fourth time. And then heard Marvin again: *Front sights on the target. Gorilla grip. Roll the trigger.*

She squeezed the grip hard. Lined up the sights on the back of the man's head. Eased out a breath. And rolled the trigger.

BAM! The gun kicked. A fountain of blood erupted from the right side of the man's head. He fell to his side.

She heard a crash and spun again. The door to the library—a man was running through it. He was holding a gun. He saw her. Evie brought up the gun, but the man was too fast—he dove behind the checkout desk.

She heard Marvin again: *Don't confuse cover and concealment. Concealment is something you hide behind. Cover means the bullets can't go through.*

Could she shoot through the desk? But if she didn't hit him, she'd be wasting bullets. And their own position was exposed—

"Evelyn!" the man yelled from behind the desk. "Don't shoot. I'm not here to hurt you. Marvin sent me. He gave me a message so you would know I am who I say I am. Are you listening? Can we talk?"

Evie was suddenly paralyzed again. Could it be true? But what if it was another trick?

In her peripheral vision, she saw Dash roll to his knees. He picked up the table leg and stood. She wanted to check him, to touch him, to make sure he was all right. And tell him to hide again, to make himself small, there was another man with a gun.

But she had to stay focused. Panting, she managed to say, "Tell me. The message."

"Marvin told me to tell you that the Orioles should never have traded Machado to Los Angeles. I don't even know what that means, okay? But that's what Marvin told me to tell you."

Manny Machado had been Dash's favorite player with the Orioles. Marvin had given him Manny's walk-off home run ball when they'd first met. And Dash had been heartbroken when the Orioles had traded Manny to the Dodgers. No one else would have known all that. It had to be Marvin.

"Okay?" the man said again. "Can I come out?"

"Yes," Evie said, her hands beginning to shake. "But . . . slowly." She realized she was still on her knees and came to her feet. The moment she stood, a bolt of pain shot through her left ankle.

"I'm going to start with my hands," the man called back. "Okay? You'll see they're empty. And then the rest of me. Now I know you're scared. If you're pointing a gun toward me, please lower it, okay?"

"Let me see your hands first." She realized her voice was shaking now, too.

A pair of empty hands appeared above the desk. "Okay? Now it's your turn. Lower the gun. We don't want to have an accident."

She was suddenly suspicious. "How do you even know I'm pointing it at you?" she called out.

"Because I would be. Now listen. I'm going to move very slowly. But I want you to tell me first you're not pointing a gun at me."

She wanted to believe him so much. But she was afraid to. Still, as long as she could see his hands, it seemed safe to lower the gun.

A little.

She lowered it. "Okay," she said. "It's down. Not that much, though. So don't try anything funny."

The words sounded strange as they came out, like something she would have heard in a movie. She had an odd feeling of dissociation. Was any of this really happening?

The hands went higher. She could see arms. Then a pair of eyes. The eyes took in the way she was holding the gun. The man slowly stood. He was Asian. He wasn't big, but there was something . . . physical about him. As though he might be stronger than he looked. Or faster.

"Can you lower the gun more?" he said, his hands still up.

And then her urge to check on Dash overwhelmed her. She took her left hand off the gun and pulled Dash to her body, touching his head, his shoulders, his back. But he seemed barely to notice. His feet were planted solidly, and he held the table leg across his body with his right hand at the thin end and his left palm up under the fat end, like the sheriff in that movie *Walking Tall*. Her little boy was suddenly gone. She'd been protecting him, and now he was protecting her.

"Do you believe me?" the man said. "Can I come out from behind this desk?"

"Yes," she said, crying. "Yes." She couldn't sign with the gun, so she put it on the floor and explained to Dash what was happening. His eyes shifted from her hands to the man and back again.

The man stopped a respectful distance away. Evie signed, *Do you think he's telling the truth?*

Dash watched the man for a moment longer. Then he nodded.

Evie looked at the man. "Are there others?"

The man glanced at the doors. "I think it was just the two of them. If there had been more, they'd be here by now."

"What about our house?"

"I don't know about that."

"Then what do we do?"

"I think you have two choices. You can take your chances with the police. Or you can come with me."

Dash had been intent on the man's face while he'd been talking, reading his lips. He said, "You're Marvin's friend?"

"No," the man said. "A friend of a friend."

"What's your name?"

"Rain. Listen, I can't stay here. Your next move is up to you."

Dash looked at Evie. But not a searching look. Or a frightened or confused one. He nodded his head. And that decided it for her.

"All right," she said. "We're coming with you."

chapter
fifty

MAYA

Maya sat in the rear driver-side seat of the car, Frodo in her lap. Her forehead was pressed against the window, and she stared out as trees and signs and streetlamps went past. It reminded her of when she had been a girl, in the back of her parents' car. Just a passenger, secure that everything was fine and always would be, free to stare out the window, her mind wandering as the world rolled by, while her parents took care of her and everything else. Only now, the feeling of just being along for the ride was bewildering and anything but secure. She didn't even know where they were going, and almost didn't care. She thought of Ali, lying motionless on the ground, police tape and flashers all over the street. All of it felt exactly like a nightmare. Except she knew she wasn't dreaming.

She'd said hi to the woman and the boy when they got in the car, and the routineness of the interaction was itself deeply bizarre. The boy, sliding over to the middle seat, gave her a small wave, looked at Frodo, and said in a slightly strange voice, "He's cute." The woman came in behind the boy, nodded, and said hello. Frodo didn't bark, or even make a sound. He just licked Maya's face, trying with all his little might to make both of them feel better.

Rain stood by the door while the boy and the woman were getting in, and Maya had seen he was holding his pistol. Delilah reached across and opened Rain's door, and was pulling away the second he was in. Maya was no gunfighter, but she'd done the training at the Farm and knew the smell of gun smoke, and as soon as all the doors were closed, she recognized it. Rain had shot someone. The boy and the woman, who Maya could tell was his mother, started signing furiously. The boy must have been deaf. "What happened?" Delilah said, and Rain told her there had been two men waiting, and they were both dead now. And Maya had turned to the window.

They kept driving. Eventually they'd get somewhere. And maybe some of this would start to make sense.

"Hey," she heard Rain say. "We've got them all. Everyone's fine."

She looked over at him. He had placed a satellite hotspot on the dashboard, and was talking on a cellphone. Probably to Tom. She listened as he retold what had happened at the school. She turned away and stared out the window again.

"Yes," Rain said. "She's right here. Hold on." There was a pause, and he said, "Maya." She turned, and he held out the phone to her.

She didn't want to talk to Tom. Or anyone. She wanted to go to sleep. Or to wake up. Whatever it took for none of this to have happened.

But she took the phone. "Hello."

"You okay?" It was Tom, as she'd thought.

"Yeah."

"They're good people. They'll take care of you. No one's going to hurt you."

"I don't care." It sounded childish as she said it. But she felt like a child. Her eyes welled up. Frodo started licking the tears.

"Listen," he said. "I think I have a way to solve this. But I need your help. I'm sorry to ask you again, because your helping me is what put you in danger. And got Ali killed."

Maya's face scrunched up and a tiny whimper escaped her throat. Then the tears were coming and for a moment, she couldn't speak. She closed her eyes and sat there, silently shaking in a car full of strangers.

When she opened her eyes, the boy was holding a tissue, extended to her. She shook her head, embarrassed. She was such a wreck that a kid was trying to comfort her. "It's okay," he said, a little too loudly. "It's clean." And his expression was so earnest that Maya couldn't help but laugh, that he thought she didn't want the tissue because she was afraid it was used.

"Okay," she said. "Thank you."

"You're welcome. I have more if you need them. I have allergies."

"Okay. Thanks again."

He glanced at Frodo. "What's your dog's name?"

"Frodo."

"Like in *The Lord of the Rings*?"

"Yes."

Frodo barked, and the boy must have realized it because he laughed. "I'm Dash."

"Maya."

"Can I hold him?"

She nodded and handed him Frodo, who immediately began licking his face. He laughed again, obviously delighted.

Tom said, "Are you there?"

She wiped her eyes and blew her nose. Took a deep breath and let it out.

Then she said to Tom, "Tell me what you need."

chapter fifty-one

DEVEREAUX

Devereaux had given the contractors strict instructions to check in every thirty minutes. It had now been over an hour, and the only explanation was that something had gone wrong.

He took a swig of Mylanta straight from the bottle, grimacing at the powdery taste. His stomach was killing him, and he'd barely slept since this thing had begun. He'd always known there would be a price to pay for what he'd done, hadn't he? For the . . . temptation he'd succumbed to. He just hadn't imagined it would be this.

He leaned forward, put his elbows on the desk, and covered his face with his hands. There had to be a way to turn this around. There had to be.

He sat like that for a few minutes. His office, the mighty command center of America's entire intelligence community, had always seemed so secure to him. So stalwart. But now it felt flimsy. As though its walls were paper, about to be shredded, leaving him helpless and exposed, to be pulled down and torn apart from all sides.

When he opened his eyes, he saw activity on the police channel he was monitoring. Reports of a shooting. Montgomery County police officers dispatched to the deaf school. Two bodies, both white males.

He laughed, more sickened than shocked. Because of course. A woman and her teenaged deaf son. Against two ex-military contractors. They must have had help. But who? Manus, back from the West Coast?

But that was a question for later. What mattered now was that the leverage he had hoped to gain over Manus had just evaporated. He needed another move. A new plan.

Well, Plan A had been to prevent the videos from ever even seeing the light of day. Even after the texts he and Hobbs had received on the Mall, he'd still believed they could stop the release.

But now, he had to be realistic. He had to mitigate. Just in case.

Okay. He had half a dozen reporters who would print virtually anything he told them on background. Rispel had probably been playing him with her talk about the Russians and Chinese. He'd been so distraught at the time that he'd bought it. But it didn't matter if it was bullshit. The truth was, it was a good idea. There was no reason he shouldn't use it . . . and every reason he should.

But that was defense. Were there any other offensive plays left to him?

Rispel had been a step ahead of him so far. That much was clear. He had been a fool to take her gratitude, her loyalty, for granted. He should have foreseen the possibility that, confronted with the potential power of those videos, she would seek to acquire them for her own purposes.

Fine. But how had she been outplaying him?

She was closer to the action, of course. She reported to him, yes, but he knew from experience that being nearer the nuts and bolts of fieldwork had its advantages. A mayor was better positioned to address potholes than a governor.

But that didn't mean the governor was powerless. Far from it.

Devereaux had been DCI before Rispel. He'd been elevated, but his network was still there. The biggest change, really, was that his ability to reward and punish had been enhanced.

Rispel couldn't make big moves on her own. Whether for intel or for ops, she'd be moving pieces on the board. Asking for favors. And calling in some, too.

It wasn't so difficult to imagine who she'd be relying on. And in a game of threats and favors, it would be no contest. Rispel reported to him. He reported to the president of the United States. All it would take would be a reminder to certain key people—people who were already in his network, after all—of how grateful he would be to know if Rispel seemed to be up to anything unusual. And how displeased he would be to learn he had been kept in the dark.

He thought of the way she'd told him to sit, like she was talking to a dog. And threatened to have him escorted out—from what she called *her* building, no less.

Well, she'd had her fun. He hoped she'd enjoyed her little games. Because now she was going to find out exactly who she was playing with.

chapter
fifty-two

MANUS

Manus watched from the lobby of the Shenandoah University Health & Life Sciences Building as the cab turned around. He waited until it had left the parking lot and disappeared down the street. Then he headed out and started walking west. The morning sky was gray, the air cold and humid. It felt good to be outside after the long, sleepless flight.

Before Manus had left, Dox had said to him, "You saved my ass at the hotel. Don't think I don't know it, and don't think I'll forget. And if I'm ever in a position to return the favor, I hope you believe I will."

The strange thing was, Manus did believe him.

His cellphone was too risky to even turn on, let alone use, and Dox had given him the credentials to a secure site. After landing and clearing security at Dulles Airport, he'd borrowed a phone from a sympathetic barista—*I'm deaf, I lost my speech-to-text device, could I use your phone to access my account*—and had found a message. Evie and Dash were safe. They were with Rain, the man Dox had sent to protect them. They were in a room at the Winchester Hilton. Rain would be waiting in the hotel restaurant. Manus should use the same bona fides he had given Rain to use with Evie and Dash.

As worried as Manus still was, and as eager as he was to get to them, it would have been a mistake to have the driver take him to his actual destination. So he'd asked the man to drop him off at the university instead, and was now walking the half mile to the hotel, navigating with a paper map he'd bought at the airport. Route 50 was already thick with early rush-hour traffic, and he doubted another cab would even have saved time.

He reached the grounds of the hotel in a little over ten minutes and circled the parking lot. He didn't see any problems and went in through the restaurant entrance, head swiveling, alert to danger.

A young woman was standing by the door. She picked up a menu and said something, but Manus didn't catch it—he was too intent on the room. About half the tables were filled, mostly by solitary people absorbed in their electronic devices, obviously business travelers. In a corner table, back to the wall, sat an Asian man, a coffee mug before him but no electronic device. Manus's gaze almost skipped over the man because there was something so still about his presence. To someone else, the man might have seemed lost in thought. But Manus sensed something else: a person exceptionally attuned to his surroundings, his transmission dial set to bland, the reception dial wide open. A long-ago instructor had told Manus of a Zen concept called *mushin*—literally meaning "no-mind," but in fact a description of a relaxed mind, a mind open to everything and therefore able to instantly react to anything. He hadn't thought of the concept in years, but something about the man made him remember it now.

He glanced at the receptionist. She said, "Just one?"

Manus shook his head and looked at the Asian man again. "Meeting someone."

He walked forward, keeping his hands where the man could see them. The man kept his hands in plain sight, too, his fingertips resting on the table.

Manus stopped a couple of feet before he reached the man's position and stood off to the side. They'd been reassuring each other so far, and this was another way of doing so—not blocking the man's view of the room, leaving him space to maneuver. "The Orioles should never have traded Machado to Los Angeles," Manus said.

The man laughed. Manus was confused by the reaction. Then he saw why—a woman at the adjacent table had overheard, and had looked up at the incongruous greeting.

"I've been saying that forever," the man said. "Do we have time for a coffee? Or should we get going?"

"We should get going."

The man nodded. "Good enough." He finished what was in his mug, stood, and left some bills on the table.

Back out in the parking lot and around the corner of the restaurant, they stopped. The man said, "Manus?"

Manus nodded and checked their flanks. "Rain?"

"Yes."

"Are they okay?"

"They're fine. We had a problem, but they're fine."

Manus's heart was suddenly pounding. "A problem?"

"Earlier this morning. But really, they're fine. They're in a room inside, waiting for you."

For a moment, Manus had to focus on the word *fine*, which was being drowned out in his mind by the word *problem*.

"You . . . helped them?"

Rain nodded and did a quick scan of the lot. "But they did a good job of helping themselves. That's a brave boy you've got. Evie, too."

Did Rain think Dash was his son?

Manus was suddenly fighting back tears. This was all his fault. Something terrible could have happened, almost *did* happen . . .

They're fine. They're fine.

He was desperate to see them. But he dreaded having to explain.

A moment passed. When he felt more in control of himself, he said, "Thank you."

Rain nodded. "So you know, there are two more people in the room with them—a woman I'm with, named Delilah, and a young woman we're taking care of, named Maya. And Maya's dog. I'd suggest you and I go in one of the side entrances and I'll take you to them. Is that okay with you?"

Manus was impressed both by the man's calm and by his manners. Offering someone options was a good way to create confidence. Trying to hem someone in tended to cause suspicion, and suspicion between dangerous people could escalate fast. Having dealt with Dox, Manus wasn't surprised that Rain knew what he was doing. But it was reassuring regardless—especially because just hours earlier he'd entrusted Evie and Dash to this man's care. And knew now they might be alive because of it.

"Yes," Manus said. "Please."

Rain used a keycard to let them in through a side entrance. They took an internal staircase to the second floor. Halfway down the corridor, Rain stopped at a door and gave a single knock. The peephole was dark—probably they had covered it, to prevent anyone from knowing if someone inside was looking out.

The door opened. It was an attractive blonde, her right hand concealed behind her back. She must have been the woman Rain mentioned, Delilah. Manus, no longer suspicious, wasn't concerned. He was glad they were armed.

Dash and Evie were standing alongside one of the two twin beds. Dash was holding a small dog. He set the dog on the floor, ran over, threw his arms around Manus's back, and buried his face in his chest. Manus put his arms around the boy and looked at Evie, speechless. She smiled, then started crying. She walked over and hugged him, Dash in between them.

Manus looked around the room. He saw a young woman sitting in the desk chair—the one Rain had mentioned, Maya. A laptop was open in front of her and she was intent on it. He glanced back. The blonde—Delilah—had closed the door and was talking to Rain.

He could feel Dash shaking. He must have been crying. *They're fine,* he told himself. *They're fine.* But what had happened?

After a few moments, they disengaged. Dash wiped his face and began signing. A man had come for them at the school. Evie had hit him with a cart of books. And Dash had hit him with a table leg. Dash held up his hand so Manus could see he'd torn up his fingers getting the bolts loose so he could detach the leg. And then Evie had taken the man's gun and killed him. And Mr. Rain had killed another man. And then they came here. Manus looked from Dash's signing to Evie's face and back again, rocked by a storm of emotions.

As Dash finished relaying the story, Evie signed, *You should have seen him with that table leg. Our brave boy.*

This time, when Manus tried to suppress the tears, he couldn't.

Dash signed, *Why are you crying, Marvin?*

Because I'm proud of you. You protected your mom.

Dash smiled. *You would have protected her, too. Probably better than I did.*

But I didn't. He looked at Evie. *I put you in danger.*

Dash shook his head in confusion. *How?*

Manus no longer towered over Dash as he had when the boy had been younger, but it felt wrong to be looking down at him now. He squatted and met Dash's eyes. No, this wasn't a little boy before him. It was a strong young man. Who was old enough to make up his own mind. And Manus would have to live with what he decided. One way or the other.

Some people wanted me to do a bad thing. They told me if I didn't . . . they would tell you I used to be a bad man.

Dash shook his head again. *What bad thing?*

They wanted me to kill someone.

Dash's eyes widened. *Did you?*

Manus shook his head. *No.*

Then you're not a bad man.

239

But I was. I . . .

He stopped, his fingers frozen in a kind of purgatory. Then he forced himself to go on. *I did kill people before. For the government.*

I don't care about before.

You should.

Why?

For a moment, Manus was stuck for an answer. *I just . . . I thought you would.*

Not if you're good now. You are, aren't you?

Manus didn't want to lie to him. But he didn't know what was true, either.

I don't know.

But you won't kill anyone anymore, will you?

I will if they try to hurt you or your mom.

That's different. Anyway, don't you want to be good?

Manus thought for a moment. And then remembered what he had been thinking about in the park, just yesterday morning but seeming much longer ago.

I want to be . . . who you see when you look at me the way you are now.

Dash gave him a beautiful, unself-conscious smile. *That's easy. You already are.*

Manus wiped his face and tousled Dash's hair. Dash hugged him.

Manus looked at Evie and signed, *I'm sorry. I was so afraid . . . they would tell him. All of it. All the things I told you.*

She glanced at Dash, then back to Manus. She smiled. *You didn't have to worry. He loves you.*

Manus nodded and started crying again. He would have signed *I love him, too,* but he was holding Dash too tightly.

chapter
fifty-three

DOX

Dox was lying on the bed next to Labee, watching her face in the dim glow from the bathroom light. He wondered when he'd see her again after this thing was over. Maybe months. Maybe never. He'd put on a brave face when she'd been asking him all those questions, partly because he didn't want her to feel pressured, partly to protect his own dignity. But the truth was, it wasn't easy for him. He wanted to be with her. All the time. He'd never thought he'd reach a point where he wasn't interested in other women. But here he was. All that nonsense in the poems and songs and movies . . . It had happened to him.

And my God, it had been good just now, too. He'd been thinking about it for a while, how maybe his natural protectiveness for her was blinding him to her needs. Not that she required protecting, by him or anyone else. It was just that knowing her history, and the way she had entrusted it to him . . . It made him look at her a certain way. But he was glad he'd gotten past that.

Maybe it was foolish to worry about what would happen next. Life was short, and he was with her now. And if he ever had a chance at the end of his life to think back to the most magical times, he knew this would be one of them. Lying in this bed, watching her beautiful, sleeping face, and wondering at the strangeness of it all. He was glad he understood how special the moment was now, that it wouldn't be only in retrospect.

She opened her eyes and looked at him. "Hey."

He reached out and touched her cheek. "Hey there. I thought you were sleeping."

She sighed. "On and off. You're not?"

"Almost. It was an eventful day."

She closed her eyes and smiled. "That's one way to put it."

"Eventful night, too."

"Mmm."

"Was it good like that?"

She opened her eyes and looked at him. God, she was so lovely in this light, half-awake, half-asleep. "You know it was," she said.

"You know, you can tell me. If there are things you want to do."

"I think it works better when you figure it out on your own."

"Oh. Well, you could give me some hints."

"You don't think I have been?"

He couldn't help laughing at that. "Oh, shit. I hate when I'm dumb."

She smiled and touched his cheek the way he liked. "But apparently not ineducable."

They were quiet for a moment. She said, "You going to sleep?"

"Yeah, in a few. I just like looking at you. I don't get so many opportunities."

"I'm sorry."

"No, I didn't mean it that way. I mean . . . I'm too happy to go to sleep. I don't want to waste it."

"That's nice."

"Just the truth."

"You know," she said, "if you're really going to be up, might be worth checking the secure site. It's morning on the East Coast. Rain and Delilah have probably landed, and Kanezaki might have found something."

"Yeah, that's a good point. Tell you what. You doze off if you like, and I'll lie here looking at you for another minute or so. Then I'll check the site."

She smiled and closed her eyes. "Wake me if there's anything."

He watched her for a little while longer. It would have been nice to just drop off lying next to her, but she was right: better to check the site first just in case.

He set up the satellite hotspot in front of the window and used a burner to log in. There was a message from Kanezaki: I know where they have Schrader.

Well, shit. So much for the rest of their idyllic night in the Silver Cloud Inn.

LARISON

Larison was dozing in a chair he'd carried to the corner of the room near the door, the Glock in his hand. He hadn't wanted to alarm Diaz, but she'd taken the precaution in stride. In fact, after hearing his explanation, she'd dragged one of the mattresses off the box frame and onto the floor. "If someone breaches a room," he'd told her, "you don't want to be in the first place they look. Randomness can buy you a second. And if you don't think a second's a long time, you've never been in a gunfight."

There was a soft tap at the door, and he was instantly awake. He stood, padded over, and looked through the peephole. It was Dox and Livia. He checked his watch. Not quite six.

He unbolted and opened the door. "Everything all right?"

"Fresh intel," Dox said quietly. "Sorry to wake you."

"I don't sleep. Come on in."

He closed and bolted the door behind them. Diaz was already awake and sitting up. "Is everything okay?" she said.

"Everything's fine," Livia said. "New information from Kanezaki. He located Schrader. We need to decide what to do about it."

"Bunking down on the floor," Dox said to Diaz. "I see you've been taking lessons from Mr. Larison. And let me tell you, you could do a lot worse for a teacher."

They pulled the mattress back onto the box spring and sat across from each other on the two beds, Dox next to Livia, Larison next to Diaz. "First of all," Dox said, "John and Delilah landed outside Washington. Manus made it back, too. John and Delilah ran into some opposition picking up Manus's woman, Evie, and his boy, Dash, but they're all together and everyone's fine."

"Opposition?" Diaz said. "You mean that UPS driver Manus was worried about?"

Dox nodded. "Apparently so. There were two of them, and when they couldn't find Manus's people at his house, they showed up looking for them at the school where Evie teaches and Dash is a student. Sounds like John got there just in time, though I gather Evie and Dash acquitted themselves well. Anyway, now it's two fewer we're up against, and that's always good. But the main thing now is Schrader. Whoever took him is holding him in a house. In a place called Lake Tapps."

Diaz looked at Livia. "That's twenty miles from here."

Livia nodded. "That's right."

"What do we do?" Diaz said. "Call the marshals?"

"That's one possibility," Livia said. "We're considering something else."

Larison had a notion of what *something else* might be. He doubted he was going to like it. "What do we know about where he's being kept?" he said.

"It's just an Airbnb place," Dox said. "Detached single-family house, backed by woods, rented yesterday morning."

"Who's guarding him?"

"Three men. We don't know their backgrounds, but we can assume they're capable."

Larison didn't respond to that. It was his habit to assume everyone was capable, until after he'd killed them. "Countermeasures?"

"No way to be sure, but unlikely to be anything extensive. Feels like a hurry-up operation."

"Hmmm," Larison said. "That sounds familiar."

Dox laughed. "Fair. Still, it's good to get a little corroboration that busting Schrader out of jail was a Plan B. We're not the only ones improvising here."

Larison wouldn't have admitted it, but he liked being around Dox because, in addition to being extremely capable, the man was always cheerful. Even when—especially when—the shit hit the fan. But at the moment he seemed a little too eager. Larison figured he must have gotten laid. He wasn't picking up anything from Livia, but she tended to be more of a closed book. Well, he was happy for them. But that had nothing to do with the matter at hand.

Diaz looked at Dox. "How does Kanezaki know this?"

"You promise not to tell anyone?" Dox said, his expression mock-serious.

Diaz nodded.

Dox shrugged. "Okay, I'd call that officially top-secret cleared. So here's the deal. To keep us all safe, the government developed a program called Guardian Angel. It was originally called God's Eye, but that upset the civil libertarians among us, so the people behind the program changed the name. The government always starts off with bad names, I don't know why. Carnivore, Total Information Awareness . . . I mean, the Defense Department was originally called the War Department, which seemed to be giving people the idea it was responsible for fighting wars or something. And then—"

"How does Kanezaki know?" Larison said. He was familiar with Dox's occasionally discursive style.

"Right, right. Anyway, Guardian Angel sucks in all the electronic exhaust we modern humans emit in our daily lives—what we search for on the Internet, use credit cards for, who we call, who we associate with, where our cellphones go . . . everything. It's how old Rispel knew you like to jog in the morning at Freeway Park."

"Jesus," Diaz said.

"Yeah, it's a powerful tool, no doubt. But Kanezaki has a young tech whiz—Maya, the one whose friend got killed last night—who built some kind of back door into the system, so Kanezaki could see what other people were searching for, and particularly what searches were getting deleted in violation of what passes for the law these days. That's how he uncovered the plot to take you out, and how he knew to send Larison and me in to foil it."

Diaz shook her head. "I can't believe this shit goes on."

"I know, it's a lot to get your head around. But like Blade said, 'The world you live in is just a sugar-coated topping.'"

Diaz looked at him, obviously not getting the reference.

"A movie," Larison said. "Wesley Snipes. Telling a human about vampires."

Dox smiled. "This is one of the reasons I like partnering with you, amigo. John never gets my cinematic references. I mean, you were the only one in the room who was with me that time when I did Cleavon Little. If you hadn't laughed, we'd probably all be dead right now."

"It was pretty funny."

"Thank you."

"You want to finish explaining how Kanezaki got this intel?"

"Right. Well, Maya got back into the system remotely. I don't know all the details, but according to Kanezaki, using Guardian Angel to maximum effect is as much an art as it is a science, and he says Maya is quite the artist. She used cellphone data, satellite imagery, Bayesian probability, and who knows what else. Apparently Evie helped—she was some kind of tech wizard at NSA. But the gist of it is, they have three guys holding Schrader right now in a house just twenty miles from here. And the question is, what do we do about it?"

"Why do we need to do anything?" Larison said. He knew the question might come across as aggressive. He didn't care. He liked to test people. If they folded from a little pushing, what would they do when they were being shot at?

Livia looked at him. "What do you propose instead?"

"I'm not sure I'm proposing anything. They'll torture Schrader, and either they'll get what they want from him, or they won't. Either way, it plays out and the storm passes. I mean, Diaz isn't in danger anymore. That was only when she was going to prosecute Schrader."

"I don't want this to be about me," Diaz said.

"Fine," Larison said. "We can make it about me."

"Nobody's keeping you here," Livia said.

Not for the first time, Larison admired her balls. "I never said otherwise. But here's the way I see it. If you call the marshals and they recover Schrader, we're right back where we started, with Diaz a target. And maybe all the publicity about Schrader's release and recapture will offer some protection in that regard, but maybe it won't. Or we can just do nothing. Schrader's the focus now. The people holding him will either get control of the videos, or the videos will be uploaded. And Schrader is toast either way. Why do we care?"

Diaz looked at him. "You don't care about powerful men trafficking children?"

That annoyed him. "What, are you going to try to shame me now? You know what these two are about to pitch, right? The three of us go to this house, kick down some doors, get in a gunfight, and drag Schrader out, sirens howling behind us." He looked at Dox and Livia. "Is that about right?"

"Hopefully absent the sirens," Dox said. "With surprise and violence of action, I think we could be in and out faster than that."

"Oh, well, that's great. Count me in, then. These things always work according to plan. I mean, look at how it went in the park yesterday."

"Look," Dox said, "I'm not saying we didn't have to adapt—"

"'Adapt'? If Manus had reacted a second earlier, that fucking sword he carries would have a new sheath. Your body."

Dox grinned. "That's why I had us hold hands. Told you it would work."

Larison shook his head. Fucking Dox. There was just no arguing with him. It could be endearing, but it could make you crazy, too.

"I don't know how to kick down doors," Diaz said. "So I can't help you. I would if I could. For what it's worth, I say we call the marshals. I have a case and I want to prosecute. I'm not afraid of the risks."

Larison looked at her. It would have been easier if he didn't like her.

"You should be," he said. "You have no idea how lucky you got yesterday."

"You're wrong," she said. "I do know. I'm just not going to let it stop me."

"Christ," Larison said, "am I the only person in this crew who ever makes any sense?"

"Maya and Evie uncovered plenty more," Dox said. "How about if I finish the briefing, and then everyone can offer somewhat more informed opinions."

No one said anything, and he went on. "It turns out that yesterday evening Washington time, a series of text messages and emails were simultaneously delivered to a whole passel of powerful men. Captains of industry, politicians, Director of National Intelligence Pierce Devereaux, and—wait for it—our very own attorney general, Uriah Hobbs."

"Holy shit," Larison said. "The dead-man switch?"

Livia nodded. "It's real."

Larison looked at her. "What were the messages?"

"Nothing incriminating this time," Livia said. "Just photos of empty rooms. Guest rooms. Maya matched them to archived real-estate advertisements. They're all in Schrader's houses. And a text, warning that the next message will have people in it, and will be widely disseminated."

Larison tried to think it through. "The shot across the bow Schrader told Diaz about."

"Exactly," Dox said. "And the people who got those messages got the message. 'You better get me out of prison right quick if you don't want video of you raping little girls all over the Internet.'"

Larison considered. "We know who Schrader is threatening now. So we can infer—"

"Right," Dox said. "My guess is, after Hamilton had her meeting with Hobbs, Hobbs went to Devereaux. Devereaux went to Rispel. And Rispel went to us—through Kanezaki, of course."

That made sense to Larison. "Can Maya and Evie reverse-engineer the distribution? See what servers the videos reside on, that kind of thing?"

Dox shook his head. "I asked the same question. Apparently it's architected in some super-distributed way, and routed through Tor."

"Fine," Larison said. "But look, this reinforces what I was saying before. The bad news is, the opposition is even more formidable than we'd feared. But the good news is, there really is a dead-man switch. Either Schrader gives up those videos, and we're off the hook, or they get released, and we're off the hook. What am I missing?"

"A conscience?" Livia said.

Mostly shit like that didn't bother Larison. But that one did.

He looked at her. "You know," he said evenly, "there's a lot we don't know about each other, Livia. The difference is, I don't pretend to know. And I don't judge you based on the pretense."

"Hold on," Dox said. "Everybody hold on." He turned to Livia. "I know where you're coming from, and you know I respect it. But you can't talk to people like that. Larison's right. You don't know him. Just like he doesn't know you. And if we fall into the habit of thinking the worst of each other instead of being generous, the Hobbses and Rispels and Schraders of the world won't have to kill us. We'll do it for them. So let's all just take a deep breath, keep talking, and most of all keep listening to each other. Okay?"

Larison appreciated the support. He'd seen Dox back Livia before and was glad it wasn't just a reflex. "The Cleavon Little version was better," he said. "But thanks."

Dox laughed. They were all quiet for a moment. Livia looked at Larison and said, "I'm sorry."

She was a proud, prickly person, and maniacal when it came to protecting children. Larison knew the apology wasn't easy for her. "Don't worry about it," he said. "But look, I still don't understand the plan. Yeah, if the intel is good, we could kick down the door, shoot some people, and drag out Schrader. We could take that risk. Hopefully none of us would get killed in the process. But for what? What's the upside, compared to doing nothing?"

Livia started to say something, but Dox, maybe worried she might be impolitic again, jumped in. "If those videos get released, it's not just the men in them who'll be all over the Internet. It'll be their victims. That's a whole lot of innocent lives permanently ruined."

The truth was, Larison didn't care. He didn't know the girls. He didn't know the circumstances. And while he might feel sorry for them in the abstract, it wasn't enough to motivate him to risk his life. And if Livia wanted to judge him for that, she just wasn't thinking clearly. He didn't see her on a crusade to feed the hungry or house the homeless or whatever. As far as he was concerned, everyone had their own shit, picked their own battles, and did their own cost-benefit ratios.

But there was no point in having that argument. So all he said was "All right. What about an anonymous tip to the Marshal Service? How would that hurt these girls?"

"I had the same thought," Livia said. "The problem is, one, we don't know how soon they'd go in. If they wait, Schrader's dead-man switch could upload something more damaging than the initial warning. And two, whenever they go in, they'd be going in as law enforcement. Playing by rules that could wind up with Schrader dead—either in the crossfire, or by action of whoever's holding him. It sounds safer, but it's not."

Larison wasn't buying it. "You just don't trust anyone else."

She looked at him. "Do you?"

It was a fair question, and there was no point in answering it. "I still don't see the endgame," he said. "Even if we break Schrader out, Hamilton says he has to operate the system himself. From one of his houses. His own voice. Now maybe you could record his voice and that would work, though maybe not, and if it didn't, you wouldn't have a lot to fall back on. So what we're talking about is his live voice, presumably reciting a secret phrase, and with no stress in it. How are you going to overcome all that? In the end, that dead-man switch is just going to do what it was made to do."

"Kanezaki can get us drugs," Dox said. "Beta blockers and other anti-anxiety agents."

"You're shitting me," Larison said.

"Nope. He says CIA has studied this kind of thing, and that with enough Klonopin and Propranolol, Schrader could have a shotgun to his head and there'd be as much stress in his voice as if he were dozing in his favorite recliner."

Larison shook his head. "Your tax dollars at work."

"So if we can get him out," Dox said, "and get him to one of his houses, and give him a beta-blocker cocktail, we can reset the system. And buy Maya and Evie time to figure out how to take control of it."

Larison still didn't see it. "To what end?"

"One possibility is evidence," Livia said. "In court, those videos will be sealed. The girls' images, their identities—it can all be protected."

"Come on," Larison said. "Look what the powers that be did when Diaz had Schrader arrested. And now you're talking about, what, prosecuting the attorney general? The director of National Intelligence? What country do you think you're living in?"

"There's another possibility," Dox said. "In my opinion, a better one."

"What?" Larison said. "Build a time machine and stop all this before it even happened?"

"Maya and Evie," Livia said. "If they can scrub out the girls' faces, we can release those videos ourselves."

The room was quiet for a moment. Larison looked at Livia. "You'd be okay with that?"

She made a fist and the knuckles cracked. "More than okay."

Larison thought about it more. It was elegant, he had to admit. Audacious. And had just the right amount of *fuck-you* frisson. "If it could be done," he said, "it could solve a lot of problems."

"And not just ours," Dox said.

They were all quiet again. The more Larison considered, the more he liked it.

"Maybe Kanezaki can get us armor," he said.

No one responded.

He shrugged and added, "I mean, if we're going to be kicking down doors, I'd like to be wearing something thicker than just my rain parka."

Livia looked at him. "Then you're in?"

"I guess so," Larison said. He shook his head. "Release the videos ourselves. I mean, what kind of plan is that?"

Dox smiled. "The chaos kind."

chapter
fifty-five

DOX

They drove in the minivan, Diaz behind the wheel. Dox would have preferred Livia, who was their best driver, but they needed three shooters. So when Diaz volunteered, even Larison's protests were pro forma. And regardless, Diaz had quickly put those to bed by pointing out that she'd been driving even before she had a license, and learned how on the streets of Washington Heights and the Bronx. "You have your credentials," she'd said to Larison, "and I have mine," earning herself a nod and a respectful smile from the angel of death himself.

Kanezaki had given them the coordinates of where to pick up the gear they needed, and told Dox his contact would be the same person who'd supplied him the last time he'd been in the area. Dox remembered a black woman so grandmotherly she was about the last person he would have made for an operator. That time she'd been waiting in a coffee shop, but this morning the pickup would be on the side of the road, along a stretch of the city known locally as the Jungle because, Livia explained, it was impenetrably forested, home to countless homeless encampments, and largely impervious to the local government's authority.

Diaz knew the exact spot—a street called Beacon Avenue South, just east of I-5. It was getting light as they crossed the overpass, and Dox could see how the area had earned its name. There was something primeval about it, brambles and pine needles and swirling, thick mist, a serpentine carpet of green that made the support pylons of the elevated roads above it look weak and temporary by comparison. Here and there, nylon tents and garbage piles appeared amid the vegetation like hilltops breaking through fog, but their presence only emphasized how much more was likely hidden.

Fifty yards beyond the overpass, Diaz did a U-turn and pulled over. Dox got out and crossed the road, his breath fogging in the still, moist air. He stopped to listen. Morning birdsong. Traffic from the nearby interstate. A dog barking in the distance. He looked around and on both sides of the road saw nothing but green. It was strange—to the northwest, he could see the cityscape of downtown Seattle, but where he stood, everything felt entirely rural.

The drop-off had been set in motion too recently for anyone to have had a real chance at an ambush, but still he had the Wilson in hand inside his jacket as he walked along the shoulder. In less than a minute he saw her, sitting on a tarp just below the guardrail. If he hadn't been looking, he would have gone right by.

"Oh, it's you again," she said. "Tom told me."

He nodded, amazed. He recognized her face, but . . . last time she had looked like a well-fed grandmother. Now she was dressed in filthy rags and seemed . . . well, not emaciated, but at least in need of a square meal. "I guess we don't need the bona fides anymore," he said, glancing around. "Pardon me, ma'am, but are you all right?"

She smiled, and for a second she looked the way he remembered. "Sonny, I don't know where you went to school, but didn't they teach you to blend?"

"I like to think so, yes, but not as well as they must have taught you."

She laughed at that. "Well, thank you."

"You sure you're all right? You don't need a ride or anything?"

"Oh, I'm not nearly as helpless as I look. If you keep walking, ten yards up, right under the guardrail, you'll see a large olive duffel bag. It has everything on your shopping list. You know, I'm always expecting you to ask for a sniper rifle, but you never do."

This time it was his turn to laugh. "Tom's been talking about me, has he?"

"A little."

"Well, he's right. I do prefer gunfights to be conducted at a proper distance, but circumstances don't always oblige. You mind my asking how you're able to get ahold of such great toys on such short notice?"

"I do, actually. A woman should have her secrets."

He shook his head, amazed. "That's fair. Please understand, I was asking out of sincere admiration."

"I know you were. Now, you should go. Good luck to you, always. Maybe we'll get to meet again."

"I hope so," he said. Then he smiled and added, "I think you could teach me a thing or two."

She returned the smile. "I'm way too old for you to flirt with, young man. But thank you anyway."

Had he been flirting with her? He hadn't meant to. Or had he? He gave her a little bow and walked off.

A minute later, he was back in the car and they were moving again. They distributed the contents of the bag. Modular breach charges and tape. KDH Magnum TAC-1 vests. Suppressors. Armor-piercing rounds—9 millimeter for Livia and Larison, .45 for Dox. Tactical gloves. Pry bar. Flashbang grenades. Hemostatic bandages and other medical supplies. Bolt cutters, in case Schrader was chained to a wall. Flexties. And a backpack-carried, Agency-issue multispectrum Technical Surveillance Countermeasures unit, which could detect microphones, cameras, and pretty much anything else that bled an electronic signature from up to fifty feet out, through a Bluetooth-connected pair of binoculars.

While Diaz drove, the three of them geared up. Dox hated that Livia was going in with them. He knew what kind of shooter she was—better than he was with a pistol, truth be told, which was saying something, though not as good as Larison—but the whole point of bringing in Larison and stopping Manus was to keep Livia out of this, not to drag her deeper in. But that ship had sailed. The best thing he could do now was to get on his game face, drop everyone in that house, and come out with Schrader.

The Airbnb website had been a big help, given that they included numerous photos of the property, interior and exterior. The plan was to approach through the woods behind the house, use the TSCM gear to confirm no cameras or other electronic countermeasures, and then for Larison to use the external stairs to a second-story porch, where he would use the breach charge to blow a hole in a wall while Dox and Livia went in through a first-floor window, preceded by a flashbang. They'd sweep the house, neutralize the opposition, and hustle Schrader out.

That was the plan, anyway. How it went would likely be another story.

chapter fifty-six

LIVIA

W hile Carl was picking up the gear, Livia connected her phone through Carl's satellite hotspot and called B. D. Little, a contact with Homeland Security Investigations. Not long before, she'd helped him solve the crime that had changed the course of his life—the loss of his teenaged daughter. They knew each other's secrets. He was one of the few people she trusted.

He laughed when he heard her voice. "Been reading the news from out there," he said. "I had a feeling I might hear from you."

She smiled at that. "How've you been?"

"Better. Thanks to you."

"I need a favor."

"Anything."

"You heard about Andrew Schrader?"

He laughed again. "Yeah. Busted out of prison. Like I said, I had a feeling I might hear from you."

"I might need to pay a visit to his Bainbridge Island house. I need to know whether it's being watched. The Marshal Service, FBI, whoever. Can you find out?"

"That's easy," he told her. "We have a central database now. I can check other federal law enforcement deployments right from my desk. Can you hold on?"

"Of course."

It took him only a few minutes. "It's clear," he said. "My guess is, it's such an obvious place, no one thinks he'd be stupid enough to go there. Besides which, there's so much interagency finger-pointing on his escape I bet no one's even put together a coherent plan for recapture. I can monitor things and let you know if anything changes."

"Yes. Please."

"You need anything else?"

"Not right now."

"I wish you did."

"Well, it's only right now. It could change."

He laughed. "Let me know," he said. "And good hunting."

Livia had Diaz pull into White River Amphitheater, a place for open-air concerts with a large dirt parking area separated by a short stretch of woods from the house where Schrader was being held. Larison set out wearing the TSCM gear while the rest of them waited.

"Wish we'd gotten the intel just a couple hours earlier," Carl said, double-checking a backpack with the flashbangs, bolt cutters, and medical supplies inside. "It'd still be dark now. Call me crazy, but I think this kind of job goes down better under cover of darkness."

Livia gave him a small smile. It had been a good night. But he needed to set aside the afterglow. "Stop worrying about me."

For a second, she thought he was going to argue. Instead, he nodded and said, "Told you you're getting to know me well."

"Remember," she added, "I've probably breached more houses than you."

He scowled. "All right, you've made your point."

"I'll be fine. And you'll be right behind me."

"I hate that I'm going in after you. Bad enough you made me ride in the damn rear on the motorcycle in Pattaya. Now this."

"I'm a smaller target. And a better shot. You toss the flashbang, clear the glass, we check, you cover me, I go in, then you. It's a good plan."

She knew that was as much lecturing as he could take. But she was still concerned. She'd seen how cool he typically was in the face of danger. His nervousness now was a measure of how attached he'd gotten. She didn't mind. She'd gotten pretty attached herself, though she found ways to fight it. But right now, they had a job to do.

They sat in silence, scoping the parking lot through the windows. After a few minutes, she saw Larison jogging through the woods in their direction. She slid open the passenger-side door and he got in.

"Good to go," he said. He pulled off the backpack and tossed the accompanying goggles in the foot well next to it. "No countermeasures. And the curtains are all drawn. I didn't see anyone looking out. Still, with three guys, they'd have to be pretty incompetent to not post at least one sentry. If we come in from the southwest side, we'll have less than twenty feet of open ground to cover from the woods to the back of the house. If someone's looking through those curtains when we move, they'll spot us. If we take fire, I'll cover our retreat to the woods and then you cover me. We good?"

"We're good," Carl said. He pulled on the backpack with the flash-bangs and other gear.

Larison looked at Livia and she repeated it. "We're good."

"See you in five," he said to Diaz. "Keep that engine running."

"I'll be here," she said.

They headed out, the sun coming up behind them. Livia couldn't deny that Carl had a point. The woods were thick, but she didn't like the twenty feet of open ground Larison had described. Even if they were seen, they'd probably make it to cover before anyone could mount an effective defense. But they would have lost the element of surprise. It all would have been easier in the dark, with night-vision goggles. Well, you couldn't have everything.

At the edge of the woods, they paused, scanned, and listened. Nothing but birdsong.

Larison looked at them. They nodded. He turned and fast-walked to the corner of the house. Livia and Carl aimed at the windows, ready to return fire if anyone spotted him coming. But everything stayed quiet.

Livia went next, joining Larison at the corner of the house. A few seconds later, Carl pulled up alongside her. Larison headed silently up the stairs. When he was in position, Livia and Carl moved laterally to the near first-floor window. Livia stopped at the edge. Carl got down low and elbow-crawled underneath it. When he was past, he stood on the other side.

They couldn't see Larison from here, but she knew what he was doing: unrolling the modular breach charges. Taping them to the wall. Retreating down the stairs. When she and Carl heard the boom, they'd break the window and toss in the flashbang. Carl would sweep any remaining glass and cover the room, and in she'd go. People in the area would hear the breach charge explosion and maybe the flashbang, too, but even if anyone called 911, by the time first responders were on the scene, the three of them would be gone, Schrader along with them.

Minutes seemed to go by, but Livia knew it was less than that. Her heart was hammering now. The waiting, the anticipation, was always the worst part. Made even harder now because when to go in wasn't up to her. She wasn't even waiting for a signal as such. Their signal would be a sudden boom.

They waited. She could see past Carl and everything was quiet. She was glad he had her back the same way. Now it was just a question of—

BOOM!

Without a second's hesitation, Carl smashed the glass with the pry bar, pulled the pin from the flashbang, and tossed it in. Another *boom!* came from the room within, along with a gigantic flash of light. Carl drew the Wilson, swept back the curtain, and aimed inside, left, center, right. He raked the remaining glass out of the frame with the pry bar and shouted, "Clear!" Livia put her free hand on the bottom pane and vaulted in, landing in a crouch and sweeping the room with the muzzle of the Glock. There was smoke from the flashbang but nothing else—just a couch and chairs and a flat-panel monitor. She yelled, "Clear!" and dashed ahead to the side of the room's open door.

Carl hit the floor behind her and raced to the other side of the door. She heard loud shots from the second floor—*BAM! BAM!*—and then a quieter answering volley. But there was no time to worry about Larison. They had the entire first floor still ahead of them—

Another *BAM!,* from the other side of the door, louder than a pistol shot. Carl staggered. She looked and saw a huge hole in the wall. Someone had shot through the other side—from the sound and the size of the hole, a shotgun. She felt a surge of fear and rage. She calculated the angle by instinct, aimed at the wall, and fired eight times in a wide pattern. There was a cry from the other side. She bolted through the door into a kitchen. There, to the right, a man with a pistol-grip shotgun. His shoulder was bloody—she must have hit him there—and his right arm was dangling. He grimaced and tried to bring up the muzzle one-handed. Livia put three rounds in his chest. He dropped the shotgun and fell backward into the dining room.

She spun. To her left were two closed doors that she knew from the Airbnb site went to a rec room and to the garage. Straight ahead were the stairs to the second floor. To her right, the dining room—

She didn't even hear it. It was more a feeling, or an instinct. She spun. She saw a man flash-check past the doorjamb. She fired three rounds through the wall and dove behind a counter. The wood looked cheap and she doubted it would provide much cover, especially against another shotgun. She pressed against the wall, dropped the magazine, and slapped in a spare. Had she hit him? She wasn't sure. And the angles here were bad. If she popped up, he'd know her position after she dropped back down. If she scuttled left, it would make for an awkward shot.

She heard three more pistol shots from upstairs. Then a much louder one—*BAM!*—from the other side of the room. In the same instant, a giant hole appeared in the cabinet next to her. Wood and porcelain shards sprayed past her.

Fuck, shotgun—

She popped up before he could rack the slide, a distant part of her mind praying it was pump-action, not semiauto—

She put the sights on center mass and pressed the trigger. She hit him. Fire erupted from the shotgun muzzle, and the cabinet to her left exploded.

Fuck, semiauto—

She kept firing, putting three more rounds into him. He got off two more shots, but he was firing wildly now, his body jerking and flinching from being hit. Her last shot caught him in the neck. A geyser of blood erupted. He tripped over the body in the dining room and went down.

She wanted to go to Carl, but she had to use whatever surprise and confusion they had left. These guys were better armed than they were. She couldn't risk getting pinned down again—her best hope was speed and mobility.

She heard more shots from upstairs. Either Larison was having a protracted gunfight with a single shooter, or Kanezaki's estimate of three men was badly off.

Come on, Livia, move—

She raced out into the hallway. Clear. No one on the stairs.

Where the fuck is Schrader?

The garage or the rec room. Had to be one or the other.

She turned and saw the garage door open a crack. A face peeked through it. She fired twice. The rounds hit the door and it slammed closed. She stepped offline, but before she could get off another round, a fusillade of fire erupted through the door. Rounds punched through the air to her left and slammed into the wall behind her. Shards of the garage door flew through the air. What was left looked like shredded paper.

She dove back into the kitchen, primally terrified. She heard another burst of fire. The guy must have decided it was safer to finish shredding the door instead of trying to open it.

How many rounds was that? Fifteen? More?

Must have been a magazine-fed automatic shotgun. She guessed an AA-12.

She got to her feet and dashed through the kitchen. She saw Carl coming in from the room they'd first entered.

"That's an AA-12!" she shouted.

"I know! Go, go!"

She tore into the dining room, leaping over the two bodies. The shooter had probably already swapped magazines. These walls would be as much cover as paper.

She turned. Carl was behind her, wrestling the refrigerator away from the wall. He must have been supercharged with adrenaline because he got his arms around it, lifted—

The man with the shotgun raced to the edge of the kitchen. She saw the weapon—the AA-12—

—drum-fed, are you fucking kidding me?—

He raised it—

Carl spun and got the refrigerator facing the other way. A staccato series of shots rang out—*BAMBAMBAMBAMBAMBAMBAM!*— and the refrigerator was jolted by repeated impacts. Carl dropped it. It landed with a thud and he dove to the side. Several slugs made it through, slamming into the wall behind them.

Livia gripped his shoulder and leaned close. "Distract him," she whispered fiercely. Before he could respond, she raced out to the living room. She stopped at the edge of the hallway, her heart hammering.

Come on, come on . . .

She heard a series of pistol shots from the dining room. And an answering series of reverberating cannon shots from the AA-12. She stepped around the corner, saw him, put the sights on center mass—

He must have picked her up in his peripheral vision. He started to turn, the AA-12 spinning around—

She pressed the trigger, hitting him. He flinched and jerked. She kept shooting, walking the shots in, firing continuously, putting six rounds into his body and a final one in his head. He fell face-forward, hitting the carpet with a meaty *thud*, the shotgun landing next to him.

Carl ran up behind her, the Wilson at chin level. They backed up against each other so they had 360-degree coverage, Livia facing the kitchen, Carl facing the stairs.

"You okay?" Livia said.

"Yeah, took the round in the vest. But you might need to minister to my bruises later."

"Schrader. He could be in the garage, but I'm guessing the rec room."

"One thing at a time," he said. Then he bellowed, "Larison! You still with us?"

Two shots rang out in response, followed by two louder ones in return.

"Damn it," he said, "he must be pinned down."

"Yeah, by another shotgun."

"Sounds like it. Cover me. Always wanted to play with one of those drum-fed AA-12s. Saw the videos on YouTube."

He went to the guy Livia had dropped, picked up the shotgun, checked the magazine, and ran to the bottom of the stairs. Livia went to the other side. She pointed the Glock at the top and nodded.

He took the stairs three at a time. Livia had been expecting him to move quietly, but apparently he was more interested in speed. She checked behind, then raced up after him. He reached the top and three shots rang out. Instantly he was proned out on the stairs. She crouched down alongside him, covering the top landing with the Glock. The walls were pockmarked with bullet holes.

"Larison!" Carl bellowed. "We're right here, with some heavy artillery we picked up. Can you fall back and get out of the way?"

"What the hell are you doing?" Livia whispered. They had the guy pinned down from both sides. Why tell him which side the attack was going to come from?

"Give me a three count," Larison yelled back.

"One," Carl yelled. "Two. Three!"

Three pistol shots rang out from ahead of them. Carl jumped up, shouldered the AA-12, and let loose a thunderclap of continuous fire. Livia ran past him to the edge of the landing and aimed the Glock, but it was too late—Larison was standing in the doorway at the end of the hall, and the shooter was on the ground, half in and half out of a doorway, his face and torso shredded, a shotgun lying next to him. Livia swept the muzzle of the Glock from side to side, searching for movement, but there was nothing, only gun smoke.

"Was that the only one?" Carl said.

"Just the one," Larison said, his gun up, the muzzle tracking as he searched left and right.

"Then it's zero," Carl said, "'cause this one is dead."

Livia realized she hadn't been giving them credit for knowing each other's moves. Carl hadn't been telling Larison to move. He'd been drawing the shooter's attention, giving Larison a chance to get the drop on him.

They went down the stairs, Livia in the lead, Larison behind her, Carl bringing up the rear with the AA-12. Livia didn't know whether there were any others, and her instinct was to slow things down. Speed and surprise had gotten them this far. Care and control were how they would see it through.

They checked the garage first. There were two cars, and it took them a minute to make sure the interiors were empty and the area was clear. Carl put his hand on one hood, then the other.

"This one's warm," he said. "Got here not long ago. Maybe to pass off Schrader, or to change shifts, or whatever. Probably why Tom's intel about their numbers was off."

They moved back through the house, fanning out near the door to the rec room. "Give me that shotgun," Larison whispered to Carl. "And go back out. When you hear shooting, put another flashbang through the window."

Carl nodded. He handed the AA-12 to Larison and went out. Larison holstered his Glock. He looked at Livia and smiled. "We having fun yet?"

She didn't see the humor. She was too aware of why they were there, and what was at stake. "It'll be fun when we have Schrader," she said.

"Then let's get him. You ready?"

She nodded. He backed up, aimed the AA-12 at the doorknob at a sharp angle, and—

BAMBAMBAMBAMBAMBAMBAM! Shards of wood flew through the air. Silence, then—

A giant *BOOM!* from inside. The flashbang.

Larison kicked open the door and pointed the shotgun. Livia dashed up alongside him, aiming the Glock—

The room was filled with smoke, but she saw him immediately. In the corner. Schrader. For a second, she thought he had two heads. Because behind him, pressing his cheek to one side of Schrader's face and the muzzle of a pistol to the other, was another man. They were both blinking and coughing.

"I'll kill him!" the man shouted. "I'll fucking kill him!"

Carl ripped the curtains away and took aim. Larison sighted down the shotgun.

"Wait!" Livia yelled. "Wait!" From where he was standing outside the window, Carl couldn't have had more than an inch of the guy's face. And the shotgun wasn't a precision weapon.

"Back up!" the man shouted. "Back the fuck up or I swear to God I'll blow him away!"

"Just let him go!" Livia shouted, pointing the Glock. She was ninety percent sure of the shot. But ninety percent wasn't good enough. "Can you hear me? Let him go and you can walk out of here."

The man blinked furiously, fighting the blinding effects of the flash-bang. "No way!" he screamed. "All of you, back up or he's dead!"

"Listen to me!" Livia said. "You shoot him and you're dead a second after. But we don't know who you are. And we don't care. We're here for Schrader. Walk away and we never saw you. That simple. Just walk away."

The man didn't answer. He was panting, his eyes darting from her to Larison to Carl and back. He wanted to believe. She could feel it. She prayed Carl and Larison would for once keep their mouths shut.

"We're going to lower our guns," she said, glancing at Larison. His eyes bulged, but she glared at him, then looked back to the guy behind Schrader. After a second, Larison lowered the muzzle of his Glock a little. She did the same.

"Lower your gun!" she shouted to Carl. "He can go. If he's smart."

Carl lowered the Wilson.

"Leave," she said to the man. "Right now. This is your chance."

He looked at her, panting, then at Larison. He eased the muzzle of his gun away from Schrader's face, relaxed his grip, started to move to the side—

Livia stepped offline, brought up the Glock, and put two rounds in his face. His head snapped back and he went down.

"Oh, my God!" Schrader screamed. Larison stepped in and kicked him field-goal style in the balls. The scream was instantly cut off and Schrader doubled over.

Larison looked at Livia and smiled. "You're good. For a second there, you had me convinced, too."

Carl rushed in. He and Larison grabbed Schrader by the arms and half dragged, half carried him out the back, Livia covering them from the rear.

She heard sirens. But in seconds they were in the woods, and a minute later, the van. Carl and Larison threw Schrader in back and sat on him. Livia jumped in front.

"You got him?" Diaz said.

"Go," Livia said, her heart pounding. "Drive normally. Head west. Yeah, we got him."

She turned around and watched as Carl and Larison flex-tied Schrader's wrists behind his back. She heard Diaz say, "Actual fact, girl: you are badass."

Schrader was crying. He said, "I want to go home."

"Don't worry," Livia said. "That's the plan."

chapter
fifty-seven

RISPEL

It was already ten in the morning on the East Coast, and still no word from the Seattle team. Of course, a benign explanation was possible, but Rispel knew something was wrong. Everything about the Schrader operation had been a clusterfuck, almost from go. Well, not everything. Getting Schrader released from jail had worked. Weirdly, it was the most audacious move of the entire game, and the only one that had gone smoothly.

She told her admin to hold her calls, then tried Sloat again. Then Tyson. No one answered. She tried them on their alternate burners. Nothing.

She checked the news feed on her desktop monitor. Nothing out of Seattle. But the *Washington Post* had a scoop: intelligence about the discovery of a Russian disinformation campaign, including deep-fake photos and videos of administration officials engaged in salacious acts. "This is the next step in the information wars," an unnamed senior intelligence official was quoted as saying. "Russia's ability to wage this kind of asymmetric, low-intensity warfare against the integrity of our government, our elections, and our way of life cannot go unanswered. America needs to develop a robust set of tools for a full suite of potential responses throughout the battlespace. Until that happens—until our adversaries pay a price for this kind of meddling—we're going to see continued escalation of fake news from the Kremlin."

Devereaux, she thought. Playing bullshit bingo with the press. Information wars, meddling, fake news, the Kremlin . . . It was actually an astute move, and she mentally kicked herself for having given him the idea. You could get the establishment media to print anything on background, and then quote it yourself later as proof of the need for whatever policy you were selling. In this case, Devereaux was indeed shaping the battlespace. Now if those videos were released, he'd be able to point to reports like the one he'd just dictated to his stenographer at the *Post* as proof that the videos were nothing but fake news. Information wars, indeed.

She paused for a moment, thinking. Had Devereaux learned something about an imminent release of the videos? Why else would he be establishing this preemptive groundwork?

Or—had something been released already?

The more she thought about it, the more she suspected he'd been lying to her about the president being in the videos. Because what was he going to do, tell her the truth? *Help me out here, Lisa. I fucked a bunch of teenaged girls at a drug-fueled orgy and now it's all going to be released as a movie of the week.* He would have been afraid she would want those videos for her own leverage. And rightly so.

But who was pressuring Devereaux? He had been vague about that when he first brought Rispel into this. Schrader himself? How could he have, from jail? Through his lawyer, maybe, but who would the woman contact? Well, given that the underlying problem was an out-of-control assistant US Attorney, it stood to reason that Schrader's lawyer would have gone to the attorney general himself. But why would Hobbs have cared enough to bring in Devereaux, unless Hobbs was implicated in the videos, too?

It didn't matter. Either way, she needed to secure the videos quickly. Every leaked report about Russian fake news would bleed off the eventual impact. Enough time, and Devereaux and Hobbs and anyone else who appeared in the videos might even be able to ride out a release. They'd cry "fake news" in unison and accuse anyone in the media who wanted to publish the material or even to ask questions about it of doing the Kremlin's *kompromat* work. It wouldn't be easy—the public, like the press, was far more interested in sex scandals than in routine corruption—but if Devereaux and the rest kept strict message discipline, eventually they'd exhaust the media, and it would move on to the next glittering object. In the end, it always did.

She went back to news from Seattle. And this time, there it was. Explosions and a shooting in a house on Lake Tapps. She felt a cold weight settle inside her chest.

She found a television station. Reporters were standing outside the house, which was surrounded by police tape. A stunned-looking uniformed cop the chyron identified as being with the Bonney Lake Police Department was briefing the press. Five bodies inside, all shot to death. A reporter asked if this had anything to do with the shootings the day before in Freeway Park and the Four Seasons, or with Andrew Schrader's escape from prison. The cop stammered that she didn't know. Rispel almost sympathized. Before this morning, probably the cop's toughest case had been a couple of teenagers breaking into an empty off-season lakefront vacation home.

She watched for another minute. A television crew had managed to get behind the house and was showing footage of one of the walls. There was a large hole blown in a second-story wall. Windows broken on the first floor. Evidence of a coordinated, professional entry by a trained team.

She stared at the screen for another moment, then exited the site. She tried to think.

Somehow, someone had gotten intel on where they had been holding Schrader.

Devereaux?

Maybe. But her gut told her otherwise. Her gut told her Kanezaki.

It made sense. He had sabotaged the initial operation. He'd lied to her afterward. And he was missing now, incommunicado. Rispel had people watching his house, and he hadn't gone home. His cellphone was off. He was a prick, but obviously he wasn't stupid.

And it wasn't just him. His little spy, Maya, was also in the wind. Rispel had sent a contractor to her house, and the idiot had shot the wrong person—another officer, as it turned out. Maya had given a statement to local police and then disappeared, probably with Kanezaki. Rispel sensed it wouldn't be long before Devereaux found a way to incorporate the shooting of a young intelligence officer into the tale of Russian disinformation he was spinning.

All right. Assume they have Schrader now. What's their next move?

Kanezaki was after the videos, of course. How could he not be? Anyone who controlled that information would have almost undreamt-of power.

She had to assume they'd learn from Schrader everything Sloat had been able to extract. So it stood to reason that their next move would be what hers was going to be. A team had come for Schrader that very morning. They were going to bring him to his Bainbridge Island house, drug him, and have him reset the system. Then more interrogations until they had enough information to take control of the videos themselves.

So. With Schrader in hand, why wouldn't Kanezaki do the same?

It wasn't a sure thing, of course. Schrader had six houses, and apparently he could reset the system from any of them. From his private plane, too. Kanezaki might not use the Bainbridge Island house.

But she thought he would. The dead-man switch meant time was of the essence. The nearest house would be tempting. Kanezaki would confirm it wasn't being watched, just as she had. At which point, he'd go for the low-hanging fruit.

In fact . . . it might just make sense to let him pick it. And then take it from him, before he'd even gotten a taste.

LIVIA

T en miles west of Lake Tapps, Livia started to let out her breath. The sirens were long gone. Realizing they were out of danger, they all got a little giddy. Even Livia was laughing. "How the hell did you move that refrigerator?" she said to Carl. "It must have weighed three hundred pounds."

"I think more," he said, rubbing his back. "But I'll tell you, when I heard the shots and realized what that hombre was shooting at us, that refrigerator felt about as light as a can of Diet Coke." He turned to Larison. "How about you? How'd you get pinned down up there?"

"Bad luck," Larison said. "The guy was in another room, so the breach charge surprised him, but he wasn't stunned. He had good cover and all I had was a bureau that seemed as small to me as I'll bet that refrigerator felt to you."

"Yeah," Carl said, "we had some shit luck, too. Dropping a flash-bang in an empty room. About as useful as shouting, 'Good morning.' And to a house full of guys with automatic shotguns, too."

They all laughed again. Schrader, his wrists flex-tied behind his back, started crying.

Carl looked at him. "You all right?"

Schrader shook his head and glared at Larison. "Why did you kick me?"

Larison looked taken aback. "You were screaming. How'd you want me to shut you up?"

"Who cares if I was screaming? There were already explosions!"

Larison looked at Carl as though expecting help. Carl said, "Well, he has a point."

"And those men," Schrader said. "They hurt me."

Carl looked at him with what seemed genuine concern. "What'd they do to you?"

"They put me in the bathtub. And wrapped a towel around my face and poured water on it. Again and again."

Carl glanced at Livia and Larison, then back to Schrader. "It's called waterboarding. I had it done to me once and I still have nightmares. Nobody deserves that." He glanced at Livia again, then added, "Well, almost nobody."

Diaz said, "What did you tell them, Andrew?"

"Can you untie me?"

"Later. What did you tell them?"

He sniffled. "I don't even remember."

"Okay," she said. "But if you want my help, you better help me."

Schrader didn't answer. He just sat there, weeping. Livia had questions of her own, but Diaz knew what she was doing. And it was generally better to have one person leading an interrogation.

"It's okay," Diaz said. "It's okay. What did they ask you? Start with that."

Schrader shook his head. "The videos. The system. What I told you about at the detention center."

"Okay," Diaz said. "What did they want to know?"

"How it worked."

"And what did you tell them?"

"What I told you. That I have to reset it. Or . . . or . . ."

"Or what?"

275

"Or the shot across the bow. Which has already happened, I think, but I don't even know what day it is. I'm so tired. Please, just take me back to jail, I don't care anymore. And I think I want to talk to my lawyer."

"Okay," Diaz said. "The shot across the bow happened all right. Yesterday. So what's coming next?"

"More shots," Schrader said.

Livia had to bite her tongue. She reminded herself Diaz was doing fine without her.

"What kind of shots?" Diaz said.

"The men. With the girls."

"What men?" Diaz said.

Schrader didn't answer.

"We know some of them," Diaz said. "The attorney general, the director of National Intelligence . . . who else?"

Schrader looked alarmed. "How do you know that?"

Diaz shook her head. "It's a long story. But those are the people who are after you now. Who's with them? If we don't know that, we can't help you."

Schrader sniffled. "It's a lot of people."

"I'm sure," Diaz said. "But who?"

"You wouldn't believe me."

"Try me."

There was a long beat. Schrader said, "Connected people. Top people."

"What are their names?" Diaz said.

Schrader shook his head.

"You're not going to tell us?" Diaz said.

"I don't want to get in trouble," Schrader said.

Livia knew what everyone was thinking: *How much more trouble could you get in?*

But that wouldn't have been a useful thing to ask.

It was obvious Schrader wasn't going to say more, and Diaz, a good interrogator, knew it was time to shift gears. "Okay, so when is the next release?"

"If the first one happened yesterday," Schrader said, "then tomorrow. Every forty-eight hours after the first one."

"What time tomorrow?"

"Eleven at night, Greenwich Mean Time."

"Which is what time here?"

"Three o'clock in the afternoon," Livia said.

"Andrew," Diaz said, "that doesn't sound good. You know, if too many shots get fired, the gun's going to be empty. What are you going to do then?"

"I don't know!"

Diaz glanced at him in the rearview mirror. "Then we better reset that system, don't you think?"

"If I do . . . do you promise you'll help me?" He started crying again.

"Yes," Diaz said. "I promise."

Livia didn't know if she meant it. But it didn't matter. It was Diaz's promise, not hers.

"I've been meaning to ask," Carl said. "What do you need to say to that system of yours? You know, is it *abracadabra*, or can you say anything at all, and it recognizes your voice?"

"It's a phrase," Schrader said.

"What phrase?"

"You'll know when I say it. I'm not telling you beforehand. Besides, there's also a retina scan, a thumbprint, and a passcode."

Carl glanced at Livia, then back to Schrader. "A lot of locks you built into that door."

"I didn't want anyone else using it."

"What if something had happened to you?" Carl said. "I mean, none of us is immortal, or immune from accident."

Schrader shrugged. "I just didn't want them to put me in jail again. It was lucky that first time, that I had the videos. And I didn't do anything wrong. I'm not even in the videos. Why should they try to put me in jail? I didn't do anything those other people didn't do, too."

You provided the girls, Livia wanted to shout. *Located them, enticed them, tricked them, drugged them, trafficked them. And after you used them, you sold them like a product to other buyers.*

Carl looked at her as though reading her mind. She gave him an *I'm okay* nod.

"What about the girls?" Livia said.

Schrader looked at her. "What do you mean?"

"If you release those videos, it's going to ruin their lives."

Schrader scowled. "They're trying to ruin mine. Diaz said they're going to testify that I had sex with them! That I . . . that I raped them. And made them have sex with other men."

"Did you?" Livia said.

"That's not the point. I was nice to them. I gave them money. Rides on my helicopter and plane. Introduced them to celebrities. I don't understand how they could be so mean."

"Most of them aren't testifying," Diaz said.

Schrader just sat there, his mouth scrunched into a pout.

"Do you understand?" Diaz said. "I contacted over a hundred girls. Most of them were terrified of what would happen if this came out. The media scrutiny. Their families. Some of them have husbands now, children, who don't even know. What about them? They didn't turn on you. They're still protecting you. How can you let those videos come out and destroy them? Who's the one who's being mean now?"

Not for the first time when she was listening to Diaz, Livia was impressed. The woman had the interrogator's knack for setting aside her own outrage, her own disgust, and addressing the subject in whatever terms he indicated would make sense to him. Speaking his own language.

"It's not . . . ," Schrader said. "I mean, I don't want to. I wasn't going to. You're the one who arrested me."

"No," Diaz said. "The release of those videos has nothing to do with your arrest. You designed the system. You automated it. The videos aren't a part of my case—I didn't even know about their existence until you told me. Do you see? You're going to ruin those innocent girls, girls who like you, who think you're nice, who are grateful to you, who are protecting you—for nothing. I don't understand. How can you be so mean?"

The interior of the van was silent. Livia knew Diaz and Carl would be perceptive enough to let the silence work on Schrader. She was only worried about Larison, who could occasionally lose his patience. Not that she could throw stones.

But this time, Larison stayed cool. After a moment, Schrader said, "Well, I don't want to. But what am I supposed to do?"

"First," Diaz said, "you help us reset the system."

Schrader nodded. "Okay. I will."

"And then," Livia said, "help us blur out the faces of those girls."

Schrader looked at her. "What? No."

"Why not?" Livia said.

"Because . . . I don't want to show you how it's designed. I don't want to give you access."

"I get it," Diaz said. "But you know, Andrew, if those videos come out, it makes your case worse. It's more evidence of the allegations against you."

"But then you could just drop the case."

"I'm just an assistant US Attorney. Those decisions are above my pay grade. But look, there are two possibilities. One is the videos never come out. The other is they do come out. If they never come out, you won't have lost anything in helping us blur out the girls' faces. If they do come out, you can impress the judge by showing how you cooperated. To protect those girls. Not the men—they're hypocrites, they deserve it.

Besides, the videos would lose their impact if the men weren't in them. But the girls' faces? Help us blur them. That's what a nice guy would do, anyway."

"I guess so," Schrader said.

"Maybe you don't believe me," Diaz said, "but I believe in you. I want you to do the right thing, Andrew. Will you?"

Diaz glanced at him in the rearview mirror, and Livia could sense how much Schrader wanted her approval. When it came to establishing rapport, Livia had worked with some of the best. And no doubt, Diaz was among them.

"Will you really help me?" he said. "Tell the judge I wasn't mean or anything?"

Diaz nodded. "Yes."

"But what if I can't?" he said, his eyes welling up. "Because . . . I'm upset. Those men . . . they really hurt me. And if someone tries to make me, it won't work. Because of the voice-stress analyzer. I thought it would be a good idea, but I shouldn't have done it. It's like when someone's watching you pee, and you can't." He started crying again.

Livia looked at Carl. He nodded. "It's all right," he said. "Andrew, it's all right." He took out a plastic water bottle. "I'm going to fix you a drink. It'll make you feel better, I promise."

chapter fifty-nine

RAIN

They were still in the hotel room, talking about their next move, when Delilah's phone buzzed. For a second, Rain was alarmed, and then remembered it was connected to the satellite hotspot.

She picked up and listened for a moment, then looked at Rain. "It's Dox. They got Schrader." She listened again, then said, "That's great. But you should brief him yourself." She looked at Rain again. "No, he's not mad at you. Hold on." She handed Rain the phone.

"Everything good?" Rain said.

"Hey, amigo," Dox said. "You're really not mad at me?"

"For what?"

"Come on, don't pretend. It makes it worse."

"All you did was go out of your way to get involved in a national freak show involving some of the world's most powerful people, drag Delilah and me into it, and ruin a beautiful evening in Paris, along with my retirement."

Dox laughed. "Anyone ever tell you you've gotten funnier with age? I think it's my influence."

"Who's being funny?"

"I deliberately didn't call you, you know. I thought the angel of death and I could handle it fine on our own."

"I know. Delilah told me."

"You forgive me, then?"

"Depends on how this thing turns out. You have Schrader?"

"Yeah, and we're taking him to his house near Seattle to reset the system."

"The house is the first place—"

"No, Livia's contact, Little, says it's not being monitored. Should be just a quick in and out."

"Why does that sound familiar?"

Dox laughed again. "Because women say it's your only means of lovemaking?"

Rain didn't answer. Sometimes with Dox, silence was all you could do.

"Seriously," Dox went on. "We'll be careful."

"What's the endgame? You reset the system, then what?"

"Then Mr. Schrader has kindly offered to advise us on how to obscure the faces of the girls in the videos. That way only the men in them will get hurt. The girls didn't do anything, and in fact quite a few of them are kindly inclined to Mr. Schrader for being so nice to them. He understands if any of the videos get released without being obscured, it could cause a lot of pain for those nice girls."

Rain understood Schrader must have been nearby and that Dox was choosing his words deliberately.

"All right," Rain said. "So the plan is to release sanitized versions of the videos?"

"Exactly."

"That's going to have a lot of very powerful people feeling irked."

"Well, they're already irked, and they have a logical motive to do us in on top of it. I'd like to remove the logical motive and just leave them feeling irked. Irked isn't too bad. I've irked lots of people and none of them has killed me yet. Look at you and Larison. I irk you all the time and we're all friends."

"Still."

"Partner, if you've got something better, I am all ears."

Rain considered pointing out that it wasn't his job to come up with solutions, given that Dox had created the problem. But that wouldn't be fair. Or helpful.

"I wish I did," he said.

"Look, it's actually a pretty good plan. If those videos get released, the men starring in them are going to have a whole lot of problems more serious than getting back at whoever pressed the publication button, assuming they even know who that was. On top of which, they might lose access to their current resources. I mean, today, Pierce Devereaux is the damn director of National Intelligence. Tomorrow, he could be the disgraced former director, and negotiating a plea deal for reduced prison time for the rape of teenaged girls. I'd call tomorrow's Pierce Devereaux a much less formidable enemy, wouldn't you?"

"And I suppose that applies to the others, as well."

"That's our thinking. So unless you have any other concerns, we're going to proceed as planned. By the way, how's old Manus?"

Rain glanced over. Manus was signing with Dash. Evie was watching Rain.

"He seems good. They're all good."

"Tom told me what happened. I really appreciate you and Delilah helping out. And I'm not trying to gild the lily here, but I think this could work out well. That Manus is a damn force of nature. He saved my ass earlier, and I for one would be proud to welcome him into our little band of brothers."

"There is no band. I'm retired. Or anyway, trying to be."

"All right, well, if you ever decide to get off the shuffleboard court, or shit happens, or whatever. I'm just saying, Manus is solid. Give him my best, will you?"

Rain nodded at Evie. "I'll give him your best."

"Thank you. And if you talk to Tom, see if he can get ahold of another of those private jets he flew you and Delilah out here on. When we're done with Schrader, Larison and I are going to need to vamoose, and I think we're a little hot right now for commercial travel."

"Anything else? You want me to order you a pizza? You need a back rub?"

Dox laughed. "I told you you've gotten funnier. I'll let Larison know. I think it's his influence as much as mine."

"You be careful, all right?"

"You bet. And you know I love you, too."

Dox clicked off, saving Rain the trouble of trying and failing to come up with a snappy reply.

Dox had a way of keeping things light, but Rain hadn't been joking about the shortcomings of the plan. Or, given the level of the players threatened by those videos, the stakes. He understood the logic. But at the same time, the whole thing felt like an attempt to snuff out an oil-well fire by dumping high explosives on it. If it worked, great. If it didn't, you just bought yourself an even bigger fire.

chapter sixty

LIVIA

Thirty minutes out from the compound, Livia said to Schrader, "All right, Andrew, time for your cocktail." She wanted to make sure it had fully taken effect by the time they arrived.

Schrader looked doubtful. "What's in it?"

"I'd like to say Bombay Sapphire," Carl said, handing him the plastic bottle. "And a dash of vermouth. But as it happens, it's mostly just beta blockers. You know what that is?"

Schrader nodded. "I know people who use them. For anxiety. And high blood pressure."

"Exactly," Carl said. "Now maybe you've gotten to know us well enough to understand we're not like those people who were holding you before. On the other hand, you've had a rough time of it, and we're not old friends who you're maximally comfortable with, either. So we need to make sure your voice is stress-free when you go to reset your system. You get it?"

Schrader didn't look mollified. He glanced at the bottle. "How do I know this is what you say it is?"

Livia wanted to say, *You don't. Now fucking drink it.* But Carl had a different style, and he was doing fine on his own.

"Why would I lie?" Carl said. "You think we're trying to poison you? Or knock you out? What would be the point?"

"I guess," Schrader said. "Could you at least untie me? How am I going to drink it?"

"I'm going to hold it for you," Carl said. "Now drink up and we'll have you back at that jail in no time."

"Couldn't you just let me go?"

"Andrew," Diaz said from up front, "where would you go? The marshals would pick you up in a day. It's much better if you cooperate."

"I guess," Schrader said again.

Livia sensed that Diaz meant it. But probably only because she hadn't thought it through. Schrader knew who Diaz was, and he could describe the rest of them. He could put them at the Lake Tapps house, where five people had been shot to death. He had no reason to keep quiet, and every reason to tell the whole story. Even to embellish it.

She didn't know what Carl was thinking. But it didn't matter. Larison was never going to let Schrader walk away.

And the truth was, neither was she.

Dox held the bottle and Schrader drank the contents. "Good job," Carl said. "How was it?"

Schrader smacked his lips. "Okay. A little menthol taste."

Carl patted him on the shoulder. "Sounds like Bombay Sapphire has nothing to fear."

It occurred to Livia that Schrader didn't understand how dire his position was. Despite everything he had done, he seemed fundamentally a child. Probably the first time he had surreptitiously filmed the men he was blackmailing, he had conceived it as a prank. Or maybe it was something he got off to sexually. Just a "harmless" hobby no one would ever even know about. But over time, as he realized there were other possibilities, it got more sophisticated, and more dangerous. Almost every home-invasion rapist Livia had ever arrested had started out peeping. And there were home invaders who had originally intended only to steal property but who, upon seeing the complete power they had over their bound, terrified victims, wound up escalating to rape.

In some ways, though, Schrader's fundamentally infantile nature made him worse than the freaks she hunted. Most of the freaks had been horrifically abused as children, their humanity methodically beaten out of them. Livia didn't care about that, either—most abused children didn't go on to be abusers themselves, instead transcending their circumstances—but at least there was an explanation. But the ones who ruined lives for money? Or status? Or as some kind of grift? The casual, thoughtless, banal ones. Yeah. They were even worse.

The property was on the south end of the island, in one of the more heavily wooded and secluded enclaves. Once they were off Route 305, with its double yellow line, the streets grew increasingly narrow and overgrown, and soon they were on a single-lane gray-top road. The sun eased out from behind the clouds, and streaks of light lit up the autumn yellow in the trees. "I feel so calm," Schrader said. "That was awful before, what they did to me. It was like I was drowning. But it's okay now. What did you give me again?"

"Klonopin and Propranolol," Carl said.

"When this is over, I'm going to get a prescription."

"Well, I know a guy who can hook you up. But first things first. Any staff in your house, or anyone else we might want to warn about our arrival?"

"Maybe. The housekeepers, the groundskeepers . . . and the cook. And the helicopter pilot. And my driver."

"But you've been gone for a while now," Carl said. "What do they all do when you're not around?"

"The maids . . . they clean when I'm not there. I don't like to be bothered."

"And the rest?"

"It depends."

"Are your people loyal to you?"

"I pay them well."

"Well, for our purposes, that's going to have to amount to the same thing. If someone sees you, are they going to call the police?"

"Not if I tell them not to."

Livia looked at him. "Andrew. Where is the encryption keypad?"

"In my office."

She glanced at Carl. "We'll be in and out fast."

"We better be," Larison said.

"What about cameras?" Carl said. "I'm guessing you have a security system?"

Schrader nodded. "There's an alarm. And Nest cameras outside."

"Are they set to record?" Carl said.

"They're more for show," Schrader said.

Livia kept a poker face to conceal her disgust. Schrader had no problem planting cameras in guest rooms to film children being raped. But his own privacy was sacrosanct.

"Give me one of your burners," Livia said to Carl. "I'll download the app and confirm nothing is recording."

"Andrew," Diaz said, "you'll have to give us your username and password. Will you do that?"

"I guess so," Schrader said.

By the time they reached the gate to Schrader's property, Livia had downloaded the app and accessed Schrader's system. She confirmed the cameras weren't recording and turned them off completely.

There was a keypad alongside the gate. The driveway beyond snaked to the right, hiding whatever might be at the end of it.

Carl and Larison scanned the surroundings. Diaz rolled down the window and looked at Schrader in the rearview. "What's the code?" she said.

"You're not lying to me, are you?" he said. "I mean, shouldn't I talk to Sharon or something? She always tells me not to talk to anyone when she's not there."

"Do I seem like I'm lying?" Diaz said.

Schrader shook his head. "No."

"Good. Because I'm not. And we'll talk to your lawyer after for sure. But we have to take care of this first. So tell me the code, okay?"

He recited six digits. Diaz punched them in. The gate swung open. She rolled up the window and they drove through.

They followed the winding driveway for almost a minute before the house came into view. It was enormous, some sort of French chateau style, surrounded by manicured lawns and topiary. Livia found it both hideous and entirely fitting.

Larison looked at Schrader. "You don't have a key. Are we going to need another breach charge? Or is there an easier way in?"

"The garage," Schrader said. "There's a keypad by each bay. The same code as the front gate. Use the far one, it's for visitors."

The garage had six bays and was attached at ninety degrees to the house. "Back up," Livia told Diaz. "Off to the side, not right in front of the door. We'll need to clear the garage first. And if there's someone in there, you want to be out of the way and pointed in the right direction. Engine running."

Diaz positioned the van. Carl shouldered the medical pack, and he, Larison, and Livia got out. There was a light breeze and the air smelled of salt water and fallen leaves.

Livia and Larison stood at the sides of the bay, guns out, while Carl held the Wilson in one hand and punched in the code with the other. There was a mechanical whine and the door started to rise. Carl tried to move in front of Livia, but she wouldn't budge. "Behind me," she said.

"Damn it, you know I hate that."

"Hurry."

He grumbled, but did as she said.

The door reached the top and the mechanical whine stopped. Larison nodded to her. Simultaneously, they swung around each end of the garage, guns up. Carl was right behind her.

Other than five fancy cars so gleaming Livia wondered if anyone ever drove them, the garage looked deserted. They squatted to check, then moved through to make sure. When they were satisfied, Carl went out and waved to Diaz. She backed in the van and they closed the garage door as soon as it was inside.

They got Schrader out. "Now can you untie me?" he said.

Carl looked at Livia. She nodded. "Okay," he said. "I'm going to cut those flex-ties off you. I really hope you're not going to do anything dumb. None of us wants to shoot you, Andrew. You've been through plenty already."

"I'm not going to do anything dumb. But I need the bathroom."

"That's fine," Carl said. "One of us will escort you."

"I have to go number two."

"As I said, Mr. Larison will escort you."

Larison shot Carl a look. Carl smiled.

"That's gross," Schrader said. "I don't want someone watching."

"Hold it in if you want," Larison said. "I won't complain."

Schrader shook his head. "I can't."

Larison glared at Carl. "Then let's get it over with."

Another keypad, and they were inside as vast a kitchen as Livia had ever seen. Stone floors, high ceilings, top-of-the-line appliances. But like the garage, it was too spotless, and somehow soulless. A space designed to impress, but not really to live in. "If we run into a problem," Livia said to Diaz, "get behind something solid if you can. If you can't, then get low and get out of the way." She turned to Schrader. "That goes for you, too."

"Why would there be a problem?" Schrader said.

"In case you haven't noticed," Diaz said, "there are a lot of people looking for you."

There were fewer obstructions than in the garage, and the kitchen took them only a minute to check. They proceeded into a hallway as long as a bowling alley.

"You always leave all the lights on?" Carl said, sweeping left and right with the Wilson.

Schrader looked up as though noticing all the recessed lights for the first time. "I don't know. I think so."

Partway down the hallway was a bathroom. Larison took Schrader in. While she waited, Livia glanced around. Marble floors, wood paneling, leather sofas in case, what, someone got tired traveling down the endless corridor and needed to sit? The notion of one person living in a place like this disgusted her. She didn't begrudge people success. But when she thought about how little there had been in the village she had grown up in, and how happy she and Nason had been, at least before what her parents had done . . . she couldn't help but find this sort of excess both sickening, and a sickness.

After a few minutes, Schrader emerged from the bathroom, Larison behind him. Larison glared at Carl, wrinkled his nose, and said, "Expect payback."

Carl laughed. "This was payback. For you mocking me for having to ride a damn three-wheeled motorcycle."

Larison half smiled, half grimaced. "Oh, we're not done with that."

They followed Schrader down the hall, passing innumerable rooms as they moved, their footfalls echoing off the high ceiling. Livia and Carl checked each room they went by, but they were all empty. Larison stayed in the hallway, making sure no one surprised them from the front or behind.

"Seems quiet," Carl said as they walked. "Would you say a little too quiet? 'Cause when they say that in the movies, the next line is always *We've got company.*"

"I told you," Schrader said, "the maids work when I'm gone. I don't know where everyone else is. I haven't been in jail before. Or at least, not in a long time."

They came to another doorway, inside of which was another enormous, overdecorated room. "My office," Schrader said.

They followed him in. Everything was dark, polished wood—the floor, the bookcases, the ceiling twenty feet above. On the walls were paintings of hunting scenes in heavy gold frames; above them, a second-floor walkway encircling the room, its bookcases filled with volumes doubtless read by no one. A spiral staircase. Chandeliers. Thick oriental rugs. Two leather couches and a half-dozen upholstered chairs. And a wooden desk as long as a city bus, two giant computer monitors perched on top of it.

And between the monitors, a keypad, a microphone, and a fingerprint reader. And a vertical, elegantly curved device of polished metal. The retina scanner.

"I get it," Carl said. "A place for quiet, solitary contemplation. Reminds me of my ancestral home in Abilene."

Larison was always quiet, but there was something especially still about him now. He was looking at the far end of the room. There was a fireplace, on either side of which was a set of thick floor-to-ceiling curtains. Drawn curtains. In the rooms they had passed, the curtains had all been open.

Livia pointed to Diaz, then swung her finger over to the end of the huge desk. Diaz must have seen the concern in her eyes because she nodded and immediately took cover. Schrader looked at Diaz, then at Livia, obviously not getting it. Livia pointed to the desk as she had for Diaz, shaking her finger for emphasis. But the idiot just kept staring at her. "What is it?" he said. "What's wrong?"

Carl picked up on the problem, too. Unlike Larison and Livia, though, he kept talking. "Not that I don't have concerns," he said, "Frankly, I'm not sure this property is adequate for my current needs. Is it equipped with a separate gymnasium, for example?"

Schrader looked at him, his expression perplexed. "Yes, but I don't really use it."

Livia and Larison eased deeper into the room, toward the windows, using the massive chairs and the edges of bookshelves for cover whenever possible, glancing up at the walkway, then back to the curtains as they moved. Livia heard Schrader call out to them, "It's okay, there's no one here."

Livia kept moving. *Carl, shut him up—*

"That's what concerns me," Carl said. "The absence of adequate staff. I mean, how do you keep it clean? Do you have one of those Roombas, or what? Been thinking about getting one for my folks for Christmas."

"Roombas?" Schrader said. "No, there's a whole staff. I mean, a Roomba would—"

"Above you!" she heard Carl bellow, followed immediately by a solid *Bambambam!* from the Wilson.

She glanced up just in time to see a man crumple behind the railing of the walkway. Then Carl was shooting again. She spun toward the curtains. Two men were racing forward, firing pistols, trying to reach a pair of chairs for cover—

A round sizzled past her, and something slammed into her chest with a thud she felt through her entire body. She was hit. No time to wonder if the vest had stopped it. She returned fire. Larison was shooting from her right. One of the men ahead of them cried out and blood erupted from his head. He went down. Livia saw movement from above her on the walkway to her right. She swung the Glock up and fired. Carl was shooting from behind her. The man got off two wild shots and twitched as she and Carl hit him. He fell back, out of her range of vision.

The last man reached one of the chairs and dove behind it. She and Larison hugged opposite walls and kept moving in.

The room was suddenly silent. The man must have realized his comrades were done and his position hopeless. A second went by, probably while he was screwing up his courage, or maybe swapping magazines. Then he burst up with a scream—

Livia and Larison put a dozen rounds in him before he'd even gotten his sights on them. He flailed, fired three wild shots, and went down.

Larison pointed to the curtains. Livia nodded and swapped in a fresh magazine. Larison did the same. They aimed and opened up with a wide pattern of shots—reconnaissance by fire. The material fluttered as the rounds tore through. She heard glass shatter.

They raced forward and raked back the curtains—nothing. Livia spun. Carl was in the doorway, sweeping the corridor. He turned back, saw her, and pointed up to the walkway. She nodded. She and Larison moved back halfway toward the door and covered the walkway while Carl headed silently up the spiral staircase.

He padded along one side of the walkway, then disappeared from her view as he crossed overhead. A moment later, he called down. "Both dead. We're good."

Diaz was scrunched up on her butt along one end of the desk, her knees drawn to her chin. Livia ran over and squatted next to her. "Are you all right?" she said.

Diaz nodded, panting. "Holy shit. I don't know how you do this for a living, girl, but I'm going to stick to being a prosecutor."

Livia glanced around. Where was Schrader? She saw his feet poking out from behind the desk. She stood and went around. "Andrew, are you all—"

She stopped. Because Schrader was anything but all right.

His shirt was covered in blood, and the carpet under him was soaked with it. "Oh, boy," he said. He was panting, but his tone was weirdly calm. "I think somebody got me."

Livia dropped to her knees alongside him. She heard a hissing from his chest. Pink froth bubbled up around a hole in his shirt.

"Sucking chest wound!" she shouted. She tore open his shirt. She saw two entry wounds—one in the stomach, one in the right side of his chest.

A moment later, Carl was beside her. He pulled off the backpack, dumped the contents on the floor, and grabbed a chest seal. "Wipe him off," he said. "Or it won't stick."

Livia tore open a package of gauze and did the best she could to mop up the blood around the chest wound. She heard Larison say, "I'll cover the door."

Carl slapped the plastic seal in place over the wound. Instantly Schrader's breathing got a little less labored. They checked his back—no exit wounds.

"We need to hurry," Carl said. "That dressing's got no vent. Don't want a—"

"Tension pneumothorax," Livia said. "I know." She tore open a bandage and placed it over the stomach wound. Schrader cried out. Carl was already sliding a roll of elastic gauze under his back. They looped it around several times, securing the bandage.

Carl looked at her, and she knew what he was thinking: without immediate medical attention, Schrader wasn't going to make it.

"Help me get him up," Livia said. "Into his chair."

Carl looked dubious, but he didn't argue. Together they hoisted a groaning Schrader into his desk chair.

"Andrew," Livia said. "Come on. Let's reset the system and get you to a hospital."

"Oh," he said, his voice still weirdly calm. "It hurts."

"Is there a sequence?" Livia said. "The access code, the biometrics . . ."

Schrader moaned. "Access code first."

"What is it?" Livia said. "Tell me the numbers."

"Oh, wow, it hurts . . ."

"Come on, Andrew," she said, her voice rising, "what are the numbers?"

"Oh," he said again. "This is what it feels like to be shot."

Diaz put a hand on Livia's shoulder and leaned in. "Andrew," she said. "You promised to help. Those girls were nice to you, remember? Tell me the access code."

"Nine . . . ," Schrader said. "Eight . . . five . . . two . . . one . . . four."

Livia punched in the digits. There was a beep, and a red light at the top of the keypad turned green.

"Which finger?" Livia said, dragging the fingerprint reader over.

Schrader extended his right hand, forefinger out. It had blood all over it. Livia swore. She turned to look for gauze, but Carl had already grabbed a roll. He tore it open and wiped off Schrader's finger. Livia pressed it down on the reader. Another beep, and a red light at the top of the device turned green.

She grabbed the retina scanner and held it to his eye. Another beep, another red light going green.

She grabbed the microphone and held it near his lips. "Say the phrase, Andrew. We're almost there. You're almost done. Just say the phrase."

He was very pale and his lips were growing blue. He was probably bleeding internally. And his breathing was getting worse again. Livia didn't need Carl to tell her. The punctured lung was leaking air into his chest cavity. Tension pneumothorax, as Carl had feared.

"Come on, Andrew, say the words!" she said.

He nodded. "Little Miss Muffet," he panted. "Sat . . . sat on a tuffet."

Livia looked at the red light at the base of the microphone. It blinked three times . . . and then stayed red.

"Is there more?" she said. "Do you need to say more?"

Schrader didn't answer. She felt Diaz's hand on her shoulder again.

"Say it with me," Diaz said, looking at him. "Little Miss Muffet, sat on a tuffet . . ."

"Eating . . ." Schrader panted. "Eating her curds and whey."

The light stayed red again. "Is that it?" Livia said.

Schrader nodded weakly.

"It didn't work," Livia said. "Do you have to say the whole thing together?"

"Y . . . yes."

Livia held the microphone closer to his lips. "Then do it! Come on, Andrew, it's just a rhyme. You've said it a hundred times before. Just say it."

He looked at Diaz. "I can't breathe. Am I . . . am I going to die?"

"No," Diaz said, though she must have known it was a lie. "You're going to be fine. And you can still do the right thing, Andrew. Don't you want that?"

"I'm scared," he panted. "Can I have more of that cocktail?"

"As soon as you say the words," Diaz said. "Just say them, Andrew. You're not a mean guy. You're a nice guy. Come on now. Little Miss Muffet . . ."

Tears leaked from the corners of his eyes. "Please, it hurts."

"Come on!" Livia shouted. "Little Miss Muffet! Just say the words, say the fucking words!"

"We need to take that seal off," Carl said. "Or vent it. Labee, look at him."

She was looking. The veins on the sides of his neck were bulging. She knew he had only minutes. Maybe seconds.

Diaz touched the side of his face and turned his head so he was looking into her eyes. "Andrew," she said, so calmly it was almost a coo. "Say the words with me. Like you promised. Just a few words and we're done. Ready? Little Miss Muffet . . ."

Schrader said it with her. "Little Miss Muffet . . ."

Livia was gripping the microphone so hard it was beginning to shake.

"Sat on a tuffet . . . ," Diaz and Schrader said together.

"Eating her curds and whey," Diaz said. But Schrader didn't finish. He made it through *eating*, then stopped, his breathing fast and shallow.

"It's no good," Carl said. "He's going into shock." He pulled a catheter out of its packaging.

"Say the words!" Livia shouted.

Carl shoved her aside. "Damn it, Labee, he's not going to be able to say anything if we don't get that air out of his chest!" He felt for the space above the third rib and plunged in the catheter. There was a loud hiss as the air around Schrader's injured lung whooshed out.

Little Miss Muffet, Livia thought, as though she could will Schrader to say it. *Little Miss Muffet, come on . . .*

Schrader moaned, and for a moment, she thought he might rally. But then his breathing got faster, and shallower. His skin went gray and his eyes rolled up.

There was a portable defibrillator in the medical kit. Livia grabbed it and tore open the zipper.

"Give it up," Larison said from the doorway. "He's not going to say the words. He's not going to say any words. Ever. And even if he could, you could give him all the beta blockers in the world and that voice-stress analyzer isn't going to buy it. We gave it our best shot. Now we need to get the fuck out of here."

Carl put a hand on Livia's arm. "Larison's right," he said. "Labee, come on. He's done."

"Help me shock him," Livia said. "It's just a few words, we could—"

"He's done," Carl said again. He started policing up the medical gear and shoving it into the pack. "He was bleeding internally. We can't do anything for him. Nobody could."

All at once, Livia felt the familiar dragon of hate flare up inside her. She grabbed Schrader by the shoulders and shook him. "Say the fucking words!" she screamed. "You created this fucking doomsday device, now help us reset it or tomorrow those girls are going to be violated all over again!"

Schrader's head lolled to the side. Froth bubbled from his mouth. She might as well have been shaking a rubber doll.

Diaz put a hand on her arm. "Livia. Come on. We did the best we could."

Livia looked at her.

"We can't win every round," Diaz said.

Livia knew that, of course. At least intellectually. But what Diaz didn't understand was that every time Livia lost a fight, every time she couldn't save someone from some horror, it was like losing Nason all over again.

But she would deal with that later. Like always. For now, there was nothing to do but leave.

And wait for what would happen to those girls, tomorrow at three o'clock.

chapter sixty-one

RAIN

Rain listened while Dox briefed him from the road. The bad news was the plan had failed. Schrader had been shot before he could get anyone into his system. The good news was no one else had been hurt. Apparently Dox and Livia had both been hit, Livia at Schrader's house and Dox earlier, but their vests had prevented anything beyond bruising.

"What's the plan now?" Rain said.

"Still under discussion," Dox said. "We already made an anonymous call about where Schrader can be found. That ought to take the pressure off Diaz at least."

"Are Rispel and the others going to know Schrader didn't help you before he died?"

There was a pause. "That's a good point. I was thinking there might at least be some upside when the dead-man switch triggers again tomorrow and releases a batch of videos. But maybe they won't be so sure it's a dead-man switch. Maybe they'll think it's us. Hard to say. I guess we'll find out if someone tries to kill us all again. Goddamn. I'm sorry I dragged you and Delilah into this, I really am."

"How's Livia?"

"Taking it hard. Most of the girls Diaz interviewed were afraid to cooperate. And now they're going to be tabloid fodder, and worse, for the rest of their lives."

"I'm sorry."

"Yeah, I won't lie to you, it feels like we won every battle but maybe . . . maybe we lost the war. The worst part is, apparently with Schrader dead, those videos might not even be admissible in court against the men who appear in them. Diaz says there are ways around it, but anyone charged will claim hearsay or lack of foundation or some such. Besides which, nobody's going to want to prosecute the men after Schrader's death any more than they did before it. I mean, the attorney general? The director of National Intelligence? So realistically, if the girls won't testify, and maybe even if they do, the men won't face charges. Well, at least maybe they won't get invited to the same dinner parties."

Rain wondered whether to say anything, then decided Dox would be hearing about it soon enough regardless. "We saw a news report. Unnamed senior intelligence officials talking about deep-fake Russian disinformation campaigns. Obviously laying the groundwork for dismissing any videos that get released as fake news, a Kremlin *kompromat* plot . . . That kind of thing."

Dox laughed harshly. "Almost can't blame them. It works every time."

Rain tried to think of something comforting to say, and couldn't.

"You talk to Tom?" Dox said. "Maybe he's got something new."

"I left him a message."

"Well, I doubt even old Kanezaki could pull a rabbit out of this hat. I'd like to think I'm missing something, but right now, I figure the best we can hope for is a stalemate. And eventually, when that system is done automatically spitting out every last video, hopefully no one will think there's any benefit to be derived from killing any of us. Toothpaste being out of the tube and all that."

"Do we even know what that time frame is?"

"Schrader said every other day, with yesterday being the first release and tomorrow at three o'clock West Coast time being the second. But we don't know how many overall. Might have to hunker down for a while."

Rain had never heard the big sniper sound so down. "Dox. It's not your fault."

Dox gave another harsh laugh. "Is this like that scene in *Good Will Hunting*? 'Cause we can't hug it out over the phone."

"You know I don't get your movie references."

"Never mind. I appreciate the thought."

"It's not just a thought. It's true. If you want to blame someone, blame Kanezaki. But come on, nobody could have foreseen this. It's just one of those things that went sideways."

"You foresaw it. You're the one with the good sense to retire. Or at least to try, despite all my interference."

"Listen, you know the only reason I keep you around is because you're funny, right? If you're going to get maudlin on me, it's over."

Dox laughed again, a little less harshly this time. "Thanks, partner. All right, let me get with the team here and figure out our next move. And tell me if you hear from Tom."

Dox clicked off and Rain briefed the rest of them. The atmosphere in the room was bleak.

When he was done, Maya said, "It's weird. I was wondering how Schrader was going to access the videos. Now we won't know."

Rain looked at her. "What do you mean?"

She shrugged. "I'd just be surprised if the underlying material were localized or easily accessible. That would risk it being compromised. Which, okay, fine, maybe Schrader could be that thoughtless or sloppy. But he wasn't. Someone put a lot of thought into this—integral biometric and encryption safeguards, the dead-man switch, the escalating series of warnings . . . Evie, what do you think?"

Rain had heard the two women talking earlier. Apparently when she had been with NSA, Evie had been involved in the creation of what was then called God's Eye, now known as Guardian Angel. And the two of them had used the program together to track down where Rispel was having Schrader held.

"Agreed," Evie said. "We're talking about a complex, robust, redundant system."

Rain wasn't sure where they were going. "Regardless of where the underlying material is kept, why wouldn't Schrader have access? He's the one who created the videos, right?"

"Sure," Maya said, "but that's like . . . Look, you know how to shoot cellphone video, right?"

The way she was dumbing it down gave Rain an odd, slightly out-of-body feeling. He realized that to someone as young as Maya, he must have seemed like a creature from prehistory. And maybe she wasn't completely wrong. Would this be what it felt like when people talked to you and assumed you were slightly senile? Christ, no wonder he'd been trying so hard to retire.

But all he said was "Everyone does."

"Right. But then if I asked you to make sure the footage was both set to automatically release if certain conditions weren't met and also unstoppable by any foreseeable opposition, what would you do then?"

"I'd ask someone like you. But I thought Schrader was some kind of technology genius."

"That's his reputation," Maya said. "Or was. But did you ever see that movie *Being There*, or read the Jerzy Kosinski book?"

Rain shook his head. "But I know the story."

"Then you get the idea," Maya said. "Sometimes a simpleton is so pristinely simple that people think it must be something else. I mean, Schrader would go to conferences and ask things like 'What do we mean really when we say *down*? Or *up*?' And attendees would treat it like it was some galaxy-brain insight into something everyone else takes for granted."

"It's true," Evie said. "People act like he's a genius, but so much of that is because of money. I once talked to him at a conference on facial-recognition technology. Everyone was fawning over him and I thought I was missing something. There was no *there* there."

"Did you read the paper he submitted?" Maya said.

Evie nodded. "Of course. It was after talking to him that I realized someone else must have written it. He got all this obsequious coverage in the press. But probably he bought that, too."

"Wait a minute," Rain said. "Why didn't you say any of this earlier?"

Maya shrugged. "You guys had this plan. They were already on the way to Schrader's house. And I thought maybe I was missing something."

"I don't know that you were," Rain said. "From what you're telling me, probably Schrader could have reset the system. But the rest . . . Now it sounds like they were asking for a tour of a building from a guy who never even went inside it, let alone drew up the plans. Is that accurate?"

Maya looked at Evie. They both nodded.

"But somebody designed it," Delilah said. "Who?"

Rain looked at her. He'd dragged her into this shitshow, and once she'd aired her concerns, she set them all aside. He'd caught the way she'd been looking at him earlier, when he was talking to Yuki. The expression somewhere between irritated and jealous. He'd been expecting a lot of questions. But there hadn't been any. In the end, all she cared about was backing him. He didn't know how he was going to make it up to her. But he would.

For a moment, no one said anything. Then Maya looked at Evie and said, "Grimble?"

Evie nodded. "Could be. Someone who could architect something like this. Someone Schrader knew and trusted . . ."

"Who's Grimble?" Rain said.

"Constantine Grimble," Maya said. "They met when Schrader was just a trust-fund baby and Grimble was a prodigy at MIT. Grimble's on the spectrum, and a lot of people think Schrader exploited him, because Schrader got all the fame, but who knows? They both got rich, or in

Schrader's case richer, and celebrity seemed to be Schrader's thing a lot more than it was Grimble's."

"Where's Grimble now?" Rain said.

"I don't know," Maya said. "He's supposed to be a recluse. With some kind of hobby he's really into, toy soldiers or something like that." She looked at Evie. "Do you know where he lives?"

Evie shook her head. "No. He gave a talk at NSA once, but for the most part he stays out of the public eye."

Rain looked at her. "Is he still close with Schrader?"

"I don't know," Evie said. "But I've never heard about any kind of rift. And when people asked him at his presentation, he was complimentary. Maya's right, by the way. I talked to him at length. He's definitely on the spectrum."

"How so?" Rain said.

Evie blew out a breath. "He doesn't look in people's eyes, for one thing. His presentation was fine, maybe because it was all about math, and that's comfortable for him, but he stared at the ceiling the whole time. And when I talked to him afterward, there were tics, some echolalia."

"Echolalia?"

"Repeated words. And instead of looking at the ceiling, he never took his eyes off my chest. And it wasn't . . . like, sometimes you'll catch a man doing that, and okay, he realizes he got busted, he'll look away. Or sometimes it'll be an asshole who'll keep stealing glances because he thinks he has the right. But Grimble . . . he just didn't seem to know better. Didn't realize he was being rude, or committing a faux pas, or whatever. On the one hand, we were engaging as peers about some pretty high-level applied math. On the other hand, it was though he was talking to a pair of breasts, not a person."

Rain nodded, wondering whether what he was thinking was too much of a long shot.

"Look," Evie said, "I think I see where you're going. But remember, even if Grimble architected Schrader's video system, the dead-man switch, all that . . . there's still the biometrics. And the passcode, which would be Schrader's."

"Unless . . . ," Maya said.

Evie looked at her. "Good point."

Rain looked from one to the other. "What?"

"Unless he created a back door," Evie said.

"Would he have?" Rain said.

"I would have," Maya said. "Any hacker would."

Evie nodded. "That's right. Or if not a back door, he might have just kept a spare set of keys."

Rain wondered whether they had both decided to dumb down the references for his benefit. If they had, it probably wasn't a bad idea. "Then it sounds like Grimble could be the solution," he said.

Delilah looked at Maya and Evie. "You found out where Rispel was holding Schrader. Can you find Grimble? And determine the extent to which he might have helped design Schrader's system?"

Evie said, "There's almost nothing Guardian Angel can't find. And I've never seen anyone use it like Maya."

Maya smiled. "Thanks."

Delilah looked at Rain. "All right. Assume Evie and Maya can find him. And that we're confident he's the architect. We can ask for his help. But what if he says no?"

"We're not going to ask," Rain said. "Larison is."

chapter sixty-two

RISPEL

R ispel sat at her desk, the late afternoon sun slanting through the
windows.

Schrader's house had been yet another disaster in what was turning
out to be the most cursed op she'd ever been involved in. Four more
contractors killed. And Schrader, dead. Police reports said there were
signs he'd received medical attention. Had he given Kanezaki's people
the keys to his system before he died? Shown them how it worked?

Apparently not. Because according to her technical team, someone
had just finished remotely querying Guardian Angel. The subject of the
queries was one Constantine Grimble. Who, it turned out, was a close
associate of Schrader's, and the apparent brains behind their former
partnership.

It had to be Maya. Meaning it had to be Kanezaki.

The queries had started broadly and become increasingly focused.
Grimble himself, to start with. Then credit card use. Cellphone calls,
incoming and outgoing, of which there seemed to be few. Cellphone
movements going back years, with trips to Schrader's various properties,
and more recently, little movement at all. Then a house, apparently
some sort of Japanese-style mansion, in the San Francisco Bay Area.
Then schematics for the house. Details about its alarm system and other
security.

Whatever Schrader had given up before he died, Kanezaki believed Grimble was part of it. Why else the extensive use of Guardian Angel? Why else the obvious preparations for a visit?

She decided it was time for a visit of her own. And this time, she wouldn't be sending a detachment of contractors. This time, she would personally lead an in-house team from Special Operations Group. The same type of team she had run at the black sites.

No more screwups. She'd risked too much, and there would be too much payback from Devereaux if she failed. She was going to get the keys to those videos. And when she had them, all the Devereauxs of the world would be on their knees before her, begging for her favor.

Or for her mercy.

Of course, the videos would be useless against Kanezaki. He wasn't involved. He was too junior. And too much of a boy scout.

Well. There were other ways of dealing with him. Maybe she couldn't make him useful. But she didn't have to let him linger as a threat, either.

chapter
sixty-three

DEVEREAUX

It was early evening, and Devereaux was about to crack the seal on a fresh bottle of Mylanta when he got the call he'd been waiting for: Dutch, the head of CIA's Special Operations Group, the Agency's blandly named paramilitary wing. Well, *wing* wasn't really the right word anymore. Since 9/11 and the advent of the drone program, the operations tail had been wagging the intel dog. Once upon a time, Devereaux had harbored some misgivings about that. Now all he cared about was having people loyal to him in the right positions.

"You wanted a heads-up about Rispel," Dutch said. The man, a legend in CIA's wars going back to Operation Enduring Freedom in Afghanistan, had a peculiar way of talking, the end of each word bitten off just before being enunciated. Dutch didn't know it, but he had a lot of behind-the-back imitators. Or maybe he did know and simply didn't care.

"That's right," Devereaux said. "You have something?"

"She just requisitioned a six-man team and a Jeppesen jet. Dulles to San Jose, California."

It was exactly the kind of thing he'd been waiting for. But what did it mean?

"Anything else?"

"She gave my guys the schematics for a compound in Silicon Valley. Owned by some *Lifestyles of the Rich and Famous* character named Constantine Grimble. You want me to find out more?"

Devereaux smiled. "I want you to find out everything."

chapter
sixty-four

KANEZAKI

Kanezaki was outside the terminal at Leesburg Executive Airport, standing in the shadows behind one of the portico's concrete support poles. If Rispel had anticipated him, he wanted some cover and concealment. But he'd have to be careful about announcing himself to Rain and the rest. They weren't a crew you wanted to surprise.

He saw a car pull in at the far end of the lot. The area was otherwise empty—the airport was closed for the night. His heart kicked up a notch, and for the dozenth time in the last half hour, he squeezed the grip of the HK Mark 23 he was holding inside his coat.

The car hit a dip and the headlights bounced. A moment later, it passed one of the parking lot's streetlights, and he caught a glimpse of the driver—a stunning blonde who must have been Delilah. And there, in the passenger seat, Rain. He relaxed his grip on the HK, took his hands out of his coat, and walked out from behind the support pole so they would have plenty of time to see him.

The car pulled up to the curb in front of him and stopped. The front passenger window went down. Rain looked at him. "Not that it isn't good to see you, Tom, but what are you doing here?"

Kanezaki glanced in back and saw Maya, holding a little dog, plus a few faces he didn't recognize. "Do I really need to tell you?"

Rain sighed. "Why didn't you give us a heads-up?"

"You might have said no."

"I might still say it."

Kanezaki laughed. "Also better to keep communications at a minimum. Not risk giving away my location unless it's really necessary. Just in case." He leaned down so he could see Delilah. "The car's fine there. And leave the keys inside. I've got someone coming to take care of it."

An extremely solid-looking man got out of the back. The car seemed to rise appreciably on its shock absorbers once he was out. Kanezaki straightened. "You must be Manus," he said.

The man nodded. "Kanezaki?"

Kanezaki gave him a nod in return.

Manus scanned the area, then looked at him. "You sent Dox? And Larison?"

Unlike Larison, who radiated danger, there was something about Manus that was as still as a bomb. Kanezaki felt nervous at the question, and how Manus might mean it. But he didn't see a way to avoid answering. So he simply said, "Yes."

There was a long, silent beat. Manus extended his hand. "Thank you," he said.

They shook. Kanezaki said, "I'm glad everything worked well."

Rain got out and did a perimeter check. It was reassuring—both substantively, and because some things, it seemed, would never change. Nor should they.

Rain held out his hand. They shook. Then Rain surprised him by offering a bow. Rain didn't ordinarily express the Japanese half of his background, even though he'd grown up in Japan and was far more "both" than half of anything. Kanezaki had always wondered whether the reticence was some way of denying Kanezaki's own heritage. Kanezaki was ethnic Japanese, but as a nisei, he'd been born in America and identified fully as American. And compared to Rain's native Japanese fluency, his own language skills were a joke.

"You know," Rain said, "the older you get, the more you remind me of Tatsu."

Kanezaki was surprised to find himself a little choked up by that. "Thanks," he managed to say.

Delilah came around the car from the driver's side. "Hello, Tom."

Kanezaki smiled. "Delilah. At last we meet."

She kissed him on both cheeks. "I've been looking forward to it for a long time. Though I always imagined different circumstances."

He nodded. "I'm sorry."

She waved a hand as though dismissing the problem. "My fault. By now, I should know better. You know, John talks about you a lot."

"Really?" Kanezaki said. "I didn't know he talked a lot about anything."

She laughed. "We'll have to work on your elicitation skills."

He smiled. "I think you might have skills I don't."

He saw Maya getting out on the other side of the car, still holding the dog. Two more people emerged on his side—a pretty brunette, and a teenaged boy, lanky but filling out. Evie and her son, Dash.

"You must be Tom," Evie said.

He nodded. "Hello, Evie."

They shook hands. "Marvin told me what happened," she said. "Thank you."

He nodded but didn't feel he deserved their gratitude. He hadn't been trying to save Manus—or, to the extent he had, it was subordinate to his desire to protect Diaz. And even that was a function of the imperative of intelligence—of learning more, understanding more, knowing more.

Dash held out his hand and gave Kanezaki's a firm shake. Kanezaki looked at Evie. "You sure you want to do this?" he said. "It's a long trip, and—"

"We stick together," Evie said. She put her hand on Dash's shoulder. Manus did the same from the other side. Dash put his arms around both their backs.

Maya came around the back of the car. When he'd talked to her earlier, after Rain and Delilah had picked her up, she'd sounded shell-shocked. Even beaten. She looked tired now. But also . . . determined.

"You all right?" he said.

She looked at him. "Let's get these motherfuckers." Her dog barked, and she added, "Yeah, boy, that's right."

Kanezaki nodded. "We will. But you've already given us all the critical intel. On where they were holding Schrader, on how to get to Grimble. On Grimble's interests, habits, everything. You don't have to—"

"Tom. I'm going."

Rain looked at him. "You don't have to go, either. You have two kids, Tom."

Kanezaki shook his head. "You've got to be kidding. I caused this." He looked at Maya. "All of it."

"No," Delilah said. "Rispel caused it. And Devereaux. And Hobbs. And Schrader. They caused all of it. And dragged us in. Now let's finish it. Okay?"

Rain looked at her, his expression unlike anything Kanezaki had seen in him before. Gratitude? Protectiveness? Love? All those, and more. He realized he had gotten to know Rain over time. But only in a relatively narrow range of circumstances. No wonder Delilah had joked about Rain's being talkative with her. When it was just the two of them, he was probably a different person. He was happy for them. But not quite happy enough to wish they weren't here.

"I got your shopping list," Kanezaki said, looking from one of them to the next. "Most of what you asked for is already on the plane. There's enough firepower and ammunition to lay siege to the Alamo. Commo's also good to go. But let me ask . . . is anyone here into bicycling?"

"I am," Maya said. "On weekends, I bike to work."

Dash seemed to have missed what Kanezaki had said, and Evie was signing to him. After a moment, he turned to Kanezaki. "I have a trail bike."

"Are you asking for the reason I think you're asking?" Rain said.

"Probably," Kanezaki said. "Grimble lives in a town called Woodside. I've attended a lot of conferences and other meetings in Silicon Valley, and they take their biking seriously. Daily waves of pelotons, not just on weekends, but on weekdays, too. For reconnaissance, it would be low-profile."

Evie glanced at Dash, obviously not liking the idea of his being involved even at the periphery. Well, she was his mother. It would be up to her.

"Another thing about Woodside," he went on. "It's home to numerous horse farms and riding trails. You see people on horseback all the time. So . . . anyone here know how to ride?"

"Yes," Evie said. "It's been a while, but yes. But . . . we're going to land at, what, five in the morning California time?"

Kanezaki nodded. "More or less."

She looked at him doubtfully. "And you're going to have a horse waiting for us?"

"I have people I can call," he said. "Whether they can deliver, I don't know. I'll need your shoe size and some other measurements regardless. But look, somehow Rispel knew Maya has been helping me. Someone made a run at you and Dash, almost certainly as a way of getting leverage over Manus. And the Seattle team had to fight their way through an ambush at Schrader's house. Rispel's been anticipating our moves. So we need to assume that when we get near Grimble's, there could be a welcoming party. If there is, I want to make sure we spot them before they spot us. And whatever they might be expecting, I doubt it's someone out horseback riding."

"I get it," Evie said. "But how are you getting ahold of this stuff? Because—"

"I had the same thought," Kanezaki said. "Outside of what you and Maya have done using Guardian Angel, it's all through my own networks. Nothing via CIA or any other official channels."

Ten minutes later, they were airborne, the cabin dimmed, the urban lights of Northern Virginia disappearing below them, the darkness of Shenandoah National Park and Monongahela National Forest coming into view. Maya stayed glued to her laptop, pillaging Guardian Angel for anything that might be useful about Grimble. But ten minutes after takeoff, Kanezaki watched while one after the other the rest of them grabbed pillows and blankets, reclined their seats, and dropped off—the aftermath, Kanezaki knew, of adrenaline and parasympathetic backlash. Napoleon had observed that the greatest danger occurs at the moment of victory, and Kanezaki was glad they had this interregnum to rest and recover.

He would have liked to join them. But the cross-country flight was his last chance to deal with logistics and matériel. And while he had an extensive network of suppliers of arms and related gear, and private jet owners, and safe house operators, and doctors, requisitioning bicycles and especially horses, particularly in the middle of the night, was definitely going to be a novel experience.

Beyond which, for the moment, he was too keyed up to sleep anyway. He'd failed to anticipate Rispel's ruthlessness or her resourcefulness, and as a result, Ali was dead. It could have been Maya; it could have been any of them. Going forward, he wouldn't allow himself to miss anything. He couldn't.

And there was something else. He wanted those videos. Preventing them from falling into Rispel's hands would feel like a stalemate, one achieved at great cost. Gaining control over them himself would be victory.

He'd always understood that knowledge is power, and he had sought knowledge accordingly. But the most powerful knowledge of all was knowledge you had—and that others lacked. Which was to say, knowledge was power only when it was *your* knowledge. What gave you power over others was their ignorance. Asymmetrical knowledge, otherwise known as intelligence. And he was in the intelligence business.

But these videos were something else entirely. They weren't knowledge. They were power itself. And power like that could only be entrusted to someone who would know how to wield it wisely.

Someone like himself.

chapter
sixty-five

DOX

Dox was standing between Larison and Labee, reviewing documents about Grimble's compound they'd printed and laid out on a table. It had been a short flight from Seattle, made shorter by the fact that Dox had passed out cold before the private plane Kanezaki had secured had even left the runway. Well, smoke 'em if you got 'em, as the saying went, and he'd learned as a Marine it was even truer when it came to sleep.

They were in an empty building now, part of a nondescript office park north of San Jose International Airport along Route 101. Another item Kanezaki had scored for them, complete with a kitchen someone had left stocked with breakfast items and plenty of coffee. Dox wouldn't have said so out of fear it would come across as condescending, but he was proud of the man. When they'd first met, Kanezaki had been nothing but a green CIA case officer. But since then, he'd been betrayed, disillusioned, blooded, and repeatedly promoted, and through it all had managed to assemble a private network that would have been the envy of any gunrunner, smuggler, trafficker, or other outlaw Dox had ever heard of.

Larison was reading a news article about the compound. "Look at this place," he said. "Twenty-three acres. A three-acre pond with two artificial waterfalls. Ten buildings, including a guardhouse, guesthouse, bridge house, boathouse, teahouse—"

"Everything but a henhouse," Dox said.

"—a barn, and a moon pavilion, whatever the hell that is. The main residence is modeled after an early seventeenth-century Kyoto palace. Thousands of tons of materials imported from Japan. Everything hand-planed and joined on the site without using nails or any other machine-made materials. Is this guy insane?"

"When you're that rich," Dox said, "I believe they call it 'eccentric.'"

"What about security?" Labee said.

Larison put down the article and picked up his coffee mug. "I know of the outfit. Gorgon Security. They're full service—threat assessments, investigations, and site security, including for estates like Grimble's."

"How good?" Labee said.

Larison sipped his coffee. "Good enough. Some ex-military, a lot of ex-cops."

Labee pointed to the blueprints on the table. "There are two posts. The guardhouse, on the northwest end at the Mountain Home Road entrance, here. And another structure on the southeast corner of the property, behind the main residence, here. How many guards in each?"

Larison flipped through a sheaf of papers. "One each. And two more patrolling the perimeter, so no fixed location. Total of four, all armed."

Dox pointed to a blown-up satellite map of the area. "The shortest distance to the main residence is here at the southeast corner. We can get there from this other road, Manzanita Way. We'd have to cross someone else's property, but these lots are all the size of small countries and there's ample tree coverage. I'm not worried about being seen. Kanezaki could get us intel on security at the various houses backing up on Grimble's property. I doubt any of them has more than an alarm system and maybe a dog, but it doesn't matter—we'd select the weakest link and cut through there."

"Speaking of dogs," Labee said, "are we sure there's no K-9 patrol?"

Dox shook his head. "No mention of it. Which is good, because you can bypass an alarm system, and you can make a person shut up by sticking a gun in his face, but for security a barking dog is hard to beat. Even a little yapper, let alone a squad of trained Dobermans. But probably Grimble figures that four gunmen on the property is plenty. I mean, what are his real concerns? Gawkers? At worst maybe a kidnapping attempt? I'm surprised he's got even this much. Tell you the truth, I was hoping all we'd have to do is hop a fence or something."

Diaz was standing off to the side, sipping her coffee. "Have we ruled out just calling Grimble, and explaining what we need?"

Dox gave her an appreciative nod. Diaz was smart, and impressively adaptable. She'd adjusted pretty fast from assuming disputes were something to be settled in a courtroom to realizing a lot of them got handled more the old-fashioned way.

"It's tempting," he said. "We have the number, it's how we know he is where he is. But look what happened at Schrader's house. Plus the hotel, plus with Manus's people. Plus with that poor girl Ali. Someone's been a step ahead of us, at least some of the time. And if that someone is monitoring Grimble's communications, we'd just be tipping them off."

"It's not just that," Labee said. "What if we were to call and couldn't persuade him? Or worse, what if he decided to do something on his own, release the videos or something like that, as a way of protecting himself. I don't want him to have time to think. I want him reacting. And I want us to be there so we can monitor how he's reacting. And press him, if he needs pressing."

Diaz nodded. "I get it."

Larison picked up the coffee carafe. "Anyone need a refill?" Diaz nodded and extended her mug. Larison refilled it, then his.

"Look at the placement of cameras," he said. "If we go in from the southeast side, there's no way to make it to the main residence without being picked up. In fact, there's no way to get to the main residence from anywhere without passing at least one camera. And according to the paperwork Kanezaki hacked from Gorgon, the cameras are monitored in real time in the main guardhouse."

"True," Dox said. "Probably by a minimum-wage guy focused more on his paperback novel or porn stash than on the camera feeds. But right, we can't count on that. We'll need a distraction."

Larison nodded, and Dox knew they were both thinking the same way: if there was one thing that could distract a man from his ostensible duties, it was the sight of Delilah.

He heard a car in the parking lot and looked up. Larison and Labee both drew their guns, then went to the window and peeked through the blinds. "Anyone here order a bicycle?" Larison said.

Dox drew the Wilson and went over. There was a van marked **PALO ALTO BICYCLES** under a streetlight in the empty parking lot. Two guys got out of the van, opened the back door, and took out a couple of bicycles. They set them down, dropped a duffel bag alongside them, got back in the van, and drove off.

"Can't say I like that duffel bag," Dox said. "But I think it's a safe bet this was all Kanezaki's idea. Recon, maybe."

He and Larison went out and brought in the bikes and the bag. They opened the bag on a table and examined the contents. Helmets, riding clothes, water bottles, and other gear. Dox looked at it all, shaking his head. "I don't get it. Bicycle cosplay, maybe."

Twenty minutes later, they heard another vehicle in the lot. They repeated the exercise at the window. This time it was a pickup truck with a trailer attachment. The trailer had **WOODSIDE EQUESTRIAN** stenciled on the side.

"Huh," Dox said, unable to come up with anything else. The rest of them seemed equally dumbstruck.

A stout man in a cowboy hat got out and went to the back of the trailer. He opened it and escorted out a horse.

Dox glanced over at Labee and Larison. "Are we all seeing the same thing?"

Larison continued to stare out the window. "I think someone is delivering us a horse."

"That's fine," Dox said. "Long as I'm not hallucinating."

Another pickup came into the lot and stopped, its engine idling. The man waved to its driver, then took hold of the horse's halter and led the animal to the front door. He knocked.

Dox and Larison stared at each other. Try as he might, Dox couldn't come up with what to do. Or even to say.

Diaz broke the logjam. She went to the door and called out, "Yes?"

"I have a horse here," a voice called back from the other side of the door in a light Mexican accent. "It's from Tom."

Diaz glanced at the rest of them, but no one seemed able to offer guidance. She gave a quick *Whatever* shake of her head. "Put your guns away," she said. As soon as they had complied, she opened the door.

"Buenos días," the man said. "I am Miguel. May I come in?"

Diaz glanced over, but again no one offered anything. She stepped aside and said, "Please."

The man came in, followed by the horse. It took a few seconds before they were both completely inside. Diaz closed the door behind them.

"Thank you," the man said. "This is Margarita. Usually she stays in the stables. But Tom told me to bring her in. You don't mind?"

Margarita swished her tail, but other than that seemed not terribly interested to find herself in an office. Diaz glanced around impatiently, and, when no one offered to help, switched to Spanish with the man. Dox followed most of it. Tom had asked Miguel to drop off the horse. The tack was in the pickup; the pickup and the trailer were theirs; here are the keys; try to get her back to us by three, when the kids arrive for their riding lessons.

Miguel turned to the rest of them. "She's a good girl," he said. "Very gentle. Give her a sugar cube and you'll have a friend for life." He turned to Diaz and doffed his hat. *"Hasta luego, señorita."*

"Muchas gracias, señor," Diaz said. She closed and locked the door behind him. They watched the man get in the second truck, and kept watching until the taillights were gone.

Dox turned and looked at Margarita. It was a reasonably surreal sight. "Well," he said, rubbing his chin, "as Nicolas Cage put it in *Con Air*, 'On any other day, that might seem strange.'"

Diaz was stroking Margarita's shoulder. Margarita dropped her head. "That's good," Dox said. "That means she likes you."

Diaz smiled, still intent on the horse. "Yeah?"

Dox nodded. "You bet. Though it doesn't exactly answer the question of what she's doing here. Maybe old Kanezaki thought this outfit needed a mascot. Well, they ought to be here to explain soon enough."

chapter sixty-six

DELILAH

Delilah slept well on the flight from Virginia. Hunger was the best seasoning, and exhaustion the best soporific.

The first pale light was showing in the eastern sky as they left the plane and walked onto the tarmac. There were three vehicles waiting. A gray Toyota minivan. A FedEx truck. And a bright yellow Porsche 718 Cayman GT4.

Kanezaki reached under the truck, felt around for a moment, and retrieved a magnetic lockbox. "Okay," he said, opening the lockbox and taking out a set of keys. "No fighting over the cars. The Porsche is for Delilah."

John was scanning the parking lot. He was attuned to good clothes, but cars meant nothing to him. Delilah appreciated both.

She looked at Kanezaki. "Your idea of a low profile?"

He handed her the keys. "More hiding in plain sight. You won't be out of place in Woodside. Shit, you can drive a stick, right?"

She cocked an eyebrow.

"Sorry," he said. "Of course you can."

Dash, who had been staring at the car, signed something to Evie. Evie looked at Kanezaki. "Are we going far?"

Kanezaki shook his head. "Fifteen minutes up the highway."

Delilah didn't know sign, but she caught the drift. "It's okay with me," she said to Evie. "If it's okay with you."

Evie smiled and nodded to Dash. The boy laughed delightedly, and he gave Delilah a double thumbs-up.

"Why don't I take the FedEx truck?" Kanezaki said to the rest of them. He handed John a set of keys. "You take the minivan. The others should be waiting for us. It's an office park on O'Brien Drive in Menlo Park, straight up 101. Follow me. I doubt anyone's going to get lost, but if there's a problem, each vehicle is outfitted with encrypted walkie-talkies. No cell towers, no way to track a signal. Good to go?"

Delilah got in the Porsche with Dash, who was all smiles. *Resilient kid,* she thought. Just twenty-four hours earlier, he and his mother had killed someone who was trying to do the same to them. Or to do them some kind of harm, anyway. If he'd been Israeli and the IDF had gotten wind, they'd be eyeing him for Sayeret Matkal. If that worked out, Mossad would recruit him for Kidon. For whatever reason, the thought made her sad.

He buckled his seatbelt. "We don't really have to stay behind them, do we?"

She smiled at him. "This time, I think yes. But maybe we'll get a chance to drive her properly later. Would you like that?"

"Yes!"

"Okay. We'll see."

They all moved out. Dash had a point—keeping the race-bred machine behind a minivan at fifty-five miles an hour, the engine growling as though enraged at being so unfairly hobbled, was frustrating.

"You're French?" Dash said.

She looked at him so he could read her lips. "These days, yes. It's complicated."

"Is John Japanese?"

"He was born there."

"Are you married?"

"What? No."

"Oh. You look like you're married."

Out of the mouths of babes, she thought. She glanced at him. "I have to watch the road."

He smiled—an innocent smile, or was there something more in it?—and said, "It's okay."

Ten minutes later, they were pulling into a parking lot behind a low-slung, unremarkable collection of office buildings. A few landscape management and auto-repair shops, others with names more suggestive of technology startups. A door to one of the places opened—Dox. Delilah killed the engine and stepped out of the Porsche.

Dox gave her a big grin. "Darlin', that car's almost as pretty as you."

She smiled back, surprised at how good it was to see him, even under the circumstances.

Kanezaki got out of the FedEx truck. Dox gestured to the Porsche and said, "No more Priuses at the rental place?"

Kanezaki laughed. "A friend with a collection."

The others were getting out now, too. Dox said, "Come on in, y'all. I've got too many hugs to give in the parking lot. The rest of the gang is waiting inside."

They filed in. The first thing Delilah noticed was a horse at the far end of the space, with a pretty Latina—Diaz?—standing alongside it, stroking its shoulder. But before she could process the incongruity, Dox gave her a big hug, then moved on to Kanezaki and Rain, switching to handshakes for Evie, Dash, Manus, and Maya. Once everyone was in, Kanezaki closed and locked the door, then stood at the corner of the window, keeping an eye on the parking lot.

She saw Larison hug Rain, cocking his head at Dox and saying, "His influence." Rain was smiling and laughing, and she realized how attached he had grown to these people—and how attached she had become, too. For a moment, she felt guilty about having tried to stop him, and was relieved he hadn't let her.

Livia came over and offered her hand. "Delilah. It's good to see you."

Delilah summoned a smile. "And you, Livia." They shook. With someone else, *la bise*, the French kiss, would have felt natural, and though they had parted that way the last time they had seen each other, in Paris, in general Livia had a standoffish air, and Delilah had no desire to make either of them uncomfortable.

They might have stood there having not much to say to each other, but Larison came to the rescue. "Hey," he said to Delilah. "Sorry again for dragging you into this. But . . . I'm glad you're here."

It was adroit of him to apologize for what Delilah still thought of as more Livia's war than anyone else's. After all, Dox had stepped in with Kanezaki in an attempt to keep Livia out of it, and the rest of the dominos had fallen from there. Delilah knew this wasn't the generous view she had managed at the airport in Virginia. The truth was, Livia just rubbed her the wrong way. Delilah had known plenty of zealots in her time—the term came from a sect of Israelites that had resisted the Romans—and no matter how noble their intentions, in the end they were always willing to sacrifice anyone else for whatever the sacred cause.

She smiled—no effort with Larison—and kissed him on both cheeks. "Daniel. I won't deny, I'm glad, too." She glanced over at Diaz and the horse. "I'm sorry, am I seeing that correctly?"

Larison nodded. "It's a long story. Actually, I don't know the story. We're hoping Kanezaki can explain."

Delilah saw Evie and Dash and waved. "Evie, Dash, let me introduce you." They came over, and the extra people diluted the initial awkwardness with Livia. Dash, who was a natural elicitor, immediately started asking Livia questions about being a cop. Larison told Evie he was glad that she and Dash were all right and that John had been there to help. It was interesting to see how relaxed Larison could be, even charming. He must never have had people he trusted. And now he did. Not so unlike John.

Delilah noticed Maya standing a bit awkwardly, holding her dog. Larison must have seen as well, because he excused himself and walked over. "You must be Maya."

She nodded. "Yes." The dog shrank back a bit in her arms.

"Daniel Larison. That was some impressive intel you got us. Thanks."

Maya gave him an uncertain smile. "You're welcome."

Delilah could tell the girl was nervous. Probably just at the collective decades of killing experience suddenly assembled around her. And probably particularly in the presence of Larison, who even when he was relaxed had an unpredictable quality, some potentially explosive thing, just below the surface.

"What's your dog's name?" Larison said.

Maya looked at the dog, then back to Larison. "Frodo."

Larison raised his eyebrows. "Frodo, huh? Well, I think I get how you're feeling, Maya. 'I wish the Ring had never come to me. I wish none of this had happened.'"

Maya's face lit up in a surprised smile. "You're a fan?"

"Of course. From way back."

Her smile faltered. "It does feel a little that way. But . . . I want to help."

There was a pause. Larison said, "I'm sorry about your friend."

Maya nodded but didn't otherwise respond.

A second passed. Larison said, "One thing I think Frodo got wrong."

Maya looked at him. "What?"

"When he said, 'It is useless to meet revenge with revenge: it will heal nothing.' In my experience? It heals plenty."

He patted her on the shoulder and moved off. A moment later, he was shaking hands with Manus, both of them smiling as though they were old comrades in arms, when in fact they had met only a few days earlier. Though in fairness, a lot had happened since then.

Delilah looked over and saw John talking to Livia. They were laughing about something, and for a moment, Delilah envied his ease with her. Not in the minor-key jealous way she'd felt about the flirtation with Yuki. This was different—more akin to, what, a teacher and a capable student? John had told her about a conversation with Livia, when they'd all been in Paris, and his sense that the questions she had asked him, about his ability to adopt different personas to blend or disarm or get close, had been the product of much more than general curiosity. That this woman had an interest in killing, an intimacy with it, and not just in the line of duty. Of course, a normal person would have been put off by that. But then again, Livia wouldn't have been interested in John if he were normal.

It was strange. John had always approached Delilah as an equal. He was the better tactician, but he never talked down to her, and though he was always willing to answer her questions, sometimes in quite personal ways, he seemed to have no particular urge to teach her, either. She wondered whether Livia struck some different chord. Maybe John thought he had something to impart to Livia of which Delilah had no need. If so, she didn't want to begrudge him that.

Dox walked over with Diaz. "Alondra, meet Delilah. Delilah, Alondra Diaz. Alondra set sail only a few days ago now, but my God, she got her sea legs quick. She's a good driver, a good interrogator, and for a city girl I think she's got a way with horses, too."

Diaz laughed and she and Delilah shook hands. "I think I need you to introduce me more often, Dox. And Delilah, it's good to meet you. He's talked a lot about you."

Delilah smiled and glanced at Dox. "He does talk a lot."

Dox laughed. "Someone's got to provide the entertainment around here. It's not like John's gonna do it."

They all spent a while getting acquainted and reacquainted, drinking coffee, taking advantage of the well-stocked refrigerator. At all times, someone kept watch on the parking lot.

After a half hour, Kanezaki said, "We should get to it. The sun's up, and if Rispel has somehow learned about Grimble, we don't want to give her another chance to get ahead of us."

"I doubt the plan would be to ambush us straightaway," John said. "Rispel doesn't know what we learned from Schrader. It might be something she needs. So the smart play would be to hang back until we've made contact with Grimble. At that point, if all goes well, we'd have the entire puzzle. Rispel could swoop in and collect it all at once."

"Great," Dox said. "Maybe she'll capture and waterboard us, like she did Schrader."

"We already sketched out an approach," Larison said to John. "It tracks with your point. But Tom, you're going to have to bring us up to speed on the transport. I mean, you did order the horse, right? The bicycles? The screaming yellow Porsche?"

"I did," Kanezaki said. "I knew that by the time we were here, it would be too late to get ahold of anything I hadn't thought of earlier. So I tried to be comprehensive—including fake license plates we'll attach to the truck and the Porsche. But listen, Maya found a few interesting things about Grimble on the flight over. Maya, you want to tell them?"

"He's into figurines," Maya said. "I'd heard something about this before, but didn't realize the extent. I mean, big-time. Obsessively."

Once upon a time, Dox would have made a crack about that— about his own interest in figurines, or at least in figures, something like that. But he didn't do that sort of thing anymore. Livia. He really was smitten. And even as the thought took shape, Delilah realized *smitten* was probably her own attempt to downplay the depth of his feeling, a reluctance that was an outgrowth of her distrust of Livia. She would have to be careful about that. If Dox was in love with this woman,

Delilah would have to come to terms with it, lest she force Dox to make a choice that ultimately would be no choice at all.

"What kind of figurines?" Delilah asked, knowing that if no one else raised the question, Larison would, and probably less delicately.

"Japanese," Maya said. "Samurai, feudal lords, that kind of thing. Something called the Battle of Sekigahara."

"How is that relevant?" Larison said, and Delilah had to suppress a smile.

"He spends a ton of money on it," Maya said. "And apparently a ton of time. Casts his own figurines, paints them, uses authentic materials like silk and leather to construct their outfits. He has a whole room dedicated to it. He's given a couple interviews, but he won't allow photos."

"The Battle of Sekigahara involved almost two hundred thousand soldiers," Rain said. "If he's serious about depicting even a portion of it, yes, he'd need some space."

Maya nodded. "The point is, we can't be sure of where he'll be on the property—only of where his phone will be. That's not the same thing. People don't ordinarily go out without their cellphones, but they do sometimes leave them on chargers while moving around their homes. And this guy's home is on twenty-three acres with ten buildings. Knowing what he spends his time on could help us narrow things down."

The room was quiet for a moment while the group digested that. Livia said, "We have a lot to plan, and not much time. Schrader said the next release is scheduled for three o'clock this afternoon."

Delilah wasn't surprised. They all had different concerns, and Livia's were about the girls in the videos more than they were about the people in this room. And while those priorities weren't indefensible, from Delilah's perspective they didn't make the woman trustworthy, either.

"We all have different puzzle pieces," Kanezaki said. "Maya knows Grimble. I've been arranging transport and other gear. You guys have the schematics for his compound. Now we need to turn it into a plan. So let's put our heads together and get this done."

It wasn't *Henry V*, Delilah thought, but she'd heard worse. And it was good to see how seasoned a player Kanezaki had become. It wasn't so long ago that he would never have presumed to take charge of a team of such formidable operators—or that any of them would have taken him seriously if he had tried.

And while on one level she was happy for him, somewhere deeper down she felt a tiny germ of concern. She considered Kanezaki one of the good guys, but of course in the intelligence business *good* was a relative term. Relative, and flexible. She'd never known Kanezaki to do anything that wasn't calculated to increase his information portfolio, or that wasn't a quid pro quo for something he himself wanted. It was possible his interest now was simply about obscuring the girls' faces in those videos and then publicizing them, and thereby neutralizing the threat the videos had come to represent to everyone in the room. But it was also possible he was playing for something more. In her experience, people didn't beat swords into plowshares, any more than governments did. No, when people came across a sword—especially one others were trying to acquire—they tended to conclude that the best possibility would be to find a way by which they themselves could wield it.

chapter
sixty-seven

EVIE

E vie rode Margarita along the side of Manzanita Way, Evie bounc-
ing lightly in the saddle, Margarita's hoofs clomping on the dirt
trail. Evie had a lump on the back of her head from the tumble down
the stairs, and despite heroic quantities of ibuprofen, her ankle was
throbbing, too, but after what had happened the pain was almost glo-
rious, a kind of proof of life. It was a beautiful day—the sky bright
blue; the canopy of leaves above the cracked, gray-top road lit in various hues of yellow and orange and red; the midday air crisp and cool
in the shadows and radiantly warm in the sun. If the houses hadn't all
been mansions at the ends of long, winding, cobblestoned driveways,
and mostly shrouded by moss-covered stone walls and dense clumps of
old-growth trees, she might have thought she was far off in the country
somewhere, rather than thirty miles south of San Francisco in one of
the most exclusive enclaves of Silicon Valley's moneyed elite. Well, she
could see why people would live here, if they could afford it, and why
so many of them owned horses. She hadn't ridden in years and promised
to make more time for it once this craziness was done. And it would be
done. She believed that. She had to.

Her task was to identify anything that looked like surveillance.
Rain had gone over a map with her, explaining where Rispel or another
enemy could be expected to set up in preparation for an ambush. The

man seemed to have a knack for getting in the head of an adversary, and Evie had been struck by how the others, who were themselves all veterans of one kind or another, had deferred to him. And she had been even more impressed by the way Marvin, who had outthought NSA Director Anders and his goon, Delgado, had periodically nodded in approval at Rain's thinking.

Good security could be thought of as concentric circles, Rain had explained, with the outer circles tending to be more cost-effective and intended, among other things, to buy more time. Think castles, he had said: moat, ramparts, walls, battlements, keep. Meaning you could gain a significant advantage by finding a way to bypass the outer circles and attacking the inner layers directly. Which is exactly what they hoped to do here, and exactly what Rispel or whoever else had been preempting them would be expecting.

Depending on her resources, Rain said, Rispel would deploy surveillance, both mobile and static. A mobile unit would have at least four miles of ground to cover—the circumference of roads around Grimble's and the adjacent properties—and would therefore be faced with too much risk of missing a small team attempting to gain entry. So there would also likely be a static unit or units, positioned at choke points. On the one hand, these teams would be impossible to avoid. On the other hand, they would be easier to spot—which is what Evie was trying to do now.

They walked along, Margarita's hoofs clop-clopping pleasingly in the stillness. As pretty a road as it was, it seemed not much favored by pedestrians—maybe because it was the middle of the week, maybe because the road didn't really lead anywhere. A few of the houses she passed had gardening crews at work, and there were two construction sites. Beyond that and some birdsong in the trees overhead, everything was quiet.

Close to the end of the road, thirty yards ahead, there was a small bridge that passed over a dry culvert. A man in a baseball cap and shades was sitting on it, eating a sandwich held in a brown paper bag. He looked up without evident interest as she passed and then went back to his sandwich.

He could have been no one—a construction worker or a gardener taking a break, a birdwatcher, someone waiting on a friend for a planned bucolic stroll. But she didn't think so. There were plenty of horses in the area—she had passed enough stables and droppings to know that—but still, his lack of interest as she went by struck her as more studied than real. The cap and shades felt like light disguise. And though outdoor work was a good way to stay in shape—Marvin was proof of that—even under the sweatshirt, this guy looked like he spent a lot of time pumping iron.

She made a right on Sand Hill Road and continued until Sand Hill became Portola, then turned onto Old La Honda until she came to the parking area for the Thornewood Preserve, the terminus to another series of horse trails. Marvin, Dash, and Rain were waiting outside the truck, and she could see the relief on Marvin's face as she came into view. She stopped and dismounted.

Dash immediately signed, *Did you see anyone?*

She nodded. "I think someone is there," she said to Rain. She held out the reins to him so she could sign. "Here, can you hold these?"

Rain started to say something, then stopped as though he couldn't figure out what. He took the reins. Margarita looked at Evie, seemingly displeased at the handoff.

"Thanks," Evie said, and then started simultaneously signing for Marvin and Dash. "Yes, I think someone is there. Right at the entrance to Manzanita, where you thought they would be."

Rain glanced at the road behind her. "You're confident you weren't followed?"

She smiled. "I didn't even see a car on Old La Honda. The only way someone could have tailed me is on a horse of their own."

Rain looked up at the canopy of leaves above them, and she knew what he was thinking: *Drones?*

"If they're using drones," she said, "they couldn't be anything man-portable or I would have heard it. Or seen it. And regardless, I doubt someone out horseback-riding would be the kind of thing they'd be looking for."

Rain nodded. She couldn't tell from his expression whether he was impressed with her analysis or doubtful, so she added, "At NSA, among other things, I was in charge of tying together distributed video feeds and facial recognition. I wasn't a field operative, but I'm not a stranger to surveillance."

Rain nodded again, though no less unreadably.

The side door of the trailer opened and Kanezaki got out. "All good?" he said.

She nodded. "Let's get Margarita in the trailer, and I'll brief you."

Kanezaki opened the back, took the reins from Rain, who seemed relieved to no longer be holding them, and helped lead Margarita inside. They all went in and closed the door behind them. Frodo, lying in a corner, watched, apparently too bemused by Margarita and all the strangers to react. Rain had wanted to leave the dog at the office park, but Maya had persuaded him by asking, "What if we can't make it back? He's chipped, he can be traced to me."

Rain had nodded reluctantly at that. And Evie had suppressed a smile. Maya wasn't just computer smart. She knew how to persuade, too, primarily by understanding what mattered to the person she was persuading. Evie recognized the skill because Dash wore her down with it all the time.

Evie told them what she had seen. Marvin looked at Rain and nodded as though to signal his concurrence that the sandwich man was not a civilian. Rain nodded back.

"Let's see how long he's been there," Kanezaki said. He worked the screen of a Stingray cellphone tracker for a minute. Dash watched, his mouth slightly open in the way he looked when he was utterly fascinated.

Kanezaki said, "Entrance of Manzanita at Sand Hill?"

"Yes," she said. "Maybe fifty feet in, on the side of the road. You're not seeing a phone there?"

He played with the controls. "That's right."

"Then he doesn't have one," she said. "Or it's turned off."

No one had to say what that meant. It was unusual for someone not to be carrying a powered-up cellphone. Combined with the other factors—the location, the appearance—it made it more likely the man was indeed surveillance.

She took off the riding helmet and field boots and pulled on her shoes. She'd change out of the jodhpurs later. She had to give Kanezaki credit—he'd wanted her to look the part, and she had.

"So what do we do?" she said.

Rain said, "Let's have Maya make a pass on the bicycle. If the guy's still there, that'll settle it."

The fascination on Dash's face changed to disappointment. He had badly wanted to be part of the bicycle countersurveillance. Intellectually, Evie doubted there was much if any danger—he would have just been biking in the area, as she had been riding Margarita. And of course Dash had made that case. But intellectually didn't matter—Evie absolutely refused. Delilah had cushioned the blow, saying to Dash, "Hey, I thought we were going to go take the Porsche for a ride." Dash had smiled in a way that made Evie wonder whether he had developed a rapid-onset crush. She couldn't blame him—the woman was certainly stunning. But it seemed that, compared to actually being involved in countersurveillance, Delilah and the Porsche were still a consolation prize. Or, more likely, Dash was wondering why he couldn't just have both.

Kanezaki unclipped one of the encrypted walkie-talkies, then hesitated. He turned to Rain so Dash couldn't see what he was saying. "You're okay taking that guy out, based just on a second sighting?"

Rain looked at him. "It's more than your outfit uses as the basis for a drone strike."

Kanezaki seemed not to have an answer for that.

"Besides," Rain said. "It's not just a second sighting. That sandwich feels like cover for action. If he's still eating it after a half hour, we'll know. And yeah, if Maya sees a sandwich, it could be his second, or even his third. Maybe he's a sandwich freak. Maybe he's just a guy who likes to sit by the side of the road for an hour at a time. Probably not, though. And besides, on top of all the other evidence, the final check is me. Before anything else happens, I'll see for myself. And I'll know what I'm looking at."

Evie was surprised to realize she had no objections. She trusted Marvin, and Marvin trusted Rain.

But beyond that, just a day earlier, someone had come for her and Dash. She wasn't going to let that happen again. No matter what.

chapter
sixty-eight

MAYA

Maya was sitting in front of a place called the Village Bakery when she got the call from Tom. She took a last sip of coffee, closed the chin strap of her helmet, got on the bike, and took off.

She'd felt silly when she first suited up—a brightly colored jersey and matching tights; padded, fingerless gloves; clip-in shoes; a pair of high-tech-looking shades. But Tom had assured her that she'd look right at home in Woodside, and he'd been right; there were a dozen riders in front of the bakery, and everything they were wearing was garishly over-the-top. The only mistake Tom had made was in getting a bike that was a little too fancy—a Trek Madone SLR 9 that had attracted some admiring commentary from the other riders. On the other hand, Tom had explained that excess was the point—as with the Porsche he'd scored for Delilah, it was important to go beyond what an op would require, or what a finance department would ever approve. Maya had noticed Rain smiling as Tom had explained, and Tom had smiled back. Maya realized there was a history there, and maybe something of a mentorship. She wondered whether Tom would tell her about it. And if things would ever be normal enough again for her to have a chance to ask.

The bike was incredibly light and responsive, and she realized that her own was going to feel forever clunky after experiencing this one. She wondered for a moment whether that was some kind of metaphor for her life, whether being part of this op was going to make everything that came before it seem pale and mundane. Certainly her non-date with Dave the trumpeter felt improbable now, even absurd. Then she thought of Ali and wished more than anything she could just go back, to when everything was routine and normal, and she'd taken it all for granted.

She crossed Woodside Road, cut behind a place called Roberts Market, and made a right on Mountain Home Road. She saw a sign about horse crossings alongside another for bicycles, with an all-caps notice in the middle admonishing **SHARE THE ROAD**, and again she gave Tom mental props for knowing his operational environment.

She came to the corner of Manzanita and made a left past a house with its own stables. She pedaled harder, and the Trek practically leapt forward underneath her, the trees pressed close to the sides of the road whizzing by. She was glad she was in decent biking shape. With this level of equipment, it might have looked odd if she weren't pushing it.

She passed another house with a stable, came around a gentle curve, and there, just ahead of the stop sign at Sand Hill Road, the man Evie had described, sitting on a bridge, eating a sandwich held in a brown paper bag. Another bicyclist, a guy in top-level gear like hers, turned right off Sand Hill onto Manzanita and rode past. The man watched him go by, then glanced at Maya going the other way, seeming not particularly interested in either.

Maya was relieved at the momentary distraction. She knew her cover for status was solid, but still it was good to see people just like her in the area. It was fine to be a fish in the water, but even better to swim in a school.

She turned right on Sand Hill and dropped a gear as she started heading uphill, her heart beating harder. In fifteen minutes or so, she would be at Wunderlich Park, where Delilah, Dox, Larison, and Livia were waiting. Her own role had been easy, and now it was done. The hard part was about to begin.

LIVIA

Livia jogged down the side of Sand Hill, keeping to the left and going against traffic. About fifty yards away she saw Rain come around a curve, running toward her on the same side of the road. Rain was wearing black 2XU compression tights and a sleeveless compression top and looked, as far as Livia could tell, like any other prosperous local serious about keeping in shape. He had grumbled uncharacteristically about the superhero-tight clothes, but Kanezaki had argued that the point was threefold: come across as a serious runner, look like you're not doing anything to avoid being noticed, and wear something under which it would be nearly impossible to conceal a weapon. All of which Rain reluctantly agreed was well calculated to help get him close enough to remove the target silently.

Naturally, as soon as Rain was suited up, Carl had taken advantage by declaiming, "Very attractive apparel, if I may say so, and shows off your package to full advantage, such as it is." To which Rain had responded only with an infinitely patient look. Maybe Rain's discomfort was about the near certainty that Carl was going to rib him. But more likely, Livia thought, it had to do with not being able to hide. Something about Rain always seemed exceptionally balanced and mobile, as though he could move instantly in any direction while being difficult to be moved by someone else. Livia recognized the characteristic as the result of decades of classical martial arts training. But though his clothes seemed high-quality and fit well—Delilah's influence?—Livia hadn't understood the kind of shape Rain was in until the running outfit left him no way to conceal it. And she realized this was something he must have preferred the world not to know, because an adversary's ignorance would be Rain's advantage.

Livia's role was backup, so she was dressed somewhat differently: standard ankle-length tights, yes, but more importantly a Lululemon oversized sweatshirt voluminous enough to conceal the Glock in a bellyband holster, and the SoMiCo Vaari, the other half of her everyday carry, in a small-of-the-back sheath. It wouldn't matter if anyone noticed her. If they did, it would be because Rain's attack had failed, at which point no one would have to suspect she was concealing weapons under the sweatshirt. She would be offering them all the proof they could imagine, and more.

She picked up her pace to make sure Rain didn't get to Manzanita too far ahead of her. They were working off maps, not the actual terrain, and there had been no time or opportunity for practice runs. In fact, they were getting uncomfortably close to three o'clock and the next video release. So there was going to be a lot of adjusting on the fly.

Rain reached Manzanita and turned right. He must have seen her coming—she was only thirty feet away when he turned—but he gave no sign of it. She felt nothing from him, no recognition, no awareness. Of course it made sense that he would ignore her, but still, somehow the totality of it, the absence of anything, surprised her.

She rounded the corner and saw the man sitting on the bridge, holding a brown paper bag as Evie and Maya had described. Rain had slowed his pace slightly. Was he breathing more heavily? Maybe. But she doubted it was from exertion. More to appear winded, and therefore less of a potential threat.

Rain was fifteen feet from the man now; Livia was twenty feet behind him. The man glanced past Rain at Livia. He seemed uninterested. But the contrast with Rain was impossible to miss. The man *seemed* uninterested. With Rain, there was nothing at all.

Ten feet. The man glanced to his right. The street was otherwise empty, but still he must have decided he didn't like the pattern of two ostensible runners closing in on him from Sand Hill, the first on his side of the street, the second angled off on the other. He stood, his hand drifting toward the small of his back.

Rain's pace and posture remained unchanged. Livia wanted to shout a warning to him—the man was going for a weapon. She reached into the bellyband and gripped the Glock.

Rain had pulled abreast of the man. She thought he was going to go right by. Instead, he shot out his right hand and clapped the man hard on the left shoulder, shoving him to the side. The man braced against the impact, and instantly Rain caught the fabric of the man's sleeve and yanked him in the opposite direction, his right foot arcing in and blasting the man's legs out from under him in *deashi-barai*, a judo foot sweep. Livia knew the move well and in fact favored it herself, but in competition no real accuracy was involved beyond taking your opponent to the mat. Rain was more precise, steering the man's head into the concrete wall he'd been sitting on. The man's skull connected with a resounding *crack!* and the gun he'd been trying to draw went flying through the air. Instantly Rain encircled the man's neck front to back, locked his arms, and arched violently away. There was another loud *crack!* and the man went limp. Before he could fall Rain shoved him back onto the wall, pushed him over it, and then vaulted lightly after him.

Despite all her experience with killing, Livia was awed. Carl had told her about Rain, about what he was capable of, and though she had been impressed by his self-control, his tactical acumen, and his ability to cohere and lead a team, she'd never seen him take direct action. The only other time she had witnessed anything like it was a freak who had attacked her in a hotel room when she'd been in college. A complete lack of warning signs was therefore something she associated with sociopaths. It didn't horrify her to see it in Rain. On the contrary, she instantly understood it as a form of power, the same way jiu-jitsu itself had struck her when she'd first seen it as a terrified junior high student beset by bullies at school and sexual abuse at home.

She scooped up the gun, stepped off the road, and dropped down behind the bridge wall into the culvert. Rain was going through the man's pockets. "Did he make you?" he said.

He was as matter-of-fact as though nothing had happened. Her awe increased. "What do you mean?" she said.

"Something tipped him. He went for his gun."

"I didn't think you saw his hand moving."

"I saw."

"Yeah, I'm getting that now. I reached for mine. He might have reacted to that. Sorry."

"No harm done." He pulled a cellphone from one of the man's pockets. "Nothing on him but this. It's turned off. Probably a burner. We'll leave it. You picked up the gun?"

"Yeah. SIG P320. Don't worry, I'll wipe it down and leave it."

They had considered wearing gloves, but decided it wasn't cold enough and that they would look more innocent without anything that could be interpreted as an attempt to prevent fingerprints.

Rain glanced at her. "I really do micromanage, don't I?"

In response, she offered a gentle shrug.

He nodded. "Don't let Dox see the SIG. He'll insist one of us keep it. He likes trophies." He used the man's sweatshirt to wipe the cellphone.

Livia looked at the man. His face was contorted and his neck was bent at an impossible angle. She and Rain had once talked about Rain's ability to shape-shift, to inhabit a legend so well he would go unnoticed against whatever background he was operating in. However he had acquired this related ability, she wanted him to teach her.

"How do you do that?" she said.

He shrugged. "It's just a neck crank."

She sensed he knew she was asking about something else. "That's not what I mean. You didn't show anything. *Anything.* The way you're not showing it even now."

He didn't respond.

She knew he was reluctant, and that her intensity probably wasn't the right way to persuade him. But she badly wanted to know. "Will you teach me?"

He started to say something, then stopped and looked away. After a moment, he said, "If you want."

She heard several vehicles pass on Sand Hill. One turned onto Manzanita, but the sound wasn't right, and they stayed put.

A minute later, she heard the rumbling of multiple wheels turning off Sand Hill. The rumbling stopped just ahead of the bridge. Livia glanced around the side of the concrete wall and saw the truck and the horse trailer.

The back doors opened, and Carl, Diaz, and Kanezaki jumped out. They were wearing tactical street clothes: cargo pants, chest rigs under zip-down jackets, light boots, gloves. All in woodland colors, and with body armor underneath. Diaz had insisted on coming, and when Livia couldn't talk her out of it, she'd made sure Diaz was carrying. A Glock 19, simple to operate. They'd gone over the basics, just in case.

Diaz and Kanezaki vaulted over the side of the bridge. Carl tossed a pair of duffels to Rain and Livia, then shouldered a third and came over himself. Evie, who was behind the wheel of the truck, drove off.

Carl set down his duffel and glanced at the body on the ground. "Well, that had to hurt. Maybe better to move him under the culvert. Little less visible. Tom, give me a hand?"

"Sentry?" Kanezaki said.

Rain said nothing, but the question—which could as easily have been stated, *You sure you didn't just kill some innocent bystander?*—pissed off Livia. "Yes," she said. "But if you have any doubts, how about next time you take care of it yourself?"

Rain looked at her, and she thought she detected the trace of a smile.

There was a pause, then Kanezaki said, "I didn't mean it that way. I'm sorry."

Rain unzipped one of the bags—the same clothes and equipment the others were wearing. "Don't worry about it," he said. "And no, no intel on him. Just a burner, turned off."

Carl and Kanezaki dragged the body under the overpass, where to see it a passerby would have to come down from the road. Then Carl unzipped the second bag, pulled out Livia's armored vest, and started helping her into it. "You know," he said to Rain, "spandex becomes you. I don't know why you don't dress this way more often."

Rain chuckled, and Livia could tell Kanezaki's faux pas had been forgotten. "Maybe I do," Rain said. "Just not around you."

Carl laughed. "Well, at least now I know what to get you for Christmas."

Livia glanced at the third bag. "Rifle?"

Carl smiled. "HK762A1, OSS suppressor, Leupold scope, twenty-round mags. Be still, my beating heart. And Manus has a suppressed HK UMP in nine-millimeter with thirty-round mags. Just in case. I didn't like the way we were outgunned at that Lake Tapps house." He glanced at Kanezaki. "We get to keep the toys when we're done, right?"

Kanezaki shook his head. "Delilah has to return the Porsche, and you and Manus have to return the HKs."

Carl patted the bag. "Hopefully unused. But we'll see."

Livia glanced at her watch. "Less than an hour until three," she said. "Starting to get a little tight."

"Just about good to go," Carl said. "Should be plenty of time."

Livia knew there should be—if things went smoothly. But nothing had gone smoothly yet.

They each affixed wireless earpieces, about the size of a pair of AirPods and connected to belt-mounted radios. Kanezaki had explained that the range would be enough for their purposes, but with less risk of being tracked than a cellphone.

"I hate these earpieces," Carl said. "They're so snug you can't get 'em out without a damn screwdriver."

"Everyone online?" Rain said, and one by one they checked in. "Delilah and Larison," he said. "You're in position?"

"We are," Livia heard Delilah say. "When you're ready, just say go."

"Five minutes," Rain said. "Tom, did you confirm—"

"Of course," Kanezaki said. "Other than the guards and Grimble himself, no cellphones on the property. Which tracks with the intel— no gardeners allowed except when Grimble is off the compound."

Rain glanced at Livia and gave her a small smile, as if to say, *Okay, I micromanage.* She gave him one back to indicate that she didn't mind at all.

When they were done suiting up, one by one they came out from behind the wall, crossed the street, and eased into the trees. First Rain, then Kanezaki, then Livia, then Diaz, then Carl. Livia looked around and saw no houses or other signs of habitation. Whoever owned the land here, it was sprawling enough to feel they were in the middle of a forest. "Stay close," she said to Diaz.

After a few minutes, they came to the edge of the tree line and stopped. Beyond it, Livia could see a long, curving stone road, beside which was perched an elaborate complex of wooden structures, some with tiled roofs and others of thatch, the corners upturned in the traditional Japanese style. And beyond that, an expansive garden with arrangements of granite boulders of various sizes, carefully raked sand, and moss-covered hillocks, all of it winding along the edge of an enormous pond crossed by several delicately arched bridges and buttressed at the far end by a waterfall. The only sounds were of the water and the

347

birds in the surrounding trees. Given what had just happened, and what they were here for, the utter serenity of the place was suddenly surreal.

"Did we take a wrong turn?" Carl whispered. "'Cause I think this must be the set of a damn samurai movie. Hey, the security people won't be carrying swords, will they?"

"If they are," Rain said, "you can just shoot them. Like Indiana Jones, remember?"

Carl smiled. "Hey, a movie reference! How'd you know?"

Rain looked at him. "That one I saw. Delilah, Larison, we're in position. Ready?"

"Been ready," Larison said in the earpiece. "Just waiting for your friend to finish obsessing about swords and samurai."

"You have no idea of my trauma," Carl whispered. "If I'd picked up one rock fewer—"

"Enough," Rain said. "Delilah. Larison. Go."

chapter seventy

DELILAH

Delilah drove the Porsche along Mountain Home Road, the sky hard blue behind a canopy of autumn colors, the gray pavement dappled in alternating sunshine and shade. The engine was growling, and she could feel the car practically begging to be unleashed, but a GT4 looked like it was racing even parked at the curb, and she had to keep to the speed limit. Still, what a waste.

She was wearing a vintage Diane von Furstenberg wrap dress: clingy fabric, open plunging neckline, and a skirt that would naturally fall open to expose a good amount of leg, especially while getting in and out of the car. High-heeled boots, gold hoop earrings, and most importantly a gold necklace to draw the eye to the décolletage. The whole thing was a throwback to the '70s, but it was in again. And besides, Delilah always liked vintage, which was why she had packed the outfit in Paris.

The road curved to the right and she slowed. There it was, on the left, a break in the thick foliage and the beginning of a stone driveway. Grimble's Japanese Shangri-la. She downshifted and turned in. Ten meters down, on the left, was the guardhouse, itself looking like something straight out of ancient Kyoto. And just beyond it, a closed electronic gate.

She stopped alongside the guardhouse, cut the engine, and got out, shouldering the Shinola leather market tote she was carrying. A middle-aged guy she made immediately as a former cop looked her up and down through the window, barely even noticing the Porsche. "Can I help you?" he said.

He seemed in no way alarmed—the Porsche, the clothes, and the fact that she was an attractive woman all tapping into a preexisting understanding of how the world worked. But she needed to get him out of the booth and away from the video feeds inside it.

"Thank you so much," she said, laying on a heavier-than-normal French accent. "I know this is irregular, but I have come a long way and I would be so grateful for an opportunity to interview Monsieur Grimble."

The guard shook his head as though confused. "Uh, I'm sorry, I can't really help with that."

"Are you sure? Don't you know him? Or at least see him?"

"Well, yes, sometimes I see him, but . . . who are you?"

"Ah, forgive me. Let me give you a card." She moved a few items around inside her bag. "*Merde*. I thought I had one. Just a moment, please."

John and the rest would know this was their moment. The perimeter of the property was blanketed with cameras. And there was a camera inside each guard booth, too. It was a thoughtful setup: a problem in or outside of one guard booth would be instantly visible in the other. The solution was speed, coordination, and distraction.

She went to the Porsche and leaned far inside, making sure he enjoyed a long and hopefully alluring view. Then she eased out and walked back to the booth, holding a card.

"My name is Laure. Laure Kupfer. I am a freelance writer and photographer, and I hope to place an interview with Monsieur Grimble and a photo shoot of his fabulous taste in *Architectural Digest* magazine."

He glanced at the card, but she didn't proffer it. "I don't think Mr. Grimble does many interviews, Ms. Kupfer . . ."

"Please, call me Laure. And what is your name?"

The guard hesitated, as though the non-male/ego/narcissist part of his brain recognized he was being manipulated. Delilah had seen the reaction many times in her career, along with the override that almost always immediately followed.

He stepped back from the window. A moment later he came through the door. He was wearing blue pants and a matching windbreaker that identified him as Gorgon Security. An earpiece and lapel-mounted push-to-talk microphone. And a pistol in a belt holster.

"I'm Larry," he said.

"Ah, our names begin with the same letter."

He laughed as though she had said something notably witty. She offered her hand and they shook.

"Thank you for coming out, Larry," she said, for the benefit of the team. "I really appreciate your help."

If he was attending to the monitors at all, with any luck the guard in the other booth would be focused on the one displaying Delilah. And why not? Guard work was boring. Watching your companion make time with a blonde in a Porsche would be a welcome distraction. Dox would need only a moment to get past the cameras, at which point he'd be at the second guard booth.

"Of course. But, the thing is, Laure, I can't really help you with this. Mr. Grimble has people who manage his schedule and such."

"And what do you do?"

"I'm just one of the guards. You know, I watch out for intruders. Trespassers, that kind of thing."

She cocked an eyebrow. "I hope you don't think I am one."

She heard John in the earpiece. "Dox is past the cameras."

Larry laughed. "No, of course not. I mean, maybe technically. But people stop in front of my post all the time. The mail, deliveries. Not so many journalists, though."

"I'm right outside the booth," she heard Dox say quietly. "Say the word and I'll leap into remarkable action."

"Now," Delilah said.

Larry cocked his head at the non sequitur. In the earpiece, she heard Dox say, "Don't go for your weapon. Don't go for your mic. Just slowly raise your hands, 'cause I'll shoot you if you don't."

She heard footsteps behind her, moving quickly. Larry looked. His mouth dropped open.

"Do not move or I will kill you," she heard Larison say.

She glanced back and saw him moving in smoothly, his gun up in a two-handed grip just below his chin, the attached suppressor intimidatingly long. "If you reach for anything," he continued, "including that push-to-talk button on your shirt, I'll shoot you in the face. Do you understand?"

Larry blinked. "What the hell is this?"

Larison stopped ten feet out. "It's an opportunity for you to stay alive."

She heard John issuing instructions—*prone out, facedown, hands behind your back.* He and the rest of the team were in the other booth.

Larry's eyes were wide, and focused completely on the muzzle of the suppresser, which Delilah knew from experience he was currently perceiving as roughly the circumference of the opening of a cannon. She slipped behind him, unfastened his holster, and removed the gun. Larry seemed almost unaware of it.

"Do you want to stay alive, Larry?" Larison said.

"Yes," Larry said, as Delilah eased the gun into the tote.

"Good," Larison said. "Then you'll comply with all my instructions. Can I count on you to do that?"

"Yes."

"Good. Raise your hands high. Palms forward, fingers splayed."

Larry complied.

Delilah unclipped Larry's microphone, pulled out his earpiece, and detached his belt radio. She disconnected the microphone from the radio and placed both in her tote. "Maya, Evie," she said. "We're ready for you."

She tried to insert Larry's earpiece into her free ear. It was too big. She grimaced and pushed harder. No good. She pulled off the silicone tip and replaced it with a smaller one from her bag. Just right. She couldn't help but smile. John had made them walk through everything, hitting every assumption with a barrage of *What if* possibilities. He did micromanage. But on the other hand, he was the one who had asked, *What if the guard's earpiece is too big?*

The channel was silent. "No chatter," she said. "John, your guard didn't get off a warning."

"Keep your hands up," Larison said. "Turn around. Walk back into the booth."

Larry was breathing hard. "Listen, man. You know what they pay me for this job?"

"I need you neutralized," Larison said. "I can do that by hand-cuffing you in the booth, or by shooting you in the head here. Tell me which you prefer, because to me it's all the same."

Delilah had to give Larison credit. She'd never known anyone who could deliver a threat more credibly. And it was true—he had voted to shoot the guards, on the simple utilitarian grounds that shooting them would have been safer and faster. Livia and Diaz immediately objected, and their refusal carried the day. Larison had tried to persuade Dox, saying, "The last time we agreed to less-than-lethal, you were an inch away from becoming a human shish kebab. You're going to risk that again?"

Dox had sighed. "Daniel, it's the right thing to do. Just a bunch of minimum-wage rent-a-cops, we don't have a beef with them."

To which Larison had thrown up his hands and exclaimed, "I am not carrying another umbrella or selfie stick. I'm going to point a gun at people, and if they follow my instructions immediately and to the letter, okay. If they don't, that's okay, too. And if that's not okay, then tell me now, because there's only so much insanity I can tolerate."

"It's okay," Dox had said. "And I for one wouldn't have it any other way."

"You're all still nuts," Larison had growled, but the matter was settled.

Larry swallowed. "Handcuff me."

Larison nodded. "Then turn around and get back in the booth. Now."

Larry turned and headed toward the booth, hands still in the air. Larison did a quick scan of the area and followed him.

Delilah heard wheels on the stone driveway and looked—Evie, driving the truck, Manus riding shotgun, Dash and Maya in back, Margarita in the horse trailer. Delilah didn't like the presence of all the civilians, and especially a child. But they might need Evie's technical skills. And with Rispel and potential ambushes in the mix, Manus wouldn't leave Evie or Dash, and of course Evie wouldn't leave Dash, either. Delilah thought back to her *one for all and all for one* comment to John. That had been in Paris. It seemed forever ago. But it was certainly the truth, and then some.

The four of them got out. "This way," Delilah said, and they all went into the guard booth.

Unlike the exterior, the inside was modern: fluorescent lights, a refrigerator, a computer on a table. There were no chairs—presumably, guards were expected to stand at their posts—and on the wall adjacent to the window was a row of monitors. On one of them, Delilah could see the inside of the other guard booth. A guard dressed like Larry was on his stomach, wrists handcuffed behind his back, legs in shackles attached to the cuffs, John, Dox, Livia, and Kanezaki standing around him. Dox looked at the camera and waved. "Tell old Larison we're faster at less-than-lethal than he is."

"I can hear you fine," Larison said. "I'd rather be faster at lethal. Larry, on the ground. Facedown. Hands behind your back."

Again, Larry complied.

Delilah reached into the tote and pulled out a pair of handcuffs and integrated leg irons. She cuffed him, then said, "Bring up your feet."

"Come on," Larry said. "I get paid fifteen bucks an hour. I'm not going to try to be a hero, I promise."

"I believe you," Delilah said. "Now please, bring up your feet. Before my partner gets impatient."

Larry complied. Delilah secured the ankle cuffs, and Larry was effectively hog-tied. She quickly examined his wrists and waistband for the remote possibility of a hidden handcuff key. Another of John's pressure checks. She found nothing.

She looked up and saw Evie signing with Dash. The boy looked troubled. Well, Delilah wasn't the one who insisted he come.

Maya went to the computer and started in on the keyboard. "Need a password," she said.

Larison looked at Larry. "Don't make her ask twice."

"Username is Kellerman," Larry said. "Two *L*s. Password is *RatherBeFishing1139*, capital *R*, capital *B*, capital *F*."

Maya worked the keyboard. "I'm in," she said.

"John," Delilah said, watching the monitors. "There are two more. You see them? One closer to us, stationary in front of the teahouse. The other closer to you, walking north directly in front of the main residence."

"We see them," John said. "How long for you to engage the one at the teahouse?"

Delilah looked at Maya. Maya said, "Hang on, hang on . . . yes. I'm into the security system. And . . . as of now, the cameras are no longer recording. It'll take me a little longer to delete and overwrite what they've already recorded and to switch the connection to my laptop so we can monitor the perimeter remotely."

"Don't forget the landline," John said.

"Yes," Maya said, "that's right after the cameras. And Tom can intercept any cellphone calls with the Stingray."

"Good," John said. "Can you open the gate?"

Maya scrolled and clicked the mouse. "Done."

"Okay," John said. "Maya and Evie, stay there with Manus and Dash. Delilah, how long?"

"Three hundred meters to the teahouse," Delilah said. "We'll need to get back in the car . . . Give us two minutes."

"Make it three," John said. "It'll take us that long to set up a pincer for the one in front of the residence."

"Roger that," Larison said, clicking a button on his watch. "Three-minute countdown in three, two, one."

Delilah and Larison got in the Porsche. She started it up and rolled down the windows. "Tell me when we have ninety seconds remaining," she said.

Larison nodded and looked at his watch.

Delilah had been able to lull Larry because he encountered her outside the gate, where visitors were by definition authorized. An inside guard would be a different story—he would be instantly suspicious to find someone on the property unannounced. And the teahouse, at the edge of the enormous pond, had no good approach other than the driveway, which beyond the gate was topped with gravel. Not only would the guard see them coming, he would hear them. But he wouldn't immediately conclude they were there unannounced. Not at all. Because if there was one thing a racing yellow Porsche Cayman GT4 did, it was announce its own arrival.

"Okay," Larison said. "Go."

She put it in gear, and they rolled slowly forward, past the gate, and into the compound.

They came to a bend in the tree-lined drive and made a left. Over the soft growl of the engine, Delilah could hear the tires crunching on gravel. Larison had the Glock out, alongside his right thigh. Delilah's was on her lap.

They crossed a stone bridge that arched above the pond. When they were over the crest, she saw the guard, forty meters ahead, walking away from them just past the teahouse. He must have heard them coming. He turned. He frowned, but Delilah saw no alarm in his expression, only mild confusion.

Fifteen meters. The guard keyed the mic attached to his jacket. Said something. Keyed the mic again.

Ten meters. The guard held up a hand to stop. But his frown still indicated no more than confusion. His free hand was loose at his side, not resting on his gun butt.

She rolled to a stop a few feet in front of him, gripped the Glock with her right hand, put her left arm on the windowsill, and leaned out. "Is everything all right?"

He walked straight to the window and looked inside. And found the muzzles of two Glocks looking back. He froze.

Larison was out of the car instantly, coming around the front, his gun up. "Hands up or die. Your choice."

The guard chose the first alternative. In the earpiece, Delilah heard a similar transaction taking place with the fourth guard, in front of the residence.

A minute later, the guard was on the ground, wrists and ankles cuffed together behind his back, his gun and commo gear in Delilah's bag.

"The residence guard is secured," she heard John say. "Delilah, what's your status?"

"Same. We're on our way. We'll be there in under a minute."

Larison leaned down and checked the guard for a hidden handcuff key. When he was satisfied, he said, "It would have been easier to kill you. Safer, too. But we didn't. We're not going to be here long, and it has nothing to do with you. You understand?"

The guard nodded. "Yes."

"I doubt there's a neighbor close enough to hear a bomb go off here, let alone some shouting, but still I want you to promise me you're not going to make any noise."

"I promise."

"You know what I'll do if you break your promise?"

"Yes."

"Good. Keep your word and I'll keep mine."

They got back in the Porsche and headed toward the main residence. Larison would join the rest of the team there. Delilah would drive Dox back to the teahouse, the highest point on the property and therefore the best spot to provide overwatch. Evie would bring the rest of the team, and Dash, and the horse and the dog, to the residence. They'd get what they needed from Grimble and be gone a few minutes after that.

If everything went according to plan.

chapter seventy-one

RAIN

Rain paused in front of the main residence, bemused at the number of people around him. Dox was positioned on the roof of the teahouse with the sniper rifle. But that still left nine of them, plus Rain, at the residence: Delilah, Livia, Diaz, Manus, Evie, Dash, Maya, Larison, and Kanezaki. Not to mention the dog and the horse. Though at least the animals had stayed in the trailer. The humans had proven less persuadable.

The residence consisted of four separate buildings, each a beautiful example of the classic *minka* style: *kayabuki-yane* thatched roofs; *hafu* gables; *kōshi mado* latticed windows, everything perfectly proportioned and obviously incorporating only the finest materials. All of it was built out over the pond, connected by covered walkways, and interspersed with gardens of carefully tended niwaki trees, gravel, and stones set in subtle *ishi o tateru koto*—"rock arrangement"—patterns. Rain had never seen anything like it outside Kyoto. But unlike Kyoto, it was devoid of telephone and electric lines, modern architecture, the sounds of traffic, or anything else that would have been out of place in the seventeenth century. There was a cool breeze carrying a slight scent of cypress, and other than the birdsong and the distant sound of the waterfall by the teahouse, the area was soundless. If Rain hadn't painstakingly built his own restored *minka* in Kamakura, he might have been envious. As it was, he was surprised at how wistful he suddenly felt. His mind rarely unlocked the box that contained memories of his mother, but it opened now. *Kyō nite mo, kyō natsukashiya,* she had said to him, holding his hand and quoting the wandering poet Bashō on a visit to the Kiyomizu temple complex in Kyoto when Rain was a boy. *Though in Kyoto, I long for Kyoto.* His mother had loved her adopted country in a way that, like Rain's father, it had never really requited. For a moment he wished she could have seen what this gaijin Grimble had built here. He wished he could have shown it to her.

"John?" Kanezaki said. "Grimble's phone is still in the residence's main building—the bedroom. What do you think?"

Rain realized they'd been waiting for him. Lost in thought in the middle of an op . . . He was too old for this shit. And too sick of it. Delilah was right, he needed to get out. And stay out. While it was still up to him.

He looked at the various buildings, at the pond sparkling behind them. He had of course tried to imagine Grimble's movements when they were back at the office, but that was when he'd been looking at schematics rather than the actual terrain.

Midafternoon. Unless Grimble was an exceptionally late sleeper or just enjoyed lounging in bed—which wouldn't fit the profile of an entrepreneur—he'd be elsewhere now. Out of the bedroom, at least.

A lot of people kept their phones with them, even when moving around inside a house. But a recluse, or near-recluse, obsessed with a hobby, wouldn't be like that. On top of which, Kanezaki had already confirmed that Grimble didn't get many calls.

So where would a non-late riser, who didn't make or get many calls, be if he were on the premises but not near his phone?

"Maya," Rain said. "I think you were right. He's got his Battle of Sekigahara setup in the northernmost building, right?"

Maya nodded. "As best as I could tell from the way the interviewer described it—the size and the view. Again, there were no pictures."

"Okay," Rain said. "Let's start there."

They walked to the northern end of the residential compound, scanning as they moved, until they came to the last of the four buildings there, a rectangle about a quarter the size of a football field, the length of it running south to north along the pond. They cut in along a gravel trail among a copse of black and white pine trees and came to a wooden door halfway along the eastern length. Rain knew from schematics that, like the other doors throughout the compound, this one was more solidly constructed than it looked. Maybe they could kick it open. A breach charge would be the surer bet, albeit noisier. But . . .

Rain took hold of the handle. It turned smoothly. The door opened a crack. And why not? The guy lived on twenty-three gated acres, with multiple cameras and a private security force. Why would he bother locking doors?

His heart kicked up a notch. "Dox," he said quietly into his lapel mic. "You still with us?"

"Of course. You didn't hear me zeroing the HK?"

"We didn't hear anything."

"Hah, these OSS suppressors are the best. About the only sound is the action of the bolt. Anyway, you're good to go. Lost you when you were on the other side of the trees, but I can see you again."

"Okay. Let's see if Grimble is in here."

chapter seventy-two

RAIN

Rain went in first, followed by Larison, with Livia bringing up the rear, all with guns drawn. Rain didn't like leaving the rest of them, but Delilah was a competent shooter, and as for Manus, Dox wasn't in the habit of handing out praise like "solid" and "force of nature" without good reason. It would be okay. Depending on how things went, the rest could come in after, with Manus staying behind as sentry and, if it came to that, trip wire.

He saw it immediately. It was impossible to miss—both because the space was enormous and because every inch of it was subsumed by a vast yet shrunken world. There were mountains and forests and rivers, the colors and textures utterly convincing. Grass and mud and rock. Hundreds of figurines, each perhaps three inches tall, fighting dozens—no, scores—of separate battles, with every manner of weapon: swords and spears and pikes, long bows, crossbows, and muskets. There were *ashigaru* foot soldiers and *bajutsu* mounted cavalry, battle flags, helmeted samurai in Azuchi-Momoyama armor of extraordinary detail. Bombs captured midexplosion, clouds of dirt erupting above the earth. Wounded men, the ground beneath them stained red, their bodies contorted so realistically Rain had to blink to be sure they weren't writhing in agony. The room was quiet—in fact, so silent it hummed with a slight cavernous echo—and yet the scene was so comprehensive that he felt sure he could hear the din of muskets firing and swords clashing and shouts of rage and cries of pain. Bathed in natural light from a long wall of glass on the eastern length of the room and overlooking the pond, in no respect did it feel like a diorama, or like any other artificial thing. Instead, the overall effect was of an actual climactic day that had somehow been sliced from the distant past, to be reduced and reanimated here in this room.

And to the right, at the far end of the space, looking bizarrely like a giant who had blundered onto the edge of the scene, was Grimble. He was staring through a jeweler's lamp, intent on something he was working on—a figurine, Rain thought, though he was too far away to be sure.

The surface of the scene was about four feet off the floor. And while there was enough space along each side for two people to pass, the interior would have been impossible to reach without portals accessible from underneath. Larison was squatting, no doubt after having the same thought, to confirm no one was lurking underneath, however unlikely that might be.

Larison stood, and the movement must have registered in Grimble's ambient vision. He pushed away the jeweler's lamp and looked up at them through an enormous pair of wireless eyeglasses, each lens half the size of a scuba mask. His thinning brown hair was held back in a ponytail, and his cheeks were so chubby they extended past his ears. There was no alarm in his expression, only curiosity.

"Who let you in?" he said.

"Larry," Rain said. "The guard." He started walking toward Grimble, the Glock low along his thigh, Livia and Larison following.

Grimble blinked. "He's not supposed to do that. What do you want?"

Evie had been right—the man was looking in their direction, but his gaze was off to the side. The effect was of talking to a sightless person relying only on sound to gauge their position.

"We need your help," Rain said.

Grimble blinked again, his eyes magnified in the giant lenses, and looked at the ceiling. He was wearing a white turtleneck, Rain saw, and what looked like a red, pleated robe.

"Are you with a startup?" Grimble said. "You can't just come to my house. There's a whole investing team; they handle that kind of thing."

Rain kept walking. "We had to talk to you directly."

"Directly, directly, directly. Everybody always says directly. It's not fair to interrupt me. To intrude on my privacy."

Rain stopped about ten feet away and holstered the Glock. Grimble must have seen it, at least in his peripheral vision, but the fact that Rain was armed seemed to mean nothing to him. Maybe he was used to having armed guards. Maybe he didn't understand guns the way people who used them did.

"If that's the Fuji River," Rain said, pointing, "I'm guessing that figurine you're working on is Fukushima Masanori."

Grimble looked out the window.

"I've always had him holding his sword in his right hand," Grimble said. "But recently, some of my people alerted me to scholarship suggesting Masanori was left-handed. One of my first pieces, and it was wrong, wrong, wrong. Is that a gun you have?"

Rain acted as though he hadn't heard. He looked at the area in front of Grimble. "Then that must be Shimazu Yoshihiro. Who refused Ishida's order to reinforce Ishida's right flank."

Grimble glanced at the scene before him. "How do you know so much about Sekigahara?"

"The books I used to read," Rain said. "When I was a boy. I wanted to be Musashi. But I wound up something else."

Grimble glanced past Rain at Larison and Livia, then at the wall behind Rain, then at the figurine he was holding. "I . . . Who are you?"

"We're almost out of time," Livia said.

Rain knew exactly how much time they had before Schrader's deadman switch released a tranche of videos, and for a moment he understood how his own micromanaging might grate.

"Andrew Schrader was helping us," Rain said. "And some people killed him for it."

Grimble blinked. "People killed him? Killed, killed, killed him? What people?"

"Bad people."

Grimble shuddered and looked at the ceiling. The tics and echolalia were obviously aggravated by distress, and probably alleviated by concentration on close tasks. The entire room was likely the expression of a desperate urge to scratch a never-ending itch.

"The news," Grimble bleated. "News, pews, views. Said he escaped from prison. Escaped, escaped, escaped."

"He didn't escape," Rain said. "Someone spirited him out. And then tortured him." He paused, then added, "To access his videos."

Grimble blinked and rolled his head. "Oh no," he said. "No, no, no, no, no, no, no."

"And if we know you helped Schrader architect his system," Rain went on, "then the people who tortured and killed him know it, too. Do you understand what that means?"

Grimble went pale and shuddered violently.

"It means," Livia said from behind Rain, "you can either help us defuse those videos, or you can wind up like your friend." Her tone was ice.

Grimble blinked and furiously scratched his arms. After a moment, he said, "Office. In my office, office, office. It's okay in my office. And then you have to go. Go, go, go. Masanori has his sword in the wrong hand. I have to fix, fix, fix it."

Rain turned. Larison was looking at Livia.

"You know what?" Larison said quietly. "You're a pretty good bad cop."

Livia was staring at Grimble. "You have no idea."

chapter seventy-three

DIAZ

Diaz didn't know what Livia, Rain, and Larison had said to Grimble, but when the four of them came out, Grimble was pale and his face was twitching. He kept muttering, "Office, office, office," and he barely even glanced at any of them, as though it meant nothing to him that his property had suddenly been invaded by nearly a dozen people.

Rain said to Maya, "No problems on the perimeter?"

Maya glanced at the laptop she was holding. "I'm looking at multiple feeds from all the cameras. All quiet."

Rain held up a hand to Manus to get his attention. "Manus," he said. "Delilah. Can you two see if there's a route off the property other than a driveway or the way we came in? This is taking longer than I'd hoped."

Delilah smiled. "I had the same thought."

"I know," Rain said. "I'm micromanaging. Ideally something that leads to Sand Hill and avoids Manzanita and Mountain Home. Satellite imagery looked promising, but we'll want to be sure. Especially with the Porsche, which is going to be limited off-road."

Manus nodded, and he and Delilah peeled off. A moment later, the rest of them came to another building in the cluster that comprised the primary residence. Grimble opened a door and they followed him in.

Diaz was surprised—the outside looked like photos she'd seen of old Japanese temples and castles. But the inside was nothing remarkable. The materials were obviously high-end, the walls all of light wood paneling, the ceiling high and with recessed lights, the carpeting plush wall-to-wall that seemed to soak up the sound of their entry. But it was sparsely furnished—just a desk and chair, a row of cabinets, and a couch. Other than a set of what she recognized as Noh masks hung from one of the walls—a smiling woman, a scowling man, and a horned demon—there was nothing Japanese about it.

Grimble went to the cabinets and pressed a button. There was a low mechanical hum and the cabinets swung slowly away from the wall. Behind them, built into the wall, was an enormous gray safe, probably four feet wide and six feet tall. Diaz noticed that the moment Grimble's back was to them Livia and Rain moved to the sides, presumably to make sure Grimble wasn't accessing a weapon, and also to be standing in a different place in case Grimble turned around holding something dangerous.

Grimble pressed his left index finger onto a fingerprint reader and inputted a code into a digital keypad. A red light on the keypad turned green and there was a loud beep. Grimble grabbed the wheel on the door with both hands and spun it, then pulled. The door was obviously heavy—Grimble had to lean back and put some weight into it to get it open.

Diaz wasn't sure what she was expecting to see inside—gold bricks, jewelry, something like that. But it was nothing of the kind. The shelves inside were nearly empty. On one of the middle ones, all alone, was a simple laptop, with wires plugged into it from a panel at the back of the safe.

"Defuse, defuse, defuse," Grimble muttered. He turned and looked at the ceiling, seeming to address all of them and none of them at the same time. "Defuse what? And how?"

Livia walked up. She checked her watch, then looked at the laptop. "Do you know what's on those videos?"

Grimble's head moved in a circle, as though he were nodding and shaking simultaneously. "Andrew's girlie movies. He asked me."

"They're on the laptop?" Livia said.

Grimble shook his head.

"Then where?" Livia said.

"Somewhere," Grimble said. "Everywhere. Nowhere."

Livia took a step closer. "We don't have time for riddles. And I promise, if you don't help us, the people who tortured and killed Andrew aren't going to have time, either. They'll pour kerosene on your sacred Sekigahara, light a match, and tell you to give them what they want or else."

Grimble actually moaned at that. Maybe it was too much, but Livia did have a way of knowing what buttons to press.

"Multitudes," Grimble said. "Attitudes. Gratitudes. Too many to defuse."

Livia's jaw clamped, and Diaz realized she might lose it. "Constantine," she said, before Livia could say anything more. "May I call you that?"

He looked at her chest. "What's your name? Fame? Blame? Shame?"

"Alondra."

"Alondra. Alhambra. Abracadabra."

Diaz had no baseline behavior to compare it to, but she sensed Grimble was decompensating, probably due to the notion that people he'd never even heard of might want to torture and kill him, or set fire to his prized Sekigahara.

She thought about what he had said. Maybe it was the first word that was relevant, with the subsequent ones being riffs based on sound.

"Multitudes," she said. "Are you saying there are multiple copies?"

"Not copies," he said, still staring at her chest. "Originals."

"How many?"

"I don't know . . . Hundreds? Thousands? There's no way to count."

Diaz had no idea what to do with that. She looked at Evie and Maya.

"Constantine," Evie said. "Are you saying the videos are distributed?"

Grimble turned to Evie and looked at her chest. "I know you."

"Yes," she said. "We spoke after your presentation at NSA. Are the videos distributed?"

He nodded. "Andrew said people might want to destroy them. He wanted them safe, safe as the sky."

Evie glanced at Maya, then back to Grimble. "They're in the cloud?"

"Yes," Grimble said. "Multiple servers. Multiple instances. Multiple multiples."

He seemed a little less agitated. Diaz couldn't be sure, but she sensed that compared to Livia, at least, Evie was having a calming effect.

"What does this mean?" Livia said. "There are thousands of copies? They're impossible to destroy?"

"Impossible to destroy," Maya said. "But . . . Constantine. Can we render them unreadable or inaccessible?"

Grimble rolled his head around as though trying to work out a kink in his neck. "If the videos are inaccessible, no one will hurt the world?"

"You mean Sekigahara?" Rain said.

Grimble nodded.

"That's right," Rain said. "If we can destroy them or make them inaccessible, no one will have any reason to hurt anyone else."

"But how?" Diaz said. "If there are so many copies distributed in the cloud."

"The file format," Grimble said.

Maya looked at him. "Nonstandard?"

Grimble smiled at the ceiling. "My own design."

Maya glanced at the safe. "On the laptop?"

Grimble nodded vigorously.

Rain glanced at Evie and Maya. "What do we do?"

THE CHAOS KIND

Evie looked at Grimble. "Constantine. Can you give us your credentials so we can log in?"

Grimble nodded.

Diaz realized the man was extremely literal. Evie must have realized it, too, because she said, "Will you tell me your credentials? Please."

Grimble walked to the safe. He opened the laptop. The screen was dark, with a white rectangular box in the center, a cursor blinking on the left of it.

"If you don't mind," Evie said. "Let me."

Grimble stepped aside.

"Username?" Evie said.

"Matsudaira Takechiyo," Grimble said.

Evie looked at him. "I might need you to spell that. Could you?"

Grimble spelled it. Rain said, "Better known by the name he took later—Tokugawa Ieyasu. The victor in the Battle of Sekigahara, and subsequently shogun."

"Okay," Evie said. "And the passcode?"

Grimble went over to the wall and removed the horned demon mask. He looked inside it and began to drone a set of numbers.

"Hold on," Evie said. "Slower, please."

Maya walked to Grimble's desk and set down the laptop she was using to monitor the cameras. "Tom. You have a burner?"

Kanezaki reached into a pocket and tossed her a unit.

"Hang on," Rain said. "Make sure the—"

"The cellphone reception is off," Maya said. "I know." She powered up the phone and tapped the screen a few times. "Constantine, can you turn the mask around?"

Grimble did as she asked. Diaz could see numbers and letters stenciled on the inside—a lot of them.

Maya held up the phone. "Okay, go ahead and read them. Thanks."

Grimble said the numbers again—numbers and letters, a long, seemingly random stream of them. Evie typed them in. A moment later,

371

the screen changed. Diaz came closer to see. It was a series of boxes, with choices like *Transcode* and *Upload* and *Reset*. The *Reset* box had a clock next to it—zero hours, two minutes, and seconds counting down.

"Reset it," Livia said. "We only have two minutes."

Evie worked the trackpad.

Maya said, "And . . . video of the passcode inside the mask, Constantine reading it, and Evie inputting it is uploaded to the secure site. So we have backup."

The clock on the screen flashed, and the numbers changed to 168 hours. "It's reset," Evie said. "We have another week."

Livia nodded with relief. But Diaz thought Evie looked troubled.

Kanezaki looked at Maya. "Are we limited to just his laptop? Or can we access his system through any computer?"

Grimble looked at him. "You're smarter than Andrew?"

"Yes," Kanezaki said.

"Smarter," Grimble said. "Barter. Farter. Andrew thought he was smarter. Everyone thinks they're smarter than everyone. But that can't be true."

"Do we need that laptop?" Kanezaki said. "Or can we access your system from any computer?"

Grimble shuddered. "Access. Andrew asked me to design this system because he thought it would be safe. And he would be safe. But he's not safe now. And I'm not safe. And you're not safe."

"We're going to do it differently," Kanezaki said. "We're going to blur the girls' faces."

"Tom," Evie said. "Running a facial-recognition program on all those copies of videos . . . It's a nontrivial task. It would take days."

Diaz noticed the use of the conditional *would*. Evie didn't like the plan. And the truth was, Diaz was suddenly having her doubts, as well.

"You reset it," Kanezaki said. "We have time."

Evie glanced at Maya. "That girl was killed. Ali. And someone tried to kill Dash and me. Or take us, for who knows what. And they almost killed Alondra."

"I know," Kanezaki said. "But that was all before."

"If we walk out of here with access to his system," Evie said, "we're all going to be a target."

Kanezaki shook his head. "We're already a target."

Evie looked at Grimble. "Is this laptop the only instance of your file format? Does everything come here to be transcoded?"

Grimble shook his head. "Three cloud backups. Decrypt and transcode. Long key. Donkey, monkey."

"So a total of four transcoders?" Evie said. "This laptop, plus the three cloud backups?"

Grimble nodded.

Evie looked at Rain. "If we destroy the laptop and the three backups, the underlying data can never be transcoded."

"No," Kanezaki said. "That's a bad idea. Rispel, Devereaux, Hobbs . . . They wouldn't even know we destroyed it. It would gain us nothing."

"Rispel's already around," Larison said. "Or whoever positioned that sentry on Manzanita. They're going to ask Grimble here what happened."

"Why would anyone believe him?" Kanezaki said.

Larison glanced at Grimble, then back to Kanezaki. "Let's just say he has an honest face."

Grimble said, "Face, place, grace."

"My point," Larison said. "And by the way, this is taking too fucking long."

"Livia," Kanezaki said. "Alondra. Don't you want to prosecute?"

Diaz didn't like it. Kanezaki was a spy. Why would he be concerned about prosecution? "Why do you care?" she said.

"We all have something we want from the videos," Kanezaki said. "I thought we came up with a good way for us all to get it."

"We've been over this," Larison said. "Good luck prosecuting the attorney general or whoever else."

"They're not all going to be that high up," Kanezaki said. "Some of them can be prosecuted."

"That's the plan now?" Larison said. "Make it about 'a few bad apples,' like those poor dopes at Abu Ghraib? Do the work of the higher-ups for them? Sorry, Kanezaki, I'm not buying your bullshit. I'm not sure even you are."

"Livia?" Diaz said. "What do you think?"

There was a long beat. Livia said, "I want to know what men are on those videos. I want them punished."

"Exactly," Kanezaki said.

Livia shook her head. "But not if there's a chance of someone else getting their hands on them. And using them. Rape videos live on the Internet forever. This one time . . . we can save these girls from that."

She looked at Diaz and added, "We can't win every round."

Diaz thought, *I love this woman.* "I know," she said. "But we'll never stop fighting."

"I don't want those girls to get hurt," Kanezaki said. "I don't want anyone else to get hurt. But if we control those videos . . . do you understand how much good we could do?"

"Tom," Maya said. "You don't want those videos. It's like the One Ring."

"The what?" Kanezaki said.

Maya looked at Larison.

"*The Lord of the Rings*," Larison said. "It's an allegory about power. And how power corrupts."

"'When things are in danger,'" Maya said, "'someone has to give them up, lose them, so that others may keep them.'"

Larison smiled. "'The Ring must be taken deep into Mordor and cast back into the fiery chasm from whence it came.'"

Kanezaki shook his head. "Are we seriously going to make this decision based on *The Lord of the Rings*?" He looked at Rain. "John. Talk some sense into these people."

Everyone looked at Rain. Diaz couldn't have articulated why, but she thought there was something sad in his eyes.

Rain glanced around the room, then back at Kanezaki. "I told you before you remind me of Tatsu."

"Yes," Kanezaki said.

Rain sighed. "He would have wanted those videos, too. No doubt. No matter the risks."

"I know," Kanezaki said.

Rain nodded. "And he would have been making a mistake."

Kanezaki's lips moved as though he was trying to come up with something to say. But nothing came out.

"Tatsu was a good man," Rain went on. "But he wasn't perfect, Tom. You can be better. He would have wanted you to be better."

Diaz didn't know who Tatsu was, but she knew a strong closing argument when she heard one. And so, apparently, did Kanezaki. His shoulders slumped and he said, "Shit."

Rain looked at Maya. "What do we need to do?"

Maya gave Grimble an appreciative nod. "Constantine stored the video files in the cloud in a unique file format. Without the transcoder, the videos are just a pile of incomprehensible bits. It's like . . . if we were talking about DVDs, the DVDs would still exist, but there's no DVD player. So you couldn't watch a movie. You'd just see a bunch of ones and zeroes."

Rain gave her a tight smile. "I appreciate your explanations. There would be no way to turn those ones and zeroes back into a movie? Grimble couldn't make a new transcoder?"

Maya shook her head. "It doesn't work like that. So no. If you destroy the transcoder and keys, and the backups, it's over."

"What about the passcode?" Larison said. "Are there other copies? Or just the one stenciled inside that mask?"

"Backups," Grimble said. "Backups, backups, backups."

Larison shrugged. Diaz had the chilling sense that Rain and Larison had been flirting with the necessity or desirability of killing Grimble so no one else could use him to access the system. He was lucky he had architected the system the way he had. Or that he was clever enough to lie.

"How long will it take?" Rain said.

Maya shrugged. "Ten minutes. Less, if Constantine helps me."

Diaz had turned down the volume on her earpiece so she didn't have to hear the conversation in Grimble's office in stereo. But suddenly she heard a loud rasping, like feedback from a microphone that's been mishandled or dropped.

"This is Lisa Rispel," came a loud voice. "And the lovely woman who a moment ago had this mic attached to her lapel now has the muzzle of a gun pressed to her head."

chapter
seventy-four

MANUS

Manus and Delilah had identified a route off the property that would avoid the main entrance and the approach from Manzanita. It was level ground, with adequate space between trees, and marked off only by a wooden fence supported by posts eight feet apart. Manus tested the strength of the fence by leaning against it. It wasn't much. Hit it hard between the posts with the truck, and they would blast right through. The Porsche could follow. They might surprise a few people by driving across the adjacent properties, but they would be gone before anyone could process it. And if anyone's security cameras picked up a license plate, it wouldn't matter. Kanezaki had supplied fakes. The man was more than competent with logistics.

He straightened and turned. And saw Delilah, a man's fist entangled in her hair, the muzzle of a gun pressed against her head. And five other men fanned out, all with suppressed pistols pointing at him. Too many to have any chance of taking out before they dropped him. And even if he could have gotten to cover, it wouldn't have helped Delilah.

A woman stepped forward, early fifties, hair back, jeans and a dark fleece. *Rispel.*

She gave Manus a cool smile. "Hello, Marvin. I'm only here for the videos. If I wanted to kill you, you'd be dead already."

It was a weird echo of what Larison had said to him in Freeway Park just a few days earlier, which now felt like months ago. The difference was, when Larison said it, Manus had somehow known it was true.

How had they made it past the cameras Maya was monitoring? They must have found a way to hack the system and loop in previous footage. Probably they had been planning to do something like that with Grimble's guards and had wound up doing it to Maya and the team, instead. And whether by luck or skill, they had approached from the southeast, where the trees would conceal them from Dox.

Delilah held Manus's gaze. He couldn't read her expression. One of the men removed her Glock. Rispel pulled out Delilah's earpiece and ripped off her lapel mic. Two of the men approached Manus from his flanks and took the HK machine pistol and the Espada. One of them checked Manus's ears and lapel. A moment later, Rispel said, "Of course he doesn't have any commo gear. He's deaf."

Rispel held Delilah's earpiece to her own ear and the mic under her mouth. "This is Lisa Rispel," she said. "And the lovely woman who a moment ago had this mic attached to her lapel now has the muzzle of a gun pressed to her head. I want you to come out, slowly, one by one, each with your hands up. None of this is personal. All I want is the videos and then we can go our separate ways."

chapter
seventy-five

RAIN

T here was an adrenaline dump, but no fear. Instead, what Rain felt were bulkheads, long disused but apparently still well oiled, sliding into place, shutting off his feelings, leaving only a cold clarity.

He pulled the radio out of his pocket and muted the microphone. "Maya. Can you put a new administrator password on Grimble's laptop? Just nod or shake, I don't want your mic to pick it up."

She looked at him, obviously still shocked from what they had all heard in their earpieces. And the failure of her camera hack.

"They must have gotten into the camera system themselves," Rain said. "Injected a loop into the network, something like that. It doesn't matter now. Can you do a new password?"

She nodded.

"Get the laptop out of the safe and do it."

Maya disconnected the laptop, took it from the safe, and started working the keyboard.

Rain looked around. Livia and Larison had their guns out and had angled off so they could see more of what was outside the window. Kanezaki had his gun out, too, and was looking at Rain for instructions. Evie had pulled Dash close and was signing to him. Diaz was looking at Rain, like Kanezaki apparently waiting for guidance. Grimble was staring at the ceiling.

"Everyone stay cool," Rain said. "That's what gets us through this. Okay?"

Evie, Dash, Diaz, Kanezaki, and Maya all nodded. Livia and Larison scanned—window, door, and back. Grimble seemed to have no sense that anything new was happening.

Diaz pulled out her radio and muted the mic. She said, "But how do they know which structure we're in?"

"I don't think they do," Rain said. "They probably tracked Grimble's phone to the residence, like we did, with the rest as guesswork. Or saw Delilah and Larison close by. It doesn't matter now."

"I know you can hear me," Rispel said. "You really don't want to keep me waiting."

"Diaz," he said, "put that Noh mask back on the wall." He would have preferred to smash the mask to bits, but that only would have drawn attention to it and interfered with the appearance of ignorance they needed to claim. They could have put it in the safe, but then there would be the empty hook on the wall and the remaining two masks, uncentered. Obviously Grimble was sharper about computers than he was about where to hide a passcode, but nothing to be done about that now.

"I'm going to give you a three count," Rispel said. "Let's hope I don't get to the end of it."

"Livia," Rain said. "Under this building is something called an *ennoshita*. It's a kind of crawl space, part of traditional Japanese architecture. This one looked tight to me, but I think if you prone out you can squeeze through."

"Three," Rispel said.

"It's concealed by lattices but they should be removable," Rain said. "Go out the window and make your way forward through the space. If we lose contact, use your judgment."

Livia nodded and went to the window.

"Two," Rispel said. "One—"

Rain unmuted the mic. "How do we know you're telling the truth?"

"Who am I speaking to?" Rispel said.

"My name is Rain." He didn't care what they talked about. He just wanted to give Maya time to lock anyone else out of Grimble's laptop. And Livia time to get under the structure.

"John Rain?"

He heard Dox in his ear. "John, I switched to only your channel. Rispel can't hear me. I can't see her from here. You need to get her and whoever she's with to move north on the pathway, past the trees. Probably no more than fifty feet. Let me know if you understand."

"John Rain?" Rispel said again.

"Yes," Rain said. And then, for Dox's benefit, "Is this going to be like one of those action movie standoffs?"

"I hope not," Rispel said. "You know, I've heard conflicting things about you. That you're retired. That you're not even real."

"Roger that," Dox said. "Put 'em in my sights and I'll take care of the rest."

"People exaggerate," Rain said. "I've heard a few things about you, too."

"I can assure you, everything you've heard about me is true. Now, please do come out as I've instructed."

"I said, how do we know you're telling the truth?"

"You don't. But think about it. The fact that this woman and Mr. Manus are still alive should be evidence both of my good intentions and of my good faith."

Or that you want to disarm us so you can mow everyone down without bullets flying in your direction.

"Come out," Rispel said. "You can see for yourself, and then you can tell the rest of your people to join you. You see? Good faith."

She'd snowed Maya, so she must have had impressive technical support. And a skilled team of gunfighters, too, to have gotten the drop on both Manus and Delilah. But there were gaps in her intel. She didn't know Delilah's name. She seemed to be surprised at Rain's presence. Most of all, she didn't know Dox was part of the team. Or at least they didn't know he was positioned somewhere with a rifle. If they had, they would have been afraid to be anywhere outside.

Maya waved and gave Rain a thumbs-up.

Rain nodded. "Okay," he said to Rispel. "I'm coming out."

chapter
seventy-six

RISPEL

R ispel glanced to her sides—a reflex, like checking the chamber in a gun you already knew was loaded. Three men left, three right—a semicircle, branches forward, Rispel at the center, the outermost man to her left holding Manus and the outermost to her right holding the blonde woman. All Special Operations Group veterans. And a seventh person, alongside Rispel, a woman from the technical branch named Fiona, who had uncovered Maya's tracks inside Guardian Angel. The shooters in the organization were all still men, it seemed. But Rispel didn't mind. Brains were more important than brawn.

Fiona had hacked Grimble's camera network and looped in previous footage. The original plan had been to take control of the network itself, but it seemed someone had already done that. Credit to Fiona for implementing a creative solution on the fly. Rispel wouldn't be able to use Grimble's cameras as her eyes, but at least she was aware of the deficit. The other group would think they could see, while in fact they couldn't. Better to be blind than to have your eyes deceive you.

Had Dutch been able to spare more men, Rispel would have taken them. Still, six operators were probably enough, especially given their skills and experience. The problem was, she couldn't be sure how many she'd be up against. Kanezaki, of course. And Maya. But they weren't shooters. The wild cards were the sniper Dox and the other man the

Freeway Park team had spotted. She had suspected Manus would be in the mix, and she'd been right. There was the blonde woman. And now it turned out this man Rain was involved. Rispel had to give Kanezaki credit—he knew how to build a private network. What a waste.

She'd heard stories about Rain that sounded like urban legends, including that he was some sort of martial arts master. Maybe he was the one who had broken the neck of her sentry. Which turned out to be not such a bad thing, as the sentry's failure to check in had alerted Rispel to the fact that Kanezaki was inside Grimble's compound. She had considered going in at the Mountain Home main entrance, and then decided Kanezaki would be more likely to expect that. She'd told the driver of the Sprinter to let them off on Manzanita, and to wait down the road from the main entrance, either for her signal or for her arrival.

The door to one of the structures opened. An Asian man came out, hands up as Rispel had instructed. Rain. In one hand he was holding a laptop; with the other, he pulled the door closed behind him. He walked down the short set of stairs, his eyes moving from side to side. He saw the blonde woman, who one of Rispel's men was still holding with a gun pressed to the side of her head. Rain didn't react to that, or to the sight of Manus in similar straits, or to the four men who were pointing suppressed machine pistols at him. His eyes just kept moving, as dispassionately as though he were crossing the street and checking first for traffic. Rispel considered herself a good reader of people, but she couldn't work out what was going through the man's head. It wasn't that he seemed calm. He seemed almost . . . past calm. As though what was happening here had happened long ago and was already over.

"This is what you want," Rain said, still holding the laptop aloft. "You can have it. Like you said, no one else has to get hurt."

Rispel's men had flex-ties with them, and she considered the merits of securing Rain's wrists behind his back. She decided it would be unnecessary. If the rest of Kanezaki's people saw her using restraints, they might doubt her protestations of good faith. They might refuse to cooperate. They might even resist. She needed them to believe that all she wanted was the key to Grimble's video system, and that as soon as she had it, they would all be free to go back to their lives. Martial arts were fine, but she had six men, after all. Armed with machine pistols. Disarming Kanezaki's people would be enough.

She glanced at the man on her left. "Tony."

Tony moved behind Rain and patted him down, then walked back alongside Rispel. "He's clean."

"Fiona," Rispel said.

Fiona walked forward, took the laptop from Rain, and walked back to Rispel. She opened the unit, glanced at it, then looked at Rain. "It's password protected," she said.

"I know," Rain said. "Apparently, the credentials are in another building in the complex."

Rispel was immediately suspicious. "Why?"

"I don't know," Rain said. "Security, I guess. Grimble told us his passcode is long and complicated, and he keeps it separate from the transcoder for the videos, which is on the laptop."

Rispel considered. "Where's Dox?"

"He's not here."

Rispel wasn't buying it. And though she couldn't prove otherwise, she'd learned at the black sites that one of the keys to interrogation was pretending to know more than you really did.

"Bullshit," she said. "We picked him up on Grimble's camera network."

"I don't know who you picked up," Rain said, "but it wasn't Dox. I guess so much for good faith and all that."

He said it confidently and readily, and she didn't detect any deception. Still, he was obviously a hard man to read. "Then where is he?" she said.

"You'll have to ask Kanezaki. He's the one who put together this crew. Look, my contract has a force majeure clause. I get paid either way. So take the laptop. Get the log-in credentials. It doesn't matter to me."

That wasn't so difficult to believe, based on his evident lack of interest in the two hostages, and in what Rispel had heard about his past.

She realized he was still wearing his commo gear. She should have thought to have one of her men remove it so the rest of Rain's people couldn't hear what they had just discussed. Well, no harm done. And he had to tell them to come out regardless.

"We'll see," she said. "Have your people come out. One by one, hands up, just like you did. Tell them anyone still inside at the end of the exercise gets a bullet."

"You're wearing the commo gear you took off the woman," Rain said. "They can hear you."

"I want them to hear it from you."

"It's not up to me."

"Tell them anyway. And while you're at it, tell them I'll have you shot, too. Hopefully they won't be as callous about you as you seem to be about them."

"All right," Rain said. "You heard her. I'd suggest you all come out."

The door opened. A pretty Latina was first. Rispel recognized her from file photos. Diaz. Tony searched her, then moved her over near Manus. Next was a large and dangerous-looking man Rispel thought fit the description of Dox's partner from Freeway Park. Then a woman and a teenaged boy, who broke the rules by coming out together. But Rispel didn't mind—the woman's obvious protectiveness might prove useful. Because Rispel knew about Manus's adopted family, and recognized Evelyn Gallagher from NSA file photos. The boy was her son.

As soon as Tony was done patting them down, Gallagher started signing to the boy.

"Stop that," Rispel said.

Gallagher looked at her, and Rispel had to give her credit, for a moment the woman looked more dangerous than any of them. "He's deaf," Gallagher said. "And he's scared. I'm just explaining what's happening."

Rispel glanced at the boy. He glared back, looking as formidable as his mother.

"He doesn't seem scared," Rispel said.

"I'm not scared of you," the boy said, his voice slightly off and a bit too loud.

Rispel had to laugh at his pluck. "You should be."

"You make me sick," Gallagher said.

"How I make you feel is irrelevant to me," Rispel said. "Manus is watching you. I don't want any of you communicating in a way I can't follow. Don't make me tell you again."

Next out was Maya. And then a chubby man in a ponytail, wearing some sort of red, pleated robe and an enormous pair of eyeglasses. He was petting or stroking the side of his face as though smoothing out an invisible beard. He was obviously no operator, but regardless, Rispel recognized him from the file photos. Grimble.

Kanezaki was next, looking at Rispel with surprising dispassion as he came through the door. Rispel had been expecting something more seething or self-righteous.

"Hello, Tom," she said.

"Hello, Lisa."

She gave him a patronizing smile. "You can't say I didn't tell you."

"Tell me what?"

"That sometimes it's safer to have nothing even to recall."

"I guess I should have listened."

"It's all right. I don't mind a certain degree of insubordination. It shows spirit. It'll be a little awkward when we're back in the office, but ultimately we'll be fine."

Another thing she had learned at the black sites: you had to give the subject something to hope for. People who had nothing to hope for could be difficult to manage. Say what you will about the Nazis, but *Arbeit Macht Frei* demonstrated a sound grasp of human psychology.

"Am I right in thinking you're the last one?" she said.

"Yes."

"Where's Dox?"

"I don't know. I told you, he isn't always reliable about accepting jobs."

"Who helped you take down the team at the house on Lake Tapps?"

"You're looking at them."

"And at Schrader's house?"

"The same. How did you get him out of prison?"

Rispel considered. The Lake Tapps team was solid. Ditto the shooters at Schrader's house. But with Manus, Rain, and the dangerous-looking character, they could have pulled it off.

"I have resources you don't, Tom. I wish you'd understood that sooner. But better late than never."

She looked at Rain, then back to Kanezaki. "I'm going to have Tony check that structure. If there's someone inside, I'm going to shoot one of you. One or more. Are you certain you didn't accidentally leave anyone behind?"

Kanezaki nodded. "I'm certain."

Tony went in. He was back in half a minute. "No one in there."

Rispel hadn't expected Tony to find anyone, but it paid to be careful. And it would be careful to test Rain's assertion that the laptop log-in credentials were in another location.

"Mr. Grimble," she said. "I'm so very sorry to inconvenience you. Can you tell us your log-in credentials please, so we can leave?"

Grimble shook his head furiously. "Can't, shan't, rant."

Even though the file had said the man was on the spectrum, Rispel was taken aback. But all right, if he wouldn't give her the log-in credentials, Rain might have been telling the truth. There was only one practical way to confirm.

"Fine," she said. "Then let's go to where you have them written down."

She muted the mic she had taken from the blonde woman and added, "I'll need all of you to remove your earpieces, mics, and radios, and set them on the ground. Not that I don't trust you about no one else being on the property, but you know the expression: Trust, but verify."

When they were done complying, she unmuted the mic. Now if there was a ringer somewhere else on the property—someone like Dox—he wouldn't know his people couldn't hear him. He might check in. If so, Rispel wanted to know.

"Walk in front of us with your hands held high. You may have noticed, some of my men are carrying machine pistols. And there are others positioned on the perimeter. Think about that if anyone decides it would be a good idea to run."

She had no additional men on the perimeter, but if anyone was listening in, it wouldn't hurt for them to believe she had more resources than she really did.

Rispel's men drifted back and they all started walking, Rain, Kanezaki, and the rest in front, Rispel and her people behind. She felt good. In control again. It had been touch and go for a while, with the stakes getting higher and higher even as the chances of success looked worse and worse. But she'd pulled it off. They'd get Grimble's credentials, take care of business, and be out of here in no time. And that prick Devereaux was going to be kissing her ass for the rest of whatever dead-end career she might decide to allow him.

And then she heard a helicopter.

chapter
seventy-seven

LIVIA

Livia watched from the dark of the crawl space. Rispel was taking no chances. She kept probing their responses, even bluffing about having seen Carl on the property. Rain handled it beautifully. If he were ever a suspect in a criminal case, he would be hell to interrogate.

Rispel's men seemed disciplined. Livia could take out one, maybe two. But by then the rest would be returning machine-pistol fire. And while the crawl space offered concealment, it was devoid of cover, and was even tighter than Rain had thought. Even bellied-out, Livia had just enough room to raise her head and look through her gun sights. No cover and no mobility was a death trap.

One by one, they emerged from Grimble's office. When they were out, Rispel had them all remove their commo gear. But first she muted the mic she had taken from Delilah. Clever. She must have been hoping that some as-yet-unseen players would speak up and give themselves away. Hopefully Carl was too smart to fall for the ruse.

Livia decided to wait. If Rispel believed Rain's story about the passcode and they moved, Livia could crawl out on the north side of the office structure and fall in behind them. Carl would open up the moment they were exposed. They'd be focused on where the sniper fire was coming from at the very moment Livia would ghost in from behind.

And then Rispel agreed to go to the other location. They all began to move. Livia felt her heart pounding. This was it. She belly-crawled to the side of the passage and looked through the lattice. She could see two of Rispel's men, guns out, close behind Larison and Delilah. She pushed out the lattice, squirmed through, and cut to the other side of the trees. It was rarely good to follow someone from directly behind—it was where people tended to check. And besides, the gravel roadway would be noisy, and she wanted the trees for concealment.

She heard something. At first she thought it was one of the suppressed machine pistols, but no one was firing, and the sound seemed farther off than that. And then she realized—she'd been so intent on the firearms that she'd misinterpreted what she was hearing. She looked up and saw a helicopter.

chapter
seventy-eight

LARISON

Larison wasn't exactly worried. Either Rispel would buy the story about the passcode being stored elsewhere on the property, in which case Dox would do his thing, or she wouldn't, in which case Larison intended to go for the nearest man's machine pistol and count on Livia to take that as her cue to open fire from under Grimble's office. Still, he was relieved when Rispel told them all to start moving. Their chances would be significantly better if Dox dropped a few of Rispel's people and had the rest of her team frantically searching for cover. On top of which, there would be the independent joy of watching some of these assholes who thought they had it all figured out have their heads converted into the proverbial fine pink mist, all at the hands of a man Larison felt lucky to count as a friend. Really, it was the little things in life.

And then he heard a sound, getting louder fast. *Shit,* he thought. *Helicopter?*

chapter
seventy-nine

DELILAH

Rispel had taken her earpiece immediately, so Delilah hadn't heard any of John's deliberations with the team. But it was clear he was trying to get Rispel to move north, where Dox would have line of sight from the top of the teahouse. And Livia hadn't come out from Grimble's office. Delilah didn't know where the woman was, but Delilah had seen her shoot before and knew she was formidable. It had been a surprise earlier to hear Livia agree to destroy the videos. Maybe Delilah had judged her too harshly. If this turned out well, she was going to make a point of apologizing.

When Rispel agreed to move, Delilah's heart started beating hard. She didn't know who would shoot first—Dox or Livia. But as soon as it happened, all of them would have to engage whichever of Rispel's people was closest. Overall, she thought their chances were decent. But it was doubtful they would make it through without at least someone getting hit. Evie was holding Dash close, and Delilah realized the woman was thinking the same thing.

Your boy is going to be okay, Delilah thought. *When this is over, I'm going to take him for a ride in that Porsche, like I promised. He's earned it. And then some.*

She heard a mechanical whine, getting louder. She looked up and blinked. It was a helicopter, descending fast.

chapter eighty

MANUS

Manus couldn't follow what everyone was saying because he couldn't see their faces. But he could see Rispel's face, which was the most important. Evie had been signing to Dash, telling him to stay close, that their plan was good and they would be all right. Rispel had told Evie to stop. Manus wanted to go to work on her for that alone. But then Rispel said Dash should be scared of her. And Manus thought, *I am going to kill you.* They'd taken his gun and the Espada. But they weren't as smart as Dox: they hadn't checked his belt. He didn't care what it took, he was going to get close to Rispel and punch the push-dagger buckle up under her chin and into her brain. Or get a gun from one of her men. Or use his hands. He didn't care which tool. Only about the work.

They all started walking. And then stopped. Everyone looked up. Manus looked up, too.

And saw a helicopter, coming down so fast that for a second he thought it was falling.

chapter
eighty-one

DOX

Ordinarily, Dox was completely calm when sniping. Of course, *ordinarily* involved choosing a hide that offered line of sight to the target. And while among the available possibilities, the teahouse, which was built on the highest ground on the property, gave the best coverage overall, there were plenty of spots blocked by trees. Like the one where Rispel and her people were currently holding Labee, John, and the rest of the gang at gunpoint.

Their best guess had been that any opposition was likeliest to come in through the main gate, the route Delilah and Larison had used, or to breach the fence along the Mountain Home side, because that approach wouldn't require crossing anyone else's property. John had favored the Manzanita approach precisely because it would be riskier, and therefore less expected. But it seemed Rispel had chosen it for the same reason. That, and maybe because that's where Rispel found her sentry dead after he'd failed to check in. Either way, it was bad luck. Rispel had used pretty much the only approach hidden from Dox.

It was obvious from her questions to John and Kanezaki that she was worried about Dox. The two of them had done a nice job of deflecting, but still, what if she didn't buy John's story about having to move? Twice Dox considered abandoning the teahouse and going in on foot.

But that might have put him out of position at just the moment the high ground would be most important.

And the woman was devious, too. There had been a pause between when she agreed to move to wherever Grimble's passcode was supposedly stored and when she started issuing instructions about how they had to walk with their hands up and all that. Dox had a feeling she'd muted the mic she took from Delilah while telling the team to remove their commo gear. Maybe she thought Dox would break radio silence and try to reach out to someone.

Oh, I'm going to reach out, all right. You can count on that.

But were they really moving, or was that more tactical deception? Well, he'd know one way or the other in just a few seconds. He breathed slowly and easily, his heart beating just a little faster than normal, watching the clearing just north of the trees through the reticles of the scope.

And then he heard it. A helicopter. Not passing overhead, but coming in fast. He looked, and saw an MD500E, small and quiet, black with no markings.

Black helicopters, he thought. *You've got to be kidding me.*

It landed in the clearing. The driver cut the engine and immediately the rotors began to slow. The cockpit glass was smoked, and even through the Leupold scope Dox couldn't make out the faces of the people inside. Then the pilot got out. Dox recognized him—a former Marine and current SOG guy named Dutch. *Rispel's ride?* he thought.

And then the passenger got out. And Dox was looking at none other than Director of National Intelligence Pierce Devereaux. Devereaux and Dutch immediately started walking toward the trees, beyond which were Rispel and the rest of them.

Dox put the reticles on Devereaux's right temple and his finger caressed the trigger. Devereaux was likely the top-level source of what they were up against. The head of the snake, so to speak. Take him out, and their problems could be solved, or at least substantially mitigated.

But Manus had made a good case back at the Motel 6 that Rispel might have been running her own game. If so, dropping Devereaux could improve her position more than it did the team's. Besides which, if Dox killed Devereaux now, Rispel and company would know there was a sniper in play.

There was risk either way. But the main thing was, killing Devereaux would do nothing to get Labee and the gang out of immediate jeopardy. And would likely make their jeopardy worse.

He blew out a long, steady breath. A moment later, Devereaux and Dutch had disappeared behind the trees. And Dox was waiting again, hoping he had made the right call.

chapter eighty-two

RISPEL

Rispel watched in shock as first Dutch and then Devereaux got out of the helicopter and started walking briskly toward her. The two of them here could mean only one thing.

She turned and glanced at her men. "Wait."

Everyone stopped. She turned back toward Devereaux and Dutch, dipped her hand into her coat pocket, and closed her fingers around the butt of her P229 Legion Compact.

The two of them stopped a few feet away. She eyed them coolly and said, "What are you doing here, Pierce?"

He glanced behind her, assessing her team, the prisoners, and probably the odd sight of Grimble in his red, pleated robe.

"I'm taking over this op," he called out loudly. Not to her, obviously, but to her men.

She couldn't believe the gall. "The hell you are, you insufferable worm."

He looked at her. "I'm ordering you, Lisa. Stand down."

"I know it's you in the videos, Pierce. Not the president. You. And Hobbs, too, yes?"

The color drained from his face and she knew she was right.

"It's disinformation," he stammered. "Disinformation—"

"You pussy," she said. "I see right through you. I always have. Now get the fuck out of here. This is my op."

"Dutch," one of her men called out from behind her. "What's going on?"

Dutch glanced at Rispel. "I'm sorry, Lisa. It's chain of command. That's all." He looked at his men. "You heard Director Devereaux. Ms. Rispel reports to him, and that means ultimately you report to him. And he has asserted authority over this op."

She caught the way Devereaux got the title *director* while Rispel was merely a *Ms.* She didn't need to glance back. She could feel her men buying it.

Devereaux looked at her and smiled. It was a smile of triumph, and disdain, and dominion.

Rispel pulled the P229 out of her pocket and shot him in the heart. His hands flew to his chest and his face contorted in shock and agony. His mouth twitched as though he was trying to say something. Then he sank to his knees and collapsed to his side.

"What the fuck!" Dutch yelled. He dropped down alongside Devereaux, who seemed too busy dying to even notice his man's attempt at succor.

Rispel turned to her people. "What you don't know is that Mr. Devereaux has been compromised by the Russians. They have *kompromat* material on him and have been running him for years. This is a counterintelligence operation, and I couldn't allow him to interfere with it."

Dutch stood, and before Rispel could react she was staring down the barrel of a pistol.

"Bullshit," he said. "I'm not buying it."

From behind her, she heard Tony say, "Drop your weapon, Dutch."

She turned. Tony was pointing his machine pistol at Dutch. She turned back. Dutch had swiveled and was pointing his own gun at Tony. Without a second's hesitation, she raised the P229 and shot Dutch in the face.

And then bursts of suppressed gunfire erupted behind her.

chapter eighty-three

DOX

Dox couldn't see what was happening beyond the trees, but he could hear Rispel's half of the conversation. It sounded like old Manus had been right—Rispel and Devereaux were definitely not singing off the same hymnal. She was dressing the man down but good, and told him she knew he was in the videos, and Hobbs, too, none of which surprised Dox a bit. And then a shot rang out, and though it was hard to believe and he couldn't be sure, Dox thought Rispel must have done Devereaux. Which was fine by him. The more of them that killed each other, the easier it would be for Dox to mop up the rest.

There was another loud shot. And then, just like that, there were a lot more, all suppressed, some single, some automatic fire.

Rispel wasn't saying anything else. And all Dox could do was listen helplessly to the surreally quiet shooting, and the occasional scream, and watch the empty clearing, and hope no one he cared about was getting hurt.

chapter
eighty-four

LIVIA

Livia crept in, moving silently behind and to the left of them, until she was about twenty feet away. She crouched behind the last tree thick enough to offer meaningful cover and concealment, and listened while Devereaux tried to assert authority over Rispel's op. Rispel wasn't having it, but the man Devereaux was with, Dutch, must have had his own authority, because he backed Devereaux's play. Livia had just finished thinking, *I don't think you want to corner this woman* when Rispel pulled a gun and shot Devereaux.

Livia almost went in, but then Dutch had his own gun out, and he and the guy named Tony were throwing down at each other. Livia saw it an instant before it happened—Rispel spun and shot Dutch, too. And Larison, who must have been waiting for his chance, lunged for the guy to his right, grabbed his pistol, and twisted. Almost simultaneously, Manus and Rain, farther forward, did the same with the men near them.

Livia popped up and moved in, aiming the suppressed Glock at the nearest target, the man Larison was grappling with.

chapter
eighty-five

LARISON

A s soon as Larison saw it was Devereaux, he thought, *Don't shoot him, Dox. This is just the kind of thing we need.* But there was no real cause for worry. The big sniper was too disciplined to go for the short-term gain. Though it must have been hard for him to stand down, knowing Livia would be in danger, too.

When Rispel told them to wait, Larison turned just enough to keep a peripheral-vision eye on the guy to his right and behind him. The guy was a long step away—closer than Larison would have stood, because action beat reaction and if anything distracted the guy for longer than half a second, Larison would be on him before the guy could pull the trigger.

And then Rispel shot Devereaux, and Larison almost made his move. But holy shit, Tony and Dutch were suddenly doing a Quentin Tarantino dance, which Rispel decisively resolved by shooting Dutch, too. And it was now or never, and Larison lunged at the guy behind him, got his body to the outside of the guy's machine pistol, and grabbed the barrel. The gun kicked and vibrated and the barrel was instantly hot as it spit out rounds. Larison twisted, but the guy adjusted and hung on. And then the guy twitched and blood spurted out of his neck and he screamed. Larison heard the suppressed shot and smiled grimly. *Livia.*

He looked up and saw her moving in, firing calmly and implacably, her Glock close to her chin in a two-handed grip. A warm and improbable thought flashed through his mind—*And they call* me *the angel of death*—and he ripped the gun out of the guy's dying grasp and spun.

Rain had grabbed the gun of the guy nearest him and swept his legs out from under him with some kind of judo throw. Manus was holding the barrel of another guy's gun with one hand and bear-swatted him so hard in the head with the other that Larison was surprised the guy wasn't decapitated. Delilah was struggling with the guy nearest her, who was short but with arms like an ape's. Larison waited a beat—precision shooting with an unfamiliar weapon was always risky—and as the guy tried to wrench his gun back from her, enough space opened between them, and Larison shot him in the head. Delilah kept the guy's gun as he fell away.

He heard bursts of suppressed fire—probably Rain and Manus— and screams. He saw Maya, frozen in place. Before he left Grimble's office, Larison had told her and the other civilians to drop down and flatten out the instant any shooting started. But Maya must have been too startled by the noise and the violence for his admonition to have taken hold. He braced to run for her, but Kanezaki beat him to it, tackling her and covering her with his body. Diaz, who was a fast learner, was already flattened out.

Movement in his peripheral vision. One of Rispel's people, trying to acquire him—

There were two bursts of suppressed shots. The man crumpled and went down—Livia and Delilah had hit him simultaneously. The last man took off running. Manus tracked him and brought him down with a short burst. Larison saw the woman Rispel had brought, Fiona, racing for the trees, too. *Fuck that.* He dropped her with a single shot to the back of the head.

Grimble, who in that red robe should have drawn a lot of fire, was staggering around unhurt, his hands clasped tightly to his ears.

Where was Rispel? He heard a scream. Oriented on it—

And saw Rispel, her arm around Dash's neck, the muzzle of her gun jammed against his cheek, dragging him backward. The scream had been Evie, who was following Rispel from a few feet away, but was obviously afraid to do more than that.

"Get back!" Rispel yelled. "Get back or I'll blow his brains out!"

chapter
eighty-six

DOX

When the shooting stopped, Dox had to work to keep the worrisome images at bay. Of Labee especially. Any of them could have been hit.

But he'd know the results one way or the other soon enough. For now, the best way for him to help was to do what usually came so easily to him, which was to stay relaxed. He watched the clearing through the scope, breathed in deeply, and slowly let it out. Breathed in deeply again—

"Get back!" he heard Rispel yell in the earpiece. "Get back or I'll blow his brains out!"

That rattled him. But he finished slowly letting out the breath.

The good news was, people didn't grab hostages unless they were desperate. And if Rispel was feeling desperate, on balance things must have gone poorly for her and her men.

The bad news, though, was that desperate people did desperate things. And given that Dox was pretty sure Rispel had just shot the director of National Intelligence, he had to admit that she had done a fine job of establishing her desperation credentials.

He had a feeling who she'd grabbed, too. And didn't like it at all.

Manus appeared in the clearing, backing up, aiming a suppressed machine pistol toward the trees.

Dash, Dox thought. *I knew it.*

"Get out of my way!" Rispel screamed. "I'll kill him! You know I will!"

Dox couldn't see her. But Manus's position and orientation must have meant she was trying to come this way. Maybe for a pickup by the Mountain Home entrance.

Manus sighted down the barrel of the gun.

Don't, Dox thought. *Manus, don't. You need a brain stem shot or her trigger finger could twitch involuntarily. A rifle shot will cause more instant damage. And you don't know that gun. You're too invested. Just let her come this way. Trust me. Trust me.*

"Last chance!" Rispel screamed. "Get out of my way!"

Manus's nostrils were flared, his face a mask of hate. He tensed to take the shot—

No, no, no—

And then Manus's arms shook, and he lowered the gun slightly. He grimaced and started to move away, seeming almost to have to drag his legs to get them to obey.

That's right. Good man. I got this . . .

Evie screamed, "Let him go, you bitch!"

Come on, Rispel. You sore loser. You cheat. Come and get what you've got coming.

And then there she was. Rispel. She was holding Dash close, a pistol pressed to the side of his face, and jerking him from side to side, doing what she could to deny Manus and the people behind her a shot. They all must have had guns pointed at her.

Evie appeared at the edge of the trees, her expression terrified. Manus looked desperate. Dox didn't know how much longer the man could hold back.

Rispel spun Dash left, then right. Maybe she wasn't afraid of just Manus and the gang. Maybe she was wondering about Dox again, and whether she was heading into his crosshairs.

Ten feet beyond her was another stand of trees. He wasn't going to have a surer shot than this. But damn it, it wasn't sure enough. Still, he would have to risk the shot, or risk losing her entirely.

He focused on Rispel's ear, but she jerked away. The base of her skull. Dox breathed out and started to ease back the trigger. Rispel spun and suddenly Dash was in the way.

And then Dash must have had enough of being whipped around like a rag doll. Because he lowered his head and clamped his mouth onto Rispel's forearm. She was wearing a jacket, but it looked like Dash got something good between his teeth because Rispel howled and jerked her arm free. Dash slipped down a few inches. The muzzle of Rispel's gun was off his face.

Dox fired. The top of Rispel's head erupted in a cloud of brains and blood. Not the brain stem shot Dox had been hoping for, but with the gun off Dash, good enough for government work. In any event, Rispel didn't get off a shot, involuntarily or otherwise. She half fell, half slid to the ground. Dash turned, and though Dox couldn't be sure, he could swear the boy actually said something to her.

Evie and Manus raced in. Evie threw her arms around Dash. Manus paused to put another suppressed round into what was left of Rispel's head, then wrapped his arms around both Dash and Evie. He looked toward the teahouse, tears running down his face. From where Manus stood he couldn't see Dox, but Dox could of course see him. Manus nodded his head. Wiped his cheeks. And then mouthed the words *thank you.*

chapter
eighty-seven

RAIN

A half hour later, they were all in the horse trailer, parked in the far corner of one of the lots at a place called El Corte de Madera Creek Preserve, an enormous outdoor space seemingly popular with hikers, bicyclists, and horseback riders. Delilah and Larison were already waiting there in the Porsche when the rest of them arrived, and Rain had a feeling Delilah had finally gotten to drive it the way he knew she wanted to on the mountain switchbacks that led to the preserve.

Evie, who was driving the truck, parked in the second-to-last space at the end of the lot. Delilah pulled the Porsche around next to it, so that it was concealed by the trailer on one side and the towering trees of a pine forest on the other. The trailer was congruent here, but Rain was concerned that at some point Larry the guard might describe the Porsche to the police. Still, Rain had explained to Grimble that the less the police knew, the more likely it was that the world—aka Sekigahara—would be left in peace.

"You might want to make sure the guards understand that, too," Rain had said. "And even pay them a bonus for a job well done."

Kanezaki placed a satellite hotspot near a window, and Maya and Evie worked on Grimble's laptop. A lot of it was technical, but everyone understood the purpose: have Grimble's cloud decoders choose their own impossible-to-guess passcodes, leaving the system technically intact but functionally useless.

There was a lot of backslapping in the small space, as there always was after a successful mission with no losses. Dash was watching Maya and Evie at work, seemingly fascinated by their easy camaraderie. He was a resilient kid, tough and smart. And maybe a little too fascinated by all the derring-do he had just witnessed, and been part of. But Rain supposed everyone has a destiny.

Dox waved to get Dash's attention. "How are you doing there, son?"

Dash came out from behind Evie and Maya, and Manus adjusted his position so he could see Dox's face, too.

Dash said, "I'm good," simultaneously signing so Manus could follow both sides of the conversation.

"I could be wrong about this," Dox said, "but did you say something to Rispel back there?"

Dash nodded. "I said, 'I told you I wasn't scared of you.'"

Dox laughed and ruffled Dash's hair. "You're going to be fine, son. You're strong, and your folks are, too."

Dash put his arm around Manus's waist and beamed. "They're all right," he said, and Dox laughed again.

Evie moved from behind the laptop to the other side of Dash and put her arm around him. "If there's ever anything you need," she said to Dox, "Anything we can do. *Anything.* You tell us." She looked at Rain and said, "That means you, too."

Rain nodded an acknowledgment. He understood Evie's sentiment. But he didn't want or expect anything. He was relieved it had all worked out. And that it was over.

Dox, unsurprisingly, was less reticent. "You don't owe me a thing," he said. "And even if you did, old Marvin here already paid me." He looked at Marvin and smiled. "I might have to acquire one of those

Cold Steel Espadas. Though I doubt anybody could deploy it as effectively as you."

Manus held out a hand. They shook.

Diaz was stroking Margarita, who seemed a little nervous at all these people who had invaded her trailer. Or maybe it was the gunshots she had heard earlier.

"Hey," Diaz said to Larison. "When you asked Grimble before about whether he had copies of the passcode he had stenciled in that mask. Were you thinking . . . what I think you were thinking?"

Rain knew for a fact that Larison had been thinking exactly that. Because Rain had been, too. But it was Larison's question to answer.

Larison gave her one of his trademark chilling smiles. "What do you think I was thinking?"

Diaz hesitated, then said, "About whether . . . it would have made sense to kill him."

Larison shrugged. "I like to consider all the possibilities."

"But in the time we've been gone," Diaz said, looking at Larison and then to Rain, "couldn't he log back in? And lock us out?"

Larison nodded. "I considered that, too. But I think he wants Schrader's 'doomsday device' destroyed as much as any of us. It's created too much danger for his samurai toys. Besides. Like I said. He has an honest face."

Maya looked up and said, "Okay, we're good."

Everyone gathered around the laptop.

Evie said, "Here we go." She typed a string of code into a box and hit the *Enter* key. Immediately a message appeared: *New log-in credentials.*

"The system itself chose the new credentials," Maya said. "Minimum of sixty characters, lower case, upper case, numerals, symbols. Uncrackable."

"Watch," Evie said. She entered Grimble's username and passcode. The screen flashed: *Invalid credentials.*

411

"So that's it," Maya said. "The only remaining instance of Grimble's decoder is this laptop. Destroy the laptop, and the ring is thrown back into the fires of Mordor."

Manus opened his Espada. Dox saw it and flinched. Rain gave him a small *caught you* smile, and Dox said, "Yeah, yeah, let's see how you deal with the psychological aftermath of a ferocious attack by Zatōichi the not-so-blind swordsman."

"A tale that will live in legends," Larison said.

"I'm sure it was very ferocious," Rain added.

Dox scowled. "Excuse me, but some of us are interested in the matter at hand."

Manus glanced at Maya. "What parts of the laptop need to be destroyed?"

Maya shrugged. "If you really want to be thorough, hard drive, memory cards, and CPU."

"Where are they?" Manus said.

"Let me," Kanezaki said. He placed the laptop on the floor, then pointed. "Hard drive," he said.

Manus nodded, flipped the Espada around so he was holding it like an ice pick, and slammed the point through the area Kanezaki had indicated, several times in a widening pattern. The blade punched through the metal easily. Margarita whinnied and Diaz stroked her, saying, "Easy, girl. Easy."

"Memory cards?" Manus asked. Kanezaki pointed and Manus repeated the process. Then again for the CPU. By the time Manus was done, the laptop had so many holes in it that it looked vaguely like a cheese grater.

They were all quiet then, the moment somehow anticlimactic. They had protected the girls in the videos, and themselves, too. Rispel and Devereaux were dead. And yet. Maybe it was Livia's influence, and now possibly also Diaz's, but Rain had the sense that everyone was afflicted by a gnawing feeling of justice left undone, of having been coerced by circumstances into protecting unknown people who were deserving only of punishment.

Kanezaki looked particularly glum. Rain understood. Though he was new to it himself, he'd discovered that doing the right thing could be like that. He patted Kanezaki on the back. "Did you know Tatsu believed in an afterlife?"

Kanezaki looked at him. "He did?"

Rain nodded. "At the end, he told me he'd always thought the son he'd lost as an infant was waiting for him. And that he was glad they were going to be together again."

They were quiet for a moment, and Rain went on. "I don't believe in that kind of thing myself. But if I did . . . I'd say you made Tatsu proud today."

Kanezaki put his hand on Rain's shoulder and looked away. After a moment, he said, "Thanks."

"What's going to happen?" Diaz said. "I mean . . . the CIA director, and the director of National Intelligence, and all those other people, too, dead on Grimble's property?"

Rain might have answered himself. But then Dox or whoever would have teased him for micromanaging. And they would have been right. He looked at Kanezaki and raised his eyebrows.

Kanezaki nodded, then looked at Diaz. "Devereaux was already working overtime to plant stories about Russian disinformation. It wouldn't be hard for a 'senior intelligence official offering information only on background' to build on that."

"Do us a favor while you're blaming it all on the Russians," Dox said. "Don't start an accidental nuclear war?"

Kanezaki chuckled. "Don't worry. No one wants that, and no one is going to want any of this to be front-page news for longer than absolutely necessary. Especially with all the QAnon types trying to make hay of it."

Maya was holding Frodo again, and Rain had the sense that the girl was feeling the weight of everything she'd just been through. Larison must have noticed, too, because he went over. Larison held out his hand, and Frodo licked it.

"Thinking about Ali?" Larison said.

Maya looked down. "Can't help it."

Larison nodded. "'Do not be too sad, Sam. You cannot be always torn in two.'"

Rain assumed it was a line from *The Lord of the Rings*. A good line.

When Maya looked up, her eyes were wet. "Tom told me you were scary," she said. "Maybe he doesn't know you."

Larison glanced at Kanezaki, then back to Maya. "Oh, he does. He just doesn't know everything."

"Does he know whether you're a hugger?" Maya said.

Larison gave a small, surprised laugh. "I'm not generally, no. But someone seems to have made me a convert."

Dox smiled and said, "It's all right, he converted me to the intrinsic delights of hand-holding."

Maya laughed. She hugged Larison, and Larison hugged her back.

Delilah moved over to where Livia was standing. "I heard what you said in the office," she said. "I . . . I don't like these men getting away with it, either."

Rain hoped Livia would recognize that was Delilah's way of apologizing for not always thinking the best of Livia. They were both proud, sometimes to a fault. Not that Rain could judge.

Livia nodded. "Thanks, Delilah. I never meant to drag you or John into this."

"I don't like them getting away with it, either," Larison said. "But we know one of the men in the videos. Hobbs. We're pretty sure he's the one who got this whole thing rolling. And speaking just for myself, I don't like the loose end he represents for us personally." He glanced at Diaz and added, "I like to consider all the possibilities."

Diaz nodded grimly, and Rain wondered what the woman might have done in the world if she hadn't become a prosecutor. Well, it was rarely too late. For better or worse.

Livia looked at Larison. "I'm in."

Dox said, "Me, too." He smiled at Livia and added, "And not just as a way of getting your attention."

Livia flushed. "Can we talk about this later?"

Dox's smile broadened. "Later sounds nice."

Kanezaki said, "Whatever you need from Guardian Angel, it's yours."

Maya looked at him and said, "Don't leave me out."

Kanezaki smiled. "I'd be an idiot to leave you out of anything."

Rain saw Delilah watching him. He knew she wouldn't try to stop him. He looked at her, then at the rest of them. He shook his head. "Sorry. I'm out."

There was a beat. Then Larison said, "Nothing to be sorry for. We've got this. Besides. You're retired. Which makes you the smartest one here."

Rain looked at Delilah again. "Or the luckiest."

Manus said nothing, and Rain hoped he would leave Hobbs to the others. Larison, and Dox, and Livia, and Tom . . . On some level, they were all addicted to the life. Rain thought Manus was different. And looking at Dash, he sensed he was right.

"Tom," Delilah said. "When do you need to have that Porsche back?"

Kanezaki checked his watch and blew out a breath. "I was supposed to have it back already. Margarita, too. And I've got the plane waiting— don't you two need to get back to Paris? I think you were having a drink when we . . . interrupted you."

Larison said, "That was my fault."

"Mine," Dox said.

"No interruption at all," Delilah said. "But if we have just a little time . . ."

She turned to Dash and mimed holding a steering wheel. "Come with me in the Porsche?"

Dash's face lit up and he glanced eagerly at Evie.

Evie looked at Delilah and said, "Thank you."

"I'll be at the airport," Rain said. "It'll be good to be back."

Delilah nodded. "Come on," she said to Dash. "Let's go for that ride."

Delilah and Dash left the trailer. A moment later, the Porsche growled to life, and the two of them were gone. The rest of the team headed out in the truck.

Rain meant it when he said it would be good to be back. He and Delilah had built a life in Paris, and Kamakura, and he wanted that life. All of it. However much of it there would be.

She was so insightful, on so many matters. But he knew now she'd been wrong about one important thing. When she'd told him that it was danger, or the edge, or some other such attachment he was afraid to lose.

That wasn't it. Maybe once upon a time, but not anymore.

It was the people he was afraid to lose. And determined to protect. And if he had to face danger to that end, then he would face it willingly. No matter what.

But until then, all he really wanted was to find that elusive peace Delilah had mentioned. And keep it.

For at least a little while. For as long as he could.

Acknowledgments

Thanks to:

The Legislative Drafting Institute for Child Protection—an organization that does work Livia would be proud of, and that deserves your support.

https://ldicp.org

And a particularly easy and effective way to support the LDICP is through AmazonSmile. It's simple to sign up and have Amazon donate 0.5 percent of your purchases to the LDICP (or other charity of your choice).

http://barryeisler.blogspot.com/2018/11/if-you-buy-from-amazon-do-it-at.html

Paul Draker and Dan Levin, for helping design the whole Schrader/Grimble system. I'm famously nontechnical, so if I got anything wrong here, it would be despite Paul's and Dan's patient efforts.

Former Federal Air Marshal Montie Guthrie, for the concept of a "reloader" as explained in chapter 9.

Nurse Practitioner Lindsay Harris and Dr. Peter Zimetbaum, for information on beta blockers and related drugs, and on how to treat a tension pneumothorax.

Mike Killman, who knows as much about how to treat an injury as he does about how to cause one, and who gives the most discursive-yet-essential editorial feedback a writer could ever ask for (and store away to use next time).

Lori Kupfer, for always knowing how to dress Delilah to kill, and for so uncannily getting in her head, too.

Rory Miller, for feedback about Diaz's freeze in the park, a scene that is itself based on what I've learned from Rory's work.

AUSA Daniel Velez, for background on assistant US Attorneys, federal detention centers, and federal law enforcement generally.

To the extent I get violence right in my fiction, I have many great instructors to thank, including Massad Ayoob, Tony Blauer, Alain Burrese, Loren Christensen, Wim Demeere, Dave Grossman, Tim Larkin, Marc MacYoung, Rory Miller, Clint Overland, Peyton Quinn, and Terry Trahan. I highly recommend their superb books and courses for anyone who wants to be safer in the world, or just to create more realistic violence on the page:

http://www.massadayoobgroup.com

https://blauerspear.com

http://yourwarriorsedge.com/about-alain-burrese

http://www.lorenchristensen.com

http://www.wimsblog.com

http://www.killology.com

http://www.targetfocustraining.com

https://www.nononsenseselfdefense.com

http://www.chirontraining.com

http://moderncombatandsurvival.com/author/peyton-quinn

https://conflictresearchgroupintl.com/terry-trahan/

https://mastersofmayhem.info

Thanks as always to the extraordinarily eclectic group of "foodies with a violence problem" who hang out at Marc "Animal" MacYoung and Dianna Gordon MacYoung's No Nonsense Self-Defense, for good humor, good fellowship, and a ton of insights, particularly regarding the real costs of violence.

Sometimes I listen to a particular album a lot while writing a book. This time, it was a playlist consisting of the soundtrack to *Motherless Brooklyn* (loved the movie and the book); Frank Morgan's *Mood Indigo* (which I think I learned about from Michael Connelly); and the song "In a Sentimental Mood," by Duke Ellington and John Coltrane, which I first came across in Alex Gibney's documentary *Magic Trip: Ken Kesey's Search for a Cool Place*, and which has haunted me ever since.

For everyone who's been waiting for this book, thanks for being so patient. I wanted to get it done sooner, but . . . it was an interesting year.

Thanks to Naomi Andrews, Phyllis DeBlanche, Wim Demeere, Alan Eisler, Emma Eisler, Judith Eisler, Ben Grossblatt, Mike Killman, Lori Kupfer, Dan Levin, Maya Levin, Liz Pearsons, Laura Rennert, Ken Rosenberg, Ted Schlein, Hannah Streetman, and Paige Terlip for terrific feedback on the manuscript, and to Laura for doing so much to help me write it. I love you, babe.

Notes

prologue

The Story of Seattle's Freeway Park.
https://www.seattleweekly.com/news/navigating-the-maze-that-is-freeway-park/

Manus's everyday carry—the Cold Steel Espada. Naturally, I bought one for research purposes, and I'm not too proud to admit that the first thing I did with it was screw up and cut myself badly enough to need stitches.
https://www.coldsteel.com/xl-espada-s35vn-62ma

Manus's, Evie's, and Dash's story is told in *The God's Eye View*.
https://www.amazon.com/gp/product/B00XT47SOK/ref=dbs_a_def_rwt_bibl_vppi_i16

chapter two

How to Not Get Slammed in the Guard.
https://www.youtube.com/watch?v=tC4W9dB7DM0

Marc MacYoung using a cut of meat to demonstrate how much damage a knife can do, at 37:00, but the whole video is worth watching.
https://www.youtube.com/watch?v=zQNeXMlSMOw

For a discussion of "my weapons don't work" dreams, where they come from, and how to overcome them, see generally Dave Grossman's *On Killing* and Dave Grossman's and Loren Christensen's *On Combat*.

https://www.amazon.com/Dave-Grossman/e/B001H6MBBM

Livia's backstory is told in the first Livia book, the eponymous (always looking for an opportunity to use that word) *Livia Lone*.

https://www.amazon.com/gp/product/B01DYC113A/ref=dbs_a_def_rwt_bibl_vppi_i14

chapter three

Journalist Julie Brown has done dogged work breaking and covering various aspects of the Jeffrey Epstein matter for the *Miami Herald*. See for example "Perversion of Justice."

https://www.miamiherald.com/topics/jeffrey-epstein

Fascinating article about how Epstein collected people, rumors he had blackmail tapes, the banality of the global elite, and much more, by a reporter who called all two thousand people in Epstein's black book.

https://www.motherjones.com/politics/2020/10/i-called-everyone-in-jeffrey-epsteins-little-black-book/

chapter four

The ambush Livia recalls happened in *The Killer Collective*.

https://www.amazon.com/gp/product/B07DL1Y4GV/ref=dbs_a_def_rwt_bibl_vppi_i8

chapter five

More on General Motors' surveillance of Ralph Nader and the company's attempt to discredit Nader's exposés of safety failings in GM cars.
https://www.pophistorydig.com/topics/tag/gm-investigation-of-ralph-nader/

chapter seven

The story of Guardian Angel, called God's Eye before the government got wise about how to make it sound benign, is told in *The God's Eye View*.
https://www.amazon.com/gp/product/B00XT47SOK/ref=dbs_a_def_rwt_bibl_vppi_i16

Maya makes her first appearance in *The Night Trade*.
https://www.amazon.com/gp/product/B07L9XXDCC/ref=dbs_a_def_rwt_bibl_vppi_i3

chapter eight

The stepwells of India—photos and more.
http://www.walkthroughindia.com/walkthroughs/10-ancient-popular-stepwells-india/

So-called "incidental" collection.
https://www.eff.org/pages/Incidental-collection

More on "loveint."
https://arstechnica.com/tech-policy/2013/09/loveint-on-his-first-day-of-work-nsa-employee-spied-on-ex-girlfriend/

Dox and Rain in Brazil (and Hong Kong and Macau) is a story told in *Winner Take All*.

https://www.amazon.com/gp/product/B00M4LHQ96/ref=dbs_a_def_rwt_bibl_vppi_i4

Dox's recollection of those false-flag terror attacks, and how Larison joined their band of brothers, is of course a reference to *The Detachment*.

https://www.amazon.com/gp/product/B005CDHZS0/ref=dbs_a_def_rwt_bibl_vppi_i7

Dox's original pursuit of the former Khmer Rouge child trafficker Sorm is told in the short story *The Khmer Kill*.

https://www.amazon.com/gp/product/B008674IA2/ref=dbs_a_def_rwt_bibl_vppi_i18

And the story of Dox and Livia's first encounters, in Cambodia and Thailand, is told in *The Night Trade*.

https://www.amazon.com/gp/product/B01LZ1MXK3/ref=dbs_a_def_rwt_bibl_vppi_i10

chapter nine

The notorious sumo fight takes place in *Extremis*.

https://www.amazon.com/gp/product/B00M4LHQBE/ref=dbs_a_def_rwt_bibl_vppi_i5

chapter ten

A cool video—the making of a belt knife.

https://www.youtube.com/watch?v=oBAHAhQsGLY&-app=desktop

Dox is understandably phobic about swords due to an incident that occurred in *The Night Trade*.
https://www.amazon.com/gp/product/B07L9XXDCC/ref=dbs_a_def_rwt_bibl_vppi_i3

chapter fourteen

"But only God can make a tree."
https://www.poetryfoundation.org/poetrymagazine/poems/12744/trees

An example of an acoustic gunshot detection system.
https://www.shotspotter.com

chapter seventeen

Livia's teachings on the freeze and how to break it are courtesy of Rory Miller, primarily from Rory's book *Facing Violence: Preparing for the Unexpected* (for which I was proud to write the foreword).
https://www.amazon.com/gp/product/B0182WEMGA/ref=dbs_a_def_rwt_hsch_vapi_tkin_p1_i1

chapter twenty

Another of the global elite accused of child trafficking, racketeering, and drugging victims before assaulting them—and avoiding accountability for decades.
https://www.theguardian.com/world/2020/dec/15/peter-nygard-canadian-fashion-mogul-arrested

Camera malfunctions, etc. on the night Jeffrey Epstein died in jail.

https://www.reuters.com/article/us-people-jeffrey-epstein-cameras/fbi-studies-two-broken-cameras-outside-cell-where-epstein-died-source-idUSKCN1VI2LC

https://www.npr.org/2020/01/09/795004811/video-outside-cell-during-jeffrey-epsteins-first-suicide-attempt-no-longer-exist

chapter twenty-three

For more on *amaeru*, the best source I know is Takeo Doi's *The Anatomy of Dependence*. As with so many other Japanese concepts, I think it's a mistake to approach *amaeru* as a uniquely Eastern thing. It's probably more a human thing. But it's also true that as with other aspects of Japanese culture, such as *mono no aware*, *amaeru* is relatively important in Japan—important enough to merit nomenclature we in the West lack.

https://en.wikipedia.org/wiki/The_Anatomy_of_Dependence

For another interesting example of "The West has it, too, it's just not as central," consider the Japanese writing system of *kanji* (a word that literally means "Chinese characters" because Japan adopted the system from China). Kanji are symbols with both sound and meaning. If that sounds confusing, just think of the symbols above the numbers on your keyboard—@, #, $, %, etc. Unlike letters, which have only a sound and no independent meaning, the keyboard symbols have both. And now you understand the fundamentals of kanji! The big difference is that while English has only a few such symbols, peripheral to the writing system, Japanese has thousands, and they are the system's foundation.

Delilah and John's first encounter, when Delilah was with Mossad and Rain was freelancing for the CIA, is in *Winner Take All*.

https://www.amazon.com/gp/product/B00M4LHQ96/ref=dbs_
a_def_rwt_bibl_vppi_i4

Delilah and John's breakup is told in the short story "Paris Is a Bitch."
https://www.amazon.com/gp/product/B004XQVKR4/ref=dbs_
a_def_rwt_bibl_vppi_i17

And their reunion is part of *The Killer Collective.*
https://www.amazon.com/gp/product/B07DL1Y4GV/ref=dbs_
a_def_rwt_bibl_vppi_i8

chapter thirty-one

Andrew Vachss on why *child prostitute* is an abhorrent and inaccurate
term, and why the accurate nomenclature is *prostituted child.*
https://www.randomhouse.com/knopf/authors/vachss/qna.html

chapter thirty-two

For a nice cinematic example of a witness check (and a subtle draw), go
to 3:55 in the jazz bar scene in *Collateral.*
https://www.youtube.com/watch?v=gshNksNweOg

And another nice one (more an *Is anyone here going to be trouble?* check,
but the principle is the same), from this clip of *Lonesome Dove*, at 0:45.
https://www.youtube.com/watch?v=nBG2IxzEn7g

chapter thirty-five

Regarding a "club" of insiders owning and running everything, as usual,
George Carlin said it best: "It's a big club, and you ain't in it."
https://www.youtube.com/watch?v=cKUaqFzZLxU

chapter thirty-eight

Maybe Delilah isn't being completely fair in blaming Livia. But then again, she never claimed to be no freakin' monument to justice.
https://www.youtube.com/watch?v=C7yK8cuP1Bw

The infamous bear joke is told in *Extremis*. Blame Dox, not me.
https://www.amazon.com/gp/product/B00M4LHQBE/ref=dbs_
a_def_rwt_bibl_vppi_i5

chapter thirty-nine

For "When order is your enemy, chaos is your friend," Dox is indebted to John Kirakou's *The Reluctant Spy: My Secret Life in the CIA's War on Terror*.
https://www.amazon.com/Reluctant-Spy-Secret-Life-Terror-ebook/
dp/B0036S4BMG/ref=sr_1_3

It's interesting to speculate whether even satellite hotspots and all the rest would be enough to counter the determined surveillance efforts of a nation-state adversary like NSA. It may be that real-time anonymous electronic communication has become functionally impossible, requiring a resort to slower, old-fashioned methods. If so, note that "impossible" isn't necessarily the goal; "slow and laborious" might be enough. More:
http://barryeisler.blogspot.com/2013/08/david-miranda-and-pre-
clusion-of-privacy.html

chapter forty-two

The story of Jim Hilger rendering Dox is in *The Killer Ascendant*.
https://www.amazon.com/gp/product/B00M4LHQ8M/ref=dbs_
a_def_rwt_bibl_vppi_i2

chapter forty-seven

As usual, I wish I were inventing Livia's points about the long-term consequences to victims of having images of their abuse online. But she's just describing reality.

https://www.nytimes.com/interactive/2019/09/28/us/child-sex-abuse.html

https://www.nytimes.com/interactive/2019/11/09/us/internet-child-sex-abuse.html

https://www.nytimes.com/2020/12/04/opinion/sunday/porn-hub-rape-trafficking.html

chapter fifty-four

"The world you live in is just a sugar-coated topping. There is another world beneath it—the real world."

https://www.youtube.com/watch?v=ih3tTprwY04

Dox saves the day with Cleavon Little in *The Detachment*.

https://www.amazon.com/gp/product/B005CDHZS0/ref=dbs_a_def_rwt_bibl_vppi_i7

chapter fifty-five

Seattle's Jungle.

https://www.seattletimes.com/seattle-news/inside-the-grim-world-of-the-jungle-the-caves-sleeping-in-shifts-and-eyeball-eating-rats/

The humiliation of a three-wheeled motorcycle occurred in *The Killer Collective*.

https://www.amazon.com/gp/product/B07DL1Y4GV/ref=dbs_a_def_rwt_bibl_vppi_i8

chapter fifty-six

The crime Livia helped B. D. Little solve is part of *All The Devils*.
https://www.amazon.com/gp/product/B07L9XXDCC/ref=dbs_a_
def_rwt_bibl_vppi_i1

Dox suffers the indignity of a rear-of-the-seat motorcycle ride in *The Night Trade*.
https://www.amazon.com/gp/product/B07L9XXDCC/ref=dbs_a_
def_rwt_bibl_vppi_i3

chapter sixty

Andrew Vachss on why *transcender* is a better term than *survivor*.
http://vachss.com/transcender.html

chapter sixty-four

For *GOT* fans—power is power.
https://www.youtube.com/watch?v=ab6GyR_5N6c

chapter sixty-five

A bit more on the actual house that inspired the Constantine Grimble compound.
https://www.airfloor.com/project/residential-larry-ellison-woodside-home/
https://www.sfgate.com/bayarea/article/The-Villa-That-Oracle-Built-Ellison-proceeds-2938199.php#photo-2257649

chapter sixty-seven

By serendipity, after finishing the first draft, I came across this photo of Manzanita Way in *PUNCH* magazine. Definitely conveys the atmosphere.
http://www.journalgraphicsdigitalpublications.com/epubs/punch-jan21/viewer/desktop/#page/34

A good surveillance/countersurveillance primer, particularly on the concepts of cover for action and cover for status.
https://worldview.stratfor.com/article/watching-watchers

chapter sixty-nine

More on the Vaari and Maija Soderholm, one of Livia's mentors.
http://www.somico-knives.com/about-us.html

chapter seventy-three

Abu Ghraib. It's never the policy, always just "a few bad apples."
https://layeredonionz.wordpress.com/2018/05/03/president-bush-blames-a-few-bad-apples-for-abu-ghraib-torture/

chapter seventy-six

I always try to depict things as accurately and compellingly as I can. And when I was writing this chapter, I wanted to listen to a helicopter to help ensure I wasn't just phoning it in from memory. I found this video with a simple search for "sound of a helicopter." Sometimes I hate the Internet. But other times I really love it.
https://www.youtube.com/watch?v=e8BAckZBQZc

About the Author

*N*ew York Times bestselling author Barry Eisler spent three years in a covert position with the CIA's Directorate of Operations, then worked as a technology lawyer and start-up executive in Silicon Valley and Japan, earning his black belt at the Kodokan Judo Institute along the way. Eisler's award-winning thrillers have been included in numerous Best Of lists, have been translated into nearly twenty languages, and include the #1 bestsellers *The Detachment, Livia Lone, The Night Trade*, and *The Killer Collective*. Eisler lives in the San Francisco Bay Area and, when he's not writing novels, blogs about national security and the media. For more information, visit www.barryeisler.com.